WE ARE
BOUND
BY
STARS

Books by Kesia Lupo

We Are Blood and Thunder
We Are Bound by Stars

WE ARE
BOUND
BY
STARS

KESIA LUPO

BLOOMSBURY

LONDON   OXFORD   NEW YORK   NEW DELHI   SYDNEY

BLOOMSBURY YA
Bloomsbury Publishing Plc
50 Bedford Square, London WC1B 3DP, UK

BLOOMSBURY, BLOOMSBURY YA and the Diana logo are trademarks of
Bloomsbury Publishing Plc

First published in Great Britain in 2020 by Bloomsbury Publishing Plc

A catalogue record for this book is available from the British Library

ISBN: PB: 978-1-4088-9807-9; eBook: 978-1-4088-9808-6

2 4 6 8 10 9 7 5 3

Typeset by RefineCatch Limited, Bungay, Suffolk
Printed and bound in Great Britain by CPI Group (UK) Ltd, Croydon CR0 4YY

MIX
Paper from
responsible sources
FSC
www.fsc.org   FSC® C020471

To find out more about our authors and books visit www.bloomsbury.com
and sign up for our newsletters

To Mum and Dad

VALORIAN CONTINENT

SCAROSSA

SCAROSSA

The Docks

University
Quarter

Jewellery
Quarter

Library

Temple
of Mythris

Palazzo
Square

Palazzo

Mascherari
House

Palazzo
Gardens

HOLY COUNCIL OF THE NINE GODS

FAUL
THE HUNTSMAN GOD
Colour of disciples' magic: **SILVER**

Disciples of Faul are responsible for policing the magical population. They are tasked with finding and bringing in rogues, despatching radicals and capturing magical criminals. Few are suited to the magic of Faul, and the life-threatening demands exacted upon disciples are sure to dissuade some potential candidates.

MYTHRIS
THE MASKED GOD
Colour of disciples' magic: **PURPLE**

Disciples of Mythris are known as spies and assassins, often employed by the state, sometimes by private individuals for the right price. Little is known about the specific content of their work, and their temples tend to be hidden away.

JOK
THE WARRIOR GOD
Colour of disciples' magic: **RED**

Disciples of Jok are combat specialists, learned in the arts of fighting and military tactics. This temple is one of the most populous – few major wars have been fought in recent times and disciples are instead well compensated as general peacekeepers and guards.

NOMI
THE EXPLORER GOD
Colour of disciples' magic: **GREEN**

Disciples of Nomi are skilled in spells of navigation and particularly scrying (the finding of lost things). Very few people are suited to this set of skills despite the lure of the exotic locations to which disciples are posted.

IMRIS
THE HEALER GOD
Colour of disciples' magic: **BLUE**

Disciples of Imris are specialist healers and physicians. Although priests of other temples may be physicians, the disciples of Imris are multifaceted and incredibly delicate in their expertise. Imris has many disciples.

REGIS
THE RULER GOD
Colour of disciples' magic: **WHITE**

Disciples of Regis are cut out for leadership and politics. They have truth-seeing and divinatory abilities, useful in both these professions. Regis is a popular temple attracting academically gifted mages.

TURAH
THE LAND GODDESS
One of the twins
Colour of disciples' magic: **OCHRE**

Disciples of Turah are skilled in agricultural magics, sensing and encouraging growth in the soil and even (for its most powerful disciples) controlling the weather. Turah was once a most revered goddess, but these days few are attracted to this temple.

JURAH
THE JUSTICE GODDESS
The second twin
Colour of disciples' magic: **BLACK**

Disciples of Jurah are rare in Valorian, although in the past they were among the most esteemed, their powers allowing them to null and manipulate the abilities of other mages. Nowadays the few remaining disciples of Jurah play a largely ceremonial role as the king's executioners.

AMORIS
THE GOLDEN GODDESS
Colour of disciples' magic: **GOLD**

Disciples of Amoris study the magics of good fortune and seduction. They are the financiers of Valorian, with their temples (which operate variably as bathhouses or the only legitimate brothels in the continent) by far the most profitable of the nine. An enduringly popular temple.

Legend has it that when the goddess Fortune was betrayed by her fellow deities and transformed into a mortal, she returned to the place that she had been born: the kingdom of the Wishes. A group of volcanic islands to the south of the continent, the Wishes was the last place faithful to her teachings. Here, before she disappeared completely, she granted the matriarchs of the two ruling bloodlines, Santini and Lupina, exceptional powers – magics she hoped would keep her faith alive as they were passed down through generations. She called these magics astromancy, for they drew their energies from the stars.

When she died, it is said, her body infused the very soil of the Wishes with her magic.

The King came to the isles from the mainland centuries later, bringing the faith of the nine gods and a demand for surrender. The isle's ruler, a queen of the Santini line, struck a secret bargain with the god Mythris – against her Lupina general's wishes.

In this secret bargain, the Queen of the Wishes promised to accept the lesser title of Contessa, ruling under the King. She promised Mythris that she and all her successors would use Fortune's gift to read and guide his future and that of his temples.

In return, Mythris would grant the Contessa a fragment

of his own power in the form of generations of triplet mask-makers. The masks they crafted would bear special powers, aiding the Contessa in discovering and destroying her enemies. But should the chain of inheritance ever be broken, should the Contessa's descendants ever lose the power of astromancy, everything would be forfeit ...

Richaro Mancini, *The Queens of the Wishes*

The Rules of the Mascherari

1. The three mask-makers of Scarossa are triplets. Taken from their birth mother, they are the adopted daughters of Mythris, destined to serve the Contessa.
2. Once the sisters have inherited their powers, they are bound together: one soul split three ways; one cannot live without the others.
3. The sisters craft three styles of mask: Ornamentals, Bestials and Grotesques. All their masks must fall under these three categories. Unidentifiable masks must be destroyed.
4. The masks created by the mascherari sisters are all called True Masks: there is thought to be only one possible human match for each mask. The masks grant unique powers to their wearer.
5. The youngest mascherari sister creates the Ornamentals, the weakest mask. The middle sister creates the Grotesques, of variable strength. The Bestials are reserved for the eldest sister alone. To deviate from an allocated style of mask is punishable by the removal of privileges.
6. The mascherari must never form a mask based on a real human face. To do so is a crime punishable by death.

ONE
The Fighter's Crown

Vico

'Vico, hurry up! It starts in ten minutes,' Elisao says, pushing me through the warm spring night and towards the warehouse. 'For blessed gods' sake,' he mutters. I'd protest, but I was late and he was waiting for me at the docks for half an hour, so I can't blame his ill-humour. I shoot him a grin over my shoulder instead. He returns a watery smile – I knew he couldn't resist – but quickly smothers it under a frown of irritation. 'Come *on*.'

I duck after him into the warehouse. The noise and light surround me in a familiar cocoon, the smells of sizzling fish and sweating bodies, of cheap fortified panacea and cheaper perfume. Yellow light spills from the huge lamps suspended from the vaulted ceiling, the wooden beams casting long shadows.

I turn my signet ring round and round my finger as I slide after Elisao through the gaps in the gathered people towards the centre of the room. I nod at a familiar woman, who smiles warmly – she's one of the stall keepers who sells grilled shrimp and deep-fried rice on the docks. A tall man with wild golden hair claps me on the back as I slide past. 'Vico! My money's on you tonight.' Gerret, one of Old Jacobo's crew. His northern accent is strong, despite the fact he's lived in Scarossa all his adult life.

'I'll do my best for you, Gerret,' I reply.

'Vico, there isn't time,' Elisao says, tugging my arm. I flash Gerret an apologetic smile and allow myself to be led forward.

We're heading for a large square space, cordoned off with ropes. The crowd is bustling with its usual mixture of fishermen, rogues, prostitutes, lovers, students, professors, tradesmen, immigrants, sailors and more – all the people who live in this city, who give life to this city. Conversation does not hum here; it roars, fuelled by panacea and shouts of laughter, and the coins exchanging hands, and the bets cried out, taunts thrown and thrown back …

I feel a rush of warmth. Scarossa is my city, but this is my world. As we reach the centre at last, I shout a hello to Old Jacobo, a crime lord and the organiser of the Battaglia, his most profitable venture. He's taking down wagers but shouts 'You're late' over his shoulder, in his usual jovial tone. I shake a stranger's hand that's proffered to my right, accept a chipped glass from an acquaintance to my left.

If only I could stay in this world always.

And then, through the shifting people, I see a cloaked

2

figure, standing right at the back of the room in a pool of calm. I'm not sure exactly what about the figure draws my eyes: perhaps its stillness; perhaps the black hooded cloak that covers its face, its entire body, so that it's impossible to tell whether they're male or female, rich or poor, young or old. But I'm sure, whoever it is, they're watching me. Despite the heat of the room, I feel suddenly cold.

'Focus, Vico,' says Elisao, pushing away a bottle of panacea poised over my cup in favour of a jug of water. 'We need to talk about your opponent.' I glance down to watch my cup filled – and when I glance up again, the cloaked figure has disappeared. Elisao's voice changes as he catches my expression – softening. 'Are you all right? You look shaken.' His light green eyes are warm but serious behind their spectacles, his skin pale for a native Scarossan – he doesn't spend much time outside. A student of law, he works part time in the city library – a warehouse at the docks isn't his natural habitat. But the Battaglia draws us all here, like moths to a flame. Its contest, the Fighter's Crown, is the worst-kept secret of the city, a glory from its legendary criminal network stretching generations into the past. Once, the winner was crowned King of the Underworld. Nowadays we fight for glory, riches and influence.

'Sorry – I'm fine. I just need a bit of fisherman's courage.' I swig back my water as if it's hard spirits, making Elisao smile. 'What were you going to say?'

'Let's talk about the Raven.'

There's a man standing opposite me, in the far corner, swigging straight from a bottle that I'll wager contains something much stronger than water. He's known as the Raven, and I can see how he got the name – though brown-skinned, like most people of the Wishes, he has bright orange, birdlike eyes, framed by a black mask, which covers the upper half of his face and beaks out over his nose. Medium build, muscular – perhaps he works on the docks during the daytime. Shaggy black hair. I'd put him in his thirties – though it's hard to tell for sure under the mask. Elisao is leaning over my shoulder.

'He doesn't look like much, but he's fast.' His voice is high and nervous.

'Mmhmm.'

'He's won his last seven fights.'

'So I hear,' I say. It's at least the fifth time Elisao has told me this. 'But I have too, you know. As has everyone else who's reached the midway point of the contest.'

'Apparently he's left-handed, Vico.'

'So am I,' I say, grinning at him over my shoulder. 'Elisao, you need to relax. You know I'm going to win, right?'

'This one's different, Vico. The others – they were just doing it for fun, or money, or women. They say this guy's obsessed. He almost won the crown last year.'

'Elisao' – I put my hands on his shoulders – 'I'm. Going. To. Win.'

He puffs out a breath. 'You'd better. I've got a frankly

4

indecent amount of money resting on you.'

The drums start to beat and I stand up, the crowd jostles, hushing, and the tension seems to draw in around us like a band of thieves.

'Welcome to la Battaglia!' Old Jacobo booms. 'The seventh of this year's twelve contests is about to begin!' His face is now nearly as red as his great velvet cloak, stained and ragged from years of use but nevertheless lending him an air of grandeur. The minor crime lord puffs up his chest, pushes back his greased grey hair and spreads his arms. 'My friends … and my enemies' – he smiles wickedly – 'you are witnessing the war for the city's greatest honour, the Fighter's Crown. This contest has been raging in the darkness for centuries. Each year, we award one winner – a man or woman who defeats every one of their opponents in single hand-to-hand combat – the grand prize of twenty thousand golden crowns.' Whoops break out across the room, a spattering of applause. 'You have paid well to be here – or you are already a part of our family. Either way, I welcome you and bid you place your bets while the odds are favourable.' He grins and raises his drink, a glass of golden panacea so brimming full that it sloshes over the rim as he lifts it. 'To this great city – to Scarossa!'

There's a roar of appreciation as the crowd answers, lifting their own drinks. 'Scarossa!' I join in, raising my water cup.

Once the commotion has died, the drums start up again, a slow, tremulous heartbeat. I'm confident – I *know* I can win – but even so I feel the adrenalin start to flow through me, sweat prickling across my back. I live for this feeling. Suddenly I feel the heat of the room in a way I didn't before, the snake of cool air from some gap in the wall like a blessing. Everything is heightened.

Then I catch sight of the cloaked figure a second time. Closer, now – a few rows back from the front. The darkness under the cloak unnerves me. *Who are they?* I shift my eyes away and push the figure from my mind, smother the feeling of coldness. I can't afford to be distracted. I am here. I am going to win. My hands curl into fists.

Old Jacobo starts to speak again. 'Tonight's contests pit some of our greatest soldiers against one another – and we begin with a fight attracting considerable attention. In the west corner, four-year veteran of the Battaglia and last year's runner up – famed for his stealth, speed and ghastly eyes, and the marginal favourite for the win tonight – we have … the Raven!' A cheer fills the warehouse, a tremor of excitement for those who have money on his victory. Those who haven't yet placed their bets are rushing to do so as the Raven stands up, cracking his shoulders and glaring at me across the hard-packed sandy floor. He looks mean; I'll give him that. 'And in the east corner, we have a challenger with all the advantages of youth. New this year, he's lean, he's scrappy, and he's hungry. We call him … the Wolf!' Another cheer fills the warehouse as I step forward, nearly as big as the first. I grin. Seven months ago, the first time I fought here, you wouldn't have heard a sound when I was announced. 'The first to remain on the floor for five counts is the loser. Are we ready?'

The crowd claps and cheers.

'Good luck!' Elisao whispers anxiously, pushing his mop of unruly curls from his face. His spectacles are slipping down his nose again. I feel a sudden rush of affection for him, the feeling I've been having, often, that I'd like to press my lips to his.

'Don't need it,' I say, instead, knowing it will annoy him.

He rolls his eyes. 'Just win, all right?'

And then it's time to fight.

I drop into a low, prepared stance. The Raven does the same. He's wearing a pair of loose fisherman's trews tied with a belt and nothing else. Close up, I can see his torso is criss-crossed with pale scars. The world narrows to me and him – we're alone in this shining light, in our own bright and tiny world, circling each other on the head of a needle. I can't even hear the crowd any more, can't even see the shapes of those watching as anything more distinct than fish in dark water.

But then I glimpse the cloaked figure – at the front of the crowd now. A few paces away. *Why don't they show their face?* I feel a coldness on my skin, prickling into goose-bumps. I notice something I hadn't noticed from a distance: a gold pendant hanging around the figure's neck, flashing as it catches the light. A flaming sun on a long chain. I frown.

'What's the matter, boy?' The Raven growls. 'Scared?'

I wipe the frown from my brow, forcing myself to focus. But I don't reply. I've found it's best not to talk in a fight; silence is more unnerving for your opponent.

He lunges towards me – he's quick, but I'm ready, and I duck under his fist. It's a test, really – he's figuring out what I'm capable of. I stick out my foot as he retreats, a move that's worked well in the past – but he doesn't trip.

I clench my fists tighter. This isn't going to be easy – but I'm glad. There's no fun without a challenge.

I duck another two blows – then send my own fist up towards his chin. He's gone, and out of nowhere I feel his knuckles connect with my stomach. I stagger away, somehow swooping ungracefully out of the reach of another blow aimed at my head.

Damn, he's good.

I see an opening and ram my shoulder into his gut, hear a satisfying 'oof' of pain.

I try to trip him, pull his leg out from beneath him with a jerk of my hands, but he recovers – and I change tack last minute, aiming a punch at his jaw, which – to my surprise – actually connects. He's dazed, staggering.

I haven't been listening to the crowd, haven't even been aware of them since we started fighting, but a shrill scream pierces through at exactly the moment I'm raising my fist again, pressing my advantage, and panic floods me, freezing my muscles. My arm drops. The air has changed – excitement has shifted subtly but surely towards fear. Some people are watching us, but others are glancing over their shoulders. There's something else too, something *other* – I can feel it. I think of the cloaked figure. *Where are they?* They were right there, at the front – and now they've disappeared.

What's happening?

A punch in my face: my nose makes a deafening crack and time slows as blood splashes on to the sand. It's broken – I can tell by how it feels, loose and wet like a sodden rag. The Raven's on me, pushing me down, my mouth in the dust, my entire face throbbing with pain. Old Jacobo should be over us, counting down to his win, but instead there are more screams, and I see a nearby lamp being extinguished by an unnatural swirl of sand, as if the desert is rising up to reclaim what man has stolen. No one's watching us now – and I feel the Raven's weight lift from me as he too realises there's something more important happening.

Sand whips up nearby – between shuffling legs I see the shape of … What is that? A shadow, a flash of yellow light like a flame behind dark glass. The Raven curses, then runs away from me, glancing once over his shoulder with an unreadable expression before he shoves his way into the crowd and disappears. Elisao is at my side, hauling me up, as more lights go out. The huge warehouse is alive with shouts.

Blood is pouring from my nose. Elisao pushes something

in my face – a handkerchief. I try to pinch the bridge of my nose shut, but touching it feels like a burning poker is being shoved into my brain. So I hold just the handkerchief there, feel it grow wet.

'Vico, we have to go! Come on!'

'What's happening?' My voice is thick, muffled. I try to walk but feel dizzy – I clutch my signet ring, turned inward towards my palm, as I always do for courage. People shove past us towards the door. The warehouse is emptying fast – those wide doors designed for wagons releasing people into the cool night. I see a body on the ground in the darkness. And another further on towards the door. Out cold or dead, I can't tell.

'I think … I think sandwolves,' Elisao says, his voice trembling with fear, tugging my arm. We start to press forward, my legs moving of their own accord.

'Sandwolves?' I frown, feel a thrill of mingled fear and excitement, tracing the outline on my ring. The emblem is a sandwolf howling up at the stars. But there have been none of these beasts in Scarossa for fifteen years or more. My whole body is sprung tight as I scan the room. But why am I bothering? You can't fight sandwolves with your fists.

'Come on,' Elisao says, looping my arm around his shoulders.

I stagger towards the door, leaning hard on Elisao as the ground lurches, guilt swirling inside me. Those bodies on the ground … I can't just leave them. We're nearly at the doors when I hesitate.

'Vico!' Elisao hisses.

'Wait for me outside,' I say, and I turn back, trembling.

'Vico, the sandwolves are probably still in there,' he says, pleading now. 'Get back here!'

I ignore him.

The first body, near the door, is a woman's. She's in her middle years and dressed in practical trews and a tunic. As I turn her over, I see her eyes flicker. There's a wound on her head, a raised red bruise – but she's all right. My relief feels like a living thing.

'Wolf?' she says doubtfully, as she focuses on my face. At first I think she's mistaken me for one of the creatures – then I realise that's how I'm known here. I help her up. 'What happened?'

'Sandwolves, we think,' I say, offering her a hand and heaving her to her feet. 'You must've got knocked down in the rush to leave. Go, quickly.'

I see her eyes widen and guess my accent has startled her. I can't help it: as much as I try to hide who I am, I can't speak like the people here do. Even through my broken nose, my station is obvious from the way I round my vowels and pronounce my consonants. She must be wondering what a rich boy is doing fighting in the Battaglia under the name of 'the Wolf'. But she nods, finding her way to the door.

I approach the second body, lit by a single lamp fallen, skewed, on to the ground. In the unsteady light I make out the face of a young girl – and even from a distance I can see her open, vacant eyes, the tell-tale lightning marks of a magical attack across her cheeks. The sandwolves didn't hurt this girl as collateral damage; they drained the magic clean out of her. No mage can survive that.

I can tell that she is dead. Even so, I kneel at her side, bend over her. Blood from my nose spatters on to her pale yellow dress. I drop the soaked handkerchief on the sandy ground – the bleeding has slowed anyway. The girl is around twelve or thirteen years old – dressed in civilian clothes, not temple robes. It's likely her powers hadn't even manifested yet. She might not have even known she was a mage, holding a feast for sandwolves inside her body.

There's nothing I can do for her now. My hands are shaking as I pull her cloak gently over her face.

'Vico?' Elisao is calling me from the door. 'What are you doing? Get out of there, you idiot!'

But there's movement from the opposite direction – deeper inside the building. I raise my head, the hairs on the back of my neck prickling. In the darkness of the ware-house, I see two pinpricks of yellow light. My heart flutters like a bird in a cage as the sandwolf swirls slowly towards me. A calm comes over me as the unsteady light falls on its strange floating body, a dust devil of sand curling into the ground, with the head of a wolf. A fur-like consistency surrounds its ears, and its eyes glow a bright, intelligent yellow. I've never seen a sandwolf before. Never seen any magical creature. I can't help the way my breath catches in my throat.

Then I snap out of it, anger rising inside me. 'What? Aren't you full yet?' I whisper, my voice mocking and cold. 'You want to eat my magic too? I'd like to see you try.' I stand up, draw myself tall. 'Go!' I say.

We hold each other's gaze for a few moments, then suddenly the sandwolf disappears, flickering into thin air, leaving me blinking in surprise. I glance around, half expecting it to reform nearby – but it doesn't. I stand up slowly, expectantly, but nothing happens.

I glance down at the girl one last time and then hurry towards the wide door where Elisao is waiting.

'Thank gods, Vico. What were you doing in there?'

'Sandwolf got someone. A girl,' I say thickly. 'She can't have been more than thirteen. Drained her magic completely.'

'Ah …' His expression softens. He starts to draw me away from the door, glancing nervously over his shoulder.

'I didn't think sandwolves killed.' My voice is shaky as we step away from the warehouse. I hate how powerless I feel. 'Aren't they scavengers?'

'It's not unheard of for them to kill if they're desperate … but you're right – wild sandwolves tend to feed on scraps of spells, old enchantments, that sort of thing. They don't tend to attack people.' Elisao is frowning. 'And what were they doing round here, anyway? Sometimes I hear of them on the isle of Silver, where it's less built up. But in the heart of the city, with Faul's temple of huntsmen right nearby …'

I lean against the wall of the warehouse as a dizziness suddenly comes over me.

'We should get out of here before the huntsmen come,' says Elisao. 'If they find out about la Battaglia—'

As if on cue, the bells of Faul's temple start to ring, cutting Elisao off. The grey-cloaked mages, sworn to protect mankind from magical threats, will hunt the sandwolves down – if the creatures haven't already disappeared beyond the reach of their tracking spells. But if we're not careful, they'll be hunting us too: the Battaglia is strictly forbidden.

We hurry towards the water, then back round into the shadows of the docks.

'I'll take you to the infirmary,' says Elisao.

'That's all right. I'll make my own way home.'

'But—'

'Eli, seriously. There's a physician in my building too. It's just a broken nose.'

He nods, but his jaw is set tight, and I feel a stab of familiar guilt. He's only trying to help – and I'd love to let him. I hate keeping secrets from him – sometimes it feels like that's all I do.

14

Soon we reach the high defensive wall at the edge of the docks. Elisao says, 'Oh my ...'

I turn to see what he's looking at. On the ten-foot wall, black paint shimmers in the moonlight. The graffiti is painted so large that it takes me a moment to recognise the spiral surrounded by stylised flaming beams.

The symbol on the cloaked figure's pendant. But it's not just that ... 'The Santini sun,' I say under my breath – it's the sigil of this city's ruling family. 'But it's incomplete – where are the nine stars?'

Elisao presses his finger to the paint. 'Still pretty fresh,' he says. 'Maybe they didn't have time to finish it before it's the sandwolf attack. Or maybe ...'

'What?'

He shrugs. 'Well, the Santini sun existed on its own as a sigil. Before the faith of the nine gods arrived on these islands. Back when the rulers of the Wishes were queens in their own right. And look, there's more.'

Under the sun, close to the ground, a line has been written in crude dripping capitals: *THE REVOLUTION IS COMING.*

'Probably just some crackpot. Gods know there's enough of them in this city,' says Elisao.

But I'm not so sure. The back of my scalp tingles with cold fear. 'I need to speak to Old Jacobo. There was someone in the crowd today ... cloaked, hooded. Wearing a pendant with this same symbol. It can't be a coincidence.' I glance over at him. 'Did you see them?'

Elisao shakes his head. 'You think Old Jacobo will know who it was? You know he's not the strictest when it comes to spectators …'

He's right. Old Jacobo sells tickets to whoever will pay – he doesn't necessarily ask questions, but he is well-informed, even so. I shrug. 'He might. If not, he'd probably be able to find out. I'll ask him.'

Behind us, voices cry out in the night. Magic flashes silver through the alleys of the docks as the mages start their hunt. We can't linger any longer. We hurry through the gates into the city.

TWO

The Inheritance

Beatrice

In the tall cellar beneath the mask-maker's house, everything is quiet but for the low drone of Priestess Alyssa's voice. The elderly mask-maker is instructing us in the art of decoration from her wing-backed leather chair. 'The quality and category of the gems is one of the factors that determine the powers available to the wearer and the character of the mask's movement.' She wavers. Her old hands are swollen and sore, folded in the lap of her purple robes, never to practise her craft again. Instead, she watches, she judges and she speaks.

Her words wash over me in a familiar, irritating drone.

The three of us sit at our desks in a semicircle facing the Priestess at the front of the room. My elder sister Valentina shoots me a bored glance as she threads a feather through the headdress of her latest practice mask. We stopped learning from the Priestess years ago. We aren't like the other mask-makers in the other temples: when we inherit our full powers, our masks won't merely be decorative or ceremonial.

'Remember, girls, yours will be living masks,' Priestess Alyssa says. 'The masks you perfect now, your practice masks, are the models for creations that will hold deep and lasting influence over the people of Scarossa and beyond. Each mask has one wearer. One match. And your practical skills determine how effective, how powerful your masks will be.' I mouth along with her next words, I know them so well. 'This is crucial, for every mask plays a role in defending and furthering the interests of the state.' She coughs drily.

Yes, when we inherit our powers, our mask-making will be threaded with magic. Our blood will be like strings, our fingers like tools – and a divine puppeteer will pull the scarlet cords that flow through us like stained lace. And our puppeteer? The masked god, Mythris. One of the nine, but the one few people know or understand – after all, he's a cloaked, faceless, ageless, genderless figure. He is no one. He is everyone. The patron god of the Wishes.

My future master.

I shiver. Part of me longs for the Inheritance, for change from this monotony. A bigger part of me has always feared it.

'The art of decoration is not to be taken lightly,' Priestess Alyssa continues, her coughing spell now passed. Her eyes are shut, as if she's speaking in her sleep. Perhaps she is. Perhaps she's spoken her various lectures over and over

18

until the very memory of her words is physically imprinted on her lips and tongue, her brain utterly disengaged. 'When you inherit your full powers …'

My mind drifts. *When we inherit.* In other words, when the eldest mascherari sister is on the brink of death, the Contessa will arrive at this house and speak the words of the Inheritance ceremony. Mythris will transfer the full magic of his powers from Katherina, Elina and Zia, the current mascherari triplets, to Valentina, me and Ofelia … and the cycle will start again. Some day, years later, new triplet babes will be born in the city, destined to inherit the powers after us … after we …

All those dead sisters. Years upon years of them.

I force my thoughts back to the present. My dummy mask lies out on the desk – a laughing face, already painted a deep forest green. I decided to ring the lower part of eyes with silver gems, like tears brimming, and a cloud of bruised purple-grey hangs over the forehead. My fingers burn with glue. The gems in the cellar are cheap cut glass, reused again and again, unsightly where old glue has crusted on their edges – but somehow it doesn't matter. In the moonlight shafting down from the high windows, augmented by flickering lamplight, even my humble practice mask looks a little bit magic.

Of course, were it ever worn, this mask would remain hard and still, like it is now. But all that will change when I inherit my powers. Then, whatever magic lies in my hands, it will react with the magic of the wearer, and the masks I make will *live*. That's what makes a True Mask. That's what makes our masks special. The other temples of Mythris have masks too, but they're only ceremonial – at best, they're enchanted. But these ones grant the wearer potent powers.

As the middle sister, it's my task to create Grotesques. These are masks that draw power from expression, and they are named things like Joy, Sorrow, Fear, Mirth, Jealousy … The magical effect, I'm told, is the manipulation of emotions.

I glance over at Valentina. Her masks, the Bestials, are the most powerful, drawing from the faces and abilities of animals. She's finishing off the feathered crown of a bird-like visage contorted into a fearsome screech of rage.

And then Ofelia. Her masks are to be more subtle in effect. They're called Ornamentals, and each one is a human face with the same blank expression but decorated with gorgeous variations of abstractions. The one she's working on is a swirl of darkness, like ink running into water. I wonder what its impact would be on the wearer. We've been told that Ornamentals can grant smaller enhancements – sharpened vision or hearing, increased delicacy of spellcraft.

Everything in the cellar is designed to mimic the life for which we were destined – a life we will spend in darkness, eventually working only while the city sleeps. We've been enduring later and later nights down here – gradually transitioning as we've grown older. Tonight, we will work until midnight – but we've hours to go yet. Suddenly I shiver, feeling as if a god were treading over my soul.

Something is coming.

Priestess Alyssa's cane *tap-tap-tap*s across the stone floor as she rises to inspect our work. 'Good, Valentina,' she says, bending over her desk. My eldest sister despises the Priestess, but somehow Valentina is still her favourite. 'Ofelia, your decoration could take a little more delicacy. Remember, Ornamentals are supposed to be particularly beautiful.' My younger sister's cheeks burn, and I see her open and then shut her mouth as if deciding against protesting. 'Beatrice ... that is an unconventional combination of colours. Remember, it is not your task to innovate. And your gem-work is a little uneven.'

I was about to argue that it was *supposed* to be uneven – like tears trembling on the brink – when I hear footsteps at the front door above us, and I drop a glass bead on my table, my hands frozen. Nobody ever calls on us: silence in the mascherari house is normally complete at this time of night, when the three sisters are at their work. I glance at Ofelia, who shrugs in confusion. Footsteps hurry across the hall overhead, the floorboards clacking, and I hear high, panicked voices.

I run upstairs before Priestess Alyssa can call out to stop me – Valentina and Ofelia close at my heels. I gasp as I reach the top, emerging into the hall. Katherina is suspended in the air, her body supine, floating in through the front door. Her brown hair is feather-like as it wisps in the light breeze from outside. Her eyes are closed, and her face pale as marble, but her chest rises and falls gently. Next to her, a high priest of Imris – the god of healing – is casting the floating spell, muttering under his breath as he slowly lifts her upstairs. The priest in his long blue robes is focused on his work and appears not to notice our entrance. Katherina's sisters, Elina and Zia, are following in her wake like a pair of black shadows.

On the bottom step, Elina turns towards us – I expect disapproval, as usual, but her face is tight with worry as she holds out her hands to stop our hurried steps. I notice a slight tremble in her fingers.

'Will she be all right?' I ask, before Elina has a chance to speak.

She does not respond at first, casting down her eyes. Valentina is stoic next to me, but I hear Ofelia stifle a sob.

'The Priest ...' Elina's voice is uncharacteristically soft – and it crackles slightly, like old paper. 'The Priest of Imris tells us she will not last the night.'

I let her words sink in like ink through blotting paper, darkening everything it touches. Tonight is the night. *Tonight we inherit our powers.* But I'm not ready. It's too soon. I glance at Valentina, who stands up straighter, pulling her shoulders back as if readying herself for battle. Beside me, Ofelia leans hard against the banister, as if she has been struck a blow, struggling to keep herself upright.

Elina composes her face into a mask of bravery – and when she speaks again, her voice is strong and clear. 'What she needs most of all, now, is peace. And that's what Zia and I need too. You can come – *should* come – but ... be quiet and calm, please.' Her eyes rest on Ofelia for a moment, who nods, her hand pressed to her mouth.

Elina turns and climbs the rest of the stairs, her black dress lapping the steps behind her one by one like a dark wave climbing the shore. The three of us say nothing, but both my sisters' hands find mine as we follow her into Katherina's room. Maybe there's been a mistake. Maybe she'll be all right.

But she isn't. Katherina lies propped up on her many cushions in the high bed we were born in, the blue lace curtains pulled back and tied with golden cord. Candlelight flickers across her face. I linger by the door, just close enough to listen to her shallow breath – in and out, in and out – like the whisper of the sea on this calm night. Her skin is flushed with fever, tight with some pain I don't understand and which appears to have no source but living itself. The Priest of Imris lays a palm on her forehead. For a few moments, a ghostly blue glow fills the half-lit room, and the tightness in Katherina's face lessens slightly, the tension fleeing from her brows.

The Priest speaks to Elina in a low voice – but I listen, hanging back from the bed.

'I have relieved her pain. She should regain consciousness long enough for you to say your goodbyes. That is all I can do. But I will remain in the hall in case I'm needed.'

My heartbeat rises in panic as I realise it's really happening. She's really dying.

'Will you send word to the Contessa?' Elina asks.

'It is all in hand, Mascherari. Gods be with you and your sisters.' His voice is gentle. He bows as he leaves the room, and as the door clicks shut, Katherina's eyes start to flicker open.

'Sisters?' she gasps with great effort.

Elina is at her side; she leans in. Katherina squints to focus on her sister's face, the momentary panic leaving her eyes. 'Katherina,' Elina whispers gently. 'Easy, now. Mythris is calling us home. Soon, the Contessa will arrive, and your pain will end.'

Zia presses her hand between hers. 'I am here, sister. We are all here.' She glances over her shoulder at the three of us – hovering awkwardly in the shadows. '*Come,*' she mouths.

We draw closer. One by one, we perch on the bedside. This was always meant to happen. It's the natural order. But no matter how many times I tell myself this, I can't help the way grief and terror are rushing through me in equal measure, molten and stinging, the way my fists clench on my lap. I shut my eyes and breathe, but the whole room smells of death.

Katherina appears to be too weak to speak any more, but she gazes at Elina, then Zia – who somehow summons a loving smile through her tears – then at Valentina and Ofelia, sat next to me on the opposite side of the bed. I can't help noticing how her eyes pass across me like water sliding over rock, as if I'm not here at all.

'Safe journey to the Godsworld, elder sister,' Valentina says, leaning over and planting two kisses firmly on Katherina's cheeks. But there's a tremor in her voice, even though she tries to disguise it.

Katherina once told me of the moment she inherited the mascherari powers. She said it was like lying upon the ocean and feeling the suck and pull of the waves, the cold of the deep at your back. I never liked to swim further out than the shallows – I didn't like the way the sand dropped off beneath you so sudden, how you could feel the darkness twisting in your stomach and creeping over your skin. I reach for her hand now, intending to say goodbye. Instead, it is she who speaks, her eyes flickering open: 'Run, Beatrice.'

Her eyes meet mine at last, and I am shocked at the impact.

'Sorry?' I say, astonished by her lucidity, unable to understand what she means.

'We had no choice …' Her breathing is laboured, her eyes roving wildly as if she's trying to fix on something behind me. She's feverish. I know she's talking nonsense – she must be – but I can't help the way my body tenses. 'We had no choice …'

My heart is pattering. 'What do you mean?' I manage.

'You should run,' she manages, 'Bea …'

I can do nothing but breathe. I shake my head, stepping backwards in confusion.

'She's out of her mind with pain,' Elina says, laying a hand gently on her shoulder. 'The fever has addled her brain.' She wipes my eyes – I didn't know I was crying – pulls me close and whispers, 'I know this is frightening. Remember, we went through the same thing the night of our Inheritance.' She pulls away, smiling. 'But all is as it should be, little sister. Your time is coming. Soon you will have Mythris's power running in your blood – use it well. Pray every day and remember we are watching over you from the Godsworld.' She lets me go, but I feel far from comforted, Katherina's warning ringing in my ears.

I embrace Zia, who sobs on my shoulder and wishes me 'goodbye, darling'. I shiver mutely, feeling sickness twist in my belly.

The Contessa enters without ceremony: this woman who watched us cut from our mother's womb; this woman dressed, like us, in perpetual-mourning black. We curtsey again, waiting for her permission to rise. I gaze up at her through my eyelashes as I hold myself low. She is an old woman: her hair entirely grey, her brown skin wrinkled. But her eyes are bright as they scan the room, and she still

holds herself tall. The cane at her side is as much an affect-
ation of the nobility, I know, as it is designed for support. Is
it my imagination, or does her gaze linger on me a moment
longer than the others? I avert my eyes quickly, heart
thumping.

'Is everything as it should be?' she asks the room.
Although she must be in her eighties, her voice has the
strength and power of a much younger woman's – someone
accustomed to obedience.

'Of course,' Elina replies. 'We are ready.'

Are we? My heart is hammering against my ribs.

But I hold Katherina's limp, hot hand, Valentina on my
other side, and Ofelia next to her. We all form a circle
around the bed. We've been preparing for this moment our
whole lives – we know what to do. The candlelight flickers
as the Contessa starts to speak.

'I summon you, Mythris, Lord of Shadows, God of Many
Faces. I summon you. I summon you.'

The back of my neck tingles in the silence before she
continues.

'We call on you to accept your three elder daughters
into your bosom.' Her voice is slow, deliberate. My senses
prickle as a breeze snakes through the room as if from
nowhere. 'Summon their souls into the Godsworld and
release their powers into these three fated vessels, their
younger sisters.'

Valentina's hand tightens on mine. I feel light-headed,

the air in the room buzzing as if it's full of flies. The candle-light flickers. Sparks dance in front of my eyes – I blink, shaking my head. Is it my imagination, or are the Contessa's eyes fixed on me, filled with worry even as she utters the ceremonial words? My face tingles.

'Honour your promise, Lord of Mysteries, Lord of Secrets, Lord of All Things Hidden. Honour your vow and grant your humble servants the gift you have bestowed upon us for generations past.'

The candles self-extinguish, snuffed out by an unseen energy.

'Stay calm,' says the Contessa in a different, lower voice. 'Do not break the circle.'

'You're hurting me,' Valentina hisses, and I realise I'm clutching her hand as hard as I can. I loosen my grip slightly. A bead of sweat runs down my cheek. I feel dizzy. I feel as if something is closing in on me. I can smell incense, though none is burning. And now, I can feel a velvety presence against my cheek.

'So mote it be,' the Contessa says. 'So mote it be. So mote it be.'

The tension in the room is unbearable. The ringing in my ears grows louder and louder, and then, in the semi-darkness of the moonlight spilling through the curtains, I watch as Zia and Elina start to tremble. Katherina's hand jerks in mine, and I have to force myself not to pull away as it goes suddenly limp.

The two other sisters drop down, like puppets with cut strings, their bodies *thunk*ing on the wooden floor.

A wave hits me – almost a physical impact, cold and dark, making me stagger and dragging me down into an unbearable deepness, stealing my breath. I feel another person standing beside me where Katherina's dead hand lies in mine – something old and cunning and cruel. A cloaked, hazy figure. Bodiless, faceless – a shadow in the corner of my eye.

Mythris is here, I think, my thoughts loud as a siren.

The god's cold laughter fills my senses like gurgling water.

I try to scream, but my mouth gapes open in silence.

Where is the air?

And I am gone.

THREE
Bad News

Vico

Elisao and I enter the palazzo square and stop in front of the great domed library, moonlight glinting off its four glass spiralling towers. The library is reserved for scholars at the university, and I've never been inside. I'd like to step through the grand wooden doors, breathe in the smell of paper and learning. I sit on the steps, gazing in the opposite direction at the masked temple looming against the star-spotted sky. It's isolated and dominating on its crags of stone.

I feel sick just looking at it.

'Are you sure you're all right?' Elisao asks, standing in front of me.

'I'm fine,' I say through the pain throbbing across my face and in my heart.

Elisao lifts his hand as if he's reaching out for me. I lean forward slightly ... but at the last moment his hand hesitates and changes course, lifting to his spectacles, which he pushes up his nose. 'I guess there'll be a rematch against the Raven,' he says hurriedly. 'Probably a good thing. You looked like you were losing.'

I snort – wince. 'That's not fair. I was distracted. Next time I'll win for sure.'

Elisao shakes his head. 'Oh for a fraction of your confidence, Vico. I'll keep my ear to the ground anyway. I can get a message to you … if you—'

'Old Jacobo knows how to reach me,' I blurt, guessing what he's about to ask and feeling my face flushing. 'I mean …' I break off, balling my fists.

Elisao's expression hardens, and he glances down at his feet. 'Look, I can tell you don't want me to know where you live. I'm going to guess from the way you speak that you're … I don't know … some kind of nobleman. The son of someone who doesn't want you running around the streets at night.'

I stay silent, my heart thudding. Of course he suspects. *Of course.*

'I just want you to know that you can trust me, Vico.'

I'd love to tell him the truth – I'd love nothing more, in fact. But I'm not sure our friendship could survive it. Would Elisao want to know me if he knew who I really was? I shrug. 'I'm sorry,' I mumble.

'When you're ready then,' says Elisao with a sad half-smile. 'I'll see you soon, Vico.'

He turns away, heads towards the university district. I watch him for a while, his slender figure disappearing between the buildings. Then I walk up towards an area in the palazzo district where the richer students take their lodgings. When I'm sure he's not following – hating myself for thinking he might – I take a sharp right and head into the palazzo grounds, via the crumbling wall by the maskmaker's house. The sea whispers on the cliffs far beneath.

As I drop down into the undergrowth of the garden, I'm surprised to notice lights in the windows of the mascherari house, the flicker of candles. Normally the house is silent at night, while the mascherari are working and the young triplets learning their craft in the basement.

No time to investigate. I'm in deep shit this time, I realise: there's no way I can magic this broken nose away before morning. But I'll have to try. If I don't, questions will be raised, secrets uncovered.

I could lose my life as Vico forever.

I head round the house and sneak into the elaborately arranged palazzo gardens, with tightly knotted beds of bone roses. The heavy-petalled, black-stemmed flowers sway slightly to their own current, unconnected to the breeze – but they pay me no mind. There's a light on in Grandmother's room, but I crouch low in the shadows, relying on her poor eyesight and my familiarity with the route to conceal me.

At last, I round the palazzo to reach the drainpipe below my own room, which overlooks the city. The bells of Faul's temple are still ringing and, as I climb, carefully avoiding the vicious thorns of the bone roses crawling up to my window, my mind returns to the sandwolf. I was angry at the beast – shocked at what it had done to the girl … And yet, despite the fact that my limited magic would have provided scarce defence against its attack, I didn't feel afraid. And the creature didn't hurt me – why was that?

I drop on to my balcony, then slide through the glass doors into my room and curl up on the floor. The marble is blissfully cool against my tired muscles. Now that I'm still, my whole face is a knot of pain.

A purple light flickers on from the chair in the corner, and my stomach sinks fast in mingled shock and horror. 'Livio,' Grandmother says, her voice dry and hard as she holds the mage-light in the palm of her hand. 'Foolish boy. Where have you been?'

I scramble to my feet, but when I am upright a sudden dizziness comes over me and I lean against the wall, knocking over one of the many piles of books I have stacked up on the floor. The histories and mythologies of Scarossa slide down in an untidy avalanche.

'Sit on the bed, for gods' sake,' Grandmother says, 'or you'll wake the whole palazzo.' With a wave of her hand, she lights the four oil lamps in my room by magic. Reflected light gleams in the large mourning ring on her right hand, woven from locks of the dark lustrous hair that once belonged to her daughter, Patience. As always, Grandmother is dressed all in black: black gown, embroidered in a deeper shade of darkness; black lace shawl, despite the warmth of the evening; and a black ribbon tied around her neck, the

golden sun-and-stars medallion upon it her only concession to colour. There's a pause of shock as she takes in the
full extent of my injury. 'Your face.'

I swallow, the taste of blood in my mouth – how could I
explain a broken nose in a way that doesn't involve brawl-
ing in the city streets? 'I ... uh ...'

Grandmother arches her eyebrow at me as I sit obedi-
ently on the bed. 'Don't bother, boy. Whatever you decide
to say, I won't believe it.'

I try to smile ruefully as she stands over me, her brown
eyes shadowed with concern, but I wince at the movement.
She starts to prod my nose with, I think, a little more force
than necessary, sending bright blooms of pain across my
vision.

She sighs. 'While you were cavorting in the streets like a
commoner, doing gods know what, the eldest mascherari
sister passed tonight from a sudden illness – and I officiated
over the Inheritance.'

My heart sinks.

'I had wanted you to accompany me, seeing as next time,
miracles aside, I won't be around – and you'll have to deliver
the knowledge to my heir yourself. But of course, you were
not here. A priceless opportunity, missed forever. When I
returned I decided to wait and see what exactly had kept
you from your duties.'

'Sorry,' I mumble, feeling hot and unhappy. I don't like to
disappoint Grandmother – ever since Father died twelve

34

years ago, it's just been me and her, the only two Santinis in this huge palazzo. I just wish she could understand that the life she's set out for me isn't the one I'm destined to live. I can feel it, sure as a heartbeat: I am meant for the city, not the political schemings of government or the magical intricacies of the temple. The city – where I can live, and fight, and breathe, and *love*, and feel like I'm part of something greater than myself. If only I could make her see.

She continues. 'Now you shall have to rely on the masked temple to relay the ceremony accurately, without ever having seen it yourself. Hardly ideal, Livio. Hold still. Gods, I can't see anything under all this blood.' She rises carefully, dips a linen cloth in the washbasin and starts to clean the mess from my face.

I swallow uncomfortably, my mouth tasting of iron.

'Your cousin knows nothing of our customs. I was relying on you for that. You are a link – a vital link – between Constance and her heritage.'

I shift on the edge of the bed. I don't like to think about the future Grandmother dreams for me, my role as my estranged cousin's right hand, the font of all her knowledge about the Santini dynasty. If Constance would only make haste and arrive in Scarossa, as she's always promised, Grandmother can tell her all this herself, and I …

I close my eyes and imagine myself as Vico, the name I carry in my other life. He's a student at the university, like Elisao. I imagine him studying in the library and attending

35

classes in the university buildings. I imagine him winning the Fighter's Crown as the Wolf, celebrating with Elisao and a big group of friends down by the docks, drinking cheap panacea until the sun sets. Maybe I don't have to give up on this vision entirely. Maybe there's a way I can meld my two lives together …

I clear my throat. 'Grandmother … I wondered if there was any chance … if maybe I could leave the temple. If I could study at the university instead? Like Father did? Magic has never been my strong point—'

'This again? Here, stay still.' The linen cloth disappears, and I feel the warmth of her magic tingling across my face. With a sharp cracking sound, and a rush of clean, nearly unbearable pain, my nose resets and my airways clear. I grit my teeth, tears running down my face, until the worst passes. I dab my cheeks on my sleeve.

'Holy twins, that hurt.'

She leans back, examining her handiwork, then sits down again on the chair opposite me. 'You've nothing to complain about – it's close to perfect. Only a mage of Imris could've done better. Were you planning on attending the temple tomorrow with a broken nose?'

'Of course not,' I say, clenching my fists in my lap as I realise how quickly she has dismissed my question. 'I was going to fix it myself.'

Grandmother laughs, a little unkindly. 'You just said magic isn't your strong point, and yet you think yourself capable of such a delicate operation?'

I feel my cheeks grow hot.

Her expression hardens and she leans in closer to me. 'Livio, I wish it were not so – for your sake – but you are second in line, after Constance, to inherit my position. Whether you like it or not, you were born with magic – and not all are so lucky. Your father wasn't. You can't simply ignore such a gift. The gods marked you out as one special to them.'

'Just not as special as virtually every other mage in the Wishes,' I mutter.

Grandmother continues as if she hasn't heard me, though I know her hearing is as sharp as it has ever been. 'You need to start taking your future seriously. Do you think you are the first Santini to escape every now and then? The first to rankle under the chains of duty? To wish for a simpler life? To think that destiny has determined a different, more important path for them?'

I blush. I hadn't meant to imply that I thought I was more important – if anything, it was the opposite. 'I … Sometimes it just feels like there's another life I should be living. Like my destiny is' – I wave my hand towards the window – 'out there. In the world.'

'Well, you are not the first – and you won't be the last. But there comes a point in everyone's life when you have to face up to your duties – and to the truth. You will never be like those people.' She glances in the direction of the city, the thin curtains blowing to reveal, just for a moment, the sparkling lights like a fiery mirror of the clear night sky. 'You are the mage-born son of a Santini. And our destiny isn't like that, my boy. Trust me. It doesn't bend to our will. It doesn't care for what's in our hearts.'

Her voice is oddly strained, full of pain.

'One in a hundred are born with magic, Livio – maybe fewer. Even on these islands, where such powers run strong and deep in the native bloodlines. The power in you is a gift from the gods. It may not be a gift that you want, but it's one you have no choice but to accept. More than that – you have a duty to realise its full potential. If anything, Livio, destiny – like magic – is a burden we all have to bear. You cannot cast it off, so you might as well embrace it.'

Grandmother looks as if she's about to continue when she's interrupted by a knock on the door. Our eyes meet in shared surprise.

'Enter,' Grandmother says, after a pause.

An older male servant in yellow livery – my grand-mother's steward – slips inside, bearing a silver dish with a letter resting on top. 'Sorry to disturb you, my lady, my lord,' he says, bowing. I watch his eyes catch on the bloody basin, the red-soaked rag. 'But this is marked as urgent.'

'Come here,' Grandmother says brusquely. The letter is sealed with purple wax, and as the servant steps closer I make out the mask insignia of the temple of Mythris.

Grandmother picks up the letter and breaks the seal.

She doesn't take long to read it, but as she does, I watch the blood drain from her face.

'That will be all,' she says to the steward, her voice weak and tremulous. She doesn't sound like her ordinary self at all.

When the servant has bowed again, and turned away, the strength appears to drain from her fingers and she drops the letter on the smooth polished marble of my bedroom floor. The door clicks shut and, as if released from the obligation of holding herself straight, she rests her face in her hands.

'Grandmother?' I lean forward too, unsure how to respond. I have never seen her in despair before. I have never watched her shoulders tremble, as they do now, the rings on her hand clinking faintly with the movement. Is she crying? The shiny black hair in her mourning ring – Patience's hair – catches the low moonlight beaming through the glass, between the leaves of the pale bone roses. When I touch her hand gently, I am shocked at how cold it is. 'What's happened?'

'Your cousin has died. You are the sole heir, now,' she says, her voice heavy but clear, suddenly devoid of all but a crushing seriousness. She doesn't normally speak to me in this tone. For all her severity, her voice has always had a lightness to it, as if I were the butt of a disappointing joke she was telling herself. But there is no humour in it now. 'It all rests on you.'

'What?' All of a sudden, my heart is pounding so hard that I can hear it in my ears.

Grandmother scoops up the letter and stands up, pacing towards the glass doors and pushing them wider. The ponderous flowers of the bone roses slowly, gently turn towards her, attracted by her magic as they are never attracted to mine. 'Constance is dead.'

My stomach twists. My cousin has been the heir to the Wishes for as long as I can remember – even though she's never travelled here. I've never met her, nor has Grandmother, but somehow her existence has been an unquestioned comfort to us both. She was always the stronger, the more talented – I was always measured against her and always fell short. But I was never really supposed to compete. Not when these islands are destined to be ruled by women. She was the heir. My role was to help her fit in.

I approach the balcony doors, realising with horror that Grandmother's face is streaked with tears in the moonlight. 'No more sneaking into the city at night, Livio,' she says softly. 'Your life is too precious. Do you understand?'

Elisao's face rushes through my mind. *You can trust me.* If Constance is dead, is Vico dead too? Can I continue my second life now that … now that …

I am the heir. There's no way I can do this. My magic isn't strong enough. I have too many secrets. I *can't* give up everything I've grown to love. I open my mouth, but no words come.

'Livio. Do you understand?' Her voice is stern.

'Yes,' I say quietly.

Once my grandmother has wiped her few tears from her eyes, she steps outside on to the balcony. From here, she turns to face me. The light of the lamps inside is so warm it is nearly red, turning the gold of the sun medallion at her neck into a dark, bleeding wound.

'We must pin our hopes on you, Livio.' The bone roses behind her shudder, as if in relief. 'Gods help us all.'

FOUR
An Unexpected Guest

Beatrice

When I wake, I am in the nursery on my bed, and Nurse is dabbing my face with a cold damp cloth. Candlelight flickers as my vision sharpens. The night is close and hot, still, but a breeze is teasing through the room, wafting the curtains open to reveal dark clouds drifting over a dazzling night sky. Nurse blinks her brown eyes, lined with fine wrinkles, and smiles at me faintly.

Perhaps … perhaps the whole thing was a bad dream.

'You gave us quite a scare, little Bea,' she says in the voice she uses only for me. Then, glancing over her shoulder, 'She's awake.' She turns back to me. 'Beatrice, dear, I'm going to fetch you all something to drink. Don't move.'

I don't think I could move if I wanted to. My limbs feel heavy and uncoordinated. My mind, too.

Valentina and Ofelia lean over me, their identical faces etched with a mixture of concern (Ofelia) and annoyance (Valentina).

And that's when I realise it was real. My stomach twists, shock spiralling through me, hard and cold as a corkscrew. 'Did I … did I ruin it?' I ask.

'Nearly,' says Valentina sharply. 'You knew how important it was. Everything was at stake, Beatrice – our whole *lives*. And yet you just can't help yourself, can you? You always have to be the centre of attention.' She's angry, now that she knows I'm going to be all right – I don't have the energy to take offence. 'For goodness sake – why did you do it?'

'She didn't *do* anything,' says Ofelia, glancing crossly at our older sister. 'She fainted! It's not her fault. Listen, Bea, everything's all right. The ceremony was a success. *We* are the mascherari sisters now – the Contessa has confirmed it. The mask-making powers live on for another generation. Whatever happened to you, it doesn't matter now.'

Relief unravels inside me. I allow myself to shut my eyes for a moment. *But what* did *happen to me?* 'Didn't either of you feel … anything? See anything?' I say, my voice soft. I remember the figure at my side – the dark, brooding presence …

Ofelia nods slightly. 'I did feel something. A sort of … *rushing* feeling. Like a current flowing through me. But see anything? No.' She frowns. 'What did you see?'

But Valentina speaks, saving me from answering. 'I thought I felt my fingertips tingle,' she says, glaring at me, 'but it might just be because your iron grip had cut off all circulation.'

43

I smile ruefully – I know she doesn't mean it. 'Sorry. I don't know what's wrong with me.'

Ofelia squeezes my shoulder. 'Nothing's wrong with you. You were exhausted – emotional. That's all. But you're fine now.'

Maybe she's right. Maybe the whole thing was an invention – a kind of waking dream.

Just then, Nurse returns, bearing a small tray loaded with glasses and a pot of hot sweet tea – I can smell the honey even from across the room. A bowl of young greenish figs from the tree in the garden are arranged in a shallow bowl. She sets the tray on the low nursery table and pours out the glasses.

'Now, bambinas. I know you've had a terribly difficult night – but … I'm afraid there is a little more sad news.' She helps prop me up, guides my hand around the warm glass. It feels so heavy, but I manage to lift it to my mouth and sip. 'You'll be expecting it, of course,' she adds. 'As was I … but that doesn't make it any easier.' The sugary herbal tea lingers on my tongue. I feel its strength slide into my blood. *Not my blood, now*, I think. *Mythris's blood. I am his tool, his puppet.* And the thought makes me shiver. Valentina and Ofelia perch on the end of my bed, their weight tilting the mattress. Ofelia nibbles on her fig; Valentina sets her tea on the windowsill. We all know what Nurse is about to say.

'I've packed my things and I'll be returning home before dawn, because … well, because that's what happens, I'm afraid. I did ask the Contessa if I might stay on, even if it's only for a few days – but any break from tradition is thought to be unlucky.' Her voice is brusque and cheerful – but tight as a harp string. 'So, they said no. And I suppose … I suppose this is goodbye.' Her eyes are shining in the candlelight.

Ofelia flings her arms around Nurse's neck, holding her close. 'I wish you could stay,' she whispers.

'There, there, dear. I wish I could too.' She pushes Ofelia away gently, squeezes Valentina's hand. She understands that Valentina does not care for hugs and kisses. But then, in a low voice, she says something we don't expect. 'Girls, listen. I'll be living on the top floor of the old grain store at the bottom of Silver Street, round the corner from the fish market. It's my husband's old property. You're like daughters to me. I feel better knowing you can find me if you need me.'

My eyes are stinging. It's true: Nurse has been more of a mother to us than anyone. She's been with us forever, since the day we were born – and even though we haven't needed a nurse for many years, not really, she has been employed to care for us until we inherited the mascherari powers. It's tradition. And tradition holds our lives together, stitching through our days and nights like an ancient, unbreakable thread.

And, with the same hand, it breaks our lives apart. Now, Nurse will leave. Now, we will leave the nursery and never

45

return. Now, we will go to the mask room at night, not the cellars beneath this house. Now, we will create the real, living masks – the True Masks.

Now, Katherina, Elina and Zia are gone forever.

As she turns to me to say her goodbyes, I study the familiar lines of her face, her kind eyes and grey-streaked hair. She plants a kiss on my cheek and, as she does, I smell the almond oil she rubs into her curls.

'Remember where to find me, little Bea,' she says softly – then she straightens up. Her gentle warning rings in my ears, and I am reminded of Katherina's unsettling command. *You should run.* Did Katherina know I wasn't suited to this life? Did she know I would feel trapped? And now, does Nurse know it too?

Of the three of us, I've always been the one who longed for stories of the world beyond these walls, beyond even the city walls … But I can't leave. I never can. I'm bound here, now, by blood as much as a duty.

'Now, you girls need your rest. You've a big day tomorrow night. The rest of your lives will begin.' Her eyes gleam in the candlelight before she blows out the flame for the last time. 'Goodnight.'

When Nurse has gone, I lie there silently, feeling the world churn and change, sweeping me into a new rhythm.

After a while, footsteps sound on the stairs, male voices – low and urgent. Several men, by the sound of it. They

46

enter the room next door: the room where the three bodies lie on the bed. Then more footsteps as they retreat, burdened this time and murmuring instructions – and then silence.

I sit up and peek out of the curtains. A huge hearse waits on the driveway, illuminated by moonlight. The men carefully slide the three long shapes inside, and the carriage, at last, bears away our predecessors, the night swallowing them up. Before dawn, their bodies will be fed to the flames to prevent their spirits wandering back in confusion. I am suddenly, painfully aware our world is never going to be the same again. I wish I had appreciated what we'd had – the small freedoms. The lightness. I thought change could be good for me, but now it feels as if my future is falling around me like a shroud.

Valentina's breathing is even and deep. But Ofelia is awake.

'Beatrice?' she whispers. When I turn to face her, she raises her covers, and I slip into her bed. 'What do you think we would have been,' she asks as I nestle against her, 'if we weren't mascherari?'

My stomach turns. The age-old question – I've thought about it time and again over the years, yet never spoken it aloud. But before I can reply, Valentina answers from across the room. 'We shouldn't talk about that,' she says. 'The masked god wouldn't like it. We should be grateful for the future we've been gifted.' But her voice is wavering, lacking conviction. Gods, the girl's hearing is supernatural – even when she's sleeping.

'We're just talking,' I say gently. 'Surely that's allowed? Just this once?'

'Come here,' says Ofelia – and for once, Valentina doesn't argue. We're too big to squeeze longways into one bed, like we used to when we were small, but we sit up and press side by side, our backs to the wall, Ofelia's covers draped across our legs.

'Actually … it's hard to imagine what I could have been,' Ofelia says softly. 'I don't know enough about the world.'

I'm sitting in the middle and – in a rush of affection – I loop my arms around their shoulders, pulling them both close. 'Silly, it's easy – especially in your case,' I say. 'See, you would be a great puppet actress, throwing voices from behind the stage.' I smile as I imagine it, resting my cheek against the top of Ofelia's head. 'Maybe you would write plays too. You've always had a talent for storytelling.'

I feel her smile against my shoulder. 'I'd like that,' she says. 'And I could make the costumes too, paint the puppets. I'd be an all-round puppeteer! Go on – what about Valentina?'

'Valentina …' I muse, now leaning against her instead. 'I can see you studying history at the university – you love history. You could be a professor some day – it'd be perfect. Your students would be so terrified of you, they'd never miss a class.' I squeeze her to show her I'm half joking.

'Or after university you could become a lawyer!' Ofelia adds, giggling. 'You always win an argument.'

Valentina snorts. 'That actually sounds like me,' she says grudgingly. 'But what about you, Beatrice?'

I pause. A million ideas rush through my mind. So many beautiful, unique futures – all of them impossible. Overwhelmed, I shake my head. 'I can't tell,' I reply. 'What do you think?'

'An explorer,' says Ofelia, after a moment's hesitation. 'You pored over that book of maps until it fell apart! You'd love to see the world, wouldn't you? Go to places no one had ever been before.'

'That doesn't sound like a career.' I laugh, though I feel a little cold with longing.

'Perhaps a navigator on a ship,' says Valentina quietly. 'That's more practical, isn't it? But you'd still get to travel.'

I'm silent for a moment. 'All these paths, closed to us the moment the Contessa's guards came for our mother.'

Valentina laughs harshly, pulling away from me and sitting on the very edge of the bed. 'Beatrice, our mother was a fishwife. Somehow I doubt these paths were ever really open to us at all.'

I shrug. I don't see it like that. Lack of money and opportunities inhibit freedom, yes, but they're hardly comparable to the limits placed upon our liberty by the Contessa. I can't help feeling that somehow, in that other life, I'd have found my way. But Ofelia's right: Valentina always wins an argument, so I let it lie.

Ofelia squeezes my hand. 'What would you have preferred? Fishwifing or mask-making?'

I can't help giggling a little at that.

'Come on. We really should sleep now,' says Valentina, returning to her bed, lying flat on her back and pulling the covers up to her chin. But Ofelia pulls me down next to her. We lie still for a while, until Valentina starts snoring softly, and my thoughts grow thick with the seeds of dreams. Then Ofelia speaks.

'They're really gone, aren't they? And one day, the same thing will happen to us. When one of us dies, the others will too. One soul split three ways.'

'Yes,' I whisper. I wish I could find some comforting words for her, but I can't.

'Did you see how they fell?' she continues, her voice so quiet it nearly fades into silence. 'All at once, like … like *toys*. Like a child just threw them down in a rage. Tired of them. Is that really our fate?'

I find her hand and squeeze it, feeling her body shuddering as she cries against my back. I shut my eyes and pray for oblivion – it can't be long until dawn.

FIVE
Cutpurse Lane

Livio

I'm sitting on the edge of the bed exactly where Grandmother left me, a puppet left hanging on its strings. I should crawl under the covers, beg for oblivion. My nose might be fixed, but it's painful, and I'm breathing through my mouth, gulping the air as if I've run for miles. Rest sounds good, physically. But the events of the night are running through my mind like an engine I can't stop: the fight, the cloaked figure, the swirling graffiti sun, the Inheritance of the mascherari sisters, my cousin's death ...

Why can't I shake the feeling that every one of these happenings is a vital link in a long chain that's snaking round my ankles, stealing my freedom?

When the clock in the hall strikes two, I snap out of my trance. In one smooth, decisive motion I stand up, walk to the balcony and push the doors open. I breathe in deep, then swing down on to the trellis.

I'm not ready to give up on Vico's life just yet. I'm finding Old Jacobo.

I walk past the palazzo square, downhill towards the docks, but veering off right before the water … and here I am – in a warren of streets known as the jewellery quarter. Once, apparently, the name suited it: a tangle of cobbled lanes decorated with bow-fronted windows glittering with gems. The statues and running fountains inset into the charming stone walls lent the place an air of aristocracy. Or so I'm told: I wouldn't know. Ever since I first visited this place, three years ago, 'the jewellery quarter' has been a fiercely ironic name for a place no one with enough money to buy jewellery would dare to venture.

Well, no one but me. I walk down the centre of the street, away from the windows and doors, the moon lighting my path. A stone figure dancing on a fountain, long dried-up, leers from a bare wall nearby.

It's quiet here. Quiet enough that my footsteps ring out on the stones. Prostitutes and drunks haunt the streets by the docks – but this … this is a place of business. I'm aware of figures behind closed windows, lowered voices muttering. But my face is familiar here: I should be safe.

I reach the corner of Cutpurse Lane and hesitate. I glace up at the street sign: officially, it's simply *Purse Lane*, written there in curling black letters, but years ago someone scrawled a bold *CUT* over the top, and – as it's more accurate anyway – it's held that name ever since. Smoke curls into the air from the shadows, and I smell the bitter-sweet tang of blacklung, an expensive imported drug I've never known anyone but Old Jacobo enjoy.

'Late night for a young wolf,' a voice says from the shadows. 'Glad to see you safe.'

'Jack,' I say as Old Jacobo steps into the moonlight, a huge pipe hanging from his lips. The outlandish red velvet cloak he was wearing earlier has been replaced with a plain black version with a glimmer of something expensive at the collar. Jack has a penchant for everything bright and spark-ling; he especially can't resist a brooch. 'Can we talk?'

His expression is grave as he puffs out another stream of smoke along with his words. 'Follow me.'

A small crooked shop stands a few buildings down – once a watchmaker's and now a pawn shop, displaying an assortment of valuables, heirlooms and oddities behind its square-paned glass. We ignore the *Closed* sign on the grimy door and step inside.

Behind the counter, the door to a small back room is ajar, spilling a narrow vein of light into the dusty shop. Old Jacobo leads me through, the candles wavering as he pushes open the door. Although small, the room is luxuriously furnished: walls covered in tapestries threaded with gold, gilt mirrors and outrageously decorated porcelain; floor-boards covered from wall to wall with luscious rugs; the table crammed with ornaments; and a candelabra dripping with beeswax. Despite the opulence, the overall impression is cluttered, incoherent, mad. I love it.

A boy slouches on the overstuffed velvet armchair by the empty fireplace but stands when we enter, his cheeks flushing red.

'Bring us some panacea, there's a good lad,' Old Jacobo says to him. 'And tell Gambo I'm back, will you? He can come down in an hour to discuss the latest shipment.' And while the boy slips out gratefully, my host gestures for me to sit down at the fine wooden table in front of the cracked-open windows.

The thing about Old Jacobo is he's younger than he pretends to be: behind the big stomach, the grand clothes, the bushy grey-speckled beard and the kindly bluster is a keen and calculating mind. He cultivates the idea of himself as 'Old' Jacobo. Perhaps people underestimate him as a result – and that suits him perfectly. But in reality, he's probably not much older than Father would've been, if he'd lived.

He leans against the mantelpiece, gazing down at me kindly. 'Now, what's all this about, Livio?'

My jaw tightens as I accept the seat. 'You shouldn't call me that,' I say.

He smiles an insincere apology. 'Slip of the tongue. Apologies.'

I nod. Old Jacobo is, as far as I know, the only person in Vico's life who has discovered his true identity. When I first started sneaking out into the city – and back again – I wasn't so good at not being followed. But, to the best of my knowledge, he hasn't told a soul in three years. Nor has he asked anything of me in return.

I know I shouldn't, but I've found myself trusting him.

'There was someone in the crowd tonight,' I begin. 'Tall, long black cloak. And a gold pendant. Do you know who I mean?'

'I saw them too,' Jack says. 'But I'm afraid I can't help you. I've no idea who they were.'

I sigh in frustration.

'But I got a good look at that pendant,' Old Jacobo says. 'Interesting, wasn't it?'

I glance up. 'The Santini sun – but incomplete. Elisao tells me it was a symbol from long ago. When Scarossa was the capital of an independent kingdom.'

He smiles genially as the door opens and the boy brings us our panacea, filling two glasses and leaving. All the while, we're silent. When the door clicks shut, Old Jacobo brings me my glass and sits down on the chair opposite mine, cradling his drink.

'I'm no scholar like your friend. But I do know we've been seeing that symbol a lot recently, around the city. Painted on to walls. Carved on to lintels.'

A chill runs through me, and I sip my drink. 'I saw it on the walls at the docks, not long after we left tonight. The paint was still wet. And there was a line of writing …'

'*Revolution is coming,*' Old Jacobo supplies. 'Yes – we've seen that too.'

'How long has this been happening?'

'Difficult to say exactly. Weeks – perhaps longer.'

I pause. 'And what does it mean?'

Old Jacobo rests back in his chair, swilling his untouched drink around his glass. An earring glitters above his collar. 'There's the real question. I have my suspicions. But I'm not sure it would be entirely wise to tell you what I've heard.'

I blink. 'Why?'

'I've been good to you, boy. Saved you from a scrape or two. Helped you train for the Battaglia. Kept your little secret. Would you agree?'

I feel cold, even my thoughts are frozen, but somehow I force myself to nod. Where is he going with this?

'Never had a son of my own,' Old Jacobo continues, then pauses, takes a sip. 'And you without a father.' He smiles slightly. 'Well, it's only natural we should feel a sort of bond. So let me tell you, Livio' – he leans forward, lowering his voice, so close I can smell the panacea on his breath – 'if the rumours I've heard are true, you do not want to be asking these questions. If I were you, in fact …'

'What?' I barely move my lips.

Something in his expression hardens. 'If I were you, I'd be thinking of … travelling.'

I frown. 'Travelling.'

He leans back in his chair. 'There's far more to the world than this walled city. Don't you want to see it? No time like the present. All too soon, your youth will vanish like panacea in sunlight. Trust me.' Despite his light tone, his face is as grave as I've ever seen it. 'I won't be able to protect you, Livio, if you stay here. And neither will your grandmother.'

I swallow my fear at the sight of his uncharacteristic expression. Run away? Never. Especially when I don't even know what I'm supposed to be running from. I down my drink, relishing the warm bravery running through me, the anger burning away all other emotions.

'Listen,' I say, standing up and leaning against the mantelpiece. I'm glad to see my reflection in the mirror appears strong, determined. 'I'm not the travelling sort. And I'm not a helpless child – I don't need your protection. So I'd be grateful if you'd tell me what you've heard. In fact, I won't leave until you do.' I lift my chin, meet his gaze.

Old Jacobo smiles – though his eyes remain sad. His fingers tighten around his glass. 'I thought you might say that. I'll tell you, then – but you didn't hear it from me.'

'Of course.'

He takes a deep breath. 'Word on the street is that Shadow has returned.'

I shake my head in frustration. 'Shadow? Who's that?'

Old Jacobo lifts an eyebrow. 'Sometimes I forget you are not from my world, boy. He's a great, powerful crime lord. Perhaps the greatest of us all … A pirate king – or so he calls himself. They say he has the biggest crew of any of us – and every one of them is a Rogue.'

I frown. Rogues are dangerous mages who aren't part of the temple system. By law, every new mage who discovers his or her powers must be initiated into one of the nine temples, first experiencing a ceremony – the Binding – which tethers their power to one of the gods, keeping it safe and controllable. Rogues, for one reason or other, have bypassed this law. But without the binding, a Rogue is in danger of losing hold over their power, of being overwhelmed by pure magic – the malign, wild energy of Chaos – at great danger to themselves and everyone in their vicinity. 'Surely that's not possible.'

Old Jacobo watches the fear and doubt pass over my face and shrugs. 'There's more. They say Shadow won't stop until he is King of Scarossa.'

I raise an eyebrow. 'Really – king? He thinks he can rule the Wishes?'

'Apparently so,' he continues, swirling the drink around his glass once more. 'Trouble is, none of us have set eyes on him – only on the effects of his presence. The graffiti, for instance. Magical attacks, too – but no evidence left for us to follow, no revenge. Yelic was assassinated two nights ago.'

Old Jacobo's gang is relatively small, despite its outsized influence in the underworld. But Yelic had a huge network which outnumbered all of his rivals'.

'Now his gang is fighting to determine who will be

leader – and who is benefitting?' Old Jacobo shakes his head. 'Not me. Not any of the others. And yet, resources disappear. Swallowed by shadows …' He smiles slightly at his play on words. 'Shadows, I suppose, are all we have. Hard to understand a shadow. Harder still to fight it, bargain with it. I'll hand him this – it's clever. We see what he wants us to see. But I'll tell you this, boy. I don't like it. He's hiding some place none of us have found.'

I'm shocked that none of the crime lords have been able to locate the newcomer – no one knows Scarossa's secret, hidden places better than they. 'Where can he be?'

'Rumour is he's found a way into Dark Scarossa.' Old Jacobo shrugs. 'Make of that what you will.'

I scratch the back of my neck, raising my eyebrows in disbelief. Dark Scarossa is the mythical city said to be under this one – the new built upon the old until its whole network of streets and buildings was buried, hidden underground. But as far as I'm aware, no one's ever found more than a room or two of the old city, concealed in cellars or off the sewers. What's been found, the crime lords already inhabit. I shake my head, dismissing the thought for now and returning to the question of motives. 'So this Shadow is responsible for the graffiti?' I think about what Jacobo said: he *won't stop until he is King of Scarossa*. 'He's whipping up fervour against the Contessa, isn't he?' I say, answering my own question.

Old Jacobo nods. 'Implying that she's under the heel of

the temples and the King, drawing on old feelings – feelings that run deep as blood ... *Revolution is coming,*' he quotes.

'He thinks he can get the people on his side. Or at least use them to exploit the Contessa's biggest weakness – her remoteness.' I shut my eyes, roll my shoulders. Suddenly I feel incredibly, witheringly tired.

'He won't stop at graffiti though, young wolf,' says Old Jacobo slowly. 'Understand? Revolution is one part of the puzzle. But it's in removing the Contessa that he'll find his true opportunity.'

'He'll have to go through fifty True Masked mages to get into the palazzo. Hundreds of mage guards.' Even I can hear the note of desperation in my voice.

Jack's face is stony as he shrugs. 'I know nothing of magic. But I know something of crime lords and pirate kings.' He stands up. 'We have our ways of finding a path through the toughest defences. I have told you everything I can for now. If you won't leave, then you need to be ready.'

I stand up too, setting my glass on the mantelpiece. 'So the figure in the crowd tonight ... it was one of Shadow's people?'

'So I'm guessing. But what they were doing there, what they hoped to achieve ...' Old Jacobo shakes his head. 'They're circling, Livio. But if they're expecting easy prey, they won't find it in me.' Unexpectedly, then, he pulls me into a hug. He smells of spices, of bitter blacklung and – faintly – of seawater. 'Be careful, boy,' he says as we pull apart. 'Keep your lips shut and your eyes open.'

Outside, Old Jacobo's boy tells me there's a young man waiting for me on Cutpurse Lane, adding a quick description including a pair of gold spectacles. I breathe in sharply. There's no one it could be but Elisao – but unlike me, he's not well known in the jewellery quarter. He's put himself in danger even being here: the crime lords don't like strangers.

'What are you doing?' I hiss as I walk up to Elisao, taking him by the arm and pulling him gently out on to the main street. 'It's not safe.'

'I had to see you. And I knew you wouldn't be sleeping tonight without answers,' Elisao says. 'You talked about asking Old Jacobo ...' He's wearing a hooded cloak. Beneath the shadow of the cloth, his eyes look scared behind his spectacles.

My heart softens. 'Come on – let's get out of here before you get more than your pockets picked.'

We don't speak until we reach the palazzo square and – in wordless agreement – sit on the steps of the library. My thoughts are spinning fast as a top – but what to say? There's yet more silence as we both measure our words. I can feel Elisao fidgeting – he *hates* silence. A clock strikes four somewhere behind a cracked window. Lights are starting to flicker on in the palazzo bakery.

'What did you want to talk about?' I ask. But at the same time, Elisao says, 'You went to Imris temple.'

We both smile a little, the tension easing slightly.

'Your nose. It's fixed.' He frowns at it. 'A tiny bit crooked, but I think it'll look roguish. Hope it wasn't too expensive.'

'Yes. Imris temple,' I say, shoulders sagging with the weight of yet another lie.

'Why didn't you tell me that's what you were going to do?'

'What does it matter?'

'It doesn't. That's the point. Why not tell me?' He removes his spectacles, rubbing the glass lenses on his shirt. 'Sometimes it feels like you're a stranger, Vico. You know everything about me – from my address to my eldest sister's middle name. But you're still a mystery to me. Why can't you trust me?'

I gaze up. The stars are shining bright, despite the late hour. The tiny pinpricks of light shimmer as my eyes fill with tears – until it appears they're a shining web of prisoners, connected and trapped by chains of silver. And I know, in spite of everything I've learned tonight, in spite of the world shifting beneath my feet … 'I can't do this any more.'

'Do what?'

I blink my tears away. 'Vico's not my real name, Elisao.'

He stares at me. I glance around the square to ensure we're alone.

'I'm Livio Santini,' I say quietly.

Elisao blinks. Laughs. Blinks.

'It's true,' I add, frowning.

'Gods,' he curses softly, shaking his head. 'I thought … I thought maybe you were the son of a nobleman … but *this*!' He meets my eyes, and I watch as he blinks again. 'The grandson of the *Contessa*!'

'I know. I'm sorry. I—'

But he's not listening – I can nearly see the cogs of his mind whirring. He interrupts me as another thought strikes him. 'Does this mean you're a mage too? You shouldn't really be fighting in the Battaglia.'

I snort. 'Technically, yes. But I'm no good at it. Even if I wanted to use magic to help me in the Battaglia, I'm not sure I could.' I feel light, floating on a cloud of pure relief. I've told him – and he's still here, sitting next to me, talking to me, gazing at me …

On impulse, I lean forward and press my lips to his, feeling the roughness of our stubble, the slightly awkward clash of our mouths. And yet, my heart is racing. I've been longing for this for so long. He relaxes into the kiss, and I feel … desire, yes. But peace. Calm.

The feeling, deep down, that this is *right*.

We pull apart, breathless. For a few moments, we stare at each other in pure delighted surprise.

'Look …' I say at last. 'You'll hear about it soon enough … so I might as well tell you. My cousin has died. I'm the heir of Scarossa now.'

Elisao's eyes widen. 'Vico … I …' He shakes his head.

'I mean, Livio. I'm so sorry about your cousin.'

'Thank you. But I never knew her,' I murmur, shrugging a little. 'Honestly, when Grandmother told me, the only thing I could think about was that I would lose this life ... lose you.'

Elisao's mouth flickers in a half-smile. 'Really?'

'Really. It's always been wrong for me to sneak out into the city, to live this other life. But now, with all my new duties ...' I reach out, lifting his hand in mine. 'But I can't give it up. I don't care. This is just as important. I sacrifice my daylight hours for Scarossa – but night-time is for me. For us. Somehow, I'll figure it out – I'll do both.'

He puts on his spectacles, a frown worrying at his brow. 'But when will you sleep?' he says with genuine concern.

I laugh. 'I've managed so far. I can do it.' And – as if to prove it – I kiss him again, long and gentle. When we pull apart, we linger close for a long moment. Reluctantly I say, 'I should go ...'

'Can we meet tomorrow?' Elisao asks breathlessly.

'Midnight, right here,' I say, a smile playing at my lips as I stand up. 'See you then, Elisao.'

His eyes shine as he smiles back. 'I'll be waiting.'

SIX
Red Magic

Beatrice

I wake suddenly, my breathing fast and shallow. It's still dark:
I can't have been asleep for more than half an hour.

Something woke me. But what?

A floorboard creaks nearby, and all of a sudden I know
that someone – someone *else* – is in the room with us. My
heart races as I try to pick out an unfamiliar shape in the
darkness. I tell myself it's a bad dream, that this old house
always shifts in the night, but my body won't listen. Every
muscle in me is sprung tight, and there's a swirling, sick
feeling in the hollow beneath my chest.

A second noise. It's very quiet – but this time, it's
unmistakeable. I peer into the gloom – the darkness is shifting, a figure separating itself from the shadows. If I scream,
the palazzo guards will hear – but my throat is tight and dry.
I can barely breathe. I clench my fists.

The figure solidifies as it nears the window, faint moonlight outlining long robes, a hood with shadow beneath.

Tall and broad, it's surely a man – but he moves with the silence of a cat.

He stops at Valentina's bed, the closest to the door. He raises his hands. From his palms, a bruised light flickers like the last rays of a stormy sunset, shifting and sparking. *A mage.* My eyes widen.

What is he doing? Another realisation jolts through me: *an assassin.*

If I have any advantage, it's surprise. Not allowing myself to think, I launch myself out of Ofelia's bed and at the figure. He turns towards me at the last moment, and I catch a glimpse of the darkness beneath the hood before my shoulder barrels into hard flesh and the light in his hands extinguishes. He staggers, grunting, but I'm not heavy enough to send him toppling. I grab the oil lamp from the table next to Valentina's bed before he rights himself.

I raise the heavy lamp – still-warm oil spattering on to my arm – and swing it round ... into thin air. I wasn't fast enough. Valentina has sat up in bed, scrambling back towards the wall. Ofelia screams. She flings the curtains open, shouting for help into the night, cold moonlight spilling into the room.

'Ofelia, go!' I manage.

Our attacker is unfazed. I swing the lamp round again, hoping to connect with his head. But he ducks easily, catching my arm mid-swing. Power pulses through his hand, burning my skin – red sparks flying into the air. I shout out in agony. My arm feels like it's on fire.

My vision is fading in and out, but from the corner of my eye, I see Ofelia lowering herself on to the trellis that trails up to our bedroom window, climbing down.

I force myself to stand up – I'm half raised, and the mage is already stepping towards me, his hands aglow again.

Valentina flings herself at him with a shout of anger, her hair flying out behind her, but he sends her sprawling with a casual sweep of his arm – the air glimmers. I hear her head bang hard against the wall and she sits there on the floor, clutching her skull, dazed and blinking. Anger sparks inside me as the mage returns his attention to me. His magic flashes, and in the split second before the attack hits me in the stomach, I realise he's wearing a mask – a black mask that covers his entire face, even his eyes hidden by a semi-transparent film.

Then, I double over in horrible, blinding pain.

Something is fizzing up inside me, some energy – it's surging through my blood, tingling on the skin of my face. I fling out my hands on instinct, and the air crackles as if it's full of static. When I breathe, it feels thick and cloying in my lungs, like the moment before lightning strikes. And then – a release. The mage staggers backwards, clutching his mask as if it's burning him, and I hear a muffled noise of pain.

Did I *do that?*

I drop my hands in shock and the noise stops, replaced by soft, laboured breathing.

The mage straightens and for a moment, he regards me from behind his mask, and there's a strange silence over everything. Even Valentina lifts her sore head to gaze at me in confusion. 'What …?' she says, her voice thick as she echoes my thought.

Then, we hear hurried footsteps on the stairs. The mage runs softly towards the window, swings himself up and on to the sill, fearless. A cloud of magic glitters under his feet, and all of a sudden he is on the roof, running out into the night.

The door bursts open. Four of the palazzo guards rush into the room, followed by Ofelia. Clutching her nightdress tightly, her hair unbound and her face streaked with tears, she looks about four years old.

'He went on the roof,' I blurt, sending the guards after him … even though – in my heart – I know he's long gone.

When I wake, it's late – the golden light arcing through the gaps in the curtains is high and bright, the sun past its zenith. Ofelia is in her bed, the covers pulled over her head, but Valentina's is stripped and bare.

In the bathroom I wash in the basin, fed with steaming water from the hot springs beneath this island. When I glance down at my stomach, I see livid red lightning-like marks spreading across my torso – from the assassin's magic, I think, remembering the burning, all-consuming pain. I touch the marks here and on my arm with slightly trembling hands: the skin is sore with an echo of the attack.

I dress quietly in a fresh black dress from the identical outfits in the single nursery wardrobe and head downstairs. Valentina, her hair pinned in a tight, neat bun, sits at the dining-room table, eating a bowl of plain rice and reading the daily bulletins, a collection of cheap printed pages produced at the palazzo and delivered each day to every household in the city. She glances up at me as I enter, nods, returns to her reading. Despite her composure, her eyebrows are slightly furrowed and there are dark circles under her eyes.

Everything looks normal – but it isn't. All of this is like stage scenery, obscuring the churning horror that unfolds unseen below the surface. After last night, *everything* has changed. I sit down, feeling like I'm part of a surreal dream.

'How are you feeling?' I ask my sister in an attempt to distract myself.

'My head hurts,' she says, her voice light, barely glancing up from the bulletin. 'And I couldn't sleep.' She fills up her cup of black coffee from the jug on the table.

'Anything in the bulletin about … what happened?'

'Not really.' She points to a paragraph at the bottom of the front page: *A New Generation of Mascherari.* 'It says we've inherited, but nothing about the attack. My guess is the Contessa doesn't want anyone to know.'

'It was horrible,' Ofelia says from the door. She's in her

white nightgown, her hair wild and loose around her shoulders, and her face tear-stained. She comes and sits at the table and buries her face in her arms in one smooth motion, continuing in a muffled voice. 'When I climbed down to find guards, there were bodies everywhere. Mage guards, too. There was this smell … like burning and blood.' She raises her head from her arms as a thought appears to occur to her. 'What I don't get is, how did he kill all those people but not us? What happened after I left?'

Valentina shrugs. 'I ran at him, he flung me aside, and I knocked my head, hard. Everything went fuzzy then.'

I feel a squirm of discomfort at the silence that follows, my sisters both looking at me expectantly. I've been turning what happened over and over in my mind – the energy that filled me, the sense of electricity, how the assassin had doubled over in pain – but I haven't found an explanation. 'I don't know,' I say. 'I think the fact I woke up, that we were fighting back, must've thrown him off. When you went to get help, he must've thought it wasn't worth it.'

Ofelia nods slightly, doubtfully. Valentina raises an eyebrow. But our housekeeper Anna-Maria opens the door, carrying a tray of food and saving me from further conversation. She's a young woman – only a little older than us, I think – and pretty. She has curling black hair and dark skin, and always wears a silver necklace strung with nine stars to represent the gods.

As she sets the food down on the table, Anna-Maria says,

'We'll be setting up your new rooms today. I wondered if there was anything each of you would like? The Contessa has provided a small budget for any extra comforts.'

'Oh!' Ofelia sits up straighter, her face brightening. 'Could I have the puppet stage from the nursery? If there's enough for an extra puppet ...?'

Anna-Maria smiles warmly. 'Of course. Valentina, how about you?'

My eldest sister frowns. I feel certain she'll refuse the gesture, but instead she says, 'Books. I can give you a list.'

'Very well. And Beatrice?'

I swallow, uncertain. 'I ... don't know.' I gaze out of the window at the garden, the lemon trees laden with early greenish fruit. 'Maybe a plant ... flowers of some sort,' I say, on impulse. 'Yes, flowers,' I say, firmer.

'Flowers ... all right.' Anna-Maria smiles uncertainly. 'I'll see what I can do.'

We spend our first night as mascherari in the temple, in the huge main building where an altar towers over a gleaming dark pool, and a high priestess leads our prayers. We're supposed to be mentally preparing ourselves for the task that will consume our lives – a task which starts tomorrow. But all night my knees are sore from kneeling, my neck stiff, and there's a strange fizzing feeling in the pit of my lungs. It's like there's a wasp trapped in there, desperately knocking up against my bones in its attempt to escape. All through our prayers I feel restless, distracted. Nerves, I suppose. In contrast, Valentina and Ofelia appear glowing and calm.

At last, we step out into the dawn, passing a lacquered black carriage coming from the palazzo, wheels rattling against the paving stones. Four guards wait for us, silently falling into formation as we start walking. The square is quiet, but I can hear the distant sounds of the market setting up somewhere. A young man peers out of the carriage at me as I hunch my shoulders against the wind. He's dark-haired and dark-eyed, a rash of stubble across his jaw, and for some reason I feel compelled to watch him pass by.

'That'll be Livio Santini, the Contessa's grandson,' Valentina says, hanging back as the carriage clatters past us towards the temple, watching the direction of my eyes. Because Valentina has stopped, the rest of us do too – even the four guards. 'He's a novice at Mythris's temple – but word is, he's not very talented. I heard it from Anna-Maria, who heard it from her friend who works at the temple. He barely attends his classes, and when he does, he always places at the bottom.'

Of the three of us, Valentina has the keenest interest in affairs of the state, which occasionally leads her to engage in a pastime she otherwise despises: gossip. I like to encourage this pursuit.

'He's not the heir though, is he? So it doesn't matter,' I suggest. 'He can do as he likes.'

'No … but the heir has never actually been here. Constance Santini isn't really a Santini at all – she's Constance Rathbone, daughter of a northern nobleman. She won't understand us. She won't know the ways of this island like a native would.'

'So people think *he* should inherit?'

Valentina gives me a withering look, as if I've suggested that a lemon might rule over us once the Contessa is gone. 'No. He's a *boy*, Beatrice. That would be far from preferable. I can't vouch for Livio Santini's knowledge of this city, but they say he returns home stinking of panacea.' She raises an eyebrow at me archly. I love how much she's enjoying this. 'You've got to think he's not spending his time in the library.'

'I see,' I reply, watching the carriage disappear. 'But there have been conte before, haven't there?'

But Ofelia is bored of our talk and is scuffling the ground pointedly with her heels, yawning and fiddling with her hair.

We start to walk, Valentina answering my question as we go along. 'Yes … men have ruled these islands a few times. But it has never ended well. The last conte managed to inflame a short and disastrous war with the north. That's the problem with men – they're too aggressive, impulsive. They've got no self-control.'

And with that thought, she steps ahead of me – taking her proper place.

We walk in a line behind Valentina, surrounded by our silent guards, and for the rest of the short journey home, we are silent too. A beggar pulls a dirty blanket over his face as we pass, and a young man setting up his stall of oranges outside the palazzo turns his face to the wall. They know who we are, the mascherari sisters all dressed in black, our fates like chains marking us out and binding us together. It is bad luck to set your sights upon us – we'll take your face for a mask, they say, steal your identity for Mythris.

Look away, or our three shadows might creep into your eyes.

By the time we reach the house, the chill of the night is gone and the sun is warming me through my black veil, despite the wind. Our house is large and old, and it near-tumbles into the wide sandstone city walls on the edge of the palazzo complex – like it was discarded by a rich courtier long ago. A line of tall wispy trees with silvery leaves separates the house from the square, and it appears to turn its back on the world, facing towards the garden at the rear. We pass through the archway between the trees and into cool shade. The house is in the shadow of the city walls for the majority of the day – a purposeful choice, for mascherari sleep in the daytime – and the front windows catch the evening sun, calling us to work.

Katherina once told me that, long ago, the house, the mask room and the temple were connected by tunnels. The mascherari sisters of old would walk these passages to their work, she said, and into the temple to pray, while novices selected for the honour of a True Mask would travel to the mask room underground to make their selection. But those ways are long lost.

I'm glad. I know I will treasure the few minutes each day we are allowed outside, savour the rising or falling sun.

Since last night, the guard around our house has doubled – I don't know how many men patrol the grounds in the Contessa's yellow livery, but it feels like we're living in a garrison. As we approach, I feel my spirits shrink. Our guards peel off as we reach the first line of defence surrounding the house. The soldiers here avert their eyes as we pass, exactly like everyone else. *How are they supposed to protect us when they won't even look at us?* I wonder. We're walking up the path to the door when a ghostly high-pitched noise rings through the air. I stop in my tracks.

'Did you hear that?' I ask Ofelia, who nearly walks into me. Valentina carries on at a brisk pace, as if she hasn't noticed.

The sound keens over the roof of our house again, plaintive and rasping, thin as the sliver of moon clinging to the sky far above. We've never heard them before, but Nurse described the sound to us and it's totally unmistakeable. She said they were bad omens, harbingers of misfortune …

'Do you think … do you think it's a sandwolf?' I whisper to Ofelia.

Ofelia catches my eye, nods, the strengthening breeze tugging at her veil.

'So what if it is?' says Valentina, turning on the top steps. 'Sound carries over the sea when it's calm. The creature is probably miles away, on Cantella.' Cantella is the southern-most inhabited island of the Wishes – you can glimpse it on a clear day from the cliffs, past the hulking shapes of our neighbouring islands, Silver and the Twins. 'Now, are you coming?'

As I follow Ofelia through the open door, Anna-Maria is waiting for us next to a tray of fresh mint tea and figs from the garden.

'I thought you might like some breakfast ... or supper, I suppose,' she says, smiling. 'And your new rooms are ready for you.'

'Thank you, Anna-Maria, but I am far too tired to eat,' Valentina says, climbing upstairs with barely a glance at the refreshments.

Ofelia can be trusted never to turn down food. 'Figs! My favourite,' she says, grinning and lifting one of the steaming cups and a plate from the tray. She hurries upstairs as fast as her tea will allow her.

'That's kind of you,' I say to Anna-Maria, taking my own meal.

'I've put your flowers in your room,' she adds to me before I start climbing the steps. 'I tried to think of some-thing that didn't need much light, as I supposed you'd likely have the curtains closed during the daytime.'

'That ... really is kind,' I say, although I would have kept the curtains open for my flowers – my bed has curtains, after all – and now I'm wondering what kind of plant doesn't need daylight. 'Thank you – you didn't need to.'

'It's nothing,' she says, although it isn't. 'Sleep well, Mistress.'

I set my food aside to open the door to Elina's old bedroom – I struggle to think of it as *my* room. The door creaks slightly as it opens. The smell of vinegar and lemon lingers in the space beyond. I blink at it, hesitating on the threshold. Anna-Maria and a group of servants from the palazzo have clearly swept through the room like a whirlwind while we prayed, stripping the sheets and beating the rugs and shaking out the curtains, burning incense and scrubbing everything ritually clean as if to erase the very existence of our predecessors.

I've never set foot in Elina's room before – only glimpsed the large four-poster with its heavy green curtains when the door swung open – and as I step inside I feel like I'm intruding. I pick up my tea and figs and put them on a side table by the door.

I spot the potted flowers on the windowsill, and I can't help it – my heart sinks. Of course, she gave me bone roses. They don't need much light because they feed on magic – or at least, that's what I've heard. The Contessa grows hundreds of these things in her hothouses to sell overseas – you can't find them anywhere else in Valorian, and people will pay handsomely for a potted bone rose. She has a whole private garden full of the things, nourished with different types of magic to bring out their myriad of colours. The King has several, too – they're a curiosity, over on the mainland, because they wither and die in ordinary soil. But here, where the very earth is magic, they thrive like weeds.

I walk over to them now, their pinkish petals veined with purplish grey. They rustle as I near them. The flowers are half closed, like heavy, sleepy eyelids. I've never liked how they look – their slender and bare black stems with thorns the size of fingernails, rising to oddly large and fleshy blooms. They are sad-looking flowers, I think: heavy-headed, closing and opening to the strange rhythms of magic, not the sun and earth and wind.

Nevertheless, I stroke one of the petals and am surprised to find it slightly furred and warm to the touch. I notice it revive – opening a little as I run my fingers over it – and I frown, snatching my hand away. If they thrive on magic, and this flower is reacting to my touch, does that mean there's magic in my hands? I stretch out my fingers, flex them gently. The masks we create from now on are infused with magic. Mythris's power is in my blood. Even so, I feel unsettled and draw quickly away from the strange blooms.

I fall into bed and pull the covers over me. My mind is racing at first, and I stare at the strange room, wishing Nurse were here to tell me everything is all right, to assure me there will be no more assassins, no more inexplicable powers flying from my fingers. *Where is she now?* I wonder. At the market, perhaps, buying food and flowers for her apartment. But soon my thoughts grow sluggish. I fall asleep watching the bone roses on my windowsill sway gently in the breeze.

SEVEN
The Masked Guard

Livio

I wake at dawn, which is highly irregular at the best of times – but especially after a night such as mine. I blink in the washed-out yellow light arcing through the half-closed window. Half-light, really. My head throbs in protest, and the air swirls with dust, but for some reason I resist the urge to let sleep pull me down, and I prop myself up on my elbows.

There's a noise on the balcony – a hiss or a whisper, so quiet that I'm not sure how or why I separated it from the ordinary sounds of early morning over the city. In the semi-light I can see a shape – a low, shifting form between the flimsy curtains. I sit up further, the bedcovers sliding from me. Instinctively, my muscles start to tense. The shape edges closer and as the curtains blow in, I glimpse it properly. It's the size of a fox, but it's nebulous, see-through – like a ghost. A miniature sandstorm in black. If I squint, I can make out two yellow pinpricks, glowing.

A sandwolf.

'You again?' I whisper softly. Instead of fear, a strange calm envelops me, just like it did in the warehouse. The creature and I regard each other, its glowing eyes steady. Is it the same sandwolf I saw last night? I don't know for sure, but I wonder if it caught my scent, somehow, and traced me here. It's sitting – hovering, I suppose – and watching. It's as if something about me has caught its attention … or as if it's waiting for me to say something, *to command it*. I don't know where that thought came from …

I stroke the signet ring I always wear, feeling the graven mirror image of the wisping creature. I'm on the verge of stepping out of bed towards it when a second shape drops down from the rooftop – a man in the Contessa's yellow livery, his face hidden by a snarling, living mask in the image of a wildcat, glittering with shards of gold in the dawn light. It roars, a high, unnatural sound like metal blades clashing in the night.

A True Mask.

The mage flings an unnaturally amplified spell at the spinning sandwolf, which lurches to one side, suddenly thrown off its axis. My heart lurches with it. The creature swirls into nothingness as a second attack zips towards it, reforming with a hissing noise a few paces to its right, leaving a wisp of curling sand in its wake. I run towards the balcony.

'Stop!' I shout at the guard. 'Don't hurt it.'

I'm too late to stop a third spell exploding on the balcony in a shower of reddish–purple sparks, the colour of a storm at sunset – but the creature spins free. In spite of my command, the guard raises his hand to attack again.

'No! Don't you dare!' Anger fills my voice. I don't know why, but I can't let this sandwolf die. The guard stops, obedient to my command, and the sandwolf appears to be unharmed – or at least unharmed enough to survive. It lingers for a second, gazing at me again.

'You need to let me kill it, Lord,' the guard says, his voice low, tinged with an accent I recognise as northern, from the mainland. The wildcat mask's lips move along with his, its whiskers glowing silver. 'It's dangerous.'

The sandwolf and I stare at each other, my heart beating fast. I step closer towards it, reaching out my hand – but then, its yellow eyes flicker and it disappears, reappearing a second later down in the gardens, then whisking itself off towards the city in a whoosh of sand.

The guard stands for a moment, watching it go, then turns towards me. He lifts his mask. As soon as it's separated from his face, it grows solid and stiff, like the painted eggshell face of a puppet. But I'm not looking at the mask any more. I thought he'd look angry or confused, but the man grins unexpectedly, a jewel on his tooth shining, his cropped black hair gleaming like a precious metal. From his accent, I was expecting him to be light-skinned, like most northerners – but his skin is a deep brown. He can't be much older than me, but his shoulders are broader, his body tightly muscled. I feel suddenly hot.

'Why didn't you let me kill it?' he asks when I don't return his smile. 'Were you … going to *pet* it?' There's a slight mocking tone to his voice. No other guard has ever spoken to me this way.

'I … No … Well …' I feel blood rush to my cheeks. What *had* I been thinking? I decided to focus on his first question. 'I didn't let you kill it because … because it wasn't doing anything.' I clear my throat. 'Why is your first instinct to kill something as soon as you see it, whether or not it's a threat?' I'm glad to hear my voice is stronger now, more confident.

He shakes his head, as if I'm a foolish child he's indulging. 'Can't trust a sandwolf, Lord. They look harmless, like they're made of nothing but thin air and dust, but I've seen 'em kill a mage in ten seconds flat. They'll suck the magic clean out of you given half the chance. Trust me – the more of those bastards we kill, the better.'

I remember the dead girl – but of course, I can't reveal that I too have seen that a sandwolf is capable of killing. 'Sure,' I say, lifting my chin. 'It certainly looked threatening, what with all that … sitting.'

I expect him to be chastened – but instead he grins again, laughs. 'You're mad, Lord,' he says. It's very overfamiliar. I should berate him. Instead, I feel an unexpected tingle of joy running through me, and I don't mean to, but I smile back.

'Well, I'd best return to my duties.' He bows slightly and turns away before I realise I don't know his name. In fact, I don't think I've seen him before – and I don't remember seeing his True Mask either. He jumps, and his purplish-red magic carries him up to the roof.

By the time I rush outside, craning my neck to find him, he's gone.

EIGHT
Triplets

Beatrice

It's still light when I'm woken by the sound of voices down-stairs. I try to ignore them, sleep tugging me back into its embrace, but the noise is insistent.

I get up and step out on to the landing in my nightgown. Something makes me hover out of sight, listening. I can hear three voices: Anna-Maria's; our cook, Marta's; and a male voice I don't recognise. I lean a little over the stairway, catch a glimpse of purple robes edged in gold. I start back-wards, my heart hammering. The mages of the masked temple all wear purple robes, but one man alone has the gold trim: the Cardinal.

'… due in less than a month,' the man is saying. 'The room will have to be prepared.'

'But the mascherari have barely assumed their new duties,' Anna-Maria protests. 'My lord, surely a different room can be arranged at the palazzo? This will be a terrible disruption for the girls.'

85

'You know how it is done – how it has always been done,' says the Cardinal firmly. 'Tradition cannot be disputed.'

Valentina opens her door, which is opposite mine. I manage to catch her eye and press a finger to my lips. She stops and listens.

Marta's speaking now in her low, hesitant voice – she's much older than Anna-Maria, in her sixties, and has served three generations of mascherari. 'He is right. It has always been the eldest sister's room in which the new generation of mascherari are born. And so it must always be.'

I press my hand to my mouth to stifle a gasp. I finally understand what they're talking about. They've found the next triplets. They've *already* found the next triplets. When I meet Valentina's eyes, they too are wide with horror. Our predecessors were mascherari for well over a decade before they found us. Katherina was in her late forties by the time she died, bringing her sisters with her. How old will we be when the masked god deems it time for the next generation to inherit and strikes us down?

When Anna-Maria speaks again, it's like she has read my thoughts. 'But, my lord … can this really be right? It is so soon. The mascherari are … so young.'

I hear the swish of robes and risk a glimpse over the banister, noticing Valentina echoing my movements. The Cardinal has stepped closer to our housekeeper, exerting his authority. 'The masked god has commanded it, and he will not be tolerant of your questioning,' he says, his voice low and tight with warning.

'Yes, my lord,' Anna-Maria replies, though anger burns in her voice.

'Now ... can I trust you to make the necessary preparations?'

'Of course.'

When the door shuts, and Marta has returned to the kitchen, Anna-Maria calls up to us. 'I know you're there, Mistresses. I heard you.'

Valentina and I exchange a glance then both step to the top of the stairs. Anna-Maria gazes up at us.

'You heard everything?'

We nod slowly. Our housekeeper's eyes are full of pity and it makes my skin crawl.

'Is there anything I can get for you?' Anna-Maria asks.

I'm about to refuse when Valentina says, 'Perhaps some fresh mint tea, if you wouldn't mind. I don't think I will be sleeping again today.'

Valentina and I linger on the landing when Anna-Maria disappears into the kitchen.

'She's not going to like it,' Valentina says, glancing at Ofelia's door.

'Do *you* like it?'

She shakes her head but doesn't reply at first. After a pause, she says, 'But ... if Mythris wills it, then we must try to be joyous. The cycle is beginning again.'

I feel my mouth pinch in annoyance at her empty words. '*I'll* tell Ofelia,' I say. 'She doesn't need …' – *your empty platitudes. Your complete lack of feeling.* But I don't finish my sentence. 'I'm going to try and get some more rest,' I say instead, rising to my feet. 'It's a few hours until dusk.'

'As you wish,' Valentina says, her eyes tired-looking. She lifts her chin at me, rallying. 'I will be in my room with the tea if you find you can't sleep. You are welcome to join me.'

Sometimes it feels like Valentina and I are little more than polite acquaintances.

I don't bother trying to go back to sleep – but I don't join my eldest sister either. I potter around my room, tidying away some books and cautiously tending the bone roses on my windowsill, my mind calmed by these manual tasks. I love Valentina, but I can't face any more of her before breakfast. I've always felt different to her – and to Ofelia, in other ways. As identical triplets, I think, we've all tried hard to focus on what makes us distinct. But ever since the Inheritance, I feel more adrift than ever. It feels like my sisters are walking confidently along a misty path, and I'm stumbling behind, afraid to lose them, longing to surrender to … To what?

I wake Ofelia a little earlier than she'd usually like, sitting on her bed and shaking her shoulder gently. Her dark hair is splayed out on the pillow, tangled and wild. I set a cup of weak coffee on her bedside table – with two sugars, as she likes it. She's a heavy sleeper, and I doubt she's stirred since she rested her head on the pillow.

She stretches out, blinking at the fading sunlight spilling through her curtains. Her room is far prettier than mine – strung with glass beads and candles and colourful swathes of silk. I admire how quickly she's transformed it, though I don't care for the puppet stage she's had brought in from the nursery. She's hung three puppets there – the others stored in a tall wooden chest at the foot of her bed, which she long ago painted with scenes from her favourite plays. The puppets on stage sway gently in the breeze from the window. The new one is a fine lady in a green gown with pink cheeks and unnervingly realistic golden hair. I recognise the fool with his colourful patchwork, and the knight dressed in tin, darkness behind his visor, from the nursery set. As they sway together and apart, subtly, I realise that part of the reason they frighten me is that they are a little too lifelike. I would not like them watching me as I sleep. There is a kind of knowing there, behind their painted faces.

I think of how our True Masks will spring to life with the touch of their wearer, and I shudder.

'Beatrice?' Ofelia says, finally waking up properly. 'Is everything all right?'

'I have some news,' I reply. 'A woman in the city is bearing triplets. The Contessa has decreed them our heirs.'

All at once, she is fully awake – sitting up and raising a hand to her mouth.

'It's early, yes,' I say, unable to hide the tension in my own voice. 'Apparently she's due in under a month.'

'The cycle starts again …' Tears fill her eyes. 'Bea … If the masked god deems them ready to inherit when they are our age, we will be dead before we are forty,' she says, voice thick with despair. 'We will barely have lived at all!'

I nod, but really I don't agree. For me, it should be *how* we live, not for how long. Ofelia longs for more time to live … but I want a different life altogether. I want to see other places, other peoples. I want to taste the air on the open sea. I shut my eyes. I always knew it was impossible, but now it feels even more so.

Fate is closing around us like a fist.

NINE
A Book

Livio

'Now, draw on your magic,' says Priestess Brora, her dark robes flaring as she stalks along the front of the class of fifteen purple-robed novices, her iron-grey hair pinned up in a tight bun. 'You have each been supplied with an inanimate object upon which to base your illusion. Inanimate objects, as you know, are relatively simple to imitate.' She casts an unimpressed glance at the novice seated at the far end of the room, who is struggling to reproduce a long, curled pipe. The glowing magic on his palm is slug-shaped and spitting purple sparks, but it's better than anything I'll be able to produce. A small cactus in a terracotta pot sits on the table in front of me. I hold out my hand and frown at it. *Come on.* Magic writhes in my belly like a cat slinking away from an outstretched palm. I sigh.

'Stop! Let's go back to basics, again,' says Priestess Brora, pursing her lips. I lower my hand, flexing my fingers – as if that will help. 'Your magic is an energy inside your body.

You were born with it – as you were born with legs and a voice. But, exactly as you had to learn to walk and talk, you have to learn to use it. With practice, you will use your magic with the same effortless ease that you speak. But it takes time. Don't try to run before you can walk – draw on your magic slowly, carefully. Now try again.'

I hold out my hand a second time, frowning at the cactus. Is it my imagination, or is it frowning back?

Priestess Brora is sweeping down the long bench again – now, she glances at the novice next to me, who is attempting to tame a fizzing ball of sparks, which bears a passing resemblance to the orange in front of him. 'Helton, start again – there's no use building on uncertain foundations.' She clears her throat, raises her voice for everyone's benefit – and to my relief, turns away to stalk towards the opposite end of the room. 'The art of spellcraft is subtle and requires great delicacy. Yes, we are practising an illusion – a trick. But the skills you exercise here will be applicable to multiple spells. Pay particular attention to the details as you work on your replica.' She stops in front of a novice halfway down the long bench. 'Beautiful, Carlotta. Novices, can you see the detail of the creature's wings – its sharp, pointed beak?'

The crow on Carlotta's outstretched hand shines with a faint magical glow, lighting her pale, sharp northern features, her copper hair. Otherwise, it is indistinguishable from the taxidermy creature on the bench in front of her – right down to its beady black eyes. I glance along the row, nervously hoping someone else has entirely failed at the task: but no – every one of them now holds an illusion of varying quality in their outstretched hands. A cut bone rose in a vase – imperfectly replicated in a novice's hand as a trembling outline of purple light but still, recognisably, a bone rose. A beautifully decorated teacup stands on the palm next to it – the pattern isn't quite right, but it's nearly there. Even the pipe is looking less slug-like.

And then there's me, empty-handed, glaring at the cactus on my bench and then at my hand as if I can do this by pure force of will. But there's more to it than that – far more. Magic fizzles inside me, but it won't obey my commands. The harder I try, the more it shrinks away – down, down further into the pit of my stomach – and the more frustrated I get …
I swallow as Priestess Brora stops in front of me, her face settling into a familiar exasperated frown as she watches me try harder, sparks flying from my fingers. *Come on. COME ON.*

There's a whooshing sound and, all of a sudden, the cactus is burning with a tall purple flame. I lean back in my chair and try not to let tears sting my eyes as snorts erupt around the room.

Priestess Brora waves a hand casually over the cactus, the fire flickering out, leaving a blackened accusatory carcass. She turns away, wordless, and I slump down on my desk. Gods, why is it so hard?

★

At the end of the session, I start to gather together my books hopefully. Priestess Brora is one of the good ones. She's firm but fair. Sometimes, on a good day, she cuts me some slack.

'Lord Livio, stay behind,' Priestess Brora says, laying a hand gently on my pile of textbooks. The huge ring on her middle finger catches the sunlight – a purple stone carved with the likeness of the cloaked, hooded masked god. My heart sinks. Today isn't one of the good days, I guess.

I'm so tired. By the time I had climbed up the trellis for the second time last night, I had barely half an hour to sleep, fully clothed on the bed, before dawn and the sandwolf woke me. I'm used to managing on a few hours' sleep, a few times a week – but *this*? I feel like I've been chewed up and spat out by the night.

When the long chamber is empty and silent, golden evening light spilling through the arched windows, Priestess Brora sits opposite me and quietly talks me through the spell again. I try to do as she says. I really do. But apart from another lone spark spinning up from my fingers, nothing happens. Even the eviscerated potted cactus looks disappointed in me.

'Lord Livio, I can tell you're trying. But I'm not sure your heart is in it.'

I shrug slightly, not meeting her eyes. Of course my heart isn't in it. My heart is with Elisao, in the city, in the fight. My heart is Vico.

'Some of us may not have been born with a great deal of natural power. But this kind of spell is more about concentration and focus than raw energy. Any mage has enough power for them to achieve a simple illusion.' Her voice isn't without kindness – but somehow, her words sting like an insult.

'Any mage but me,' I mutter, hating how sullen I sound.

Her mouth flattens in disapproval. 'I suspect part of it is confidence, Lord Livio. You have to believe you can do it. We all know you can – but you have convinced yourself you're not good enough.'

'I wish it were that simple,' I say. I try to smile, but it falters on my lips. 'Look, I understand what you're saying. Confidence would help. But it's a vicious circle, isn't it? I'm not confident, so I can't do it. I can't do it, so I'm not confident.'

'Exactly. But it's up to you to break that circle, my lord. No one can do that for you.' She leans forward on the table, forcing me to meet her eyes. 'You look tired. And something tells me you weren't up all night practising your spells. Perhaps it's that injury of yours.' She raises an eyebrow, and I lift a hand self-consciously to my nose.

Is it still that obvious?

'I'm sorry, Lord Livio, but poor performance comes with consequences – I can't make exceptions, not even for you. You'll work in the library for an hour today. And might I suggest you put what's left of the evening to better use? Sleep should definitely be a priority.'

Relief floods my body. Working in the library is a regular punishment for poor performance – but for me, it's ineffective. See, I actually *like* the library. 'Very well,' I say, trying to sound disappointed. I hold my books to my chest and head for the corridor, glancing over my shoulder before I leave – but Priestess Brora is staring at the blackened corpse of my cactus, frowning as if in puzzlement. I shut the door behind me.

Outside, in the bright courtyard, Carlotta is holding court among a group of her admirers. Her hair is shining copper, the breeze turning it to flickering fire. She's the daughter of the Cardinal, the head of the masked god's temple in Scarossa. She stands out, like me – but unlike me, she turns it to her advantage. She is nearly as tall as I am, though slender and pale as bone.

Jurah's tits, I hate her.

I try to slide past towards the library staircase, but she catches sight of me and says loudly in an exaggeratedly affected accent: '*Lord Livio*, of course, prefers battling plants to practising illusions.' Carlotta's admirers snigger, hardly bothering to hide their smirks behind their hands. 'Fighting a cactus is probably the only way he can guarantee victory,' she adds in a lower tone, but perfectly loud enough for me to hear.

Normally I'd ignore her. But today is different: I'm too tired, maybe; too mixed up between Livio and Vico to resist the urges of the night. Rage pulses through me and something snaps. I step forward unthinkingly, my shoulders squared and fists clenched. 'Speak like that about me again,' I say, heat simmering through my voice, 'and I'll—' I break off as I catch sight of the shocked faces of my classmates. I'm suddenly flooded with cold and let my shoulders drop. I try to think of the right words, but nothing comes.

'Were you about to *punch* me?' Carlotta says, raising an eyebrow.

I turn away, breathe deep. I'm not in the Battaglia. I'm not Vico. I'm *Livio* in the temple, surrounded by mages who are stronger than me in the way it really matters: magically. Besides, it might not be public knowledge yet, but I'm heir to the Contessa. I can't threaten the Cardinal's daughter. I shake my head and set off towards the library again, the jeers of my classmates following me like wasps.

And although my fists are clenched so hard my nails bite into my palms, I don't let myself turn back.

I start to relax a little as I climb the spiral staircase, leaving behind the bustling courtyard in exchange for a cool, stony silence. Even so, I hesitate outside the huge double doors, leaning hard against the wall. As an ineffective mage, I'll never command the respect of my peers in the temple. Perhaps that's all right, for the *second* in line to the Contessa. But that's all changed, now that I'm the heir. When I am Conte, I cannot be trampled upon.

The temples are themselves political bodies with their own agendas, headed by the Holy Council in the northern capital. And then there's the King, to whom I shall swear fealty – he has his own interests to consider. I rub my forehead. If I am not respected, if even *novices* speak to me as Carlotta did, how will I stand up to the temples, to the Holy Council, to the King himself, and protect the interests of my city?

Enough. I cannot think of this now. I stand up straight and push open the doors.

The temple library is in an ancient part of the complex, set in the tall archway over the huge wooden gates. Enchanted windows – charmed to protect fragile books from the sunlight – range across the curved room, the slanted glass panes spilling a steady but oddly glittering light on to the tall shelves. Steps separate the room into three different levels.

The space is tiny compared to the huge library in the palazzo square – however, every tome in here handles the subject of magic. And if I shut my eyes and breathe in, I can smell the paper and dust and the indefinable scent of knowledge.

The librarian – a stern-faced high priest in late middle age – barely nods at me these days as I enter. As usual, he's hunched over a huge ledger spidered with blue-inked handwriting. He glances at the wheeled case of books, which it is my task to shelve, and returns to his accounts.

Without bothering him further, I start to push it down the first row.

I've replaced around ten books before I pick up a slim volume missing a label on its spine. I turn it over and blink in shock, my breath catching in my throat. The emblem embossed in silver foil on its cover is the Santini sun, but without the nine stars. Exactly like the graffiti and the pendant on the mysterious figure. I flick it open to read the title: *The Queens of the Wishes*. The book was published a hundred years ago, and there is no slip of paper inside to show who has checked it out and when. In fact, I don't think it's a library book at all ... But if that's the case, how did it get here?

I open the plate section, curiosity piquing. The first image depicts a mage, his robes a deep, brilliant blue, dotted with stars. The caption reads: *An Astromancer in traditional Scarossan garb. Evidence of ancient Astromancy is rumoured to be hidden in Dark Scarossa.*

Astromancer? I frown. I'm aware of myths about a native magic to the Wishes, of course. A different source of magic, they say, unrelated to Chaos – a magic drawn from an old goddess known as Fortune ... but those stories have long since been proved nonsense. Before the time of the gods, magic was inherently varied and Chaotic; little wonder some called it by different names.

Dark Scarossa. That's the second time I've heard those words in as many days, I think, as I recall Old Jacobo's rumours about Shadow.

I flick over to the next plate: a crowned woman surrounded by stars. *Fortune, the goddess worshipped by the ancient peoples of the Wishes,* says the caption – but it's at that moment I hear a light cough from behind me. The librarian has risen from his desk and is glowering at me. He says nothing – he never does. The spell of silence in this place is seldom disturbed. I smile apologetically, replace the book on my trolley and continue in my task.

Once I'm alone again, I reopen the book and flick through the front trying to locate the contents page – but it's a small line of pencilled handwriting across the top of the page that captures my attention.

This book belongs to Sera Lupina. Do not steal or I will CURSE YOU.

I raise my signet ring to my lips in shock. Sera Lupina. Serafina Santini. My mother.

I glance over my shoulder, but I'm alone in the history section, the light from the sinking sun turning into molten gold as it hits the enchanted glass. Was this simply chance? Or, more likely, did someone leave this book for me to find? If so, who? And why? All my life, the only scrap I've had of my mother is the signet ring, tucked in my cradle the night she left. And suddenly, this.

One thing's for sure … someone is watching me; someone knows my life is changing. My mind spins as I hold the slim book close to my chest: the cloaked figure, the Battaglia, the sandwolves, the mascherari Inheritance …

I don't know what it all means yet – but it means something.

I slide the volume under my robes and continue my duties.

I return from the temple sore and exhausted and late, the book hidden, pressed against my stomach. As I step from the carriage and hurry up the palazzo steps in the long evening shadows, longing for my room and the privacy I need to study my discovery, I notice a servant waiting for me inside.

Grandmother wants to see me.

She is sitting alone at the tall windows overlooking the south side of the gardens, where every variety of bone rose imaginable grows in tightly ordered beds. Bone roses are naturally a kind of fleshy pink – that's how they appear in the wild. But they can change colour depending on whose magic nourishes them – and my grandmother's gardeners are assisted by mages who hail from each of the nine temples. The result is a rainbow of golds, ochres and reds, velvety blacks, purest brilliant whites and smoky greys, bright greens and deep, azure blues – flowers echoing the colours of each god's magic. The sun is sinking, and the shadows stretching over the garden are staining the grass like grey ink.

The roses she has chosen to grow on the trellis outside her window, so tall and so close they are pressed against the glass, are a bruised, thunderous purple. Like my magic, hers, Constance's ... and my mother's too, so I hear. The people of these islands have a unique connection to the temple of Mythris – nowhere else does the masked god dominate the magical population as he does in the Wishes.

Despite the warm day, the window is only cracked slightly, allowing the barest breath of fresh air inside the room, carrying the roses' cloying smell. As usual, Grandmother is wearing a long-sleeved black dress and layers of dark shawls, and Patience's mourning ring is on her finger. Today, she wears a second ring, nearly as large. Instead of hair, it contains a likeness of my cousin in profile – I can tell who it is even from a distance by the pale skin colour and the severity of her expression: Constance. How did she have it made so quickly – or does she have boxes of these mourning rings ready-made, lying in wait for the next of us to die?

'Sit down,' she says, gesturing at the chair opposite hers. I lower myself on to the overstuffed silk cushions. She sighs and I feel a sudden pang of remorse that I am not the grandson – or heir – that she longed for, or deserved.

Her face is drawn and pale, her wrinkles deep – I never think of her as an old woman, but today she looks every one of her eighty-five years. I think of what Old Jacobo told me, about the threats facing the city – about Shadow. I suspect she knows as much or more than I do – but I'm reluctant to introduce the subject. Grandmother knows I've been sneaking into the city, but if she guessed the extent of my involvement in the criminal underworld … She may look older than usual, but even as I watch, she draws herself up, her eyes hardening as she fixes me with one of her stares. I am still afraid of her, as much as I love her. I still seek her approval. Finally she speaks. 'You like book-learning, Livio. So tell me, what do you know of the early origins of our house?'

I lean forward, resting my elbows on my knees, surprised by the question. Has she really summoned me here, after all of last night's upheaval, to talk about history? I think of the book tucked under my clothes – I'm burning to open it again, to discover what secrets it holds. Does she know, somehow? I'm sure she has plenty of informants in the city and the temple … I swallow, my throat suddenly dry as I attempt an answer. 'I know we are one of the two mage families that have been here since even before the nine gods: us and the Lupinas.' *The Lupinas: my mother's family.* I stroke the signet ring, tracing the outline of the sandwolf with my thumb.

'And what magic did those Ancestors practise? Before the gods, that is?' Grandmother asks.

Before the gods …? No one really talks about those times. Where is she going with this? I clear my throat. 'Is this really …?'

She smiles slightly. 'I promise you, there is a point.'

'Well … it is said that they practised an older magic … called astromancy.' I don't think I have spoken the word aloud before – it feel alien on my tongue, uncomfortable. I try it again. 'Astromancy was rumoured to be the native power of this island, separate from the powers of the nine gods. It was drawn instead from their mother, Fortune, who is said to have died here, her magic infiltrating the soil itself – creating the strong magical energies of the Wishes.' I shake my head. 'But astromancy was disproved long ago. There is no magic but that which we draw from Order and Chaos.'

'Even so,' she says, leaning back. 'Tell me more about the two families.'

'They were rulers of Scarossa, but not in the way we now know. The Santinis were queens. And the Lupinas were generals. They ruled side by side, and both used the old magic in different ways – the Santinis had the ability, they say, to determine and manipulate the future, and the Lupinas to fight and suppress their enemies.' I glance up at Grandmother, and she gestures at me to continue. I grope around for the rest of what I've learned. 'When the gods made themselves known to mankind, they established a loyal king on the mainland to the north. And the King started a holy war with the Queen of Scarossa. The Queen at last surrendered, accepting the King's and the gods' supremacy, who in their mercy granted her the title Contessa …' I stop, casting another look at Grandmother.

'That is certainly the story we've all been told,' she says. 'But you must know there is more to it than that. What of the god Mythris's role?'

'It is said that Mythris brokered the peace, striking a bargain with the Queen against the wishes of her Lupina general, who wanted to continue the war. The Queen agreed to pledge allegiance to the gods and to the King, demoting herself to Contessa, and to build a temple for Mythris, the greatest temple on the Wishes. And in return, Mythris granted her the power of the True Masks – the greatest assassins and spies in the world were to be under the new Contessa's command. The line of mascherari sisters was started.'

'And that's it?'

I nod slowly. 'That's all I know.'

Grandmother smiles. 'Now ... as my heir ... the know-ledge of what *truly* passed between Mythris and our Ancestors can be passed on to you.' She sets down her cup and stands up with some difficulty, leaning on her cane. 'Come – this is best seen, not told.'

She leads me across the room towards a curtained alcove I've always assumed led to a dressing room or wardrobe. The room grows hotter as we leave the window, and I realise there's a fire burning in the small grate. Even so, when Grandmother holds out her hand for me to support, her skin is cold.

Grandmother reaches up with her other hand and pulls

the curtain back, revealing a narrow door. She stops before opening the door.

'Of all the gods, Mythris was the most sympathetic to the magic of our Ancestors – to astromancy. There *is* power, Livio, that runs deeper than the energies of Order and Chaos – the colourful magics we draw from the nine gods. They don't teach you this at the temple – but perhaps you have known it all along, somehow. It is in your blood, after all. There is more in this world than the gods care to admit.'

I feel a thrill run through me as we hesitate on the threshold. Another path. Another magic. Another chance, perhaps. How many times have I longed for someone to tell me that there are more than two choices in this life – magic or none? Livio or Vico? But instantly I quash my excitement, not daring to hope. 'I don't—'

'Just listen,' she says, cutting me off. 'One of these other magics is this – a power that threads through time itself, connecting the past, present and future. It is the force we once worshipped as Fortune and manipulated through the stars. A force drawn from the very earth of this island, where Fortune's remains lie.'

She can't be telling me that astromancy … is real? 'Grandmother, believing the non-magical parts of the histories is one thing, but this is—'

'Impossible, I know.' She smiles tightly. 'Ridiculous, even? Everyone knows that there is only Order and Chaos, and the gods to help us navigate their waters. I said the same thing to my own mother when she brought me here, nearly seventy years ago.'

She slips a silver key on a long chain out from under her clothes, inserts it into the lock and opens the door. I catch a glimpse of a blue gem on the key's bow as she hides it again. Beyond the door is a narrow spiral staircase leading upwards. Grandmother turns away from me, holds on to the metal banister determinedly and starts heaving herself up on to the first step, then the second, slowly. I know better than to offer to help, but I can tell this journey is causing her pain. When she continues to speak, her voice is rough with it.

'Our Ancestor agreed to bow to the nine gods, yes. But Mythris wanted something from us too – knowledge of the magic we used to pull the strings of fate. And that gave us some bargaining power. The negotiations lasted for days, but at last, a bargain was struck. Mythris granted us the True Masks. His power was to be divided among three human girls, triplets to be born on the Wishes – Mythris feared bestowing the power on a single person, so he divided it, hemmed it in, gave it to what he saw as the weaker sex.' The tone of her voice perfectly conveys what she thinks of this notion. 'The triplets would be confined to the palazzo grounds, too. There could be no overlap between two generations – when one sister died, the others would too, and the power would pass on to the next generation.

The masks were permitted to be used as a weapon for the protection and furtherance of the Contessa's power.'

She pauses to catch her breath, and I notice we have nearly reached the top. When I gaze up, I realise we are climbing the largest of the spiralling glass towers in the palazzo. I didn't know it was even possible: from the outside, the glass is tinted such a bright shade of blue that you can't see inside at all.

Grandmother continues to climb. 'In return, our Ancestors agreed to grant him the benefits of the old magic, of astromancy – while, at the same time, hiding its true powers from anyone else. The religion of Fortune was to be buried.'

She is quiet for a few moments while we scale the last few stairs and step out on to a polished wooden floor. The room opens up above us. The ceiling over our heads soars up to its apex easily thirty feet above and entirely wrought of glass, twisting itself into the distinctive Scarossan spiral that feels so familiar … and yet … there is something different here. The panes of glass are smaller, less transparent. The blue tinge floods the room with an ethereal light, as if it's being filtered through water and we are miles under the sea. The dying sunlight falls through it unevenly. A large round marble platform is set in the middle of the floor, and somehow I can tell with a glance that it's older than the gods: a huge image of a sun has been embedded in mosaic on its surface, the colours faded yellows and reds.

My mind leaps back to the graffiti, the pendant, the cover of my mother's book … 'Is this part of a temple … to Fortune?'

'Clever boy. This is the oldest part of the palazzo, hidden from all but the Contessa, her close family … and the Cardinal.' Her mouth flattens to a thin line. 'Every month, the Cardinal of Mythris's temple visits this place to hear the temple's fortune, and I am tasked with adjusting it to his specifications, as far as I am able.'

'You … *you* are an astromancer?' I blink, feeling my whole world jolt and turn.

'Of course. What have I been telling you, boy? We Santinis always have been, stretching back to that very first generation. Why do you think we are always so eager that our children be gifted with magic? Not all mages are astromancers, but all astromancers are mages. The magic within you, after all, is what connects you to both of these powers. Without that inborn talent, there can be no spells or visions.'

I nod slowly. 'The bargain relies on it. If the contessa or conte were to be a non-astromancer, the agreement with Mythris would end. No more masks. So I'm here to …' My eyes widen with realisation. 'You're going to teach me astromancy?'

'Why did you think I'd brought you all the way up here – for fun?' she snaps, walking over to the huge table, her cane tapping loudly on the floor.

I feel blood rush to my cheeks.

She continues. 'The balance is delicate, and I am growing old. It is difficult for me to climb up here, as you have seen, let alone control the powers of astromancy with the accuracy and delicacy required. The older I grow, the more the stars seem to slip from my power like coins through outstretched fingers. My link to the future fades as my own future shrinks.' She rests her cane against the table top and slowly pulls a chair from beneath it. Every one of her movements is laboured – she is clearly in pain – but when I start forward to help her, she shoots me a glare that freezes me to the spot. 'Meanwhile,' she continues, 'the signs of Mythris's favour appear to melt before my eyes. My line of heirs grows ever weaker. And the masked god did not exactly favour you with outstanding magical talents, Livio.' I feel the sting of the comment, but I try to ignore it as she lowers herself into the seat. 'And now, with this assassination attempt on the mascherari sisters from gods know who …' She shakes her head.

I freeze. 'An assassination attempt?' I repeat softly.

She sighs. 'Yes. Hours after the Inheritance. Even the True Masked guards did not detect the intruder. One has to ask, is Mythris as committed to upholding his side of the bargain as he once was?'

'What does all this mean?' I ask shakily.

'I fear … I fear it means the agreement with Mythris is in trouble.' She places her hands flat on the table's surface. The rings on her fingers catch the dying sunlight, reflecting back on her face in a golden glow. For a moment I can see how she must have looked when she was my age – when she was first in this temple, as I am now. Beautiful and stubborn. 'But for now, it means that you must learn astromancy. Come, sit beside me.'

I can feel my heart racing with nervousness. I'm no good at magic, and I've been studying it for three years. How am I supposed to master a whole new craft? 'Grandmother, I …' *I can't do this. You know I can't.*

'Livio.' Her voice is sharp. 'Hold your nerve.'

I sit at the round table next to her and follow her gaze, up into the stars, warped through the twisted glass of the minaret. I mirror her posture, my hands flat on the cold marble table. We are quiet for a few moments as the sun finally dies, the stars sapping its light. At first my head's just spinning with disbelief, with questions and fears and general unease. But at last, a peacefulness fills me as I stare up into the sky. When I speak again, my voice is quiet.

'What if I can't do it? I'm no good at magic.' I lower my eyes to look at her. 'You said it yourself – I'm not gifted.'

'Perhaps not, in the ordinary sense. But astromancy draws on something different. You are the product of two great Scarossan bloodlines – the Santini … and the Lupina. This power should be in your very heart.'

Her words ring through me like bells, setting my nerves jangling. I feel my mother's book pressed against my torso – the *Starlight Throne*, the astromancer queens. 'Was my

111

mother an astromancer too?' I ask quietly.

Grandmother hesitates. She doesn't like to speak of my mother ... but finally, she answers. 'If she was, she never told me. But that didn't mean she didn't carry the power within her, pass it on to you.'

Suddenly, after years of feeling untouchable, shrouded in darkness, my mother feels closer than ever. 'But ... what if she didn't pass it on?' I ask. 'What if I'm not an astromancer at all?'

She is silent for a moment. 'Then, Livio, the art of astromancy will die with me, and the bargain will too. Gods only know what that would mean for our family, for Scarossa ... but it can't be good.'

I swallow, my throat dry. I think of Shadow, out there in the city, waiting to claim his kingdom. Our enemies are willing us to fail.

'Now, we are going to start with something simple. You are going to look into the near future. You will change nothing of that future, Livio. Do not pull on any of the cords.'

'The ... cords?'

'Some astromancers think of them as cords – others as strings. Some have called them twists or ribbons. You have to see it to understand. When you touch them with your magic, with intent, you gain an understanding – a vision of what has to be done to change an undesirable outcome. But that's advanced astromancy. For now, you will simply try to see.' She runs her hand over the surface of the table. 'This is an altar, Livio. An altar to Fortune. For the best effect, you should lie on it – partly because touching it with your entire body can amplify its power, and partly so you don't have to strain your neck when you're stargazing.' She smiles slightly.

I touch the cold stone gently, my heart pattering. 'Right.'

'Well then, what are you waiting for? Lie down, Livio.'

Slowly, I climb on to the table – the altar – and lower myself down until the back of my head rests against the stone. I feel self-conscious – exposed, as if the stars are staring back at me. I also feel a kind of resonance emanating from the stone. Objects with magical purpose – or objects that have been used numerous times in spells – often retain a kind of echo of magic. But I can't help feeling there is more here – some deeper note. Whatever it is, I listen to it, my grandmother's voice drifting from somewhere further away.

'Gaze up at the stars. The glass is enchanted. The more you look, the more you will see. The first stage is simply to *see*. Not only with your eyes, although that comes first. But with your heart.'

At first, I'm gazing up just as she says, feeling a mild sense of panic when all I see is stars, and more stars, twisted up in the spiralling blue glass, caught like fireflies in a net. How am I supposed to see anything but what is there? But gradually a kind of calm seeps into me again, as it did when I first lay my palms against the altar. The stone against my back grows warm with that note – not magic as I know it, slinking away in my stomach like a reluctant beast, but yes, *another* magic, something higher and brighter – and the stars shimmer. Grandmother must see a change in my eyes or feel something shift in the air.

'That's it.' She sounds a little choked up – with shock, perhaps, that anything is happening at all. 'Can you see them – the cords?'

I draw on the sensation – the new magic I'm feeling. Stable, serene – not shrinking from my touch. My vision deepens, and I realise the night sky is not a flat cloth strewn with lights, as it sometimes appears. It is layer upon layer of stars – some closer; some further away – with gradations of colour. The helical dome of the glass ceiling helps me see this, somehow. And between all the stars, and stretching down towards me, are … are …

'Chains,' I say. That's the word that springs to mind. 'The stars are bound together with chains.'

Grandmother pauses before she responds. 'Very well … Chains.' She clears her throat. 'Now I want you to pull back slightly. The layer closest to you is the near future. All you have to do, for now, is touch it with your magic. Exactly as you would send a trickle of power into a spell. You will experience a vision of what is to come.'

This bit feels more tricky. As I try to refocus, the stars blur, and whatever power I've tapped into seems to falter, the high note quavering in my chest. I try to retain my sense of calm, but I've started to panic again – to feel like I normally do when I practise magic. Useless.

'Be calm, Livio. You are close.'

I slow my breath. When the first layer of stars sharpens, I am so elated, so relieved that I reach out instantly towards the chain with my power. A spark flies.

'Careful—'

I gasp as a bright, crackling light fills my vision, a roar of flame – the heat real and blistering on my skin. A face burns in front of me – not a real face, a wooden, painted face. A mask? The paint blackens and crinkles and melts grotesquely, the hair of the grinning mask is wreathed in smoke.

Horror fills me, thick and black as tar. Then – there's a loud snapping sound, like new wood popping in a fire.

I wake on the floor, my ears ringing, my skin hot – somehow, I rolled off the altar. By some miracle, the book remains pressed against my stomach, under my waistband. I raise my hands to my face, expecting blisters, surprised to find the skin apparently unmarked. Grandmother is standing at my side.

'Can you get up?'

Slowly, I raise myself to my elbows. 'What happened?' My vision is swimming and I blink.

'You went in too deep, I think. You panicked. Next time, you must remain calm. What did you see?'

I rake my hands through my hair. 'I saw … fire. There

was fire. A face, burning. But not a human face – it was a mask, perhaps.'

She pauses. 'The power of the stars can be blinding,' she replies softly. 'It was your first try.' But her voice isn't full of disappointment, or some attempt at consolation … It's something like wonder that I hear. She sits down on the chair she had used before. 'But this is … good. You have the power. You saw something – it might not have been clear, or in our near future, but it was a vision. You *are* an astromancer.' For someone who was so sure of it beforehand, she sounds very relieved. When I look up into her eyes, the mirror of my own, they are full of tears. 'You are, already, a much better astromancer than you are a mage.'

I feel hope spark inside me. 'Do you think … Do you think I can do this?'

'Livio, we've barely ever had a ruler who wasn't a woman – the last conte was two hundred years ago, and he served for only eighteen months.' I know this, of course. The tale of the Red Conte is a cautionary tale for children on the dangers of masculinity and power. Grandmother continues. 'We've never had a ruler who wasn't an astromancer – so, you are that, at least.' She smiles wanly. 'But … we've also never had one who wasn't a mage.' I've never heard Grandmother sound so frail, so human.

'I am a mage …' I say gently.

'No, Livio. You have magic, but you cannot call yourself

116

a mage until you can control it. And without control, you will never be able to perform the duties of a conte. Being an astromancer is necessary … but it isn't enough. Do you understand? You have to be powerful. You will be expected to show authority over the temples … particularly over the Cardinal of Mythris's temple. Mythris's temple knows it has a hold on us. We cannot show them our weaknesses.'

I rub my eyes wearily, her words echoing my thoughts. I think of Carlotta jeering at my retreating back. Doubtless Grandmother has already heard of the incident with the cactus – she has regular reports from my teachers at the temple.

'Do you see why I need you to try harder at your lessons, Livio? Not only try harder, but excel? Do you see why I need you to be safe? No more of these nights in the city, doing whatever it is you do there, whatever brings you home bloody and exhausted and in no fit state to learn. The very survival of this family, of Scarossa's heritage, is at stake. It is a lot of pressure to place on your shoulders – but there it is. I have no choice but to rely on you.'

I sit there, feeling the stars swirl around me again, my heart racing. Maybe I can do this, after all. For the first time, I *want* to do it. I don't want to disappoint Grandmother. I don't want the destruction of the Santini line to be my fault. But it's more than that.

The vision of fire flashes in my mind, the grotesque burning mask. It was real: I can feel it. I really saw the future. Perhaps there *is* a path for me in magic.

'This is my fault,' she continues, mistaking my silence for refusal. 'Because we had Constance, I never worried. I knew she would be capable of this. I felt secure, thought it would be easy. I let you get away with too much. I have spoilt you, Livio.'

'I'll do it,' I say quietly. I look at her to make her realise I mean it. 'I'll be Conte, grandmother. I can do it.'

An unexpected warmth flashes over her face, and for a moment, I am certain she will reach out and hug me. But in the end, she only nods and stands up, her knuckles tight around her cane. 'Tomorrow we announce Constance's death and your ascendancy as heir. Tomorrow everything changes. I want you to be at your lessons, at the temple, when the news is announced – it'll be good for people to see that you are working hard to develop your magic.'

'Yes, Grandmother.'

'Remember, the following night is the fiftieth anniversary of my rise to the title of Contessa,' she says, using the table to help herself to her feet. 'There is to be a puppet perform-ance. The Mezzanotte company shall be playing a new, special production in a temporary theatre in the palazzo square. And you, my boy, shall be appearing at my side.'

I nod.

'Now, I'm afraid you're going to have to help me down those stairs,' she says, smiling sadly. She takes my hand, squeez-ing it with surprising strength. When she draws away, I realise she's left something in my palm – a silver key on a long chain, exactly like the one I saw her use to open the door. I hold it up to the light, noticing the star on the bow, a single blue jewel gleaming at its heart. 'A copy of my own,' she explains. 'The two keys and the door are enchanted – the door cannot be opened without it, by force or even by magic. Keep it with you always, around your neck and under your clothes – as I do.' She lifts a hand to her collar, showing me her own chain, peeking from the top. 'And, Livio, you mustn't tell anyone of this – any of it. The power of astromancy is a secret kept between us and the Cardinal – do you understand?'

I lift the chain over my neck, tuck the key under my robes. 'Yes, Grandmother,' I say softly.

More secrets, I think, as I help her down into her chambers. Despite my new determination, I can't help feeling fate close around me like a monstrous hand.

I throw the library book on the bed as I return to my room, glancing at the clock – I'm longing to read it, but it's midnight, and I'm already late for my meeting with Elisao. I tear off my purple Mythris robes, pulling on a clean pair of trousers and plain shirt and jacket. Guilt twists in my stomach: guilt at keeping Elisao waiting; guilt as I swing out of the balcony and climb down the trellis, knowing every action is a broken promise to Grandmother.

Knowing that this will be the last time I see the man I've come to love, just as I've finally found the courage to show him how much he means to me.

I was so certain I could live two lives at once. But I can't cope with the feeling I'm letting *everyone* down. I keep replaying my first experience of astromancy – the vision, the chains between the stars, the feeling of a new magic … a whole destiny opening up before me. The unfamiliar expression of hope on Grandmother's face. By the time I've reached the mascherari house, snuck past the guards and scaled the crumbling wall, the knowledge of what I have to do feels heavy in my heart.

Elisao is sitting on the library steps, exactly where I left him last night. The square is busy with groups of students staggering between bars, and at first he doesn't notice me – I'm a few steps away when he finally glances up, his face brightening. 'I thought you weren't coming,' he says. We stare at each other for a few moments, heat rising in my cheeks. I'm longing to kiss him – but I shouldn't. I won't. He stands up and leans forward, but I turn aside, sitting down on the steps abruptly.

'Sorry, I got held up,' I say. 'It's been a long day.'

'Well, I'm glad you're here now,' Elisao says, disappointment tinging his voice as he sits back down. 'Do you want to go somewhere a bit more …?'

'Here is all right,' I say, running a hand through my hair nervously, bowing my head. 'Listen, Elisao—'

'I heard from my contact at the Battaglia,' says Elisao, cutting me off, his voice high and nervous. 'The rematch is the night after tomorrow night. I was thinking we could meet down at the docks – around seven, or eight. Time to warm up beforehand – maybe grab something to eat?'

I struggle to speak. Knowing that what he's proposing can never happen is choking me.

'See, Livio,' he turns towards me, and I think how my true name sounds amazing in his voice, how I didn't get to hear him say it for years, and now I never will again. 'I've been thinking about you and me, about what we could mean to each other, for a long time.' He's rushing now, the words streaming from his mouth like he can't hold them. 'Ages, really. Almost since we met. Can you believe it's been three years? And I want to say …'

'Elisao …' I manage hoarsely, sensing the words hovering on his lips.

'I love you,' he says at last and presses his mouth to mine. I pull away.

'Elisao, I can't do it,' I blurt. Tears are stinging my eyes, but I won't let them fall. I can't even look at him in case they do.

'The fight?' His voice quavers.

'Any of it. The fight. This second life … You.' I clench my jaw, determined not to cry.

The silence that follows is painful to endure. Out of the corner of my eye, I notice how he hangs his head, slowly removes his glasses. Across the square, a drunk man sings a love song at the top of his lungs, and I wish he would stop – I wish I could punch him once, hard, and silence his warbling of hearts and passion and beauty. My jaw clenches.

'Look, Elisao, I'm sorry. I'm really sorry. I wish it weren't so.' Even to me, my voice sounds stiff and strange. 'I wish I really was Vico – if I were, all of this would be different. But it's just not possible. I was wrong – I can't have both lives. I can't ignore my duty for the sake of a fantasy.'

Elisao's face is stony. 'You're sure? This is it?'

I nod once, tightly.

'Right.' His tone is curiously flat, unemotional. 'It's just that literally *yesterday* you were so sure you could do it. You said you didn't care about everything else. That you couldn't give this up. So what's changed? You've had time to think? Realised you didn't like me as much as you thought?'

'No,' I say, my voice heated. I'm holding back tears, my throat thick and sore. 'That's not it at all. Something happened today …' I trail off. 'Something important. But—'

He cuts in, his voice brutally impatient now. 'Let me guess. It's something you can't talk about? More secrets, Livio, even after everything you said about being honest? About not being able to lie to me any more?'

I bury my head in my hands, wishing all of this was a bad dream. I'm surprised at how much his comment stings. I wish I *could* tell him the truth. But I shouldn't even have told Elisao my true identity – how can I tell him about astromancy, too? Grandmother swore me to secrecy: it's a power shared between me, her and the Cardinal – no one else but the masked god himself.

He stands up after a few moments of silence. 'If you've got nothing else to say to me, I guess this is goodbye.'

'Elisao …' I stand up too – meeting his eyes, a powerful force is urging me to hold him, to kiss him, to tell him I won't leave. But destiny is stronger. I glance away. A thousand phrases run through my mind: *I'll miss you. Remember me. Kiss me one last time. Don't go yet.* But somehow what leaves my lips is this: 'Please don't tell anyone about me.'

'Don't worry,' he says coldly. 'Your secret is safe.'

And he turns away, walking down the library steps without a backwards glance, and my heart feels like a burnt-out wreck.

TEN
The Room of Many Faces

Beatrice

A quick breath, a squaring of her shoulders: these are the only signs that Valentina is nervous as she twists the key and opens the door of the mask room for the first time. The hinges are silent and a cool gluey smell drifts from the space beyond – a space, not a room, because you can tell by the feel of the air that it's vast, and that it's like no room I've ever known.

We cluster round the door, peering in, reluctant to set foot over the threshold. Like we're intruding. As if in opening the door, we've interrupted a conversation, voices still humming into the quiet ... But no – this place is empty of any living thing but us three.

And yet ... the masks cover every wall. Some even peer down from the ceiling far, far above. In the dim light cast by an oil lamp that Valentina is carrying and the moonlight falling through the high windows, my eye skims tall ladders attached to rails along the wall, and long hooked sticks for hanging and removing items. We descend the final four steps from the doorway to a stone floor so old, it has worn shiny, and Valentina settles her lamp on a hook next to the staircase door.

'Well, are you two going to help me, or do I have to light all these lamps myself?' Valentina says, breaking the silence.

Ofelia and I spring into action, first lighting the lamps over the three generous desks set against the short wall near the door – and then we work our way around the room. A doorway in the panelling leads to a small, plain ante-chamber – the place we're to wait in the unlikely event that a Choosing, the ceremony in which mages select a True Mask, should occur during the hours of our work. I note a small privy by the back wall, set behind an elaborate screen, painted with the faceless cloaked figure of our god – but this seems to be the only concession to our human needs. Otherwise, it is only the masks.

But, as I suspected, these aren't like the practice masks at all. As I brush past them, I can sense their power, conferred by the hands of generations of sisters past. If I run my hands close to their surfaces, it feels like I'm touching a kind of invisible foliage – a grassy, static energy. They watch me as I light the lamps and fill their world with shadows.

When the lamps are lit, we three turn to face each other in the centre of the room. 'So ... this is it,' says Ofelia softly, her voice trembling a little as her eyes comb the room. 'This is where we spend the rest of our lives.'

I feel a slick of something like horror run down my back.

But Valentina nods. 'We'd better get started.'

I finish the mask on my work bench by brushing it carefully with egg white – a technique designed to dry the mask hard, set the decoration, and lend its surface a slight sheen. The grimacing mouth gleams in the candlelight, and I find myself shivering, a little unnerved by this, my first creation. It's a sad mask – painted a blue that speaks of leaden clouds and heavy hearts. Crystal tears trail down the mask's cheeks; an angry bloom of purple rings its eyeholes.

At last, I set my brush down – then, noticing a small imperfection, reach to lift an escaped hair from the mask's surface.

A spark of electricity runs through me as my fingers approach the mask, and I jolt backwards. I blink. I think I saw the tiniest glint of green. I open and close my hands, uneasily, frowning. Mythris's power flows through me now – it's no wonder I'm feeling different. But I didn't expect *this* … I glance over at my sisters, examining their fingers for sparks.

'Beatrice? Taking another break?' Valentina's harsh voice rings out in the quiet, interrupting my thoughts.

'It's nearly dawn,' I say, feeling my cheeks flush red even though I've barely stopped working since sunset.

'Not yet, though. Clear up your workbench at least – it's a mess.'

Ofelia and I exchange an eye-roll. A few moments later, Valentina stands up to visit the privy behind the screen. When she is out of earshot, Ofelia leans over.

'It's different, isn't it? From the practice masks. Can you feel it?' Her eyes are glowing. 'It's real in a way it never was before.'

I feel a little throb of relief. 'Yes … yes it is.' I shake my head. 'I'm glad you feel it too. I've been so … mixed up. Like there's all this energy churning up inside me. I was beginning to think there was something wrong with me.'

Ofelia looks thoughtful. 'Actually … I wouldn't say I feel mixed up, Bea. It's more like … like I'm stronger and calmer.' She shrugs, unconcerned. 'I guess it affects different sisters in different ways.'

Valentina is returning from the privy, and we both turn away. I feel more unsettled than ever. I think back to *that* night, the night the assassin tried to steal our lives. What happened when power surged through me and I pushed him away? The only people who know are me and him.

Tonight was the first night of the rest of my life: the fulfilment of my destiny. And yet … even beyond the physical toll of my sore neck and hands burning with glue, the task has left me aching and exhausted and confused. I thought this was meant to be our fate. I thought it would feel *natural* … but it doesn't. Instead, I feel more drained and out of control than ever.

When we step into the red-tinged dawn, there's an escort of four guards waiting for us – but unlike yesterday, one of them steps forward, keeping his eyes fixed on the ground.

'A message from the palazzo,' he says, bowing and holding out a scroll stamped with the Contessa's crest in purple wax: the Santini sun surrounded by its nine godly stars.

Valentina and I share a glance of confusion. She steps forward to accept the scroll … and then starts to walk off, holding the letter at her side, unopened.

Now it's Ofelia and I who glance at each other in frustration as we hurry after her towards home, following the straight, quieter street at the back of the palazzo square. In a few moments, we'll be veering off, climbing a narrow stepped path along the cliffs to our walled compound alongside the palazzo. The morning is already quickening, voices rising from the square beyond the mask room, the smell of oranges carrying on the breeze.

'Aren't you going to read it?' I ask, catching up to Valentina.

'It's unseemly to open private post in the street, Beatrice,' she replies, her jaw set, eyes fixed as she walks. 'Besides, this message is from the Contessa's household and must be of the utmost importance.'

'But how can you wait? We've never received a letter

before.' My stomach churns. 'Do you think it's about the new triplets?' I whisper. 'Maybe the mother has gone into labour ...'

'Don't be absurd, Beatrice – why would they send us a *letter* about that?'

As we're talking, I barely see Ofelia darting to Valentina's other side and snatching the folded paper audaciously straight from her hand.

'Hey!' Valentina says, two bright spots of colour rising on her cheeks as she stops and spins to face Ofelia. We're at the turning off towards the house, where the path narrows and steepens, and the sea crashes somewhere beneath. Valentina reaches to snatch the letter, but Ofelia darts up the narrow steps away from her. Our escort of guards shuffle nervously – but they're too afraid of us to say anything. 'Give that back! Don't you dare open it, Ofelia!' Valentina hisses.

Ofelia runs, and we all follow – a hurried procession of girls in black and guards in bright yellow. I find laughter rising in me, bubbling out in a fit of breathless giggles as my feet pound the stony path – if Valentina was worried about appearing *unseemly* before, she'll be burning up with embarrassment now. We're about thirty paces from the gates to the mascherari grounds when Ofelia stops, climbing up on a rock beside the path.

'Get down from there! Get down!' Valentina says.

'Make me!' Ofelia cries, waving the letter triumphantly.

I can see both of their faces are flushed even beneath

their black veils. The line of silver trees hiding our house rustles in the wind behind Ofelia, the sea crashes beneath us. My heart lifts. Our guards stand a few paces further back – and for a moment, we're not surrounded.

'Give it back this instant!' Valentina says, her voice cracking with frustration.

But Ofelia has already broken off the seal, which separates from the paper intact and drops to the paving stones at my feet, and is scanning the text of the unravelled scroll. Suddenly she shrieks and throws the letter up in the air.

'Oh blessed many faces of Mythris!' she exclaims, bringing her hands to her mouth, and I can't tell what other emotion is mingled with her obvious shock.

The letter is fluttering away on the breeze. Valentina is close to fainting with rage – it's beneath her dignity to hurry after it, especially after our crazed chase – but it's not beneath mine. Two of our guards – one of whose mouths I swear is twitching in amusement – step aside for me to catch it where it's landed on a fragrant rosemary shrub.

I retrieve the letter and unravel it. 'It's an invitation,' I say, scanning the text. 'We're invited to the puppet theatre tomorrow night for the Contessa's fiftieth-anniversary celebrations.' I glance up at Ofelia, suddenly understanding. 'The puppet theatre!'

'The Mezzanotte company, Beatrice!' she squeaks, jumping off the rock, skirts flying. 'An original production!' She's whirling and dancing like a spinning top.

I return to the letter. 'We'll have the night off,' it says. 'Some escorts will arrive for us at dusk.' I glance up at Valentina – an offer of peace in my eyes. 'Isn't that exciting?'

But her face is pinched and pale. 'Exciting? What is wrong with you both? I shall have no part in it. Better, if I am not to work in the mask room, to spend my night in prayer. Now, if you're quite finished with your ludicrous display?' She turns and walks up towards the house.

We hurry after her, enclosed again by the guards – but even Valentina's foul mood cannot wipe the smile from Ofelia's face. I step on something as I walk and lift my foot. It's the purple seal – the sun encircled by stars – turned face up and curiously intact but for the neat crack down its middle. I'm not sure why, but something in me makes me bring my heel down hard, crushing it to dust.

My mind spins the rest of the way home. Inside, Valentina is already in her room by the time Ofelia and I climb the stairs, the door slamming behind her. Ofelia opens the door to her room, humming, lost in her dreams of puppets and plays. Then, on instinct, I catch her arm, pulling her after me. We enter my room, and I click the door softly shut.

'Ofelia …' I take a deep breath. I'm not sure that what I'm thinking should ever be voiced – but then I remember her face when I told her about the new triplets, and my resolve hardens.

'Beatrice?' she says, her face creased with worry. 'What's the matter?'

'This could be our chance.'

'What?' She doesn't understand. I lower my voice, drawing closer to her.

'Our chance ... to leave.'

'Leave?' It takes a few long breaths before her face settles into understanding. My heart thuds with hope and terror in equal measure.

'Bea ... no ...' she shakes her head, clearly shocked. 'We couldn't.'

'What have we got to lose?' I reach out and take her hands in mine, pulling her towards me, certain I can convince her. 'Ofelia, you're like me. You and I have always been frustrated that we didn't choose this life. We've always wondered what our paths would have been – if we weren't born triplets on this island, if the Contessa hadn't plucked us from the world before we were old enough to decide. Remember? Well, now we'll have a chance to find out.' I'm sure I see a glimmer in her eyes – hope? Inspiration? But then she pulls her hands away, leaving mine cold and empty.

'What about Valentina?' she says gently. 'She'd never agree.'

'We'd convince her,' I said. 'If it were both of us against her, she couldn't say no. Look, Ofelia. We won't have another chance like this – all three of us out in the city, away from the house, surrounded by crowds ...'

But Ofelia is shaking her head, and the words fall away from my lips. 'But it's more than that, Bea. Scarossa is relying on us. We are part of an unbroken chain stretching back for generations. Our masks keep the people here safe, helping the Contessa protect us from our enemies. Do you really want to be the ones responsible for breaking that chain? The consequences for us would be bad enough—'

'*If* we were caught!' I say desperately. 'We'd make sure we weren't!'

'But the consequences for the Contessa, for the people here would be dreadful,' she says firmly. 'No, Beatrice. I can't accept this and neither should you.' Her words are final.

When I close my eyes, I see myself sailing on a ship across the waves … I can't let go of this dream, not yet. I open my eyes and blink a fat, hot tear down my cheek.

'The people hate us,' I tell Ofelia, my voice barely more than a croak. 'They won't even look at us. And the Contessa only cares about her own power.'

'But this is our duty. Our fate.'

'You sound like *her*.' My eyes dart in the direction of Valentina's room.

She shakes her head. 'I know … I'm sorry. She's insufferable. But sometimes, just sometimes … although I hate to admit it… . I think maybe she's right. I think …' her voice is gentle. 'I think this is just a symptom of your mental state,

Bea – all your worries and anxieties rising up, making you panic. And who can blame you? Everything has changed, so quickly, and with such upheaval. The Inheritance. Nurse leaving. The assassin.' She smiles at me. 'Somehow, you fought him off. You're my hero, Bea. But that's a lot of pressure on one girl.'

I think about telling her that there's more. That fighting off the assassin has raised further questions in my mind about the power I now hold … Instead, I say quietly, in a voice that already sounds defeated, 'It's more than that. It's not just anxiety. This life is so full of darkness, Ofelia. How is that something I can love? And the rest of the world is out there, shining like a jewel.'

She is quiet for a moment, as if she's turning my words over in her mind. Then, she places her hands on my shoulders. 'What you have to remember is that this life is your destiny. This is what you were born to do. Is it a hard burden to bear? Yes, of course it is. But it's also full of opportunity. I truly think that the life we live here, together, in the service of the Contessa and Mythris, will be a happy one. Come here,' she says, and she pulls me into an embrace. 'I'm upset about the new triplets too. I didn't expect it to come this soon.'

I relax in her arms. I know I've lost this argument, such as it was. 'You're my little sister. *I'm* supposed to comfort *you*,' I mumble, my face pressed into the black veil pulled back over her hair.

'We support each other. One soul split three ways – remember?'

For some reason, tears wrack me harder than ever. She holds my trembling body tight. 'There, there, sister. You can't fight against fate and win. So surrender gladly.'

ELEVEN
A Lesson

Livio

I open my wooden locker, the muted roar of my fellow novices' voices filling the changing room next to the arena. As usual, I am in my own silent corner, ignored, my stomach fizzing with nerves. I'm frustrated already – wishing I could summon the bravado that filled my heart in the Battaglia, wishing I could be the Wolf, just once more.

But my life as Vico is over now, for good.

After Elisao left me last night, I lingered in the palazzo square for a while, watching the people – *my* people, I suppose – as they laughed and stumbled and talked and drank and *lived*. I thought I was one of them, thought I could be part of their world. I was wrong. If I am to protect them from Shadow and the other dangers that face us, I have to embrace my destiny. I have to be a mage strong enough to earn the respect of my peers; an astromancer skilled enough to retain the ancient bargain with Mythris; a ruler detached and smart enough to judge clearly.

Grandmother was right. To be the people's champion, I have to set myself apart from them, however much it hurts.

And, holy twins, it hurts.

Shrugging off my formal purple robes, I bundle them into a ball and replace them with the loose trews and tunic assigned for my least favourite lesson: combat.

The irony isn't lost on me.

I sit down on the low pitted bench to tie my sandals. My mother's book lies under my pillow at home – I read a few pages last night, distracting my mind from the memory of Elisao's sharp words, before sleep pulled me under. Now, I turn one passage over in my mind …

This form of magic consists of two main strands – astromancers inherit one or the other. Half of astromancers possess the ability to conjure visions of the future in the stars. The other half can command the natural magical creatures of the Wishes.

The 'natural magical creatures of the Wishes' … is the author referring to sandwolves? Surely not … no one can command creatures of Chaos. I pull the leather cords of my sandals tight, frowning as I puzzle it over. I can't wait to return to the palazzo tonight to read on.

But first, somehow, I have to endure this godsdamned day.

I lean against my locker and shut my eyes. Today is the day of the announcement – today everyone will find out that Constance is dead and I am heir to the Wishes. Grandmother didn't tell me what time it would happen. I've already sat through an hour of lore, expecting the door to burst open at any moment with a message from the palazzo. What will the others think when they find out that I am to rule over them?

I glance up through the hair flopping over my face, scanning the locker room. I'm sitting on the far end, right by the corridor – no one is paying any attention to me, as usual. I stand, gripped by a sudden thirst, walk out into the corridor and over to a nearby fountain. I bend, drinking the cool water gratefully. My fellow novices are busy chatting to one another, voices raised, jokes thrown from end to end of the narrow room behind me. But a little down the corridor, through a slightly ajar door, I hear a confrontation. I wipe my mouth and, on instinct, edge closer.

'… must do better,' a cultured male voice is saying quietly. I lean slightly to one side to catch a glimpse of who's speaking through the gap in the door. My breath hitches in my throat as I recognise the back of the gold-edged robes of the Cardinal, his flame-bright hair tied at the nape of his neck. Carlotta is standing opposite him, facing me, her head bowed, expression unreadable. 'Your ascendancy within the temple is far from guaranteed. You do still wish to follow in my footsteps to be the Cardinal, some day?'

'Yes, Father,' Carlotta says, her voice unenthused. I frown, leaning into the shadows.

'Then you must prove your worth and loyalty with utmost obedience and perfect performance – no less will do.'

'Yes, Father.'

'Be prepared tonight. Events are coming to a head, and we have to be ready to seize our advantage. Now, go. I will be watching.'

I step quickly back to the fountain, bending down to sip again as the door opens fully and Carlotta's footsteps approach. *Be prepared tonight ... Events are coming to a head... .* What did the Cardinal mean?

Whatever's happening, Carlotta's not happy about it: her footsteps are sharp and fast, and she doesn't even hesitate long enough to throw me an insult. I stand up, watch her disappear into the locker room, instantly greeted loudly by a group of her friends.

She's lonelier than she looks.

Outside, the sun is burning and the heat feels like a living thing draped around my neck. It's the hottest spring I can remember, and as we trudge on to the hard-packed sand, the grains whip up and singe the skin of my ankles.

Priest Talon starts his lesson. I try to pay attention, I really do. I know he's talking about defensive shields, and shielding tactics – how to minimise the use of energy. But the sun is hot, my skin is itching, and my mind wanders to Elisao – the memory of our last encounter a fresh scab I can't stop picking – and every few moments, my eyes dart to the arena entrance, expecting a messenger with news of the announcement.

'Now … a little demonstration,' Priest Talon is saying. 'Carlotta Rosso. And … Lord Livio. Could you take the centre, please?'

I feel the blood drop from my face – my sweat prickles. The other novices snigger and whisper. Priest Talon appears to be oblivious to the reaction rippling across the room, and I suspect he's picked us for no other reason than we happened to be standing in his line of vision.

'Come on, novices – we haven't all day.'

So, I find myself standing opposite Carlotta, her eyes burning with obvious hatred. *Why does she despise me so much?* The buildings of the temple circle us like spectators in cloaks of stone, our fellow students watching from their shade. Above, the sky is a burning disc of blue.

Priest Talon walks over to us. He is a thin, bald man with a wiry frame and lined brown skin. 'This is a simple contest of attack and defence,' he says, 'to demonstrate how magical attacks can be shielded. Are you both ready?'

'Yes, Priest Talon,' Carlotta says.

Talon now turns to me.

'Mmmggh,' I manage, my eyes fixed on Carlotta, who is sending sparks flying between her fingers behind his back.

Talon signals the start of the fight. Even standing ready, I can't muster a magical attack quicker than Carlotta. I duck under her first strike, which is close enough to singe my hair before exploding into the ground at my back, sparks flying. Her magic is the deepest of purples – so dark that rumour has it she was nearly assigned to Jurah's temple, where the magic is black as coal.

I recover my footing on the compacted sand, my sandals skidding. In the split second I'm able to think, I run through all the training I can remember: breathe deep, draw on your power, aim and fire. But when I throw the attack, a pale lilac spark fizzes chaotically through the air – misaimed and hardly strong enough to stun a cat. Most first-year novices could produce a better attack. I curse in frustration as someone behind me snorts. Carlotta steps closer – she's not yet broken a sweat – and sends a confident strike towards my feet. I stumble, hear laughter as I drop to one knee. She's not even trying to win: she just wants to humiliate me.

'Lord Livio's bending the knee,' a female novice calls mockingly.

'*Defence*, Lord Livio,' Priest Talon is saying, failing to disguise his exasperation. 'At least *try* to throw up a shield.'

Carlotta smirks, another attack forming in her open palm. I'm angry, now – desperate. I feel my muscles tensing, urging me to run, to punch, to *fight* – but I can't. I'm not the Wolf. He's gone forever.

The hope in my Grandmother's eyes flashes through my mind. I *have* to do this right. If I can't win the respect of my peers, if I can't show them I can defend myself magically, what hope is there for Scarossa?

Time feels like it's slowing down as I reach down deep for my magic. *Too deep*, I realise, too late to stop myself. Suddenly my vision blurs … the peaceful, powerful feeling I experienced in Fortune's temple fills me up. I can hear my heartbeat in my ears, so slow it's like a drum …

Boom—boom …

There's a lurching sensation in my stomach.

Then, a shape barrels into Carlotta, a swirling darkness, oddly glittery in the bright light of the quickening morning. The attack she'd prepared spins from her palm, exploding uselessly against the arena wall, dark sparks flying. She's knocked prone by the thing, and Priest Talon steps in front of me, facing the creature. He sees it for what it is before I do, even though I've seen two only recently: 'Sandwolf!' he cries. 'Everyone get inside – now!'

I stare wordlessly at the sandwolf, unable to move.

My fellow novices flee inside the arena buildings, but I remain kneeling. The sandwolf stops its frantic spinning briefly and settles in the sunlight, fixing me with its burning yellow eyes. Then I watch the strange glittering blackness of its whirling body as it retreats, sizing up its new opponent. A magical dust devil with a wolf's head and eyes like lamps … I should be scared, but I'm drawn to it. Instead of fear, I feel a sense of wonder.

Then Priest Talon throws an attack at the creature, which disappears and reforms a few paces away – and it's looking at me expectantly, as if it's waiting for me to do something. 'Get inside!' Talon barks at me.

The attack and his voice snap me out of a trance. Finally I notice Carlotta lying on the arena floor, clutching her ribs. I can't see any visible injuries or blood, but her face is twisted in pain. I hurry over to her, try to help her up. Of course: magic is strong in her – the sandwolf sensed a feast.

'Get off me,' she growls, gritting her teeth as I reach down and take her hands gently in mine, but she looks afraid and allows me to pull her to her feet, looping her arm around my shoulders. We make it to the shade near the wall before her legs buckle. She's ashen. I let her sit down – I could probably carry her, but I don't think she would like it.

Talon has turned back to the sandwolf, and as I watch, he shoots another attack. This time, the sandwolf isn't quick enough. I hear a sound like a howl of pain, and when the sandwolf reforms, it appears slightly smaller, diminished. I feel a flash of fear for its life.

'Go,' I whisper. 'Just go.' It glances at me again, and for some reason I feel like it's listening. On instinct, I nod slightly. Priest Talon's next attack melts into thin air – the creature is gone. I watch a swirling shadow reform high above us, on the roof, then disappear over the sides of the arena.

I glance down at Carlotta. 'Are you all right?'

But Priest Talon arrives, kneeling at her side, and she

doesn't reply. Soon, others rush into the arena: first, Mythris priests and priestesses dressed in purple, checking the arena's safe. Then, mages in blue robes from Imris's temple, here to help Carlotta on to a stretcher and transport her to their hospital. Then, at last, other mages dressed in grey – huntsmen from Faul's temple – scouring the walls for traces of the sandwolf and tracking the creature's magical traces into the city beyond. All of this within minutes.

I'm sent inside, where the rest of the novices are gathered in a worried huddle. Priest Talon announces all classes for the rest of the day are to be held in the auditorium, the room with the highest security – and it's as we're filing in that the messenger arrives from the palazzo.

The woman was likely expecting a room of rapt students, for whom her announcement would be the most interesting thing to have happened that day. Instead, she is met with a pale-faced, frightened crowd. A few of the younger novices are sobbing. A space has formed around me. There's a rumour going round the room that I did it. That I summoned the sandwolf and set it upon Carlotta.

'Nonsense,' I hear Priest Talon saying, a few paces to my left. 'It's impossible to control creatures of Chaos. And it's irresponsible to spread rumours.'

'Besides,' someone else whispers, 'he's hardly got the magical talent to manage something like *that*.'

Don't they know I can hear them? I think they do. I don't think they care. As the messenger reads out the scroll,

I feel eyes settle on me, and my hands curl into fists as I silently will the ground to open up.

Change is in the air as the carriage brings me home, in the rolling clouds now gathering over the sea. It feels as if the tide is turning – and I know which way I'm being pulled. Inward. Into the heart of Scarossa, where my destiny lies.

But I can't help the way my heart is tugging me back. I think of Elisao and shut my eyes.

We've arrived. The sun is hot on my back as I walk the short distance into the palazzo. I climb the stairs, passing the ferns draping their grey-green fronds between the white banisters like soft, coaxing fingers.

I open the door to my room and step inside. As usual, someone has made an attempt to tidy and fallen short. Piles of books are pushed against the walls, but the bed is made, and the windows let in the evening sunlight. I walk over to the bed and check under my pillow, intending to read my mother's book for a while on the balcony before I am called for dinner. But my stomach lurches: my hand finds nothing there but cool cotton.

'You sure have a lot of books.'

I nearly fall back against the bedside table, my heart thudding wildly. There's a man sitting in the chair by the fire, my mother's book is open on his lap. 'What—?'

He flicks closed the cover of the book and reads out

the title in an accented voice I'm sure I recognise from somewhere. '*The Queens of the Wishes*. Gods, I hate history – but looks like that's all you read.' The sun sigil embossed on the front cover is gleaming in the dusk. He casts the volume down on a nearby pile as if it's nothing, and I feel heat rise to my cheeks. He doesn't know how special the book is, and I'm torn between relief and anger. He stands up. I'm tall, but he's an inch taller, his shoulders broad as he rolls them back – utterly relaxed.

'What are you doing in here?' I say coldly. 'And who gave you permission to search under my pillow?'

I recognise him, now: his dark skin and curly hair; his nonchalant, northern voice. He's the one with the wildcat True Mask, the one who dropped down from the roof when the sandwolf was on my balcony the morning after the Battaglia.

He speaks now. 'I'm here under the Contessa's orders. The book was on the bed when I came in, not under the pillow. I guess whoever tidied the room left it there.' He smiles, the gem on his tooth glinting, and goes on. 'By the way, you really need to work on your observational skills. I wasn't even hiding. Why do you read so much history, Lord?'

I draw myself up in outrage. 'Only by studying the past can we understand the present.' I hate the prissy, defensive tone that's crept into my voice. Why do I feel the need to explain myself to this man?

146

'Oh? I'd have thought studying the present would be more useful. But what do I know?'

'Who are you?'

'My name is Hal. We sort of met the other morning ...'

'I know – I remember,' I snap.

'I'm your new personal bodyguard.'

There's a pause as I let this sink in, my guts squirming in some unholy mixture of humiliation and horror. I stare at Hal dumbly.

'Don't look too pleased – it's embarrassing.' He shrugs. 'Anyway, I'm here because the Contessa also wanted me to give you some extra lessons. I mean, in combat.'

'Extra lessons?' I feel blood rush to my cheeks and turn away from him towards the window and the sunset. 'Well, send Grandmother my thanks for her concern, but I don't want any extra lessons.'

'I've been warned about this.' I glance over my shoulder, and Hal shrugs. 'I've been told to insist.'

'So you're going to force me to learn?' I shake my head ruefully. 'The temple has been trying that for years, Hal. What makes you think you'll have more success?'

He flashes another smile at me, the jewel on his canine gleaming once again. 'I'm more fun,' he replies. 'Come on, follow me. I can't teach you anything in here.'

He steps out on to the balcony and, ignoring the spiral staircase leading up, leaps on to the roof, magic glittering around his feet to power his jump in a way muscles never could. I follow him by foot, curious in spite of myself.

In the luscious rooftop garden, Hal is frowning and staring at the potted plants and raised stone flower beds scattered liberally around the ample round space, forming reading nooks and sun traps. The small glass spiralling tower of my room rises up from the centre, reflecting the warm red sunlight. Grandmother's taller blue minaret towers over it about fifty feet away, hiding its true identity under jewel-blue glass. I don't often come up here, and I'm surprised at how green and cool it is, the sounds of the city blowing up on the breeze.

Right now, a bell is ringing over in the temple of Faul in the university district – an alarum for the sandwolves, I think. It's official: the city is infested with the creatures again for the first time in over fifteen years. I shiver at the thought of the danger that has crept up on us all while we were half asleep. Now the whole city is at risk – and unless I can master my two magics, there's little I can do to help.

I turn away from the rooftops and instead watch the sun setting heavily over the shimmering sea. I should give Hal a chance. What if he really can help me?

'Yes. This'll do.' Hal's voice brings me back to the present. 'Though I'll have to clear a little space.' He raises his arms, and the air flickers a bruised, purplish red. All at once, several of the pots rise up, scoot towards the roof edge and clatter down, a couple of them cracking, dirt spilling on to the clean golden stone. I flinch at the noise.

'What do you think you're doing?' I demand.

'What does it look like I'm doing?' says Hal, brushing his hands in satisfaction. 'I'm clearing a practice area.' He rubs the heel of his hand across his tightly curled hair. 'Sorry about the pots, but it's not an exact art.' He grins. 'Are you ready?'

'Ready for—?' A shimmering attack cuts me off – I fling myself to the ground as a pot of hanging ferns explodes over my head, scattering me with soil. 'What the—?!'

'Lesson one – always shield yourself.' I'm even more annoyed to see him laughing. 'If you'd shielded yourself, you could have avoided that. Every good combat mage prepares a defence *before* the fight. I watched you in the arena, too. Your instincts are always to defend yourself physically rather than using magic. I can see your fists clenching, your muscles twitching. It's a pretty common thing for new mages, actually.'

My mind's racing to keep up. 'Wait – you were *there*?' I feel the familiar sharp sting of mortification as I brush the dry soil off my purple robes, rising to my feet.

'Of course. I had to see you in action to know what I was working with. But my point is that we need to change your instincts. For now, you try. Attack me.'

I'm outraged, my hands balling with fury. 'Seriously, I—'

'Just do it,' Hal says, cutting me off.

Fuming, I relent and muster my magic, attempting to focus my anger into something helpful. Sparks fizz at my fingers. I already feel frustrated, knowing the attack will be weak. Sure enough, when I aim and fire, an arrow of pale purple darts through the air in a curve. Hal raises a shield at the last minute with an effortless flick of his hand.

'Your problem is focusing your energy. Did you notice those sparks? You had some extra power there, but you didn't use it. You ...'

He trails off, his expression suddenly changing. In the corner of my eye, I catch sight of a dark shape as it leaps on to the rooftop. I turn to face it. The figure is dressed in black, loose robes; it's hooded, and beneath the hood is a dark, blank mask. I don't have time to wonder who they are, what they're doing here on the rooftop, or how they got past the guards. Before I know it, their hands are raised, and the blackest magic I ever saw – so dark it's almost the *absence* of colour – is shooting a curved dagger towards me.

Black magic. Jurah's magic.

Executioner's magic.

I throw myself to one side – the dagger and the magic deflect on a shield Hal has already raised, flashing red. The dagger shoots back into the assassin's hand, gleaming in the dying sunlight.

'Find cover!' Hal shouts at me. In one fluid movement, he's deflected a second attack, reached into his uniform and pulled his True Mask over his face. When he glances back at me – still sitting on the ground in shock, unable to move – his face is a snarling wildcat's, glowing gold and glittering with moving gems. 'Go!' he roars, his voice somehow changed: not only muffled and rough, as you'd expect under a mask, but animalistic – full of a raw and dreadful power.

I stagger to my feet. Dimly, I think I should shout for help, but it feels like all the breath has been drawn out from my lungs. *Someone wants me dead*, I think blankly. The assassin tries to leap over Hal's head to reach me, distracting him with a feint, but Hal manages to trip him up with an attack that explodes on the ground, sending rubble flying. I can't see anywhere to hide, but finally my brain's frantic instructions reach my feet, and I start running to the furthest end of the garden. The assassin is in pursuit – moving so fast, so close to me, he's like a shadow.

Hal's right behind him and he's fighting all the while, slowing the assassin down. By the time I reach the far wall, ducking behind some huge pots of palm trees, he's leaped between the assassin and me, deflecting another spinning strike from the magic-fuelled daggers, then darting back behind the attacker to strike him from behind. Then Hal's in front of him again, and I realise he's trying to draw him away. The rooftop is alight with red flashes – the other guards must've noticed by now – but no one runs. What's happening? I gaze up at the stars as if hoping they'll answer.

I blink. I don't decide to do it consciously, and I don't know what I hope to achieve, but suddenly I'm reaching for the new power – *astromancy* – and a sense of calm and clarity fills me, fear draining from my body. My heart-beat slows.

As I'm watching the sky, crouching behind the palm trees, a shape materialises on the edge of the roof at my side. A sandwolf. I face the creature, the fight between Hal and the assassin fading into the background. I run my finger around the seal of my sandwolf signet ring. The creature is watching me closely, but I don't feel afraid: exactly as before, I'm drawn to it. I feel a tug in my chest, as if the sandwolf is trying, somehow, to communicate …

I *pull* on the magic. It feels safe and instinctive in a way that magic never normally does, for me. A tingling sensation fills my body, and the stars appear to grow brighter. The sandwolf, I realise, is speckled with tiny flecks of light – inside. Is it … made of stars? *No, not* it. *She.* I know that with a sudden certainty.

She wisps forward, lowers her swirling body until she's right next to me – we're nearly nose to nose.

'Are you …?' I whisper. But I'm not sure what I'm asking.

I hear a soft susurration somewhere in the back of my head …

Then, I'm suddenly aware of the sounds of the fight growing alarmingly close – and of other voices and foot-steps approaching. Half a moment later, the sandwolf leaps at me. There's a heavy *thunk*, right over my head, and I feel a rasping, biting heat against the exposed skin of my neck as

I am knocked down, an extraordinary raw power settling against my chest. My magic sparks in response – and then the weight lifts. I'm woozy, but as I open my eyes, I notice the assassin running off across the roof, escaping. I piece together what just happened: the assassin leaped at me, and – I'm nearly certain – the sandwolf pushed me out of the way. The creature sits on the edge of the roof again, regarding me with her yellow, glowing eyes, as if waiting for my instructions.

But Hal is standing on my other side, I realise, and his masked face is snarling and murderous as he stares at the sandwolf.

'Go now,' I whisper under my breath, scared for her life now that she's saved mine, and even as Hal shoots an attack, she disappears, wisping into nothingness. Hal's spell falls into the night, dissipating into the air. Several True Masked guards in yellow livery are belatedly arriving on the rooftop, pressing their masks to their faces – but both sandwolf and assassin are out of reach now.

Hal kneels at my side, removing his mask. 'Lord? Are you all right?'

I don't answer at first. I'm too lost in my thoughts, convinced now that the sandwolves are listening to me, obeying me, even protecting me. And somehow, it's all linked to astromancy. Are they the *natural magical creatures* referred to in the book? What if they're not creatures of Chaos at all? After all, they're only found in the Wishes, nowhere else …

But if I can read the stars, there's no way I should be able to command sandwolves too. According to the book, you inherit one power or the other: never both.

'Lord?'

'Yes. I'm fine.' I hold my head. I've knocked it, but I don't feel any blood. 'Just bruised, I think.'

'That's good.' He gazes out over the roofs as he helps me up. He seems annoyed, for some reason – distracted.

'That sandwolf saved my life,' I breathe. My head is spinning, and I clutch it in a futile attempt to regain my balance. 'It pushed me out of the way before the assassin could get to me.'

'No, Lord.' His voice is harsh as he meets my eyes – not at all like the light tone he has been using till now. 'It took advantage of the fight to attack you – you were weak and distracted. It's pure luck that it happened to knock you from the assassin's path. Sandwolves are dangerous. You must not think otherwise.'

I frown. 'But it felt like ...' I can't tell him about astromancy though – Grandmother made me promise to keep it secret. And while Hal might've had *The Queens of the Wishes* open on his lap, I don't get the impression he absorbed what little he read. So how can I explain? I shake my head, mumbling, 'Never mind.' Hal isn't my friend: he's my bodyguard – a tutor at best. I don't have to explain myself to him.

My grandmother is approaching from the direction of her own balcony, flanked by a couple of her True Masked guards – two Grotesques. One mask's expression is a flexing, maniacal smile that sends a shiver down my spine. The other mask is angry-looking – fiery gems streaking across its twisting, rageful expression. But it's my grandmother's face that chills me most: lined with worry and exhaustion. I stand up, and she folds me in her arms in a rare show of affection. I'm startled but hug her back, realising perhaps for the first time how very small and frail she is. When I was little, she was the strongest, scariest person in the world. But now …

'Thank Mythris you're all right,' she says, pulling away. She spins to face the nearest of the yellow-liveried guards. 'Why in the nine gods' names did it take you so long?'

'My lady.' The young woman bows, her face a rictus of terror. 'Five of the closest guards have been murdered. The alarm wasn't raised until the spell lights were spotted from the grounds.'

'Five guards,' Grandmother repeats. Her hand tightens around her cane. 'And what colour was the assassin's magic?'

Hal answers the question. 'Black, Lady. It would've been my magic the guards noticed from the grounds.'

Grandmother's face is grim. After a moment, she turns to the angry-looking Grotesque. 'Double the patrol across the palazzo – a mix of mage and civilian guards are to be on duty at all times. And send a contingent of ten True Masked guards to bolster the ranks.' The guard bows, leaving with quick footsteps. 'You saved him?' Grandmother asks Hal.

He inclines his head. I decide now isn't the time to mention the sandwolf – something tells me Grandmother won't believe me anyway. She removes a small purse from her belt and presses it into Hal's hands.

He blinks. 'My lady—'

'I know. I already pay you well. But remember that I've plenty more where that came from, as long as my grandson is kept safe. Now – a little privacy, please.'

Hal bows, retreating – the others following, orders ringing out across the rooftops, footsteps pounding, and lights bobbing as the Contessa's orders are relayed. Grandmother, meanwhile, loops my arm in hers and draws me further aside. We stand on the edge of the rooftop, gazing out in the direction of the temple, its dark hulk – dotted with purple lights – crouching on the neighbouring hilltop. For a while, we are silent, and I find myself scanning the skyline, my fists clenching and unclenching at my side as if I'm expecting the assassin to return. But at some point, I have to face the reality that all the physical power in the world can't defend me against magic. Perhaps that time has come. I was useless without Hal, without the sandwolf. As helpless as a child.

I shut my eyes for a moment. There's no doubt in my mind who is responsible for this attack. Old Jacobo's warning runs through my mind. Shadow is out there and he wants our city. The question is, how much does Grandmother already know? I hold a hand to my head, which is starting to throb now where I hit it against the ground. Should I tell her everything Jack revealed to me? To do so would expose the extent of my second life and its links to a criminal underworld that Grandmother has been fighting for decades – and possibly put Old Jacobo in danger too. But are we beyond that, now that our lives are truly at risk?

I'm about to speak when at last, Grandmother sighs. 'I was hoping not to have to burden you with this along with everything else … but it appears a powerful crime lord has arrived in Scarossa. What happened here this evening and the attempted assassination of the mascherari sisters are both his work.'

She knows. I feel a slight sense of relief and hope – perhaps she is already dealing with the threat in ways Old Jacobo was unable to detect. 'Shadow,' I say quietly. A single word – but its utterance changes everything.

Grandmother stares at me, her eyes widening slightly. She turns to face me fully, reaching up to rest her hands on my shoulders. Her expression is grave. 'Livio … I have underestimated you. I should remember that you know this city better than I do. I shouldn't be surprised you have heard of Shadow before. But I need you to tell me everything you know.'

My short-lived flicker of hope twists and plummets. *Grandmother is asking for my help.* I've never been in a position where I can help her before, and I don't like it. The fear in Grandmother's eyes is unmistakeable: whatever she's been doing to fight Shadow, it hasn't been working. I swallow, my palms prickling. 'I don't know too much. I know he wants us dead, our power crippled. He's determined to take over this city for himself – he wants to be King of Scarossa.'

She nods slowly. 'That much I knew. What else?'

'Every one of his crew, they say, are Rogues. I don't know how many. A lot, I think.'

Her face grows grim. 'Rogues often have unusually strong, if chaotic magic. I suppose this accounts for the power of his assassins – no bound mage could overcome a True Masked guard. Anything else?'

I think for a moment. 'Graffiti has been cropping up all over the city. A Santini sun, but no nine stars to represent the gods. And often there's a motto to go with it – *Revolution is coming.*'

'You think Shadow is responsible for this?'

I nod. 'The symbol without the nine stars is from a time before the rulers of these islands were subservient to the King. Perhaps Shadow is whipping up those old sentiments – that you're under the King's heel, doing his bidding and not what's best for the Wishes. I think sometimes …' I hesitate. 'Sometimes people see you as remote, inaccessible – not one of them. He's trying to capitalise on that.'

'Rulers are supposed to be above their people, not among them,' Grandmother snaps, turning away from me. But she quickly lowers her tone to a worried whisper. 'Shadow is

158

attacking the pillars of our authority – the mask-makers, the heir, and even our closest ally, the temple.'

'Shadow sent assassins to the masked temple?' This is news to me. 'That's the stupidest thing I've ever heard.'

'No, Livio – these attempts are far from amateurish. And each one has been alarmingly close to successful. If you, the mascherari, or the Cardinal were removed, we'd be in trouble. But that's only one part of his assault on our island, which has been steadily progressing for years without us even noticing. I believe our officials are corrupt more often than not – many of them already in Shadow's pocket – and consequently revenue has been gradually sinking. Businesses and merchants' guilds have long been threatening to move elsewhere. And suddenly we find ourselves even less able to defend ourselves. We can't even find where he's hiding out.' She pauses as we both contemplate the city lights and the invisible evil lingering among them. 'I don't suppose you know?'

I hesitate before replying. 'The rumours are that he's based himself in Dark Scarossa.'

She laughs, a cold sound that quickly falls into silence. I feel my cheeks colour – I shouldn't have mentioned it. It's like suggesting that Shadow might be hiding in a storybook.

'Grandmother, I want to help,' I say. 'If you like, I can dig deeper – find out if anyone in the city has heard more—'

'Absolutely not, Livio. You are not to venture into the

city again. The best thing you can do to help, right now, is stay safe and improve your magic … both kinds.' She smiles slightly. 'I had hoped for an opportunity to teach you more astromancy tonight – but I think we've both had enough for one evening. We'll meet again after the puppet perform-ance tomorrow, in my rooms.'

'All right,' I say.

'In the meantime, we should get some rest. Another big day tomorrow. Fifty years.' She holds out her hand, her eyes narrowing as she examines the prominent tendons, the age spots, her wrinkled knuckles beneath the gleaming mourn-ing rings. Her voice is sad as she continues. 'How on earth did I get so old? Fate is an assassin. It has crept up on me, Livio – soft-footed as a cat. One moment, I am twenty years old, my whole life ahead of me, the stars lighting my path. The next, I am struck down by a strange spell. Time has disappeared – my body is failing … and the future so diminished …' She shakes her head, a smile playing at her lips. 'Never get old, Livio.'

'If things go on like this,' I say grimly, 'maybe I won't get the chance.'

TWELVE
Disguises

Beatrice

The night before the fiftieth-anniversary celebrations, our work in the mask room is disturbed.

A knock sounds on the door at the top of the staircase, breaking a deep, concentrated silence. All three of us jump. I drop a glass bead on the floor, listen to it rattling across the stone and into the darkness under my table. I'm uncomfortably reminded of the night everything started: the night Katherina died.

Valentina stands up, and we follow, three shadows climbing the winding steps, lowering our veils over our faces as we go.

The door at the top is open. A high priestess of Mythris stands in the night outside, holding a purple mage-light in her upturned palm, which casts an ethereal glow across her dark skin. Her purple robes are edged in black, a signifier of her rank. She lowers her eyes.

'Apologies, Mascherari, for disturbing the masked god's

161

work. We require the mask room for a Choosing.' I notice someone behind the High Priestess – a tall young woman in plain robes stands nervously, her head bowed and hooded, fiddling with her sleeve. The skin of her hands is white as milk.

We were warned about the Choosings. Occasionally, we were told, the ceremony in which talented novices of Mythris were permitted into the mask room to select a mask is by necessity performed by cover of darkness.

'Of course,' Valentina says. 'Give us a few minutes.'

Downstairs, we tidy our things a little, retire to the small, dark antechamber and wait.

It's not long before we hear footsteps on the stairs, voices in the mask room. Purple light slides under the door as the High Priestess passes. I fidget. Ofelia yawns. Valentina sits still as stone, her face serene in the moonlight filtering through the window high above. I stand up and press my eye to the crack in the door.

'Beatrice!' Valentina hisses, her serenity shattered in an instant. 'Get back here!'

'Shh,' I reply softly.

The High Priestess and the young novice are standing in the centre of the room. The girl pushes back the hood of her robes. Her hair is a fiery, beautiful red, cascading down her back in loose curls. As she lowers her arm, she winces, gently touching her side. An injury?

'Are you sure you're well enough for this?' the High Priestess asks.

'Father thought so,' she replies with a tight half-smile. 'He said it has to be tonight. I'll be all right.'

The High Priestess shakes her head slightly, as if she disapproves but doesn't care to admit it. 'Then let's begin.' She kneels on the stone floor. 'Come, kneel next to me.'

The girl does as she's told, facing away from our little antechamber.

'Now, as I'm sure you know,' says the Priestess gently, 'there's a good chance this won't work – mostly, it doesn't. All we can do is pray for the masked god's favour. Whether he chooses to guide you or not is up to him.'

'Beatrice,' Valentina hisses again from behind me. 'You're not supposed to—'

'Move over,' Ofelia whispers, closer to me. I shift down slightly, kneeling on the floor to allow her room to bend over me and press her eye to the gap.

Valentina exhales her disapproval sharply.

'I understand,' says the red-haired girl, her voice quivering with nerves.

The High Priestess starts a low, sonorous chant in a language I don't recognise – and yet, I feel it repeat every so often, the rhythms of the phrases growing familiar to my ears even if the words are senseless. I feel Valentina join us, at last, leaning round Ofelia to peer through the top of the door.

Finally, the chanting stops.

'Mythris,' says the High Priestess in a calm, steady voice, 'your novice, Carlotta Rosso, kneels beside me in the hope of your favour and guidance.'

The mage-light dims and our lamps flicker, as if a breeze has swept through the room. Although the lamps remain illuminated, the darkness in between appears to deepen – velvety and thick. Suddenly, it feels hard to breathe. I remember the Inheritance ceremony, the presence I felt pressed up against my ear. My ears start to ring, nausea trembles in my gut, my lungs constricting as if bound by an invisible cord. Is this Mythris? Is it happening again?

I *do* feel dizzy now, darkness edging my vision – but I'm already kneeling. I gently rest against the door, closing my eyes. I breathe deeply, willing the feeling to pass. My fingers are tingling and, as I crack open my eyes, I watch in terror as a small spark of light jumps from my palm, lands on the stone floor and dies. I glance up. Ofelia and Valentina have their eyes pressed to the gap: they haven't noticed. They seem totally fine.

What's wrong with me?

I feel better now, though – well enough at least to be sure of my hold on consciousness. I press my eye again to the gap in the door.

The red-haired girl is standing now, though the High Priestess continues to kneel, head bowed, lips moving in prayer or spellcraft, I can't tell. The girl is scanning the walls, slowly turning, step by step, as she peers at the masks. When she's facing our wall, I glimpse her face – tight with hope. Her hands are curled into fists at her side. What's she waiting for? Can't she choose her mask now?

I notice it before she does.

One of the masks, half hidden in the shadows, is *glowing*. My breath catches in my throat, and I feel Valentina and Ofelia stiffen in surprise as they notice it too.

We've had it all wrong, I realise: it's not the novice who chooses the mask, at all. It's the other way round.

The mask is a Grotesque – hung on the wall above my desk. My stomach twists. It's one of mine – the first one I made. A blue spark fires from its face, flitting through the darkness – and another ... and another. As if it's reaching out for her.

The girl notices the mask at last, and all of a sudden, her body is strung tight with visible tension. She steps towards it. I can feel her excitement as she gets closer, summoning a mage-light and holding it up to the Grotesque.

Now I can see it properly. A crying face – a beautiful one, its expression calm and sad in equal measure but changed, now, by whatever magic has been activated by the girl's presence. I lean forward even further, pressing my eye right up to the gap in the door. The mask's surface is decorated with a swirl of grey and blue, which brings to mind an early morning mist over the sea. Gems sparkle across its brow like droplets. The girl opens her hand. The mask lifts from the wall, drifting towards her with an odd circular motion, like some celestial body orbiting its sun.

As she holds it in her hands, she turns it over, wonderingly.

The High Priestess stands. 'Excellent, Carlotta – Mythris has shown you great favour. Your father will be happy.'

'He wanted me to have a Bestial,' says Carlotta. 'He won't be happy at all.' But her face is glowing with delight as she stares down at the mask in her hand, and I can't help feeling a shiver of pride. *I made that.* 'Can I wear it now?'

The High Priestess's mouth twists into an indulgent smile. 'Go ahead.'

'What will it do?' Carlotta breathes, already lifting the mask to her face but hesitating.

'Try it. The masks are all different, even within their types. You'll experience some enhancement of your natural powers. And ultimately, when you wear the Grotesque, you should be able to sense and manipulate the emotions of those around you.'

Carlotta presses the mask to her face – but her back is turned towards us. 'Oh,' she says, voice slightly muffled. 'Everything looks so ...' She trails off as she glances towards the High Priestess. 'There's colour all around you,' she says.

'Not colour – thoughts or feelings. You'll learn to read them in time – even to change them. But don't try anything yet, Carlotta. Wait until it feels like you aren't wearing anything at all, until you and the mask are one.'

Carlotta continues to turn until she – and the mask – finally come into view. I blink in wonderment, inhale sharply. The surface of the mask has liquefied, the beautiful weeping expression coalescing with her own features as she gazes at the door hiding us. Mist appears to rise from the mask's surface. Tears fall down its cheeks. It's really *moving*. I knew it would happen, but somehow actually seeing it is different. I hear Ofelia gasp, too, her weight shifting … and suddenly we three are hurtling forward, the door swinging wide and banging against the wall.

I'm pressed between my sisters and the floor – for a moment, I can't breathe. Then, Valentina is hauling me up roughly by the armpit, holding Ofelia's arm in her other hand.

'My apologies, High Priestess,' she is murmuring. I can hear the mortification in her voice. 'My sisters …'

The High Priestess arches her brow as she averts her eyes. 'It is not I to whom you should apologise, but our god.'

'Of course.' Valentina sounds as if she's about to cry.

Carlotta is staring at us through her mask – at *me*? Then, she's ripping it off her face, the pale freckled skin beneath flushed. Her eyes narrow as they meet mine – then, as if remembering who and what I am, she glances away quickly.

'Are you all right?' says the High Priestess.

Carlotta blinks. 'I'm not sure …' she says. Her eyes drop

to the mask in her hands. 'I thought I saw something …
different.'

The High Priestess sighs and gently grasps Carlotta's
arm. 'Come. Let's go.' They head towards the door, mage-
lights bobbing behind them. On the threshold Carlotta
turns slightly, as if she's wishing it was all right for her to
look back … But it isn't, so she carries on. Their footsteps
fade as they climb the steps.

We hold our collective breath until the door at the
top clicks shut. Valentina, Ofelia and I stay in the antechamber for a few long moments, staring at each other in
the dark.

'Oh blessed Mythris,' Valentina says, burying her face in
her hands. 'Why did you do that, Beatrice?' she murmurs.

I blink, my mind elsewhere. I'm thinking about the spark
in the darkness, the way Carlotta looked at me. But I muster
enough annoyance to retort: 'We were *all* watching.'

She raises her head. 'You started it. I suppose at least *you*
weren't stupid enough to lean on the handle.' She glares at
Ofelia, who snorts.

'If they didn't want us to see the Choosing, they would
have made us go elsewhere,' she says. 'And why shouldn't
we see it?'

Valentina glares at her. 'If the masked god wanted us to
see it, he would have had us sit in the same room instead of
behind a closed door, you fool.'

My younger sister blushes. 'What's the harm, Valentina?

We're the mask-makers – doesn't it make sense for us to know what we're creating?'

'That's not the point. It's like the High Priestess said – we disobeyed the masked god's wishes. We deserve some kind of punishment.' She lifts her chin defiantly. 'I don't think any of us should be attending the puppet theatre tomorrow.'

Ofelia snorts. 'You do what you like,' she says. '*I'm* going. And Mythris knows I'm not going on my own.' She grabs my hand.

I run my other hand through my hair. What did the novice see when she looked at me? The Priestess said that when she wore the mask, Carlotta would be able to sense and manipulate emotions. Could she tell I was different to my sisters? *Am* I so different? I guess part of me was hoping that, inside, they're as much in turmoil as I am. But maybe I'm more alone than I thought. They're staring at me, now, waiting for me to take sides – but I've forgotten what we're even arguing about.

'Shouldn't we get back to work?' I suggest softly.

Valentina blinks at me. Ofelia sighs demonstratively. But neither of them protest as I lead the way back to our benches.

We emerge from the mask room a few hours later. The sun has risen on the Contessa's fiftieth anniversary of rule. Tonight, the puppet theatre awaits. As we pass the palazzo square, I hesitate to watch two dozen workers erect a giant wooden framework in front of the library. A stage has emerged at one end of the frame, and reams of material, bundled up in thick ropes, await their purpose on a series of carts nearby.

Back at home I try to sleep, as we're supposed to during the day, tossing and turning in Elina's bed for an hour or two, thinking of everything that's passed. Yes, I have the magic of Mythris in me now … but if it was the mascherari powers causing sparks to fly from my fingertips, wouldn't my sisters have felt it too? Wouldn't Carlotta have fixed her gaze on all three of us, rather than on me specifically?

I abandon the idea of rest entirely when Ofelia sneaks into my room. 'I wonder what the new play will be like,' she says, curling up next to me on the bed. 'The letter didn't even say what it was called!'

'It'll be something like the *Evil Seductress's Grisly Revenge*. Or *The Bloody Murder at Midnight*,' I say, mouth quirking as she thumps me playfully on the arm. It's true: puppet plays are unfailingly bloodthirsty – it's always struck me as oddly wonderful that sweet, kind Ofelia loves them so much. Nurse would buy her the penny scripts from the market, and Ofelia would put on private performances in the nursery at every opportunity. I didn't care for the stories, but I enjoyed it anyway – she's good at the voices.

I try to share Ofelia's excitement. But as the day fades and we change out of our nightgowns and into our ordinary uniform of black dresses and veils, a quietness settles over our preparations, and even Ofelia can't keep hold of her joy. Something about the stiff black clothes casts a darkness over our moods, too. Perhaps we're both thinking about the conversation we had yesterday, my suggestion of escape, and how – at least for me – destiny seemed to close its hands even tighter around us afterwards. When we shadow our faces with the veils, our trans-formation is complete, and I feel myself shrink. We look completely ... ourselves. Looking like this, everyone will know who we are: we will never truly escape the prison of our lives. People will avert their eyes. In the puppet theatre, in the special seats the Contessa has reserved for us, we will stand alone, a circle of emptiness spreading around us like a stain.

'We should check she really doesn't want to come,' I whisper, nodding to Valentina's room as we step out on to the landing. There's no sound from inside.

Ofelia frowns but nods her agreement. I knock hesitantly. 'Valentina? We're going out – for the puppet theatre. Are you sure you'd rather stay here?' After my second knock, I open the door slightly. Valentina is in bed, the covers pulled over her body and most of her head. Only a dark tight braid of hair is visible, snaking over her pillow.

'Just go,' she calls. Her voice sounds high and strained. 'I told you, I'm not coming. I will be spending my time in prayer.'

'Valentina … we made *one* mistake,' I try. 'And this is only one night. The masked god can forgive you that, can't he?'

Nothing. I blush, find myself thinking back to Ofelia snatching the invitation. To us, it was fun – just a game – but was Valentina truly hurt? And yesterday night, tumbling into the mask room … these small humiliations are felt deeply by my older sister. Valentina is a lot of things – but more than anything, she is proud.

'I know stealing the invitation was unkind, but it was just for fun. We didn't mean to upset you. And—' I try, but she cuts me off.

She sits up, pushing the covers off her and glowering at me with red-rimmed eyes. 'You're right. It was unkind – and immature. Just like your behaviour in the mask room last night. As the eldest sister, it's my job to be the adult, to be an example to you both, advise you and show you how to be. But you make it nearly impossible. I'm sick of both of your childish attitudes and have no wish to spend any more time with you than I must. Now, leave me alone.' Her voice is prim, and I feel irritation rising in my chest along with pity and hurt.

'Valentina …'

'Go,' she says, her voice cracking slightly. She lies back down, pulls the sheets over her head. I close the door, maybe a little louder than I need to. I take a deep breath, then join Ofelia at the top of the stairs, shaking my head. She hesitates, her expression at once hardening and brightening. Suddenly she grabs my hand and pulls me into the nursery, opposite Valentina's room, the door squeaking slightly as it opens.

'What are you doing?' I hiss, a little shocked at her flippant breaking of an unspoken rule: no one should be in here, not until the new triplets are born. But at the sight of the old, familiar room – can we only have left it a matter of days ago? – my shock is swallowed by sadness and nostalgia at the life we once lived here. The walls and ceiling are painted light blue, dotted with yellow stars, suns and moons; and the four beds – three for the triplets, one for their nurse – are bare, their wooden frames arced over with white dust sheets. A paper mage-light chandelier floats over everything, a huge boat with yellow sails surrounded by tiny fish, birds and puffs of cloud, the whole thing draped over with a dust cloth too – the mage-lights now faded and gone. It was always ironic to me: a boat chandelier in a room of children who were going nowhere. Someone has rolled up the rug, and the pale wood floorboards are exposed. The room smells musty already, and the sunlight arcing through the window illuminates the floating dust like a kind of magic.

Ofelia shuts the door softly and spins to face me. 'Why should we have to dress like this?' She tugs in annoyance at her long veil and dark dress. 'Everyone can tell who we are. We stick out.' Her voice is low, a mere whisper. 'We can't even *pretend* to be normal, dressed like this.'

'That's the point,' I agree, frowning. 'Besides, we don't have any other clothes. Why are we here, Ofelia?'

She pulls off her veil, and underneath she is smiling. 'Follow me,' she whispers. 'I'm glad Valentina isn't coming. She would never have let us do this.'

'Do what?' I'm worried, even as I follow her across the room, treading softly. 'Ofelia ...' One of the four beds is slightly larger, set into an alcove. 'Nurse's bed?' I ask. In a flash, I remember her dark hair and warm brown eyes, her gentle voice. I miss her. I wonder how she is.

'Come on, help me,' my sister says.

Ofelia is reaching underneath the bed, fiddling around. I kneel beside her – but with the sheet lifted, I can see there's nothing under there but dustballs. 'Ofelia,' I start. 'What––?'

She grabs my hand. 'Here, push down.'

When we both push together, there's sudden click, a creak. One of the floorboards tilts upwards. Ofelia tilts the one next to it, too – and something is exposed, something covered in what I can tell is years and years of dust – though a few recent-looking finger marks show around the edges. A wooden chest.

'What is it?' I ask, dropping to my knees. 'How did you know it was here?'

'I found it months ago,' she says, her eyes glittering. 'Priestess Alyssa sent me to fetch an extra cloak or blanket – she was cold.'

I think I remember the day, last winter. The cold doesn't reach Scarossa, not really, but sometimes when the wind is sharp and the clouds roll over, you can half imagine how the bite of frost must feel in the north. 'Nurse kept a few spare things under her bed,' I say.

Ofelia nods. 'So I looked under here and I noticed the loose floorboard. I couldn't resist having a peek at what was inside. I didn't know what to make of it at the time, but now …' She smiles. 'Now, it feels like fate.'

I nearly laugh with shock and joy as she plants new fingerprints in the dust and lifts the lid of the chest, exposing the brightly coloured materials within. But I don't. I press my hands to my mouth in silence.

Together, we lay out the clothes on the narrow bed. They smell musty, but they've been packed with a sprig of ancient, sweet-smelling lavender. Three white cotton petticoats. A bright red dress of old silk, a little damaged at the sleeves – the stitching unravelling – but beautiful nonetheless. A lovely light blue dress in linen, printed with white flowers. A deep green velvet gown with wide bell sleeves, stitched with bright yellow foliage. Three silver necklaces: one draped with a constellation of nine glittery stars set with white glass, a popular design like Anna-Maria's; one hung with a single sliver of moon; the last with a pretty blue pendant in the shape of a flower. At the bottom of the chest, we unearth three pairs of shoes: lace-up brown boots with dainty heels; a pair of silver-buckled black slippers in a style that I'm sure was last fashionable decades ago; and plain dancing shoes in green velvet, matching the green dress.

I know at once that they are not the clothes of a rich woman – but to us, they're magnificent. *Three full outfits.* I wonder what is the significance of this? We run our fingers over the dresses as if they're made of gold. We've never worn clothes like these. We've always worn plain black dresses, ever since we were babies, and slept in plain white nightgowns. It's tradition.

'But why?' I breathe. 'Why are they even here?'

'I've been thinking about this for a while … I think they're disguises, Bea. I think a set of triplets decided they wanted a second life, one outside the mascherari compound. Maybe they bribed a servant to bring the clothes, then used them to escape into the city every once in a while.'

I feel my heart lurch, and I glance over at Ofelia, unable to disguise the hope in my eyes. But her mouth straightens and she frowns.

'Now, Bea, I'll have none of what we talked about before. I'm not suggesting deserting our duties altogether. But I've been thinking …' She strokes the long skirts gently, lovingly. 'As long as we complete our duties, I can't see the harm in exploring the city outside every now and then. You were right about one thing – this life is full of darkness. Whatever superstitions people have about us, they aren't true. And doesn't everybody need a little light? Wouldn't that make this fate of ours easier to endure? Perhaps we will even take more pleasure in our work this way, produce better masks. Be better mascherari. Because we'll have balance.'

'Should we?' I say, my words lingering in the air. But I already know we shall. 'How will we get away from the chaperones?'

Ofelia's already thought it through. 'We'll wear our veils and cloaks over the top. It'll be busy in the city – we'll find a chance to slip away and stow our black clothes somewhere safe. They'll never recognise us in these outfits. We'll have a lovely time, then pick our cloaks and veils up afterwards and come home, claiming we were simply separated from the chaperones and got lost in the crowds.'

Or, I think to myself, *we could just run down to the docks. Get on a ship. Sail across the wide blue sea and never look back.*

'Valentina will be cross if she finds out,' Ofelia adds. 'And maybe the Contessa too, but I think she'll be angry at the chaperones rather than us. She needs us to make her masks, doesn't she? What's the worst she can do?' She shakes her head. 'Besides, they won't find out. We'll be careful.'

I'm already nodding.

'The red and the green are the prettiest,' Ofelia says, gazing down at the dresses.

'You found them. You pick your favourite.'

She chooses the green velvet with the matching slippers. I help her into a petticoat and then slip the dress over the

177

top, fastening the little buttons at the back – it fits so beautifully, it could've been made for her. We choose the moon necklace for her, and I fasten it carefully around her neck. When she turns around, she is transformed. I undo her severe plait, and her dark hair spills over her shoulders in shining waves. I can't help the way my eyes prickle with tears. I wipe them fiercely.

'Silly Bea,' Ofelia says gently, but her eyes are shining too. 'Your turn now.'

We dress me in the red silk. This dress fastens with ties, like a corset, and is pleasingly tight around my waist without feeling stiff or constraining. Once it's on, I turn up the sleeves, slightly, and you can't even tell they're damaged. In the heeled boots, I stand a little taller, too – and the nine-star necklace glitters across my collarbones.

'You look amazing,' Ofelia says gently. And of course, I know I do: after all, she is my mirror. And her face is glowing with excitement.

We stuff our old dresses and sensible shoes into the box and push it under the bed, not bothering to hide it in the hole in the floor – after all, we'll have to replace it all later, and no one would have reason to go looking there. My hands are trembling as we pull on our black cloaks and veils to hide our dresses. We'll have to step carefully to hide our shoes. We hear the doorbell ring, our housekeeper answering. The chaperones are here.

Except for this night, every night in between now and

my death will be the same. Perhaps we'll find a day, here and there, in which to escape into the city again … but I already know it won't be enough. Not for me. Because for the best part of my life, I'll be trapped in my tight, dark fate like a body in a coffin, buried under the earth. Unless things change, I might as well be dead already. I shudder.

So for now … just for now … I will live.

I wipe my palms on my cloak as we step outside, praying the soft wind leaves the folds of black intact. One gust, and our disguises would be revealed to the world. I'm starting to doubt whether this was a good idea, but Ofelia flashes me an excited smile from under her veil.

I smile back, pushing aside my worries.

Our chaperones are two women in the yellow uniform of the Contessa, the great sun symbol bordered by nine holy stars emblazoned in red on each of their backs. Masks are tucked into special pockets on the insides of their jackets – if I glance to either side, through my veil, I can see the glimmer of beading on one, a tuft of feather on the other. If the Contessa is sending two of her True Masked guards, she is clearly worried about our security … but I try not to think about that.

Near the mask room, a sheet of paper blows gently into my skirts – I bend to retrieve it, mid-step, and realise it's the front page of the daily bulletin. Scanning the headline, I raise my eyebrows and glance over at Ofelia. 'Lord Livio is the Contessa's heir,' I tell her, hesitating. Our two guards hover beside us uncertainly. I frown down at the words, thinking back to my conversation with Valentina. 'This is huge …' I mutter.

Ofelia rolls her eyes at me. 'Valentina will be in hysterics. Come on – who cares about all that?' She snatches the paper from my fingers and throws it to the wind. Then, she grabs my hand, pulling me round the corner into the palazzo square.

My breath catches in my throat.

The square is thronged with floating mage-lights and is uproariously busy, buzzing with people and colour and stalls selling delicious-smelling food. Opposite the palazzo itself, in front of the library, the huge marquee has now been completed. It's easily the size of our house, though its walls and roof are blue velvet dotted with golden stars.

'The puppet theatre!' Ofelia says, clapping her hands.

'The performance starts in half an hour,' says one of our escorts, the taller of the two women, her eyes fixed somewhere over our shoulders. 'And the Contessa has reserved you some very good seats. Shall we?'

We nod, catching each other's eyes beneath our veils. Between here and there, we will have to find a place to slip away, blend into the crowd. But as we walk down into the square, a pool of quiet spreads around us, people drawing back to let us pass. Eyes are averted, voices lowered.

We are horribly conspicuous, like a well pulling everything down into darkness. I feel blood rush to my cheeks.

If I were those people, I would wish we hadn't come.

Ofelia grabs my hand suddenly. She's noticed a scuffle breaking out beside a jewellery stall to our left – someone unhappy with their purchase, perhaps. The jeweller has snatched up her wares and is holding them to her stomach defensively.

The customer, a brawny northern-looking man with pale skin and a shaved head, isn't interested in arguing any more – he wants to fight. He overturns the table, sending crystals and trinkets crashing and skittering across the ground in a crash that shakes the air. The crowd presses in, and Ofelia grabs my hand, drawing us backwards.

It's like the gods are on our side. Our chaperones are rushing towards the commotion, and when the customer raises a fist to attack the jeweller, the taller of our guards grabs his arm. He turns to her, scowling at her uniform. He's not going to back down quietly.

Now's our chance.

Ofelia pulls me, but I'm already hurrying to the nearest side of the square. We draw curious glances at first, but the fight is attracting more attention than us. My heart is hammering as we slip into a side alley, which winds into another. Here the houses are so close that the balconies on the third floor are almost touching. The abrupt quiet is surprising, as if we've been suddenly submerged in water.

'Quick!' Ofelia says. 'We can hide our cloaks here.' She's already bundling her veil behind a stack of empty crates – I follow her lead and then, hand in hand, we walk back towards the square transformed, our faces flushed from adrenalin. We hesitate for a moment, glance at each other, then plunge into the colourful crowd.

Wherever our chaperones have gone, we don't see them as we slip between the people of Scarossa. Everything is different, now – brighter, closer without our veils. Instead of the crowd parting for us, we are part of it. A stranger jostles me, and a thrill runs over my skin as I clutch Ofelia's hand. I'm terrified, elated. Eyes are drawn to us, not repelled. We're just a pair of twin sisters, pretty and excited and on our way to the puppet theatre. We join the queue to the sparkling tent flaps, drawn wide open, welcoming us in.

The performance tonight is free, by the grace of the Contessa, and it feels as if everyone in the city has piled into this marquee. We find seats near the back, climbing several steps to the level where a few rows remain empty, and gaze down on the stage. It looks quite small from here but is brightly illuminated. Ofelia squeals when she sees the puppeteers' company sigil – a large hand in black silk on blue, with trails of stars emanating from its outstretched fingers.

'They're called the Night Company, run by Giovanni Mezzanotte,' Ofelia says. 'They are the finest puppeteers in the world,' she explains when I look at her blankly. 'Most of the time they're touring, but when they're here, they usually only perform in the palazzo. Anna-Maria said they've only just returned here from the City of Kings – performing for the King himself!'

'Will we really be able to see everything from all the way up here?' I ask, gazing down on the distant stage.

'For performances like this, the puppets themselves will be very large compared to our toy puppets at home,' Ofelia replies. Her eyes are glittering in excitement. 'They can be four or five feet tall. They make them hollow, out of light wood or sometimes metal, so they're not too heavy to handle. Often, they're enchanted too. The Mezzanotte family has a magical bloodline, and the company contains *lots* of mages – more than any other, they say. Their special effects are supposed to be dazzling.'

I look at her excited face, smiling affectionately at her enthusiasm, and she elbows me in the ribs.

As the theatre fills, the energy and expectation grows. I feel an echoing energy building inside me, and I watch as the Contessa and her grandson file into a grand box to the left of the stage, which is draped with golden velvet and emblazoned with the red-star-encircled sun of their house.

At last, the huge floating mage-lights dim, and an answering hush falls over the audience. The stage is lit up brightly instead – by candlelight, a softer, gentler and somehow more lifelike kind of glow.

Music starts. A trumpet flares up a familiar tune against a background of violins, and Ofelia claps along with the rest of the theatre. Beneath the clapping, whoops and stamping feet are murmurs of anticipation. At last, a huge banner unravels, declaring in elaborate letters the title of the play: *The Hand of Fate*.

Ofelia squeals – the audience cheers. I beam at my sister, her exuberance infectious. The play is one of her favourites – an old, established classic.

As the music quietens, the banner is dropped, pooling on the floor beneath the stage, and in the split second it takes for this to happen, the puppets have appeared.

A figure steps across the stage – a woman in a fine red gown. Her movements are at once fluid and jerky, an unsettling cross between lifelike and inanimate. Her wooden feet, hidden under the long skirts, *clack-clack-clack* against the boards in a strange galloping rhythm. A sword is strapped to her back, gleaming silver.

I can't even see the strings holding her up.

The light grows brighter, and the backdrop scenery springs into view: a desert, beautifully rendered and glittering with sand; a harsh blue sky overhead; cacti leaning into the distance. It's the kind of landscape you can find on the less populated islands of the Wishes, a landscape that must've been here before Scarossa was built.

I wonder if the dark hair cascading down her back is real human hair.

I jump as a chorus of voices emerges from somewhere behind the stage, clear and ringing.

'Hail, citizens of the Wishes, these holy ancient isles! Our story begins over two thousand years ago, before the gods and the king came to Scarossa, in the time of mages and heroes, when Scarossa's only deity was Fortune.'

Music rises, a sweeping score of violins, the moan of a cello. The woman on stage lifts her hands – the air between them sparkles and glows with beautiful yellow magic like fire. The audience gasps as the lights float upwards, separate outwards into constellations. They're *stars*. The puppet appears to watch the magic, her head swaying as the glittering lights gently shift and turn in the darkness. Ofelia shivers next to me as images flit across the conjured stars – impressions of two figures embracing, one figure falling to its knees in death.

At this apparition, the puppet onstage appears to stiffen and cry out. She turns from the sky – the magic falters and falls. The lights onstage brighten. The music stops.

The woman stalks across the stage – already, I have nearly forgotten she is a puppet. She drops to one knee as if in prayer, facing the audience. 'I am Alana, Queen of the Wishes, the greatest mage in the world, and I have seen the future in the stars. My apprentice and lover, Ruggio, is destined to fall in love with my mortal enemy, Bradamante, and die young, killed at my enemy's hand. Fortune has decreed it. *Fortune.*' Her face can't show expressions, but somehow I feel her anger, hear the way she spits the word as if it's a curse.

Drums start up, a low, thrumming war-beat that reverberates in my very bones. The puppet stands up, squares her shoulders. 'I cannot let this stand.' The music grows in volume and drama, the whine of violins rising again from somewhere beneath us. 'What does Fortune do but sit on her throne of stars and declare that things shall be thus? What right does she have to decide? No more of this tyranny. I declare *war*.'

All the lights black out, candles and all – the theatre fills with gasps and murmurs.

All of a sudden, that energy is rushing through me again now, stronger than it did last night in the mask room – I gasp. I feel ill, faint, my pulse sounding in my ears as the drums start up again somewhere in the theatre. *Not here, not now.* A voice is speaking from behind the dark stage, but I can't listen any more, I have to focus on suppressing this, on *not letting go.* I clench my fists to ground me, my eyes darting around. There's no way I can slip out – we're hemmed in by people, all of them staring rapt at the dark stage. I'll have to get through this, like I did before, leaning my head against the mask-room door. I press my hands together, willing the feeling to die down – and it does, a little. Perhaps I can keep this under control. Perhaps it'll be all right.

The stage lights blare on again, and the scenery has changed. Now, a young man stands at the base of a tall sandstone tower – not simply painted into the backdrop but actually *on* the stage, stretching up to the height of two men. He wears a suit of bronze armour, visor raised, revealing a handsome dark-skinned face. The mage Alana joins him as he examines the building.

'Alana, my love, your mortal enemy Bradamante is on our doorstep – shouldn't I be fighting at your side rather than hiding in this tower?' Ruggio demands.

'This tower is impregnable, sweet warrior. Unscalable, unbreakable, fortified by magic. In here, you will never meet Bradamante. She will never be able to kill you, as Fortune has decreed.' She turns aside and, in a voice intended only for the audience, adds: 'Nor will you give your heart to her, betraying mine.'

But Ruggio shakes his head. 'You have taught me many things, Mistress. But one is that you cannot fight Fortune. Nobody can. I will not go. I will face our enemy – if I die, so be it.' He lifts his chin. 'I am not afraid. But I will not sit out the battle in this tower like a coward.'

The air fizzes with energy. Sparks surround Alana like a halo as she draws her sword. 'You *will*, or I will make you. I will not let you die.'

A cold wind blows across the theatre, rustling the puppet's clothes and causing the hairs on the back of my neck to prickle. As Alana and Ruggio start to fight, their swords clashing as the music rises once more, the scene feels too real to me. I want to scream as Alana's sword severs Ruggio's hand, a spurt of red blood – not blood, *silk* – flying on to the stage. Next to me, Ofelia gasps in delight, claps along with the rest of the audience. I dig my nails into my clenched palms to remind myself what is real and what is not.

The sharp pain in my hands is real. The cold wind in my hair is real. The story played out onstage is just that – a story.

The energy building again inside me isn't, *can't be* real.

Alana kneels in front of Ruggio, lays her hand on his forehead. 'May your memory desert you, my sweet, until you are safe again.' The air shimmers with her magic.

Despite my efforts, the sick feeling grows – the energy returning twofold. A shiver of electricity runs through me, and I breathe deeply, focusing on the stage. I can't look at the puppets, not any more. I focus on a blank piece of the curtain, trying to calm myself, but instead my heart beats fast as a spark appears out of nowhere, right where I'm looking …

And curls quickly into flame.

Before I quite understand what I'm seeing, the flame is spreading fast across the old curtains, and soon others notice and rise to their feet in alarm and point.

'What the …?' Ofelia breathes beside me.

'Injured and safe, my love, is better than dead,' Alana says, standing over Ruggio's unconscious form as two bronze-armoured men join her on the stage – her guards. 'I shall conquer Fate. Take him—' Her voice falters, stops. The puppets continue to stand for a few moments, edged in flame ripping up through the fabric curtains – and then the stage itself ignites, the tower shimmering with sparks. The puppeteers must drop their strings, because the puppets slump down suddenly, lifeless, with a rattling bang that I already know will haunt my dreams.

I think of Elina and Zia, my breath tight and fast in my throat.

A woman at the front screams and starts to run – and that is a spark of a different kind. A spark of panic that spreads through the audience faster even than fire.

I did this, I think. *I started the fire.*

Suddenly I'm being pushed along the aisle by Ofelia, but there's someone in front of me, and there's nowhere for me to go. The puppets themselves are burning now, and I catch a horrible glimpse of the Alana puppet, hair a blaze of gold, the paint on its face crinkling and browning before the flames catch, and it's too bright to see.

People are climbing over the seats, drawing knives and slashing through the material of the marquee to get outside. The flames are spreading so fast, it doesn't feel possible, arcing up the walls and ceilings in a roar of yellow. I spot the Contessa being ushered down from her box, bowed over her grandson's arm, before Ofelia tugs me over the back of a seat, and another, and then we're moving towards the marquee opening and fresh air, just as smoke starts to clog my lungs.

The panic continues to rage in the square. People are fleeing in every direction as the Contessa's guards struggle towards the marquee, bearing laughably small buckets of water. Billows of black smoke are blown all around us, and I clutch Ofelia's hand almost as tightly as she's clutching mine. All I want is to be home, but we're being borne in the opposite direction and there's nothing we can do to stop or turn around. People are jostling me now and I keep stumbling over the hem of my dress, but this time I don't like it – this time I wish people would leave us alone like they usually do. Suddenly there's a violent jerk as someone crashes into my back and I lose Ofelia's hand. I'm coughing, black smoke surrounding me as I am carried helplessly along with the crowd. A woman next to me is sobbing. Somewhere further away, there's a scream.

'Ofelia! Ofelia!' I shout, my voice hoarse.

And then her hand clasps my arm. Her eyes are wide and frightened, her face streaked with tears.

'We need to get home,' I say to her.

But she shouts in my ear, 'We won't be able to fight through. Let's just go into the city. We'll loop back later when it's quieter.'

A child is crying nearby as we shuffle along with the crowd down into the city streets. It takes a long time for the roar and heat of the fire to fade, and I can still see it if I glance over my shoulder, still hear a muffled continuous groan like the fire is a suffering beast. The crowd around us thins as people peel off to other streets, but we push on, wordless, until we reach the sea.

THIRTEEN
The Fire

Livio

Scarossa is burning. My city is burning.

Outside the marquee, Grandmother clutches my arm and panic fills my heart as the crowd heaves around us, pushing us forward, carrying us like a great, slow wave. Smoke writhes through the air, my eyes stinging, and the night is punctured with screams – behind us, the roar and heat of the fire is growing. I hold Grandmother close, try to ease us forward in the direction of the palazzo – but the way is blocked by hundreds of panicking people.

'Livio, where are our guards?' Grandmother says, her voice ragged.

I blink. She's right. We were slow escaping the marquee – Grandmother had struggled down the steps from our box – but I swear a second ago, we were flanked by yellow liveries. For a few long moments, unbelievably, it's as if we are alone: the Contessa and her heir, forgotten in a shuffling, shoving crowd of their people – our guards, wealth, power and status vanished in the smoke.

'A shield, Livio,' she says with a gasp. 'Now!'

My heart lurches as I realise what she means: she thinks the fire is Shadow's work. She thinks any second an attack will part the cloud, hidden until it strikes and kills us both. My heart pounds with adrenalin as I shakily attempt to summon a shield around us, breathing deeply as I try to draw on my magic. A weak film of pale light shimmers in the air … Useless. If a spell bursts through the smoke, my shield will shatter in an instant.

I have to get us out of here.

I cough, my throat burning as I attempt to stagger forward, holding Grandmother close. We must reach the palazzo before the assassins reach us.

Then, the crowd is roughly parted. Yellow-liveried guards push people aside as they head towards us, alternately revealed and concealed by black smoke, unheedful of treading on a woman's foot, knocking a child prone.

'Careful!' I say as the foremost guard shoves an elderly man aside. The guard is Hal, mask snarling over his face. Why is Hal wearing his mask in a crowd of non-mages? To intimidate?

I angrily let go of Grandmother's arm and step past Hal to help the man to his feet. 'Are you all right?'

The man doesn't have a chance to reply. 'Lord, we have to go,' Hal says, tugging me towards Grandmother, towards the other guards – and I find myself tightly escorted in the direction of the palazzo.

Once we're in the gardens, the sense of space is over-whelming – in spite of the smoke wreathing the trees. The guards start to shut the gates as Grandmother begins to climb the six marble steps up to the door, her hand tight on the banister.

'Wait!' I say, my voice hoarse. 'We should let people in here – until the fire is put out. To relieve the crowd. People can barely move out there.'

'Absolutely not.' Grandmother turns on the middle step, draws herself up and meets my eyes. 'Are you mad, Livio? You want to let hundreds of people into the palazzo gardens, *without knowing who is among them*?'

Her lack of compassion angers me. 'Weren't you just out there? People are going to get hurt – crushed in the panic, choking on the smoke. And we can hardly tackle the fire if we can't even access it. I should be out there – I should be—'

'*We* are going inside right now, Livio. I can assure you the fire is being dealt with – there is no need for your assistance.' Grandmother's icy tone is the kind I wouldn't have dared argue with a few short days ago. But now, for some reason, it makes me even more determined.

'They're *our* people – *we* have a duty to help them!'

Grandmother glowers at me. At last, she turns to one of her True Masked guards – the sneering Grotesque mask now removed from her face. 'Please supply my grandson with a full status report.'

'My lady.' She bows to Grandmother and then turns to me. 'My lord, we are following the city procedures for fire emergencies. The temple of Imris is already dousing the fire from a safe distance, as well as supplying medical aid to those in need. The temple of Faul is evacuating the nearby buildings and transporting the weakest to safety by air enchantment. Our own palazzo guards are bringing water to assist in these efforts.'

I swallow, wetting my burning throat. Of course. Of course they're doing something. But that doesn't mean I shouldn't be out there, showing the people that we care. Grandmother turns to me. 'Good government is a series of precautions and procedures, set in motion for every eventuality. It is not a knee-jerk reaction, however compassionate the motives for that reaction. Now, go inside, Livio.'

I bite my tongue. I can't win this fight. I can't seem to win any fight that isn't with my fists. I step past Grandmother – but she rests a hand on my arm, stopping me halfway up the stairs. 'I'll see you after your studies with Hal,' she whispers, 'as we planned. There's no time to lose.'

I nod curtly, pull away from her, and climb the stairs to my room.

Half an hour later, I'm standing on the rooftop, Hal at my side, gazing out over the palazzo square. The fire is under control now, but an angry orange glow continues to burn against the huge library, reflecting in its great glass domes, and smoke spews into the night. The air smells acrid.

I watch the figures bustling to and fro, the crowd now dispersed: the mages sending magical streams of water to quench the blaze; the fire-fighting machines brought up from the lower town. From a distance, they're so tiny it's nearly unreal. A voice floats up here, now and then – but it all sounds so far away.

I should be down there. I should be helping.

Hal's voice pulls me from my inner turmoil. 'Time for our lesson, Lord – remember?'

His voice is gentle, almost apologetic, but I'm not in the mood to humour him.

'Not tonight, Hal. Not after everything that's happened.'

'But, Lord—'

'It's *my* lord, Hal,' I hiss. I know it's petty, but I turn towards him and continue through gritted teeth. 'You keep saying "Lord". But it's "*my* lord".'

'Yes, of course. You are mine.' A slow smile, the familiar glint of the jewel on his tooth, and I feel my heart beat faster from a different kind of emotion. 'If I'd known it meant so much to you …'

I turn away, watching as the fire finally dies out. An oily flag of smoke is snaking into the sky, still, like the banner of a defeated enemy. But it's darker, all of a sudden, colder. 'Whatever, Hal,' I say quietly. 'A lesson it is. As you wish.'

I close my eyes, replaying the vision, the heat, the melting puppet face. It happened. It wasn't a mistake: I had seen the future, after all. *I am an astromancer.* The stars appear to dance around me as I realise this … and then I feel something cold and sharp against my throat. A blade. Fear jolts through me as I remember last time, the assassin …

'Lesson two. Don't stand on an exposed rooftop with your eyes shut,' says Hal, his mouth so close to my ear, I can feel the heat of his breath. I'm relieved it's him … but for a few seconds I just stand there, my heart pounding, as if I really think he'll do it. But then he lowers the knife from my neck. He doesn't let go of me, though – not at first. I can't help the way I like his arms around me, the way I wish I could sink into his warmth, turn and …

He steps away at last, keeping one hand on my arm as if he's afraid I might fall.

Reluctantly, forcefully, I shrug him off me and turn to face him. I want to say something mean, something to push him away, but nothing comes. I just look at him: his smooth black skin; his dark curls nearly silvery in the moonlight; an odd intensity in his eyes. He's looking at me – really *looking.* For some reason, I think of Elisao.

'So … the lesson?' I manage hoarsely.

'Right.' He teases a flicker of red–purple magic between his fingers, breaking eye contact and taking a step backwards. 'Your problem is control. You've got a temper on you. I saw it a lot at Jok's temple, back in Port Regal.' Jok – the god of warriors. 'Full of hot-headed mages like you. My theory? The temple of Mythris doesn't know how to deal with control issues. The character of a Mythris mage is usually control-obsessed, you see?'

Like Grandmother, I think ruefully. 'That's where you trained – Jok's temple? Not with Mythris?'

He's wandering away from me now, twirling his dagger in his palm. 'Mythris's temple was an apprenticeship at first. Couldn't decide which path to choose. Mythris got me in the end – better jobs. Better pay.' He shoots a smile at me over his shoulder. 'Anyway, lots of Jok's disciples are like you – aggressive. You've got to focus all that energy.'

'I'm not *aggressive*,' I protest. 'I can fight, but I'm not aggressive.'

'Right.' He raises an eyebrow as if he doesn't believe me. I feel myself colour. 'But you have to admit you get aggressive when you're nervous. First thing you do is tense up for a fight, Lord. See?'

He reaches down, takes my hand – clenched tight – in his. I blink, uncurling my fist. I suppose he's right. As my hand relaxes, he lets go.

'You see an attack coming and you panic. You try too hard. Half your energy just flies from your fingers in sparks. Same with other spells, I reckon, though I haven't seen you try. If you think you're being watched or tested, you're bound to fuck up.' He sits down on the edge of the roof, cross-legged, smiling. 'And you've picked up bad habits as a result. Relying on your body. You're strong, Lord, but no human body is as strong as magic.'

I bow my head, rub the back of my neck, ashamed at how well he's summing me up. 'I don't know. My magic doesn't feel strong at all.'

'You're better than you think. All you need to do is relax,' he counters, nodding down at my hands. I'm clenching my fists again — didn't even realise I was doing it. I sit down opposite him on the wide wall, cross-legged, like him. The city sprawls to my right, the palazzo rooftops to my left. We're sitting close. Not touching, but close enough to do so if we wanted. Why did I sit so close to him? I nearly shuffle away, but then he says, 'Now, do you trust me?'

I blink. 'I …'

But he's already reached out, and then he's holding both my hands in his. He is so warm, his skin dry and calloused. I can feel power coursing through him along with his blood. 'Shut your eyes. Breathe deep.' I do as he says, although part of me is afraid and wants to pull away.

I feel the warmth of him spreading through me, relaxing me as I focus on the air moving in and out of my lungs, tugging at my hair, caressing my skin. I can't tell if this is magic or simply the way he makes me feel. He turns my right hand palm up. 'Keep breathing,' he whispers. 'Just keep breathing.'

We stay like this for a few minutes that feel like hours, my heartbeat slow and steady, my breath echoing the sea's. And then he says, 'Now, let magic flow into your palm, Lord.'

And then, for perhaps the first time, I sense that the power doesn't slide away from me. It feels different, smoother, as I draw on the place my magic sleeps and let it trickle through me into the open palm of my hand resting in his.

'Very good. Take a look.'

When I open my eyes, I see a light violet flame flickering there – steady, bright and true. I hold on to it, keeping the flow of my magic. I'm afraid to shut my eyes, or move, or breathe, in case I break the spell. At that thought, there's a flicker.

'Just relax. Turn it into a globe.'

I do as he says, and the flame steadies again, evening out. Euphoria fills me. I'm doing it. I'm really doing it. A ball of purple light is floating between us.

'See?' he says softly. 'That's as good a mage-light as I've ever seen.'

I close my hand and the globe remains, hovering beside me in a physical manifestation of my power. Tears sting my eyes. It's a small thing, a simple mage-light – the sort of spell I should have mastered in my first year as a novice. But it's also something I've never been able to accomplish properly or reliably. I pluck it out of the air, hold it in my hands.

'Your magic is a nice colour – so pale. Unusual,' says Hal softly. 'You should do an apprenticeship at Regis temple, no? Where the magic is white.' But it's me he's looking at. Not the glowing mage-light.

Gently, instinctively, I extinguish the light by closing my hands around the globe. Only then do my eyes meet his, my vision bursting with colour as they adjust to the darkness once more. Hal is so close to me that I imagine I can hear his heartbeat – so close that I can't help gazing at him.

'Thank you,' I say. 'That was … I haven't been able to …'

Tentatively, he reaches out for me. His hand grazes the stubble on my jawline, brushes through my hair. A voice in my head warns me of danger, but I can barely hear it over the eager thudding of my broken heart. It broke so quietly, in such a storm of life-changing events, that I hadn't realised it until this second. I think of Elisao again: of the life I have lost with him, the life I never had.

I need this. If I can't have that life, I need this. My heart seems to say, *Yes, yes, yes.*

I lean a little closer, feel Hal's breath on my lips. Now, it's the fire that's rushing through my mind. The stars. The Raven's burning gaze, the mascherari sisters with their black veils pushed by the wind, the sandwolf's yellow eyes. I'm staring into Hal's, now, and they're the brightest blue I've ever seen, and I wonder if he's looking at me – the *real* me – like Elisao did. Can I ever be in love with someone the way I was with him, even when I didn't realise it?

'Lord?' Hal whispers slightly. A question. An invitation. He leans forward, presses his lips to mine.

For a second, it's simply good – comforting and gentle and a blessed relief from *thinking*. But the next second,

Elisao is flashing through my memory again – the kiss we shared on the steps of the library, how my heart leaped, how *right* it had felt. This … doesn't feel that way. I pull away, leaving Hal leaning forward, lips slightly parted, a frown denting his brow. I swallow.

'I'm sorry,' I say, feeling heat rise to my cheeks. 'It's not y—'

'Don't say it,' Hal cuts in, his tone light. 'Worst cliché ever. It's all right, Lord. Shouldn't have done it. I have to say, though, I'm not used to being turned down.' Of course he isn't. He's ridiculously handsome. He grins his usual, easy grin – but am I imagining the hurt in his eyes? The … anger?

Of course he's angry. I definitely invited that kiss. 'I'm sorry,' I mutter again, rubbing the back of my neck. 'I don't know why … I just …' I'm blathering now. I breathe deeply – start again. 'I—'

'I'd better go, Lord,' Hal interrupts, standing up – clearly losing patience. 'Good work today … on the magic.' And he walks away across the rooftop, leaving me standing there, feeling like the biggest fool in Scarossa.

FOURTEEN
The Reckoning

Beatrice

The docks stretch along the northern side of the island, in the sheltered waters facing the mainland. But, somehow, we've found our way to the south, where steps lead down to a series of stony beaches.

The Contessa's celebrations are city-wide, and here the effect of the fire appears to be muted. Stalls still line the beach, selling delicacies like crispy squid, roasted nuts and bags of sweets, and the people walking around seem calm and unhurried. I reach into my pockets expecting nothing, but I find an old silver coin and buy us each a cone of sugared almonds, my hands shaking as I take the bags from the vendor.

Ofelia and I pick our way right down to the shore, until we can't walk any further, then we sit down on a pair of sea-worn rocks and eat our hot almonds in silence. I can see the lights on Silver, our nearest neighbouring island, where the minor noble families of the Wishes tend their

202

estates. The next islands beyond that are the Twins, connected by a slim tidal isthmus and home to bustling fishing towns and charming villages. There's tiny Cantella beyond, then the three tiny isles of the Coins – they're largely uninhabited, except for a few small houses that the nobility use for holidays in the summer.

And then, there's just the sea, for miles and miles and miles. I shut my eyes, listening to the water as if I can hear that distance, as if I can *be* that distance. Then, I hear Ofelia sigh – the sound draws me right back to earth.

'I'm sorry,' I say quietly. 'You'd been looking forward to that. Now it's ruined.'

Ofelia shrugs. 'I know what happens next. Do you remember?'

'Ruggio is trapped in the tower, isn't he?' I say.

'That's right. Alana's gravely injured him so he's weakened, unable to escape. Then there's a big battle between Alana and Bradamante. Of course, Bradamante wins, though Alana survives, slinking off in exile.'

'Bradamante finds Ruggio, then,' I supply, enjoying how strong her voice grows as she tells the story.

'That's right. He's helpless and confused – he doesn't know his own name, or how he came to be in the tower. Bradamante assumes he's Alana's enemy. Gradually, Ruggio falls in love with her, and she with him – but when their relationship is consummated at last, his memory returns … and so does Alana, who inadvertently reveals the truth.'

Ofelia scrunches her empty paper cone into a small, tight ball. 'Bradamante can't let him live after that. She kills him, breaking Alana's spirit – and her will to fight. Bradamante claims the kingdom and is crowned queen.'

'What a cheerful tale,' I remark with a wry smile.

Ofelia doesn't smile back, gazing out at the star-tipped waves. 'The thing is, if Alana had just let Ruggio and Bradamante meet on the battlefield, they'd never have fallen in love.' She glances up at the moon. 'In trying to beat Fortune, Alana only made her prediction come true.'

I laugh thinly: the story of characters trapped by their destinies feels a little close to home. We stare out at the sea, momentarily silent.

'What happened back there?' Ofelia asks softly. 'It was … It was you, wasn't it?'

I glance over at her, my heart beating hard in my ears. 'What do you mean?' I ask. She can't know – can she? Even I don't *really* know that I did it …

'You think I don't notice things. You and Valentina must think I'm stupid or something. But I've thought about how you passed out during the Inheritance. How you fought off the assassin. I noticed yesterday, in the antechamber, when a spark flew from your fingers. And I was watching you in the marquee. Whatever *it* is, it always happens around magic.'

My voice is high and fast as I reply. 'Ofelia, the stage must've been thirty feet away. It can't have been—'

'But it was you, wasn't it? It was some kind of magic.'

'I honestly don't know.' I pause. 'Yes, I think so,' I add softly.

'What does that mean?' After a short pause, she answers her own question. 'You're a mage, aren't you?'

'I don't know,' I whisper. 'I can't be.'

She's frowning. 'Mascherari aren't mages – they just aren't. Besides, we're triplets – one soul split three ways. If you have magic, Valentina and I should too.' She gazes down at her hands, circling the scrunched-up almond cone, and I can't tell if it's confusion or disappointment in her eyes. 'We have the power of Mythris in our blood – but it's only for mask-making. We shouldn't be able to do anything else.'

I take a deep breath. 'I know. I wasn't sure, truly – I'm still not. The first time … it was when the assassin came. Something happened – I hurt him – but I wasn't sure how. But now … Now I think maybe you're right. Magic is the only answer. But it still doesn't make sense. I just keep getting this feeling … rising up inside me …'

Then I'm silent for a long time, we both are, just breathing in the warm air of the night. I don't understand what I did, or how I did it, or any of this. Suddenly it all rushes back to me, the heat, the screams, the hurry to escape, the way the puppets dropped to the stage in flames. I wipe two stray tears from my cheeks.

'We'll figure this out,' Ofelia says, taking my hand suddenly. 'Whatever happens, you're not alone.'

Warmth rushes through me, and I squeeze her hand. 'Thank you.'

She glances over her shoulder. 'I can't see the fire any more. Perhaps it's safe to head back. Unless …' She gazes out at the sea. 'If we strip off our dresses, we could probably swim to Silver. And from there, perhaps we could find a ship. We'll probably never have another chance,' she whispers very quickly, under her breath.

My heart could break. 'I want to. But … Valentina,' I say softly. We look at each other, and we both know we can't do this to her.

'Valentina,' she echoes.

With that, we turn away from the sea, the pebbled beach crunching under our heeled shoes as we pick our way back into the city.

After collecting our cloaks and veils from the alley, we traipse up the stairs of the mascherari house, our hearts as heavy as our feet. The guards were so relieved to see us alive that they barely questioned our story of crowds and confusion, but it's clear that our brief dance with freedom is now over. Security around the house is tighter than ever.

If I am going to get through this, I will need both my sisters at my side.

I knock softly on Valentina's door, Ofelia hesitating a step behind me – but Valentina's voice comes from the door opposite, from the nursery.

'In here.' Her tone is flat and angry.

My stomach plummets. I already know that we have been discovered. Ofelia nods slightly as we meet eyes.

Valentina is sitting on Nurse's bed, her hands neatly folded in her lap, a small lamp burning on the bedside table. The chest is open on the floor in front of her. Our black dresses are laid out on the bed opposite, our sensible black shoes arranged beneath them. The other contents remain neatly folded in the chest itself.

I feel as if I've been plunged into cold water.

'What exactly did you think you were doing?' Valentina says, her lips pursed tight. She stands up abruptly and goes to Ofelia, pulling the tie of her cloak and revealing the green dress beneath. She does the same to me. Both of us just stand there. I feel naked, tingling with shame. The sweat on my skin feels icy, and my ears are ringing.

I start to explain, opening my mouth before I know what I'm going to say. 'We—'

'Don't you dare try to justify what you have done,' she says, her voice calm and firm. 'Don't you *dare*.'

I glance at Ofelia, but she's just staring at her velvet slippers, her bottom lip trembling.

'Valentina, we're sorry,' I venture softly. 'But it was just one night.'

'One night? You have broken every rule, cast aside everything our order stands for, and shown a total disregard for the people we are supposed to help protect. How would they feel knowing they had looked upon you both, the mascherari sisters? How many would think themselves tainted?'

I shake my head. 'But it's not true,' I manage. 'It's just superstition.'

'It's what they believe, and we must respect that. These are the people we serve, Beatrice – you know that. I was praying when the Contessa's guards came here late last night – they'd been looking for you for hours – and then I heard about the fire … I was so worried …' Her voice breaks, but she pulls herself together quickly, as if she's slamming shut a door on her emotions. 'But I thought I'd heard you in here before you left, so I checked. That's when I saw how Nurse's bed was dishevelled, and I discovered the chest underneath.'

I think of her in our empty house, worrying about us, following our trail in the dust … and I feel ashamed at how we left her here. Deep down, does she wish she could've joined us? Can she really be satisfied with her piety, or does she too wish for freedom and beautiful things? If so, why can't she just admit it? Why does she put on a face in front of us, her only family, as much as she does for everyone else? She is my sister, a mirror of myself, and yet sometimes I feel I don't know her at all.

Her face hardens – perhaps she senses my pity. 'What do you think the Contessa will do if she finds out what you've done?' Valentina continues. 'We have plenty to lose. A comfortable house. Lots of food. Luxuries, even. I almost expect it of Ofelia,' she says, glancing at her coldly. 'But you, Beatrice? I always thought you were smarter. Instead, we'll all be punished for your stupidity.'

Finally, my temper rises and I lift my chin, forcing my voice to remain calm. 'Valentina, there is no need for the Contessa to know. The Nurse's clothes are well hidden here. No one recognised us. As far as the guards are concerned, we simply got separated in the crowds. We're not stupid.'

'And what if I tell the Contessa, Beatrice? What then? Would you still feel quite so clever?' Her eyes are full of tears, and her voice loses a little of its steadiness. She picks up the chest, which looks too heavy for her, even though it's nearly empty, and sits awkwardly against her torso. 'It's not right that you shouldn't suffer any consequences for your actions. I'll bring this to her and show her what you've done.'

'Don't you dare take that chest,' Ofelia says, at last raising her head. Her eyes are glowing, her body shaking with indignant rage. 'That's mine! *I* found it!'

Valentina ignores her and moves for the door, but Ofelia blocks her path, grabbing the other side of the chest.

'Let go,' said Valentina, her voice cold and calm once again.

'No, *you* let go!' Ofelia hisses. We're all aware that if we shout, Anna-Maria will come running. 'You think I'm stupid – fine. It was *one night*. You're just jealous because your stubbornness stopped you from coming with us.' She pulls the chest towards her, but Valentina's grip is too strong. 'Give it to me!'

'What possible use could you have for a chest full of clothes, anyway?' Valentina says through clenched teeth. 'You both look like common whores.'

'I wish I were,' I say quietly. 'At least then I'd be free. At least then I could walk the streets in sunlight and dance at night, and feel love, and hope, and dream that one day my life might be different.'

Neither of my sisters reacts to my words, they're so focused on each other. 'You are bitter and cruel and shrivelled up inside,' Ofelia says, eyes fixed on Valentina. Tears are streaming down her face as she pulls the chest towards her with more force – but she and Valentina are evenly matched. The lamp casts their long grey shadows across the floorboards. If they're not careful, they're going to hurt themselves.

'Stop this,' I urge, stepping forward, but they ignore me.

Valentina sneers at Ofelia. 'You've always been an ungrateful fool. Do you know how many people would kill to live the life we live, to enjoy our fate, to have the masked god's power in their veins?' Her voice is rising with emotion for the first time – Ofelia's words have touched a nerve. 'Our mother was a fishwife, Ofelia. Where do you think we would be now if the Contessa hadn't lifted us from poverty and granted us a god for our father?'

They pull the chest between them, and I hear a faint creaking, cracking sound. In spite of their efforts, anger amplifies their voices – I'm afraid the guards outside, or Anna-Maria downstairs, will hear and come running, and they'll burst in and see us standing here in our bright dresses.

I step yet closer. 'Valentina, Ofelia, don't shout. Please don't,' I try. But they're focused on their battle, their eyes locked, and I feel completely alone, completely separate from them both. It's like I'm not even here.

'I'm not saying we shouldn't be grateful!' Ofelia is saying. Her voice is choked with emotion – her rage shifting again to tears of frustration. 'I *am* grateful. But I'm asking you to let me have this, Valentina. Just this one thing. Please.'

'Valentina, Ofelia, *please* ...' But they're not listening to me.

'No. You're acting like a spoilt brat. You need to learn to face the consequences of your actions. Now – *let go!*'

Both of them tug hard – that sound again, the old chest buckling. Suddenly there's a loud crack – the ancient, poor-quality wood surrenders at last, breaking in two. A jumble of the remaining clothes and costume jewellery falls out, clattering on to the floorboards with the now-scentless sprigs of dried lavender, the colour of dust.

'You've ruined it!' Ofelia shrieks, casting aside her useless portion of the chest. She steps forward and clutches

Valentina so hard around the shoulders, I can see her knuckles whiten. 'Why did you have to do that? Why couldn't you let me have it?'

Ofelia's tear-stained face is distraught. Valentina is gritting her jaw.

'Now look what you've done,' I say softly, feeling close to tears.

A voice from downstairs. 'Mistresses? Is everything all right? I heard shouting.'

I reply quickly, willing her not to climb the stairs. 'Fine! Sorry, Anna-Maria. I dropped … I dropped a pile of Valentina's books.'

A pause. 'Very well.'

The silence that follows is the deepest and coldest I've ever felt. Valentina sits on the floor, holding the pale dress in her lap – the dress she could have worn. Ofelia is slumped against the wall, sobbing quietly into her sleeve. I'm the only one left standing.

'I just wanted one night, every now and then,' Ofelia says again quietly. She glances at me, red-eyed. '*She* wanted to run away forever.' Despite her words, her voice is completely unaccusatory – as if she's simply stating fact.

'Is that true?' Valentina sounds weary now. As if she can't summon enough energy to be angry at me too.

I don't reply. Instead, I start to pick up the broken pieces of the chest, tidying them into the space beneath Nurse's bed.

'Well, Beatrice?' she persists.

I sigh, stopping and sitting on Nurse's mattress. 'Yes, it's true. But … don't you feel the same sometimes?' There's an edge of desperation to my voice. 'Don't you ever sit there at your work and wonder what else you could be doing if the Contessa hadn't taken us? The people you could have known? The things you could have seen?'

'This is our destiny. This is what we're meant to do,' Valentina whispers, like a prayer.

'Who decided that? Because it surely wasn't us.' I feel a sudden jolt of determination. 'Why don't we do it? Why don't we just go?' I raise my eyes. 'Right now. There are three dresses here. Everyone is distracted by the fire. We could …'

But Ofelia stands and heads for the door. 'I'm going to bed,' she says without looking back. 'I'm too tired to do this any more.'

Valentina stands up to join her. 'I'm going too. And truly, Beatrice, I don't feel trapped. I feel lucky to be living this life, with my sisters beside me, creating beautiful and useful things. I can accept our lack of freedom as a price for this life of comfort and purpose.' The way she says it, I actually believe her – and for some reason, that makes me angry. 'I'm truly sorry you don't feel that way too,' she says piously.

'Don't be so godsdamned superior,' I hiss at her. 'Do you feel like that as well?' I say to Ofelia. 'I know you don't. When we were out on the beach, it seemed like you were ready to go, if only Valentina had been with us.'

She turns to me. 'I won't deny that it scares me, what we have to face. And I won't deny that running away has crossed my mind too, more than once – and that I wish for another life, sometimes ... But' – she shakes her head – 'I would never really do anything. I would never leave. I just ... I guess I just want to find a balance to this life. Is that so bad?' She meets Valentina's eyes.

Valentina shakes her head slightly. 'We've only been mascherari for three days,' she says. 'I think we all need to allow ourselves time to find a balance.'

They both look at me now – inviting me to join them where they stand beside the door. But instead I turn away, shame stinging my throat. I don't agree. I'm not happy to let things stay as they are, pacified by vague words about getting used to it. I'm not like them. I'm different. The realisation has never been stronger or clearer than it is at this moment. 'Just go to bed. Get your rest,' I say, the words bitter in my throat.

'Beatrice ...' Ofelia says softly.

'Just go.'

It's the early hours of the morning. I lie awake, staring at the canopy above my bed. I've not slept – my thoughts are too loud, memories of the night screaming and chattering through my mind like gulls.

For all my frustration, I know Valentina and Ofelia are right. I have to learn to accept this life – even if I can never

214

love it. After all, it's the only one I'll ever have. One look at my sisters' faces, mirrors of my own, tells the truth: I may be different, but I am not special. I am part of a chain of inheritance stretching back centuries – millennia, even. Nothing can change that – not me, not the Contessa, perhaps not even Mythris himself.

In the morning, I'll make up with Valentina and Ofelia. In the morning, I'll work hard to accept the hand we've been dealt, once and for all. But right now, I need to let go. I need to sleep.

It feels good to surrender responsibility like that. Tension falls from my body. At last, my eyes grow heavy, and I start to drift away …

I hear the soft, soft creak of a floorboard and jolt awake, my heart pounding. It's still dark, and I know with sharp, undeniable instinct that someone else is in the room, standing by the door. A breath of air tickles my face – colder air from the corridor. Somehow, I'm certain it's not one of my sisters. I know it's a stranger … I feel the realisation tingling down my spine—

The assassin.

All at once, my breath is shallow, my heart racing. How did he get past the guards?

If I'm alive, I think, *Valentina and Ofelia are too. That means he's come here first, and I have a chance to stop him.*

I ease myself out of the side of the bed furthest from the door, the side in front of the window where the bone roses are ghostly in a shaft of moonlight. The bed with its closed curtains now stands between the intruder and I.

But it's only a temporary solution. I have to *do* something ... Can I try to sneak out, fetch help? No – there would be no way to pass the assassin in the corridor unseen. If I scream, the guards will hear me – but so will the assassin. By the time the guards get here, it may be too late anyway. Could I fight? I shake my head in frustration. I may have the element of surprise, but I'll be weaker than the assassin, and I don't have a weapon ...

Or do I?

I remember Ofelia and I sitting on the docks – it feels like years ago. *You're a mage, aren't you?*

I fix my eyes on my hands, flex them gently. *If I can set a puppet theatre on fire, I can set a man on fire too.*

Silence. And then a whisper of material as the bed curtains are pulled back.

My heart is racing. I don't know how to summon my magic. Every time it's risen in me, it's been unbidden. I close my eyes and remember how I felt at the theatre, how I felt when specks of light flew from my fingers in the mask room, how I felt last time the assassin tried to kill us ... What's the link? My magic sparks when I feel threatened, trapped and hopeless – like a kind of defence. So I think of the argument with my sisters, the life I'll never live, the sea I'll never sail, the Contessa and the god who've forced this fate upon me – and now, yes, the feeling is rising inside me.

That power, surging closer to the surface of my skin than ever before.

I'm so *angry*.

The assassin's soft footsteps creak over towards the window – and now he's standing right in front of me. He hasn't looked this way yet – he's too busy peering under the table in front of the window. I have to strike now – *now* – while he's distracted. I hold out my hands, but they're trembling, thin and pale in the moonlight. The power that felt so close a few seconds ago has drawn back inside me …

How dare *he try to steal the life we never chose to live.*

I take a deep breath and rise from my hiding place, letting a stream of … of *magic* loose into the darkness. For the first time, it has a distinct colour – a bright, livid green that sends shadows arcing across the room as it hits him in the shoulder. He staggers, grunting, then spins, barely hesitating before he sends an answering flash of deep orange light across the room towards me. I duck, crying out instinctively, the attack smashing a mirror on the wall then ricocheting into the bed, where a cloud of feathers plumes into the air.

The assassin crosses the room, grabbing my throat with his hand and pressing me against the wall. I watch the bone roses turn towards us, slowly, like a many-headed creature roused from deep contemplation. I'm too slow. Too damn slow – and I can't breathe … But that only makes me angrier. I press my hands against his chest, and although I don't know how I'm doing it – or *if* I'm doing it – I feel my power surge.

The room spins as the magic breaks free, my hands glowing green where they're pressed against him. A muffled bang sounds, and the assassin is flying across the room – he hits the opposite wall and slumps to the floor.

Like a puppet with cut strings.

I gulp air in the ensuing silence, as if I've surfaced after being held underwater. Oh gods. Oh *gods*. What happened here? My hands are shaking. The assassin does not move.

Trembling and drained, I hurry over and touch his black mask, which feels dead and cold under my fingers. Oh Mythris, how am I going to explain what I've done? There's no doubting it now. I am a mage. A mask-maker *and* a mage. But how?

I lift off the mask. The face beneath is warm and – to my relief – I can feel my assailant is still breathing. I've knocked him out, but he's not dead. He's fair-skinned, his brown hair cropped close to his skull. A man of perhaps thirty years. Apart from being a northerner, there's nothing distinctive about him at all, except – and I only notice it because his head is turned slightly – there's a tattoo behind his right ear. A tiny sun – like the sun in the Santini crest, but this one isn't rounded by stars.

I don't have time for this. I stand up, backing away.

No guards have come running. No Anna-Maria. I'd have thought the struggle was loud enough to wake the dead. I have to get Ofelia and Valentina. Only my sisters can help me figure out what to do next.

I hurry out into the corridor, the mask still clutched in my hand, loathe to leave the assassin out of sight in case he wakes and follows me. I open Ofelia's door. She's lying in bed, the moonlight sliding across her face, her eyes shut. I feel a stab of impatience: after everything that's happened tonight, I'd have thought even she'd have trouble sleeping. I run to her side and shake her, hard. 'Ofelia, wake up!'

She doesn't move. I jerk my hands away instinctively. Ofelia's puppets sway and rattle on their stage, their eyes impassive.

'Ofelia?' I manage, forcing myself to reach out, shaking her harder. Nothing. She's so still.

Suddenly, violently, I step away from her bed, my movements so clumsy and uncoordinated that my wrist collides with the unlit lamp on her bedside table, sending it crashing to the floor.

She's dead. She's dead.

Tears obscure my eyes as I sprint into the corridor – I burst unsteadily into Valentina's room, and what I see there sends the world spinning. A scream runs through me, but when I open my mouth, nothing comes out.

My eldest sister has been brutally killed. She's on the floor, reaching for the door as if she is still trying to escape, blood running from her nose, her eyes open, the lightning-like red marks left by a magical attack spread across her face and down her bare arms. The stench of blood fills the air, blood mixed with electricity, the heaviness before a storm … My stomach twists and I blink my eyes, as if this is something I can wipe away with my tears. How … how could he do this to Valentina? I'll kill him. I'll *kill* him. Sparks start to fly from my fingers. Something rises up inside me … the *power* again …

With difficulty, I wrestle it down. I'm in trouble. How can this be? I am still alive, and we are *one soul* – one power split three ways. *One cannot exist without the others.* And yet, here I am.

I'm not who I thought I was. There's been some kind of mistake … some kind of mix-up. Because I shouldn't, I *can't* be alive. Maybe … maybe Ofelia and Valentina were twins. And I was a third sister, born in the same womb. Is that possible?

I don't know.

I don't know.

I don't know.

There's only one thing I *do* know.

I have to run.

FIFTEEN
The Sun and the Storm

Livio

Once Hal's footsteps disappear, I turn to the sky. The stars swirl overhead, the moon hidden. I feel oddly elated, light-headed. A thought reaches into my mind, clear and bright and true.

I love Elisao.

The words fill me up like a magical kind of air.

But then I remember what happened – how he tried to tell me he loved me, how we can never truly be together. I sag, deflated, rest my head in my hands. A low groan of frustration escapes my lips. *Why* did I let Hal kiss me, anyway? I can't exactly ask Grandmother to assign me a different personal guard without telling her why ...

'My lord?' A voice from the balcony below – my grand-mother's steward.

'What is it?' I walk across the rooftop towards the staircase, peering down.

The man's face is pale in the light cast from my room. 'The Contessa has asked to see you now, if you please.'

I open the door to Grandmother's room as the clock on the mantelpiece strikes eleven. The room is empty, the bone roses pressing mutely against the glass. I shut the door behind me and pick my way across the room to the secret door leading up to the blue glass tower, the ancient temple hidden by time – and here I find her, sitting at the marble table with her hands flat on the surface, her head tilted back, gazing up towards the stars.

'You shouldn't climb those stairs alone,' I say quietly, remembering how she struggled last time.

'And yet, I must.' She smiles, the blue light of the moon filtered through the tower glass softening the wrinkles on her face. 'My servants tell me the fire in the square has been extinguished. There were only a handful of casualties – given the size of the blaze, we should count this a victory.'

I nod, wondering if she will chastise me again for challenging her authority out in the gardens.

But her face is grave and calm as she continues. 'Unfortunately, one of the casualties was the mother bearing our three new triplets.'

My hands tingle with cold. 'What happened?'

'The woman was there with the rest of the city. In the hurry to escape, she fell and was trampled in the confusion. By the time my people found her, it was too late for the babies.' Her voice is flat, unemotional. But I feel my stomach lurch in mingled pity and horror.

I try to breathe deeply, running a hand through my hair. 'What now?'

'Now, we seek guidance. Lie down, as you did before. You saw a burning face. The next evening, the puppet theatre catches fire.' She smiles slightly. 'After today, I am beginning to think you are an even better natural astromancer than I gave you credit for – you saw something I didn't. So, let's see what else you can tell us.'

I feel the press of the altar, cold as a tomb against my back, and gaze up at the stars again. I slow my breathing as she instructs. I find it easier, this time, to see the first layer of stars, and I feel the same place inside me respond, thrumming in time with the shimmer across my eyes. The chains ring softly like bells, calling me in. I stay calm. But this time, I can feel two distinct paths open to me, two different ways to reach for this power – this, I was not expecting. But I wonder … I choose one, tug softly, but there is no vision this time.

Instead, I hear my grandmother inhale sharply.

'Livio, what …?'

I sit up abruptly, my head spinning. Sitting on the altar in front of me, quite calm, is a sandwolf, its yellow eyes glowing.

'Oh,' I say, blinking. 'I didn't mean …'

'Impossible,' Grandmother breathes. She appears to

gather herself together, standing up and backing slowly away from the altar. 'Send it away, Livio. At once.'

But I'm not listening. I'm watching the swirl of the creature's body, the little dust devil of sparkling sand, and – without realising it – I'm reaching out. My breath catches. The sandwolf's head is surprisingly warm and soft against my fingers, and its eyes narrow at the contact, as a cat's eyes close when it purrs. I push my fingers over its body – firmer than I'd expected. The sensation of sand running across my palm feels like nothing so much as fur. I can feel something else too – but not with my hands. With my heart. I can feel its fierce, questioning intelligence: its willingness to do my bidding.

'Livio, *now*,' Grandmother's voice interjects – her obvious fear bringing me to my senses. 'Send it away … if you can.'

'I can,' I breathe. I remember the sandwolf in the arena – it had appeared to listen. Is this the same sandwolf, I wonder – the same one as on the rooftop, too? Or has it been a different one each time? 'You … You can go now,' I say to the beast uncertainly. And, in a spinning whirl of sand, it disappears, leaving my hand outstretched and empty. I let it drop. 'So I was right. They do listen to me. And on the rooftop … it did save me from the assassin.'

But Grandmother isn't listening; she's sitting down as if she's suffered a great shock. 'It appears you have inherited the … the *other* kind of astromantic powers, Livio, alongside the ability to read the stars,' she says, her voice sounding strained with something ... Fear? 'I didn't think it was possible. In fact, I thought powers over the sandwolves died even before your ...'

Your mother. That's what she was going to say, I know it – but she trails off. I stroke the signet ring without meaning to – the sandwolf emblem suddenly holding more meaning than I'd realised. I remember the line in the book – the two powers, carried separately. Two families: the Santini and the Lupina. The visions of the future in one. The command over *the natural magical creatures of the Wishes* – sandwolves, I know now – in the other. *And those bloodlines are combined in me.* 'So ... Mother couldn't do this?' I ask softly.

Her eyes widen. 'How ...?' But then Grandmother falls silent – as she always does when I raise the subject of my mother. I feel a jolt of anger. Why has she been kept from me my whole life? Apart from the ring – and now the book – I own nothing that belonged to her. Isn't it strange? She lived in the palazzo – she must've had belongings here – why is there no trace of her? I don't even have memories – I was far too young when she disappeared – or stories, because Grandmother will not speak of her, and Father is long dead.

But *I* won't stay silent any longer.

I finish her question for her. 'How did I know? I read it in a book.'

'What book?' She's holding her breath, her whole body visibly tense.

'I found it in the temple library. I've read how the Lupinas, Mother's family, were granted the other branch of astromancy by the goddess Fortune. Command over *the natural magical creatures of the Wishes*, it said. That means sandwolves, right?'

Grandmother is silent.

'Tell me …' I ask, leaning forward. 'Could my mother do this too?'

She sighs – and when she finally speaks, I feel the words are dragged out of her from somewhere deep and cold. 'I don't know anything, Livio, truly. There is so much that Serafina kept from me – the nature of her magic, her thoughts, her pain … But now … Now I am almost certain she could summon sandwolves. It's unlikely she couldn't, if you can.'

I fall back into the chair, the anger fleeing from me all at once. I gaze up at the twisted stars through the blue enchanted glass. 'What if she's still out there?'

Grandmother reaches out, grasps my hand firmly. 'You must not think like this. It's too cruel to yourself – too painful.'

'But her body was never found,' I say. I hold her hand tightly, her mourning rings pressing against my fingers. Tears fill my eyes for a reason I can't quite fathom. 'And if … if she were alive, she'd be the only one in the world who knows about this kind of astromancy. The only one who could help me make sense of it.' I blink, feel my cheeks turn wet. 'Gods, did she not …? Did she not love me? Why did she have to—?'

'No. Enough of this.' Grandmother's eyes are firmly fixed on mine. 'Livio, your mother loved you – any fool could see that. And she cared deeply for your father, too. I was certain, at first, that she would return in time – that perhaps she only needed respite from her duties as mother and wife. But it's been close to sixteen years, now – there is no doubt in my mind that she is dead. Don't torture yourself with maybes and what-ifs.' She squeezes my hand again. 'I think we've had enough excitement for one night, don't you?'

I wipe my eyes, nod once, tightly. Together we leave the temple, hiding the entrance behind its curtain, and once back in her room, I settle Grandmother in her armchair before sending for her maids.

I finally fall into bed past midnight, my head swimming. Feeling a hard shape under my pillow, I pull out my mother's book. I hold it to the lamplight, open the cover, run my finger over the inscription written in her childish hand.

Who left this book for me? And why? How did they get hold of it?

I open a page at random – a line illustration of a great carved chair. A throne. I read the inscription below, my eyelids heavy.

The throne upon which the queens meted out law and justice was known as the Starlight Throne. Carved of volcanic stone, it is said to remain in the ancient throne room, buried somewhere beneath Scarossa.

Beneath Scarossa. In Dark Scarossa, then. The graffiti. Shadow. Old Jacobo's warnings. The city beneath. A throne. Astromancy. I feel as if I'm teetering on the edge of something. But as my eyelids droop, the questions circling my mind feel less and less urgent …

I close the book and flick off the light. The curtains are open, and I watch the stars for a few moments. Do I need to be in the temple to read the stars, or can I do it right here, right now? I tug gently on my astromantic magic, and my vision shifts. The stars stretch back in layers, past, present and future, rattling their chains. I wonder, are they the prisoners, or are we? And with that lingering thought, I fall asleep.

I am in a dark room. Suddenly, a great flash of lightning throws the room into ugly brightness, and I distinguish – for a split second – wooden faces peering down at me from every angle.

And again, a pregnant darkness, leaving me panting as if doused in a great wave. I wait a beat, unable to run – although I wish I could. And then, a loud rent of thunder splits the air and lightning flashes a second time.

The light's icy visitation reveals a changed scene. Now, the faces – the masks, *I realise – have been swept from the walls, lying destroyed on the ground as if discarded by the raging ocean—*

I gasp, open my eyes to sunlight, gritty and dry, my heart pounding as if some part of me is already aware of what's going to happen next – and perhaps it is. The remnants of a horrible nightmare cling to my mind: masks; lightning; destruction. But was it a nightmare? Or a vision?

I breathe deeply as the adrenalin slowly drains from my blood, my body clammy and cold. There's no doubt the dream had the visceral feeling of the vision from before – the burning wooden face … But what does it mean?

I can hear the wind whistling round the glass towers – the sound of a storm blowing in from the ocean. Hurried footsteps sound outside my room – low, panicked voices. Something is wrong. Before I can get up to investigate, my bedroom door flings open and Hal is in the doorway.

'The mascherari sisters have been assassinated,' he says. 'Get dressed – quickly, now – and meet in the back parlour. You and the Contessa are in grave danger.'

The door shuts, and I'm left with a freezing, sinking feeling as the curtains blow in from my window like wild spirits. I get up, shut the glass doors and prepare to face this day.

The palazzo is in upheaval. Servants are heaving chests from room to room, packing valuables in swathes of soft sheets. Two guards collide on the stairs transporting a pair of finely carved chairs I recognise from Grandmother's rooms – a pot of shadow ferns is knocked over, soil scattering over a half-rolled-up rug. Curses and commands ring out across the hall.

'Did you see it – the graffiti in the square?' one of the maids is saying to another as they manoeuvre a huge porcelain vase into a sheet-padded box outside my room. I stoop outside my door to tie my shoelaces and listen. 'Everyone's talking about it.'

'Saw it on my way in. That sun – over and over, in bright red paint. Almost every wall covered with it. No stars though.'

'Doesn't make sense, does it?'

I stand up, feeling oddly light-headed – I slump against my doorframe. The graffiti outside the Battaglia that night was identical. What had Elisao said? *The Santini sun existed on its own as a sigil. Before the gods. Back when the rulers of the Wishes were queens in their own right.* I feel suddenly cold. It's no coincidence that this huge graffiti statement was scrawled across the palazzo square the very night Shadow had the mascherari sisters assassinated. No: one thing is clearer to me now than ever before … Shadow seeks to overthrow the order established by my family thousands of years ago – the alliance with the masked god, as embodied in the mascherari – and to replace it with something older … And it's happening *right now*.

And then I remember how my mother's book, *The*

Queens of The Wishes, has the exact same image on the cover. Did someone leave it for me as a warning? Or – I feel cold at the thought – did *Shadow* leave the book for me?

'Stop dawdling!' someone yells nearby. It's not directed at me, but I jump and hurry away nonetheless. I have to see Grandmother. Disorder fills the air like a flock of frightened birds. I descend the stairs, weaving between the servants and guards, the huge arched window in front of me framing a cloudy, bruised sky.

Nobody notices me as I reach the foot of the staircase and wait for a group of guards to pass before I head towards the back of the palazzo. I've dressed not in my novice robes, as usual, but in the plain clothes I generally wear in the city at night – cream shirt, black trews in the close-cut northern style, an open dark blue jacket of fine wool. I could be a scholar or a merchant's son. The Cardinal emerges from the back parlour, Carlotta at his side – their red hair is the brightest thing in the grey hall. I stop in the shadows and listen.

'It was unseemly to express disagreement in front of the Contessa, Carlotta. Do not disrespect me again,' says the Cardinal, his voice stiff and cool as he fastens a purple cloak brought by a yellow-liveried servant.

Carlotta's voice is pleading. 'But, Father, don't you think we should be helping—?'

The Cardinal nods the servant away and pulls Carlotta into a small alcove. I lean forward, straining my ears. 'We must present a united front. Your opinions, such as they are, are irrelevant. You must learn to control your emotions.'

I peer around the side of the staircase. Carlotta is facing me – I can see two crimson spots rising on her cheeks. 'It is not *emotional* to do the right thing,' she mutters. I'm reminded uncomfortably of my own discussions with Grandmother.

I can't see the Cardinal's expression, but I watch as he reaches out, grabs Carlotta's arm. I watch her face stiffen with pain. 'Why do you insist on defying me? Always one step away from what you should be. If you are not more careful, I'll send you to some backwater temple to finish your education where you can't do any harm.'

'Please,' says Carlotta, and, mercifully, her father lifts his hand from her arm. Before she pulls down her sleeve, I see how little lightning-like impressions have surfaced on her skin. I feel a jolt of shock – he was hurting her with magic.

'Come, we've wasted enough time here,' says the Cardinal and, stepping into the corridor, he stalks towards the door. Carlotta follows but hesitates. Suddenly she glances towards me, her eyes locking on mine. Her face wavers expressionless for a moment … But then she scowls, following the Cardinal outside.

Hal meets me right outside the parlour, his expression rigidly professional. 'Go in – the Contessa is waiting. I'll be in your rooms afterwards – there's lots to do.'

'Thanks, Hal.' I feel an impulse to apologise for what happened last night. 'I ...'

'Don't mention it,' he says, smiling tightly. 'There are more important things to worry about now.'

Before I can reply, he's slipped away and is climbing the stairs.

When I finally step into the back parlour – a room constructed nearly entirely of salt-spotted windows over-looking the ocean – I find a haven of quiet, the only sound the waves hissing and thrashing at the rocks. Grandmother is sitting in a high-backed chair with her back to the door, a pot of tea and an empty cup on the small table beside her. The large round table has four chairs pulled out around it, and I guess that's where Grandmother sat with the Cardinal and Carlotta.

'They were right here again, Livio. Shadow's people. The mascherari sisters are gone. The chain of a thousand years is broken, and all the True Masks have lost their power. The bargain with the masked god is null and void, and Shadow knocks on our door, ready to destroy us entirely.' Her voice is flat and cold. 'Sandwolves roam the city streets. Our people are dying. Our trade fading. Our powers both secular and magical are severely diminished. I have failed.'

I take a seat beside her in a chair gazing out to sea. 'Grandmother, what's going on? Are we leaving?'

But she doesn't seem to notice my question. She looks paler and older than I've ever seen her: her face heavily lined; her eyes tired; her hair a cloud of steel grey around her head. 'Why didn't the stars tell me *this*?' she asks in a whisper.

Gently, I reach out and take her hand. 'Grandmother … what's happening? Why is the palazzo being packed up?'

At last, she looks at me. 'If I cannot defend my own people, and I cannot turn to Mythris for help, I must rely on secular powers. I must appeal to the *King*.' I can tell it pains her to speak it from the way she spits the word.

My mind is racing. 'I just saw the Cardinal leaving … Did they refuse to help us?'

'The servants of Mythris are slippery creatures, Livio. They have offered to assist us, but only in exchange for a granting of greater powers – *secular* powers.' She shakes her head angrily. 'If I agree, we would no longer rule Scarossa, in truth – the temple would. I cannot accept it.'

'I see …' I nod, wishing I could feel more surprised. But everyone knows Mythris's temple is full of mages whose particular talents tend towards control, deceit and unbounded ambition.

'To the King I must go. He may be bought with other advantages. Trade. A closer political alliance. A marriage, perhaps.' At this, she glances at me. 'The King has a niece who may be of age …'

I swallow, my throat suddenly dry. 'Can't you send an envoy? Why pack up the whole palazzo?'

Her voice is suddenly impatient. 'You really don't

understand, do you, boy? Perhaps, like all young people, you think you are invincible. Well, you are not. Shadow's assassins are everywhere. They are powerful enough to defeat several of my True Masked mages and a whole battalion of highly trained guards – and to do so without detection.'

I run a hand through my hair, feeling my heart pounding in my chest. 'Grandmother, this graffiti that's been drawn everywhere … it's an old symbol. The symbol of Scarossa's old queens. And there's the book I found … It was left where I could find it. Do you think Shadow—?'

'We don't have time for this talk of books and symbols. We've discussed this, Livio. Shadow is exploiting an ancient movement in our city, yes – whipping up popular fervour. And gods, it seems to be working – my guards are stretched thin, calming unrest in the streets.' She shakes her head, and I nearly press my point – but she is already speaking again. 'We are in grave danger if we stay here … and yet, that is what I must ask of you.'

I blink, and everything I was trying to piece together – about Shadow, about the symbol – flees from my mind. This wasn't what I was expecting. 'But the palazzo …'

'No, you are not to remain in the palazzo. As soon as I am gone, this place will be the most dangerous place in the city. The temple will send its mages to protect it, ostensibly in my name. And Shadow will likely want to seize it as the seat of power. No, I need you to disappear in the city. I trust you have friends there?'

I baulk, my throat seizing.

'There's no point lying to me, Livio – it was clear the broken nose wasn't a result of your first time in the city. We might as well use this to our advantage. Now, do you have someone you can turn to – a place you can stay?'

I think immediately of Elisao … But I couldn't – not after how we left it. Old Jacobo, though, perhaps. I nod once, sharply.

'Everyone beyond my closest household circle will be told you are leaving with me. We set sail at dusk – the worst of the storm will have passed by then. In any case, the light will be low. I shall dress one of my servants as you, and this double shall accompany me on the ship. But in reality, you will remain in the city. I have something I need you to do.'

'What is it?' She's starting to scare me with her serious eyes and thin, sharp voice. Thunder rumbles outside, a counterpoint to the whistling wind and the waves' restless turning.

When she speaks again, her voice is tremulous. 'Livio, I need you to burn the mask room. Will you do that for me?'

I stare at her. The nightmare – the *vision* – I had last night plays through my mind. In the second strike of lightning, the masks were destroyed. But Grandmother's request makes no sense: with the mascherari sisters dead, the masks are useless anyway. 'But the masks have lost their power. What's the point?'

She shakes her head. 'It's a long story. When all of this is over, I will tell you everything. But for now, I need you to promise me, Livio. Will you do it?'

I swallow, nod. 'Of course.'

'At dusk, then, when the city is distracted by my departure.' She stands up and – my manners ingrained – I stand too. 'By whatever means necessary, destroy the mask room, and afterwards, hide until my return,' she says, holding her cane white-knuckled. 'And this must remain secret. You tell precisely no one. Do you understand?'

'Yes,' I say.

'Then this is goodbye. I have much to prepare. Things will be … unstable in my absence. You mustn't try to fight Shadow, Livio. Remember, if I return, I will have all the power of the King at my back. And if I do not return …' She sighs. 'Well, a Santini will remain in Scarossa. Perhaps you can find a way to win back our city, in time.' Her posture is stiff and upright, her gaze challenging.

I nod. 'Come back soon, Grandmother. I promise I'll be waiting.'

SIXTEEN
Nurse's Story

Beatrice

I daren't return to my room, where the assassin lies – instead, I brace myself and enter Ofelia's. Her green dress is crumpled on the floor, and I need a disguise. Although everything in me screams that this is wrong, wrong, wrong, I lift off my white nightgown and pull it on, fastening the buttons with trembling fingers, throat choking with tears, my back to the bed. To Ofelia. The puppets sway before me in the darkness, regarding me with their gleaming painted eyes, but I'd rather that than to watch my lifeless sister.

I pull on her sensible black shoes, leaving the dancing slippers for practical reasons, and her ordinary black cloak because I'm too scared of being recognised. My hands are shaking. I feel like I'm dreaming. Maybe I'll wake up soon. Maybe everything will be as it was before.

You didn't want that life, a small, hard voice says in my mind. *And now you've lost it. Aren't you happy?*

The faintest, greyest light is starting to creep through the curtains as I hurry downstairs. Out of the corner of my eye, I spy a form laid out on the threshold of the kitchen – Anna-Maria – and stifle a sob. I have barely enough of my wits about me to grab the empty basket lying on the door-step. Once I am out in the city, heading for the market, I need to look natural. I need to look like I have a purpose.

The light of dawn is a bright, thunderous red. Corpses of guards litter the narrow path down towards the mask room, a path which I choose because I'm less likely to run into any staff from the palazzo. One woman's body clutches a red Ornamental mask with a crack down its centre. One of the Contessa's elite True Masked fighters – by all accounts, masked guards are not easily defeated. I gulp and continue, the sea struggling and roaring like a chained beast on the rocks.

In the palazzo square, I encounter my first living people – servants on early duties, eager scholars waiting for the library to open, even housewives on their way to the market for the best of the produce – like me, I think. Just a house-wife, or a merchant's daughter, on her way to the market. Everything feels oddly normal – everyone going through the motions of an ordinary day. Except, I'm out at dawn, dressed in my dead sister's party gown, and my throat is throbbing with a suppressed scream. I clutch my basket, white-knuckled.

I barely notice the graffiti until it's right in front of me, painted in stark black on the wall of the library as I'm passing by. I stop, nearly tripping over my own feet in shock. A swirling Santini sun – but without its consort of nine stars. *Just like the tattoo behind the assassin's ear.* Someone has painted it over and over again, as high as a person can reach, all around the square. I look up. Painted prominently across one of the shops that sells snacks to the tourists are four words:

THE REVOLUTION IS HERE

The matching symbols suggest the graffiti was painted by whoever killed my sisters. I breathe deeply, blink slowly, the world spinning, the strange energy rising up … I wrestle it down. I hate whoever did this so much, I have to stop myself from attacking the stark, bloody words with my basket as if I could beat them off the wall. I clutch the handle tighter and walk on.

By the time I reach the docks, the storm has hit. The clouds are roiling and black, though thunder sounds some way off. I recall Nurse's directions: *I'll be living on the top floor of the old grain store at the bottom of Silver Street, round the corner from the fish market.* Even so, it takes me a while to find the right building, all the while the early vendors are yelling prices at the girl with the empty basket, and my mind replays, over and over, memories of my sisters – first in the nursery, the argument, the last words I spoke to them, in anger and bitterness. *Just go.* Then images of their cold bodies. Ofelia's dreadfully peaceful – Valentina's ravaged.

I duck into the shadow of the doorway and climb the

stairs. The stairwell is quiet and damp, and my steps feel heavy under the velvet skirts.

I knock on the door at the top and wait – and suddenly, Nurse is there on the threshold, smelling of almonds and sunshine. Surprise pales her face, her expression stiffening as she stares at me for two long breaths. Then, her eyes soften.

'Beatrice, my bambina. You'd better come in.'

The apartment spans the top floor of the warehouse – it is comfortable but sparsely furnished. A fire burns in a small hearth, which serves, I can see, for both warmth and cooking. A kettle is already bubbling above the flame, and Nurse lifts it out, sets it on an iron stand.

'Sit down, dear.'

'They're dead,' I blurt, unable to hold it in. 'Valentina and Ofelia are dead!' She stands up and folds me in her arms, and I feel like I'm about to cry – but somehow, the tears won't fall. Instead, a horrible knot of tension twists inside me until I shudder silently in her arms.

'Oh … sweetheart …' She pulls away, tears in her eyes. 'Sit down, now, and then we will talk. You'll be needing this breakfast before you hear what I have to tell you.'

She refuses to say another word until I've sat at the wooden table and eaten two pieces of dark bread, a small bowl of figs, and drunk half a pot of sugary tea. I'm hungry, my stomach groaning emptily, but somehow the food tastes of nothing, and a grainy, dusty texture coats my mouth. It's a chore to finish the meal.

241

'Now then,' she says, pushing my plate to one side. 'You must be wondering what on earth is going on.'

I nod. Thunder rumbles outside, the clouds roll across the big windows. I can hear the sea churning along with the food in my stomach.

She reaches for my hand. 'You have figured out, by now, that you are not who you think you are. If you were, you would have died along with Valentina and Ofelia.'

'One soul split three ways. One cannot live without the others,' I whisper. 'But what can you mean?' I catch sight of my face in the darkened window – my sisters' faces look back. 'We're identical triplets. How can I be different?' I think of what crossed my mind earlier. 'Were they twins, and I, somehow, a third sister born from the same womb? Is that possible?'

'It's not that, my love.' Nurse breathes deep. 'The truth is, bambina, the middle child of those triplets did not survive. When the Priestess of Imris left, and the two younger mascherari sisters, all three of the babies were living. But minutes later, the middle child ...' She averts her eyes, and I realise she is weeping. She dabs her eyes. 'It was so mysterious ... and it happened so fast. The Contessa, Katherina and I, we could not save the baby.'

I hang on her words, my heart fluttering with the suspense.

'The Contessa turned to us. It was morning, by then, the room was filled with light – but her eyes ... they were

242

the darkest thing I had ever seen. She said she could not let this happen. She told Katherina to take the dead infant and create … and create a True Mask of the babe's face. She told me to remain in the nursery with the other two babies. She would handle the rest.'

I can't speak, struck dumb with what I am hearing.

'We protested, of course. Katherina especially. To create a True Mask based on a real face is a crime, as you know, explicitly forbidden by the masked god. But the Contessa was determined. She said it was worse to let the chain of inheritance be broken. One deception, she said, and then next time it would all return to normal – no one would know. Not the temple, nor the god, nor even the imposter herself.'

I can barely breathe. My world is crumbling as I sit there, wordless. Nurse squeezes my hand and continues her tale.

'And so, off Katherina went in the sunlight, carrying the dead child in her basket. And when she returned, at dusk, the Contessa brought another child into the nursery. That child was you, Beatrice – only a few days old. We laid the mask over your face, and ever since …' She rubs a curl between her fingers.

'I'm wearing a mask? That's impossible. I can't be.' My voice is tight with panic.

Nurse's face is sad and serious.

Lightning streaks across the sky as my heart breaks, and I lift a hand to my face. *No*, I think. *Not* my *face*. 'Then … who am I?' I manage, my voice broken and hoarse.

'That, my dear, I do not know. The Contessa swore us to secrecy on what we had seen, of course, and she told us nothing that we did not need to know. But I always knew her great deception could not go undiscovered. You cannot trick the gods.' She shakes her head. 'I thought the truth would be revealed on the night of the Inheritance. I was convinced the masked god would not grant you the mascherari powers, along with your sisters. But he did. The Contessa's plan worked ... for a short while.'

I rest trembling fingertips on my cheeks. Horror creeps over me as I let the truth sink in: I am touching not my own flesh and blood but materials that lay upon the face of the dead triplet, the triplet whose life I stole ... I snatch my hands away as if they've been burned. My head is reeling, and I don't know why but I stand up suddenly, the chair thumping back on the wooden floor.

'Beatrice ... please. Look at me.' Nurse stands too, holds out her hands and rests them around my face, forcing me gently to meet her eyes. 'You, Valentina and Ofelia are like daughters to me. I love you and I want you to be safe. Now is your chance to start again. If you take off that mask, you can board a ship to wherever you please. I will pay your fare. Nobody will know who you are.'

'Nobody will know who I am,' I echo faintly.

SEVENTEEN
What the Heart Desires

Livio

I leave Grandmother, my mind heavy and disoriented, and glance up the stairs towards my room, where Hal is likely still waiting for me. No time to apologise. No time to explain.

I walk straight out of the palazzo.

My heart is thundering along with the sky, the warm rain lashes down around me – and although I glance over my shoulders several times, no one is looking at the young man in plain dark clothes, heading for the city.

I'm soaked through by the time I've crossed the square, my ears ringing. Down in the jewellery quarter, the wind buffets through the narrow streets like a trapped bull.

The quarter is different by day – tired, small and run-down, none of the air of mystery and excitement it holds in the dark. The boarded-up shops and empty windows are sad, not threatening. A few pedestrians walk hurriedly through the streets, clutching hoods and soggy baskets as the wind whips their cloaks. A woman leans out of an upstairs window to grab a blown-out shutter and pull it into place. The cobblestones shine as I slip down to Cutpurse Lane.

I'm so hunched over against the storm, I don't notice anything amiss until something hard crunches under my boots, and I look down to see shards of scattered glass. I glance up, a few steps from Old Jacobo's den. The pawnshop's window is smashed, its door hanging off its hinges.

I watch and wait for a few seconds. Everything is silent and still – whatever happened here, it's over now. The rain patters on the rooftops in an endless random drumbeat. I peer through the broken window. The clutter of pawned items, normally arranged neatly on shelves in the window or behind the counter, lies strewn across the floor. Beyond, the shop is dark.

When I step inside, papers swish under my feet – old receipts and ledgers. I pick my way to the counter. A smell assaults me – wet and iron through the rain dripping down my nose – and now I'm afraid, truly afraid, of what I'll find in the back room.

I push open the door. The armchairs where Jack and I sat days ago are ripped up as if they've been attacked by wild beasts – the stuffing spilling out in clouds of yellowish wool. The table is cracked down the middle. The mirror is shattered.

On the far wall, a huge sun glowers down at me, daubed not in its usual black but in dry, crusted red.

Blood.

My stomach twists in anxiety as I wonder whether, somehow, it was speaking to me that put Old Jacobo in danger. I hope he's all right – pray to the nine he got out before any of this happened. As I stand staring at the wall, I'm sure I hear a noise somewhere near – upstairs or in an adjacent room. Voices. Footsteps.

If he's alive, Old Jacobo can't help me now.

I've got to get out of here.

I walk fast through the storm and, thank the nine, I don't think I've been followed. Even so, I'm stuck. I can't go home. There's only one person left who can help me – and he, rightly, hates my guts.

But I've no choice – I'll have to take my chances. My feet are already carrying me there, as if they knew the truth before I cared to admit it.

I've visited Elisao a couple of times in his apartment in the student quarter. The houses here are tall and crooked and extremely old. Elisao's family is of middling wealth, and he has a room to himself, high up on the fourth floor. As I stand outside his building, a tile slides from the roof with the force of the wind and smashes on the paving stones at my feet.

I squelch up the four steps to the front door and study the cord for the bell to his apartment. The last time we spoke … *Holy twins*. I feel a sting of shame at everything I failed to tell him, at the promises I made and broke within a day. I wonder if seeing me will cause him pain – or if he simply won't care. I wonder if he'll punch me in the face. I'd deserve it, if he did. Gods, I can't do this. I turn away – but as I do, the door opens and Elisao is standing on the threshold, spectacles slipping down his nose, brown eyes widening. He's dressed in a long brown rain cloak, hood pulled up, a leather satchel slung over one shoulder.

I open my mouth, but nothing comes out. Heat rushes to my cheeks. Then, we both speak at once:

'I'm sorry, I—'

'I was on my way—'

We stop. Can't help smiling at each other, just slightly – and for a second, it's like old times. Then Elisao's face grows serious.

'What are you doing here?'

'I want to talk to you,' I say.

'I can see that.' His voice is harsh, icy. 'Doesn't answer my question.'

'Please?'

Something in my face convinces him to step aside. I swallow as we enter the cold but blessedly dry hallway, the door swinging shut behind us. He doesn't invite me upstairs, though. Silence rings in my ears.

'What's this about?' Elisao says gently but firmly.

I force words from my throat, but they're strange and stilted, my eyes fixed on the puddle spreading around me on the flagstones. 'I'm sorry – I shouldn't – I was about to ...' I run a hand through my soaking wet hair, feeling water dribble down my spine, and take a deep breath. 'Everything's gone to shit, Elisao. I know this is a bit rich after how we left things, but ...' I glance up at him. 'I really need your help.'

Four floors up, in his small, high-ceilinged room, Elisao lights the fire he'd already built in the grate. The warm cheerful glow disguises the cracks in the ceiling, the scuffed paint on the rattling window frames. An iron bedstead is pressed up against the far wall, a desk scattered with books and papers beside it. In front of the fire, a low threadbare couch beckons invitingly. I stand just inside the door, dripping.

'Look, I think we're going to have to get you out of those clothes before you catch a chill,' Elisao says, his voice brisk and matter-of-fact. His spectacles have steamed up, so he sets them on the desk, blinking – his light green eyes are brighter without the lenses. He hangs his cloak on the back of the door, drops his satchel on the bed. 'We can hang them in front of the fire. You can borrow something of mine to wear in the meantime. And ... I'll make us some tea.'

'Thanks,' I say. As he bustles around the room fetching tea supplies, I peel off my clothes until I'm in my shorts. Without looking at me, Elisao brings me a threadbare towel and a big old darned nightshirt. Once I'm dry, I slip it over my head, grateful for the worn, soft material.

At last, we sit down on the couch, side by side – and still, the words won't come.

'You're so quiet,' he says. 'You're really starting to worry me.'

I swallow. Where to start? Facts. Start with the facts. 'I went to find Old Jacobo. But the shop is trashed. There's one of those suns painted on the wall – in blood. I … didn't know where else to go.'

Elisao blinks, pales. 'Gods, things are worse than I thought. What do you think it was – some kind of gang feud?'

'Not exactly. It's bigger than that.' I take a deep breath and start to explain everything that's happened. *Everything*. Anything less would feel wrong. I tell him all about Shadow, the two branches of astromancy, the visions and the sand-wolves, the assassination attempts, the masked temple, how the mascherari sisters were killed last night. I take a deep breath. 'Grandmother is going to seek help from the King – but she wants me to hide here in the city. I guess she's afraid that if we're together, and the assassins find us, the Santini line will be wiped out entirely. So that's why I went to find Old Jacobo, to ask him to hide me. And that's how I ended up here.'

Elisao stares at me. I think he's processing everything I've said, but then he comes out with: 'So I'm your *second choice*?'

I can't help laughing at that, and though he doesn't join in, he smiles sheepishly.

'Elisao, I didn't even think you were a choice, after how I left things. It was sheer desperation that drove me here. I thought you'd hate me. I was about to run away when you appeared on the doorstep right at that moment.'

'I couldn't hate you. Now that I know everything that's been going on, I can almost understand why you left it the way you did.' He half smiles, then adds briskly, 'So, what is it exactly you need? A place to lie low?'

'Yes. Some place to stay. And I have a task to carry out this evening, at dusk. Something tells me my clothes won't be dry by then, so I'll need something to wear.'

'A task?'

'Don't ask me why, but Grandmother wants me to burn the mask room.'

Elisao frowns. 'But if the mascherari sisters are dead, the masks are powerless.'

I shrug. 'It's what she wanted. She was very insistent.'

'I'll help you,' he says. 'You'll need a look-out.'

'No, Elisao ... You're already doing enough for me letting me stay here. It could be dangerous.'

He grins. 'Sounds exciting. Seriously, I insist.'

And slowly, I smile in return, feeling a surprising relief flood through my body. It's at this moment the kettle boils over, steam hissing on the hearthstone. He leaps to his feet. Now it's he who's nervous and quiet as he pours the water into the pot, heats the cups. I feel … unburdened. Calm. As I watch him, that knowledge fills me again – nothing I can voice, nothing I can even arrange into words. Except …

'Eli, stop,' I say.

He sets the tea things down and turns towards me, his eyes full of doubt. I remember what he said in the palazzo square the night I thought I was leaving him for good. It's high time I replied.

'I love you too,' I say.

There's a moment of stillness. He steps closer, his eyes bright – and without hesitation I lean forward and kiss him. A sense of *home* fills me – of peace, of love. And longing, too. I pull him closer. A teacup rattles on to the floor, rolling across the floorboards as we sink into each other on the couch.

When we pull apart, I gaze into his eyes, and I know this is real in the way a kiss with someone else could never be.

He says, breathless, 'You really love me too?'

I nod, smiling. 'I wanted to say so before … But I knew I was lying to you – about who I really was … except …' I smile as I realise something. 'Vico always was the real me. It's Livio who was the lie. That's how it felt, anyway. Like I was never the self I wanted to be, except in this life. With you.'

'But you'll always have to choose, won't you? One or the other?'

I shake my head, a smile spreading across my face as I realise the one shining silver lining in this whole big mess.

252

'The masks are gone, the bargain with Mythris is broken, the masked temple's knives are out, Grandmother is pleading with the King, and the whole foundation of Scarossa is threatened by a crime lord. Elisao, all bets are off – the world has turned upside down. Maybe I can be whatever I want to be – as long as I survive.'

And as we kiss again, I really think it's true.

EIGHTEEN
Decisions

Beatrice

Nurse draws me a bath in the copper tub set in front of the fire. She leaves me to soak while she sets out for the port: she's determined to buy me a berth on a ship to the continent.

'I've a sister in Port Regal, little Bea. She'll look after you.'

I'm leaving this place forever. And isn't that what I've always dreamed of? A new face. A new future. The chains of destiny broken at my feet. A ship sailing on an open sea, into a new world – a world of possibility.

But my sisters …

Grief fills me – cold, dark and heavy. I sink down into the hot water until I'm fully submerged, breath held, eyes shut, feeling sobs rise in my chest as the images replay over and over in my mind. If I had only woken sooner, before he … Before …

My lungs start to burn. I surface, heat streaming from my scalp as I let out my breath and rub my face.

Not my *face: the* dead sister's *face*.

My hands freeze, repulsed.

Take off the mask. Nobody will know who you are, Nurse had said.

'Including me,' I whisper into the steam. *I won't know who I am, either. And if I leave Scarossa, I'll never find out.*

The Contessa alone knows the truth. The Contessa, who started everything because she couldn't bear to lose her power. The Contessa, who stole the life I should have led and trapped me in another fate. The Contessa, who granted me my two beloved sisters and then failed to protect them from her enemies. Despite the heat of the water, my muscles are tensing up.

Who gave the Contessa the right to play god like she did? To treat my life like it were just another move in her game of power and politics? I remember how she looked at me during the Inheritance – the expression of cold concern, as if I were a chess piece she was considering toppling. She didn't know what effect the ceremony would have, and – as long as the transfer of power worked – she didn't even care.

Anger rises in my heart, burning hot, scorching away a little of my grief. I cling to the feeling as I raise my fingers to the mask.

I feel for an edge, for a hold, and after a lot of probing I think – *I think* – I find one. I pull. Pain scorches through me like a hot summer sandstorm. Am I pulling off the mask, or my face? I try again – but it's not happening. I sag against the copper tub, weak and exhausted. *Not today. Not now.*

What did the Contessa steal from me, the day she lifted me from one life and placed me in another? What if my parents are out there? A whole family, even? What if there's another destiny waiting for me – the destiny I should have had?

And shouldn't I find out before I run away forever?

When Nurse returns, I'm sitting at the table, dressed in the clothes she left out for me. Trews, shirt and jacket. Boy's clothes – for safety while travelling, she'd said. She stops in the doorway, pushes back her hood, drenched with rain, her eyes suddenly sad as she examines me.

'Once your hair is up under that cap, you'll do,' she says softly. She wipes her eyes. 'Sorry, dear. The last person to wear those clothes was my son. He died of the fever that took my husband too – over seventeen years ago, now.'

My hair is damp around my shoulders. I shake my head, forcing the words 'I'm sorry' through my lips – although my own grief is too raw for me to feel hers too.

'Right,' she says briskly, now bustling into the room and shutting the door. 'I'm glad you're already dressed. I've arranged a berth on a good ship, but it leaves in two hours. We've got lots to—'

'I'm not going,' I interrupt quietly. 'Not yet, anyway.'

Nurse's face falls. She walks over, sits beside me at the

table. 'Why, sweetheart? I know it's frightening to leave everything you've known but … Don't you see how much danger you're in if you stay?'

'I'm not frightened. I have to speak to the Contessa – I need to know who I am, Nurse.' I stand and walk over to the window to watch a torrent of furious rain lash the market-place, the sea beyond. I press my hand against the glass. 'I can't start a new life without knowing what I'm leaving behind. And I need to ask her why she did what she did. If I don't get answers now, I never will.'

'Bambina, this is … You can't …' Nurse's hands are trembling as she fiddles with the material of her skirts. 'The Contessa is weakened, but she is surrounded by a huge household of guards. You won't be able to get close to her. Besides, word is she's leaving at dusk tonight – to seek help from the King.'

'I have to try.' I pace to one end of the table and back again, mind racing. The upheaval of the Contessa leaving might work to my advantage. 'If I can somehow disguise myself as a guard, it shouldn't be too difficult to get to her … The fact that she's leaving could actually help. The palazzo is probably in disarray …' I stop as an idea occurs to me. 'The Ornamentals and the Bestials will be destroyed, now that my sisters are gone. But the Grotesques should still be functional, as I'm still alive. I'm going to guess that the Contessa has surrounded herself with Grotesque-wearing True Masked guards. If I can sneak into the mask room, get one for myself ... of course, it won't be matched to me – it won't *move*. But I can tie it in place. Perhaps, in low light, I can blend in for long enough to get close to her.'

Nurse stands up and when she speaks, her voice is firmer than I've ever heard it. 'Beatrice, this is foolish. If you go ahead with this plan, you'll put yourself in terrible danger. You should leave while you can. You may not get another chance!'

'I've made up my mind.' I lift my chin, sounding braver than I feel. 'Are you going to help me or not?'

After a pause, she says, very quietly, 'I suppose the one thing you've not been allowed to do, my dear, is choose. So I must let you have that at least.' She glances out of the window, which is rattling in the wind. Sea spray is whirling over the market – its reluctant vendors battling through rain to pack up their wares – and thunder roars. 'Do the masked guards wear the same uniform as the ordinary guards?' she asks at last.

'Yes, they do. Why?'

'My husband was a guard. It was how the Contessa knew of me – why she hired me to look after you. His uniform is still in his chest. It'll be big for you, but perhaps ...'

My heart leaps. 'If I have a uniform *and* a mask ...'

She smiles sadly. 'Then perhaps you'll have a chance.'

I straighten my trews, shirt and jacket as I step out into the street, my hair tucked under a cap. The storm is spent, now, the sun glancing out from her watery veil. Everything feels calm – but not me, not inside. My heart is like the thrashing, restless sea. Thoughts, memories and imaginings churn in my mind. But I have a purpose – I have direction – and so I push everything aside, hitch the battered leather backpack over my shoulder and start walking.

Hands in my pockets, I pick my way through the streets towards the palazzo square. I hesitate as I reach it, my heart pounding at the changes wrought by the past night. The remains of the puppet theatre have been partially cleared, but some larger items destroyed by the blaze – the blackened posts and a number of angular, ruined seats – remain cordoned off from the public, stark against the watery sky. I shiver, imagining a ghostly audience sitting there, waiting for a show to begin in which we, the living, are the puppets. The storm has left the scorched wood sodden and stinking, and those who hurry past, heads down, press handkerchiefs to their noses. The library steps are emptier than usual – the few students clustering into small groups, voices lowered – and no one is attempting to clean up the black graffiti all over the walls.

The whole place, the heart of this city, has a disconcerting air of abandonment. Where are the Contessa's men? I shudder, then pick my way towards the mask room. Here, outside, I hesitate in the shadows for a few minutes, wondering if anyone is watching this place – but it doesn't seem like it. And so I slide my old key into the lock, open the door, and walk down the staircase.

This time it's different as I descend the steps into the soupy, cold darkness. This time, for the first time, I'm alone – and I feel my sisters' absence like a physical pain, acutely aware of the missing footsteps in front of me and behind.

But they weren't my sisters anyway – and somehow, that makes it even worse. As if they've been taken away from me twice over: by death and by the truth.

When I open the mask-room door, thin light filters through from the windows at street level far above – it's barely enough to see by, but it's enough that I can tell there's something wrong. That the neat, orderly rows of masks have been disturbed. I know my sisters' deaths will have stolen the Bestial and Ornamental masks' powers, but I don't know how that will manifest itself. My hands are trembling as I light the oil lamp by the door and hold it aloft – the scene leaps out at me as its golden glow bursts forth.

The floor is littered with masks. I step forward, carefully nudging aside a smashed Ornamental, its face caved in as if crushed by a heel, glittering cheeks catching and reflecting the light of my lamp. Further along, a Bestial snarls up at me with sharp canines, a crack running down its forehead. I lift the lamp higher. On the walls, the Grotesques alone remain, grinning and leering and grimacing from their hooks.

That's what I'm here for, I remind myself. No need to linger – just get a mask, change into the uniform in my bag, and hurry to the palazzo before dusk, when the Contessa leaves. Demand my answers. I don't have long – the shadows were already lengthening when I descended the mask-room steps.

But as I'm picking my way through the debris towards the wall, I hear the sound I've dreaded the most: footsteps on the stairs. Someone has followed me. I flick off the lamp-light and feel my way across the mask-strewn floor towards the antechamber. Softly, I shut the door and press my eye to the keyhole. I feel a shiver of sorrow as I remember the last time I spied on the mask room in this way, my two sisters bickering at my side.

The shadows shift as light spills through from the stair-well. Then, two young men enter the room. The first is tall, broad and dark-haired – handsome with a sharp stubbled jaw. He holds a lamp high over his head as he enters, examining the scene with an expression I can't quite fathom. The second man is slender, shorter, paler, and he wears a gleaming pair of spectacles.

'Gods … it's just like my vision,' says the first man, running a hand anxiously through his hair. Then he freezes. 'Except …' He walks over to the wall, where the Grotesques hang intact. 'Gods …' he breathes again. 'Now I know what Grandmother was holding back when she told me to destroy them …'

Destroy them? My eyes widen.

'What is it, Livio?' the second man asks, hesitating by the

door. He glances up the steps, as if he, too, is afraid of pursuit.

Livio. The heir to the Contessa?

Suddenly the pieces fall into place. The silhouette I once glimpsed in the carriage. Livio Santini, Valentina had said. A young man with instructions from his grandmother – the Contessa – to destroy the mask room.

To cover up the evidence of her crime.

My anger burns brighter, answering sparks lifting from my fingers. *No.* I press my hands into my sides, gritting my teeth as I push the energy down, down into the pit of my stomach until nausea sings through my skull. I need to stay hidden – for now. I press my eye to the gap and watch.

'The Grotesques … they're intact. Elisao … one of the mask-makers must be alive,' Livio says.

'But … how can that be?' Elisao says, his voice taut. 'I thought they always died at the same time? Look, if we're going to do this, we should hurry. I swear someone was following us round the palazzo square.'

'Right,' Livio says. 'Let's get some more light in here. We need to set this fire and get out.'

Fire? They're going to burn *the masks?* I take a shuddering breath, my eyes running over the wood-panelled walls, the desks, the boxes of flammable material. This place will go up like a bonfire. What am I going to do now? If I don't think fast I'll be trapped in here.

Livio holds out his hand, frowns as a flickering mage-light appears on his palm. He breathes deep, as if the spell is costing him considerable effort – but slowly the mage-light brightens and lifts up into the air.

The floating pale purple light illuminates the scene brighter than lamplight – but in its cold glow, everything is ghostly and colourless. Elisao isn't watching the staircase any more – he's watching Lord Livio, a tender smile playing at his lips. And that's perhaps why I see the dark shadow before he does – a few steps up, through the half-open door. The shadow holds out its hand and—

I have to stop myself from crying out, clasping my palm against my mouth. Instinctively, I jump away from the keyhole, stagger against the bench at my back as a purplish-red flash illuminates the room, light shooting through the gaps in the door.

The colour of that mage's magic is seared into my memory forever. All at once, I feel as if I'm back in the nursery, the night after the Inheritance, hearing soft footsteps in the dark.

The assassin is here.

NINETEEN
Deception

Livio

I spin around when I hear the thud – every muscle in my body wound up tight.

Elisao is lying on the floor. I rush towards him, kneel at his side. His chest is rising and falling – he's alive – but I can see lightning-like scars creeping up his neck … the scars of a magical attack. But from who? My stomach lurches as I glance up at the open doorway.

A dark shape is descending the last few steps as I watch. My heart hammers. I rise to my feet, my muscles tensing.

'Shadow?' I breathe.

The figure laughs – a male voice to match the tall physique, taller than mine. His face is hidden, I realise – like the assassin on the rooftop, a plain black mask covers his features. But I recognise his tightly curled black hair, his tall, broad build … *No. It can't be.*

The figure reaches up and removes his mask. Beneath it, he is dark-skinned and handsome – a strong, determined jaw, high cheekbones, beautifully curved brows. And when he smiles, a gem flashes on one of his canines.

'Hal?' I choke out the word.

'Lord Livio. There you are,' he says, his voice softly accented.

Hal. My heart is racing as – at last – I realise how I have been deceived. A new recruit, a stranger, assigned as my personal bodyguard – unusually friendly, even seductive. *Somebody told him to get close to me.* I feel my cheeks colour. Now Elisao is caught up in my trap, out cold on the mask-room floor.

'Gods,' I say, my voice as calm as I can manage, though I'm shaking with anger. 'You were working for Shadow all along.'

'There are no gods here, Lord. Not any more. Only Fortune.' He smiles – dazzlingly, cruelly. 'Now, are you going to come quietly?'

I'm not done. I step forward, closer to him – to the door. 'You tricked my grandmother into hiring you,' I say.

He shrugs. 'I *am* one of the most skilled mages from Mythris's temple in Port Regal – I never lied about that.'

'She trusted you.' My mind is racing. 'You did everything you could to get close to me, to gain my trust. The assassin on the rooftop that night ... was it some kind of set-up?'

''Course. *I* was supposed to save your life from the assassin. If the damned sandwolf hadn't interfered, I would have.'

'And what about that kiss? What was your plan, Hal?' I'm

265

shouting now. 'To make me trust you, then persuade me to … what? What is Shadow's game?'

Hal glances at Elisao, lying on the floor among the broken, smashed detritus of a thousand years of tradition. His lip curls. 'Not for me to say, Lord. Besides, you'll soon find out.' He steps closer to me – so close that I can feel his breath teasing my hair as he says, 'Are you ready to embrace your fate?'

'Why don't you just kill me here?' I ask, tilting my chin.

Hal laughs. 'You think Shadow would go to all this trouble just to kill you?' His eyes gleam in the mage-light. 'No, we could have done that in an instant. That's not your fate, Lord. Come with me, you'll see.'

I step back. 'I won't.'

Hal's expression shifts, growing mean and determined. 'Oh, you'll come, Lord, willing or not,' he says, opening his palm as he summons a sparking ball of purplish-red magic. 'We both know you can't beat me.'

I clench my fists, drop down. My body is readying itself for a fight – but not a magical one.

I can't help it. Old habits die hard.

Hal notices it too, his eyebrows rising. 'When will you learn?' he says. 'You can't beat me with your fists.'

'I can try.' I swing a punch, fast and true – colliding with Hal's jaw. I feel a jolt of pure euphoria. Everything slows down. I watch Hal raise a hand to his face, scowl at me. The mage-light floating overhead casts weird shadows as Hal summons a spell, throws his attack.

I leap aside, faster, roll on the floor – masks crushing under my body. The force of the spell pushes me, skidding, against the wall. My head bangs against smooth stone – pain exploding through my skull. I'm vaguely aware of a spell bursting through a wooden door opposite the entrance, shattering it entirely, and then—

And then the room falls strangely silent and still. I blink, my ears ringing, feeling hot wetness on the back of my head, my knuckles throbbing where they connected with Hal's jaw. Hal stands across the room, hand pressed to his face, but his head is turned away … He's watching …

Someone *else*. A figure is staggering out of the small antechamber once hidden by the broken door, coughing, falling to their knees. Someone dressed in boys' clothes – but when their cap falls off, long straight hair unravels about their face. A girl. Around my age.

She glances up, fear written in her dark eyes as they lock on Hal's with unmistakeable recognition. I try to push myself up to a seated position, but the room spins, and I fall back against the wall. I hear a groan. Elisao is nearby, a few paces away, stirring. If I can reach him, somehow – if I can help him out of the door, up the stairs, while Hal's back is turned …

But when I try to stand, the ground pitches like the deck of a ship, and the room turns black around the edges.

As the dust settles, I watch as the girl's expression shifts from fear to pure rage. 'You tried to kill my sisters,' she screams at Hal. She holds out her hand in front of her, palm facing Hal. 'Now I'm going to kill *you*.'

Magic bursts from her palm – a strong, true attack, glittering green. But Hal is ready. His shield deflects the spell, which skitters harmlessly into a pile of masks. Then, he holds out his hand. Purple-red magic glitters around her throat – she gasps, clutching her neck. He's strangling her. I try to push myself up, but I slump forward, dizzy.

'The last mascherari,' Hal says. He peers at her curiously. 'One of a kind, aren't you, now that your sisters are dead?'

I gasp silently at the revelation, watching as the girl's face turns red, and real pain flashes in her eyes.

Hal pulls his Bestial True Mask from his jacket, tosses it on the floor with the others, all the while holding his choking spell steady. The mask-maker's lips are losing colour. 'These ones might be useless … but as long as you're alive, the Grotesques work just fine. Maybe … maybe you could make more. Would you like that?'

The girl falls to her knees, swaying.

'Yes,' says Hal softly. 'I expect Shadow would like to see you too.' He lowers his hand, the spell breaks, and the mascherari lets out an ugly gasp.

'I'm going nowhere,' she rasps, pushing herself to her feet. She holds out her palm as if to attack again.

'Oh?' Hal raises his hand, twists his fingers. I watch as the girl's wrists are pinned magically together behind her back, as if fastened with invisible ties. She tries to run but stumbles – falling hard on her knees without her arms to break her fall.

'Let me go!' the girl shouts hoarsely.

'Scream all you like, little mask-maker – there's no one to hear you down here but people like me.'

Hal turns to me. I try to stand, and this time I manage to stagger to my feet, leaning heavily against the wall, breathing hard. I hold out my hand, try to summon my magic – any kind of magic will do. But I'm woozy – slow. Hal repeats the gesture with which he bound the girl, and instead of fighting back, I find my arms pinned exactly like hers.

'Right – now you're both set, let's go.' He starts forward. But – to my confusion – he's not heading towards the stairs but towards the far wall. I feel my feet stumbling after him, against my will, as if pulled along by invisible chains.

Hal appears to be searching for a door in the panelling, pushing and feeling for gaps in the woodwork. I glance over my shoulder at Elisao, desperate to know he's all right. He lifts his head gently. Relief floods my body: he's conscious, at least. Once Hal has led the mask-maker and me to wherever we're heading, Elisao can find a way out of here into the city. He blinks. I see blood smeared on his temple, the scars of a magical attack running down his neck. At last, he focuses on my face. I wish I could tell him to be quiet. I wish I could tell him I love him – and that when I get out of this mess, coming back for him is the first thing I'll do.

'Livio?' he whispers. 'What ...?'

'Oh,' Hal says, pausing at his work. 'I almost forgot.' Casually, he turns and shoots another glittering red–purple attack at Elisao.

'No!' I scream, my voice ragged and broken. But it's too late. I watch in horror as the magic runs through the Elisao's body, tensing all of his muscles. The veins on his forehead swell – his eyes full of fear, like a horse about to bolt. And then the magic leaves him – and now he is limp and empty. His beautiful green eyes fixed on the ceiling.

Everything feels muffled, distant. I stare at Elisao, willing him to blink – to move. But he's ... he's ...

Dead, a flat, cold voice supplies in my head.

TWENTY
Beneath the City

Beatrice

The man, Lord Livio's friend, lies dead on the floor. I blink at the strange scars over his neck, echoes of Valentina's. I struggle, but my hands are bound by an invisible force, tingling and burning my skin as I wrestle to break free. My throat throbs where magic squeezed my windpipe; my head feels light and spinning, like a falling feather.

Next to me, Livio has fallen to his knees, tears streaking his face. I know how he feels. Numb. Like he's trapped in an impossible nightmare. It's how I feel, too.

Hal pushes one spot on the wall, then another. A click. 'Got it,' he says triumphantly, pulling the panel aside.

Beyond is a deep, cold blackness – I can tell by the quality of the air that there's a whole passage beyond, not simply another cupboard or antechamber. I feel my heart lurch with fear. Where does it lead? Nowhere good – I know that for sure. All the time the mascherari have worked in this room, passages winding into the earth beyond their walls. *Like when you're swimming in the ocean, feeling the cold beneath you but not knowing what lurks in the darkness.*

'Where are you taking us?' I ask in a small voice. I wish I sounded stronger – instead I sound about five years old. He doesn't answer. He slips into the darkness, leaving his magic to hold us.

As our captor's footsteps retreat. I glance across at the Contessa's grandson. His head is bowed. He wipes his eyes awkwardly on his shoulders, appears to gather himself together. And then, he glances up at me. 'You're … one of the mascherari sisters? How did you survive?'

How to explain? I have to be brief; we don't have long. 'My name is Beatrice. I always thought I was a mascherari sister … But it turns out, I'm really someone else wearing a mask. The original middle sister died.' My words feel stilted, but Livio pales, shaking his head, and I know he understands.

He speaks in a low, wondering whisper. 'So you're wearing a True Mask based on …?'

'Based on the dead infant's face,' I finish softy. 'On the Contessa's orders.' I can't help the anger that creeps into my voice as I speak her name. 'She didn't want the line of inheritance to break, so …' I shake my head.

'She tried to trick Mythris,' he says quietly. 'Of *course* she did. She would never give up her power willingly. It's her legacy. She's determined to pass it on intact.'

'You were here to burn the place down?' I say.

'Yes.' He nods, as if he's worked something out. 'She must have wanted the mask room destroyed to cover up the evidence. If the masked temple finds out, she'll lose their allegiance once and for all. And they'll have a case against her. They're already manoeuvring for more power ...' He pauses. 'And you were here because ...?'

I swallow. 'I wanted to get close to the Contessa, to ask her who ... who I am. I thought if I could get a Grotesque, I could maybe get close enough ...' The plan sounds foolish now, but Livio flashes me a sad smile.

'What were you going to do after that?' he asks gently.

I blink. 'I ... I don't know any more. I've always dreamed of sailing somewhere, seeing new things, exploring new places. But now my sisters are gone ...'

'I'm so sorry.'

I'm so taken aback by his apology that, for a second, I can't speak. When I've gathered myself, I say softly, 'What for?'

'For what my grandmother has done. She stole you away from a life you never knew. Gave you another identity, then failed to protect it – protect you.'

He understands. I feel my eyes sting with tears – but I glance away, blinking.

He goes on. 'I love my grandmother, but I'm not sure I always agree with her approach.' He smiles slightly, fondly. 'If I ever get the chance, I'll try to make amends. I promise.'

Hal's footsteps are returning already. Livio and I meet each other's eyes and, in spite of everything, I feel calmer. I nod slowly, acknowledging his apology.

'If you're going to make amends,' I whisper, 'we need to get out of this alive.'

TWENTY-ONE
In Dark Scarossa

Livio

I don't think I have ever hated anyone before – I can't have. Because I've never felt like *this*, as I stare at the back of Hal's head, his tight curls casting wisps of shadows on the tunnel wall as the reddish mage-light bobs at his side. The sensation is filling me like it's a living being, a parasite inhabiting my very soul. Stronger, even, than my grief.

We've been walking for ages, through the dark. Beatrice follows me, the scuff of her footsteps as quiet as the rats who emerge from time to time to escort us into their domain. She's so quiet, in fact, that I sometimes forget she is there, and have to glance over my shoulder to reassure myself that the presence behind me is a living, breathing human – not the ghost of someone I've left behind.

Elisao's body, forgotten in the mask room among the ruins of my family's power, flashes in my mind.

If only I'd understood my vision for what it was – a warning from the stars. I brought him with me, into danger.

It was me who killed him, as much as Hal. And that knowledge will weigh on my soul for as long as I live.

We've been traipsing for what feels like hours along tunnels I never even knew existed. Every now and then, the passage widens, and I have the sense of cold air – of deep space – wafting around us into places the mage-light doesn't reach. Once, I catch sight of an opening in the side of the tunnel – a window, I think, its ancient lintel carved into intricate swirls. The mage-light casts some of its glow inside, and I swear I see a room in there, with rotted furniture shrouded in cobwebs – but then we pass by, the shadows lengthen, and the room is plunged into its darkness again.

One realisation cements itself in my mind: Dark Scarossa is real – and the rumours Old Jacobo heard were right. *Shadow is here*.

And then I start to see lights further ahead.

'Nearly there,' Hal murmurs, and he picks up the pace. From the tremor in his voice, I think he's scared of this place – or at least it makes him uncomfortable – and that thought makes me glad. Voices murmur, the chattering increases, and I realise we're heading for a crowd.

An archway off to the right reveals a huge hall full of mage-lights in various colours hovering near the cracked ceiling. Hal leads us inside. The wide circular space contains at least seven or eight other doorways and appears to be something of a meeting place. The hum of voices fills the room, and the members of Shadow's gang surround us. A few eyes are drawn towards us briefly but drift away, as if they're quite used to seeing captors from the outside.

Hal grabs my and Beatrice's arms, tugging us through one of the doors off to the right. Another narrow passageway, propped up by wooden pillars, gradually opens out until we face a grand set of double doors guarded by four women. After a short exchange, we're inside.

We're standing at one end of a long, enormous hall, partially lit with a combination of floating mage-lights and lanterns. The far reaches of the hall are shrouded in darkness. The scale of it snatches my breath away – how can *this* be underground? I feel dizzy, and for a moment I sway dumbstruck in awe, standing on the threshold of a lost world.

Hal tugs me forward, my shoes scuffing the half-destroyed mosaic on the floor. The ceiling soars above us, mottled with huge damp patches like black constellations. In the centre of the room, a cracked fountain trickles with hot sulphuric spring water – I can see steam drifting off it in plumes. The same springs, I assume, that fill the palazzo baths. The windows, lined on one side of the enormous room, are high and arched. A clump of thin-stemmed mushrooms is growing on one of the windowsills, fleshy and pale. Some of the windows are reinforced with iron or wooden bars, holding up the crumbling stonework, but all of them open on to … yes, on to a whole *street*, lightless but for the glow spilling through from the hall … I see a broken cobblestone pavement littered with bits of fallen masonry – a crumbling arch, a statue missing its head – before Hal yanks me on again.

And suddenly we have stopped beside the fountain – Hal is shoving us down to our knees. He kneels between us.

'Lady Shadow, I bring you Livio Santini and the surviving mask-maker. There are at least a hundred surviving Grotesque masks through the east passages, too.' His voice is thick with pride, and I feel a fresh jolt of revulsion before I register his words. *Lady Shadow?* I raise my eyes. Shadow is a woman.

She stands beside the fountain, trailing the tips of her fingers in its waters. Her dark hair flows loose, lightly streaked with grey and clasped back from her face with jewelled ornaments. Her face is typical of a Scarossan – brown-skinned, brown-eyed. She's beautiful – her lips a perfect bow shape; her brows strong and serious – but there's a cruel, determined set to her jaw. She's dressed in a close-fitting black tunic and trews in the continental style, an assortment of knives, pouches and trinkets strapped to her body with leather bindings. Her boots are fine brown leather, decorated with delicate stitching. Her hands are heavy with rings, and I think of Grandmother – but whereas Grandmother wears mourning rings, this woman's fingers are laden with ostentatious jewels.

'The false mask-maker? Good work, Hal,' says Shadow in her soft, low voice. 'I've half a mind to kill her … She left one of my best assassins mortally injured.' Her hand moves to one of the knives at her belt. 'Do you know he died, girl? It was a painful death – a head wound. You left him to bleed out where he lay.'

I see Beatrice's eyes widen – her mouth opens, but nothing emerges.

'But then, maybe I won't kill her,' Shadow continues, eyes flicking back to Hal. 'She will make a fine bargaining chip. What do you suppose the temple will want to do with her?' She looks Beatrice up and down, as if she is livestock she's considering eating.

Hal replies without emotion. 'When they find out the truth, I expect the masked temple will want her dead. The forbidden mask she's wearing has powers they don't want out in the world.'

'In other words, they won't want her in someone else's hands. In *my* hands.' She slips a ring from her thumb – a great golden circle set with a huge glittering emerald – and presses it into Hal's palm. 'That's a powerful card to hold, Hal. Good work. You know how I treasure a strong hand when I gamble.' He bows his head in thanks, sliding the ring into his pocket. 'Now, take her away. I have much to discuss with Lord Livio.'

As her eyes settle on me for the first time, ice shivers down my spine.

Hal stands up and tugs Beatrice to her feet. I glance over at her. Her face is a grimace of determination. Hal can't be expecting any resistance – after all, what could the girl possibly achieve? – but suddenly, crazily, she pulls away from his grasp and starts to run straight towards Shadow, her hands outstretched.

In a split second, something flickers in the darkness at the hall's far end – two pinpricks of red light. I feel its energy – huge and restless and bound with unbreakable power to the woman standing in front of me.

I try to warn Beatrice, but I'm not fast enough – the red lights blink out, and a hurricane of a sandwolf appears on the mask-maker's chest, catapulting her backwards and pinning her to the ground.

The huge creature's hissing susurrations sound like nothing so much as a growl. It happened so fast, my heart is leaping in my chest.

The sandwolf is bigger than the other ones I've seen; its eyes red, not yellow. And rather than glittering black, its body has a bronze hue, which catches the lamplight in darts of bright gold.

And it's under Shadow's command. I frown. Isn't the control of sandwolves part of astromancy? Grandmother appeared to think we were the only two astromancers left in the world, she and I. But clearly she was wrong.

'Easy, Silas,' Shadow says, her voice as soft as it was before. The beast's spinning form lifts away from Beatrice, her face pale as she gasps for air. Shadow appears to notice my interest. 'Beautiful, isn't he?' she says in a low, confiding voice, meeting my eyes. 'Did you know, the more magic a sandwolf consumes, the more powerful they grow? Their eyes start out a pale yellow. With time, they turn darker – a beautiful amber. And eventually … red.'

I swallow, my throat suddenly feeling tight. How many mages had the beast killed?

'Hal,' Shadow says now, her voice sharper, 'pay closer attention to your prisoners. I should not have to rely on Silas for protection while you are in the room. From now on, the mask-maker is your personal responsibility.'

I can feel the humiliation rolling off Hal like heat. 'Yes, my lady. Apologies.' I never thought I would see Hal grovel like a scolded boy.

'Now go.'

Hal tugs Beatrice out of the room with unnecessary force, her feet stumbling on the mosaic floor. I'm left alone with Shadow.

Shadow – whose orders killed the mascherari, attacked Old Jacobo's base, stole the lives of countless palazzo guards. Shadow – who tore away the last of my family, my grandmother. Shadow – who tried to bring me close by tricking me into trusting Hal.

Shadow – whose orders as good as killed the man I loved.

TWENTY-TWO
The Mirror

Beatrice

I lie panting on the filthy floor, listening to his footsteps retreat. Hal has thrown me in a dark, dusty room, carrying away the leather backpack Nurse gifted me containing the old guard uniform that was to be my disguise.

If there were any hope left of me confronting the Contessa, it's gone. The sun must've sunk by now, although time is impossible to trace in the constant darkness of this place. The old woman is likely on her ship, sailing to the mainland.

Like I would've been, had I done as Nurse advised.

The paths we could have taken are so quickly lost in darkness, unreachable, leaving only the one we are walking.

I blink, sitting up, and the room shifts into focus. In the light of the oil lamp Hal left burning next to me, my eyes find old mouldering puppets hanging from hooks. Others lie decomposing, crumbling on the floor, their outfits chewed by rats and worn to rags, only their porcelain heads peering up from the detritus with a semb-lance of what they once were.

I wish bitterly for my sisters. I imagine pressing my face into Ofelia's hair, closing my eyes; Valentina sharply telling me to stop wallowing. Then I remember how they were tugging the old chest between them, how I'd felt suddenly separate, cut out. I didn't realise how true that feeling was. Tears pool in my eyes, and I sob into my shirt. Now they are together in death, and here I am, alone.

Nurse was right – my plan was foolish. I will never know who I *really* am under this identity the Contessa gave me. I might as well have fled when I could. What does it matter who I was, anyway? What mattered was the people who loved me, the dreams I could have followed. Now all have forsaken me.

When I feel strong enough, and the crying has passed, I lift my head and examine my surroundings more closely. The room is small – no larger than a closet, really. I could walk across it in three short paces, if it weren't for the debris strewn across the floor. Ancient spotted mirrors are stacked up against the walls, laden with cobwebs, alongside panels painted with various kinds of landscape, the paint chipped or blooming with mould. Stage scenery. A storage room for a puppet theatre, I suppose – and yet, I am far under-ground. Whatever theatre this once was, it has long been forgotten.

There's another face staring straight at me, ghoulish and

pale, and I start back – only to realise it's my own reflection framed in ancient, cobwebbed gilt.

The only working puppet here is me. And now Shadow holds my strings.

Shakily, I crawl to the mirror in front of me on my hands and knees. I sob again as I see my face close up, because in myself I see Valentina and Ofelia, and their dead faces return to me so fresh and full of horror that it feels like there's a knife twisting in my heart.

Unthinkingly, I gently raise my hands to the mask.

I tentatively push my fingers into the skin around my face, like I did before at Nurse's place. I still don't know what I'm feeling for – but here, alone, is a good time to find out. The tips of my fingers tingle. I feel … something odd. Like before. Is it an edge?

In my excitement I lose concentration, and the sensation slips away … but I'm determined. I try again. And again. On the fourth time, I dig my fingers in when I feel the *something*, and I start to pull. Hard. It's so painful, again, that I wonder if I've made a terrible mistake. Am I lifting my own face away, somehow, exposing only the bloody mess that lies beneath all skin? *No. Keep going.* A burning sensation pulses through me. Energy seems to swirl inside my heart, quickening as the mask pulls away.

I give one last tug, crying out as the mask comes free and drops to the floor. I lift my hand up to my cheek and touch … skin. Not blood. Skin.

Still in shock, I pick up the mask and examine it. From the back, it looks like any other mask I have made during my short time as a mascherari, or during the training of my childhood – a smooth white underside with eyeholes cut out. My hands tremble as I turn it over. Now, *this* is different from the masks I know – the realism is startling. The brownish flesh, the gentle flush of the cheeks. I'm looking at the eyeless face of my sisters.

So … what exactly is the face underneath? *My* face?

Slowly, slowly I raise my eyes to my reflection.

At first, I fix on the trembling, grazed hands holding the mask – these are not so different. My eyes comb the grubby shirt and travel up, up to the tangled mass of hair draped over my shoulders. And then I'm looking at a girl I don't recognise – or perhaps I do, vaguely. It's the type of face I've passed many times in the street, eyes averted: brown skin, perhaps a half shade darker than the skin of the mask; slightly darker eyes; and thinner, higher arches of brows.

I feel anger surging inside me as my thoughts tumble and curl in my mind like crashing waves. The Contessa stole away *this* girl's life. She gave her the face of a dead baby so that she could keep her mascherari triplets, her masks, her power. I see the face in the mirror contort with rage. There's a flash of green light, and with a huge splintering noise, the mirror cracks.

I scramble away in terror, my heart pounding. Magic has never come to me that effortlessly or powerfully before.

Could the mask have been suppressing it? I listen in the quiet, afraid the sound of the mirror breaking has alerted Hal or some other guard ... but no one comes.

The energy has drained from me, and I'm left staring at this stranger's face in a mirror criss-crossed with lines.

I'm panting with the exertion of whatever I just did, with the thoughts spinning round and round in my mind. This face is softer than the mask's – more childlike, more confused. This girl is still a girl, even though she's clearly a Rogue too, and therefore dangerous, and now her face is crumbling once again into tears.

'Who are you?' I look into the girl's dark eyes, and I feel like she has an answer, if only she could speak it. And then without warning, the lamplight extinguishes, its oil exhausted, and I am flung into darkness.

I'm on the edge of hysteria, in a room of hanging puppets, imagining how they're swaying, their eyes watching me as they watched Ofelia die in her sleep.

But something has risen in me. I'm not a puppet. I'm not ready to give up. Not yet.

Hal knows I'm a mage, yes. And he knows I was wearing a mask. But he doesn't know the mask was suppressing my magic. He doesn't know I've managed to remove it.

I crawl in the direction of the door, my hands sliding on the gritty, dusty floor until I find the pitted old wood. I feel for the handle, turn it – of course, it's locked. I expected as much. I lay my hands against it – and the iron lock beneath.

I breathe deep. Reach for the energy inside me, clearer than ever before.

Magic leaps through me, electrifying my senses. I feel a rushing sensation. My hands jerk against the iron and there's an almighty green flash, lighting the room momentarily—

I am flung backwards as if kicked by an enormous boot. I crash into the monstrous puppets, my head ricocheting against the wall. Dimly, I see a red-purple glimmer hovering over the door before it fades again to nothing.

Of course. He's protected it.

Clinging on to consciousness, holding my throbbing head, I crawl, coughing, away from the detritus, until I'm positioned in front of the door again. All right – I can't break out. What else can I do?

I can wait until he comes.

I hold the mask, feeling its oddly fleshy contours, cold and hard but somehow retaining the consistency of skin. Hal said the temple would want me dead. He said the forbidden mask would have powers the temple wouldn't want out in the world.

What kind of powers? I wonder.

TWENTY-THREE
The Starlight Throne

Livio

When Beatrice and Hal are gone, the great gilded door shuts behind them, and the ensuing silence is thick as water. I'm still kneeling on the hard mosaic, my knees sore. I look up at Shadow and am surprised to find she's searching my face.

'Follow me,' she says after a time. When I stand up, my legs are shaking – my hands too.

'What do you want with me?' I demand.

But Shadow doesn't reply. My eyes catch on one of the necklaces hanging around her neck – the longest, a gold pendant in the shape of a sun. I remember the necklace clearly from the Battaglia, when the sandwolf struck. My eyes slide over to the huge red-eyed beast, Silas. Was Shadow herself there in the crowd, watching? If so, why?

She walks to the opposite end of the hall, the end hidden in darkness – and I follow. She effortlessly conjures a small purple mage-light, which floats up and brightens simultaneously. In the light, her huge red-eyed sandwolf swirls at the foot of a raised dais, growling softly.

The light still rises. Now I can fathom why the fountain's trickling water echoes so loudly, resonating around the room like an orchestra. Above this dais, the ceiling soars up so high that I wonder exactly how deep we are standing. And on the dais stands a chair.

'Go – look at it,' says Shadow. 'Silas will not harm you.'

I don't want to, but somehow I find myself passing the swirling creature and climbing the four worn steps. Am I dreaming? It feels as if I'm walking through honey – an invisible rope pulling me inexorably forward through the ether. The chair, like the rest of the room, is clearly very old – hewn of stone, it reaches to my full height, or a little taller.

Why is it so familiar?

I round the chair slowly. Elaborate carvings cover its surface – images engraved by hands that turned to dust and bone centuries ago. On its lower reaches, on one side, are stylised curls of sandstorms. A large sandwolf's head snarls in the midst of its dust-devil body. On the other side of the chair's lower half are crashing ribbons of waves. On its back is a carving of a great castle in an ancient style, and above, around the whole chair and dominating its decorations, are a myriad of stars: some as large as the palm of my hand; others the size of fingernails and clustered into constellations.

And suddenly I know where I've seen this chair before.

'Is this … the Starlight Throne?' I ask, voice trembling, remembering the passages I read in my mother's book. My head is pounding, now – pain needling in my left temple. I lean on the throne for support, the smooth arm cold under my hand as I face her. Silas spins at her side, lazy and slow.

Shadow does not respond to my question. 'Long ago in Scarossa, we did not bend the knee to *foreign* kings or *new* gods.' She spits the words dismissively. 'We had astromancer rulers, masters of the ancient magic drawn from the very soil of these islands, nourished by Fortune's body. We were lords of our own destinies, in more ways than one – we had been chosen by Fortune.'

I draw myself tall, thinking of the graffiti – the sun, unbounded by stars. *Revolution is here.* Anger steadies me. 'Why are you telling me this? If you want your pirate kingdom, kill me and take it.'

'We are not enemies, Lord Livio, and I do not want a *pirate kingdom*,' Shadow says. She lifts her chin, meeting my eyes. 'I have brought you here to give you the greatest of gifts. This' – she gestures to the chair – 'the Starlight Throne. You are to be King of the Wishes.'

My head is spinning. I clear my throat and croak out the bizarre words. 'You want me to be … King?' She does not reply. 'You're insane!' I blurt. I find myself sitting down on the throne, dizzy, resting my head in my hands. 'Why do you need me? Can't you just crown yourself Queen?'

'When she returned to Scarossa, Fortune chose the scions of two great families to receive the two branches of her power – the two kinds of astromancy. In you, for the first time, the blessed ancient bloodlines are combined. The Santini and the Lupina. Livio, this has always been your fate.' She smiles, her eyes glittering. 'Haven't you been reading the book I left for you?'

The idea of Shadow somehow leaving me the book would, I suppose, make sense – the symbol on the cover was a direct replica of the sun graffiti around the city, the pendant hanging around her neck. But it doesn't explain everything.

Shadow climbs the dais steps, dropping to one knee at my feet. Her voice is low, now, taught with excitement. 'Do you know why Fortune died, Livio? She was a mother, forsaken by her children: the nine gods. When their father was murdered, they wrongly turned against her, stripped her of her powers. Turned her into a mortal. She died here, on Scarossa, her body infusing the soil itself with magic – her legacy to us.' She grasps my hand – I'm so shocked, I don't pull away. 'We owe it to Fortune to cast off the shackles of the new faith. We owe it to the people, too.' She squeezes my hand, her rings hard against my fingers. 'You are a man of the people, aren't you, Lord Livio? I've been watching you. You fight for them and with them. You speak to them. You help them. They want this too. You know how they feel about the Contessa. They don't want a ruler like that – a mere intermediary between them and a foreign ruler. They want a king of their own. Someone they can love.'

I shake my head slightly. 'What are you saying?'

'I don't want to force you to do this. I want you to be inspired – as I once was – to change the world. We shall have no gods. No king that is not ours. We shall be unbound by promises to false deities, or subservience to foreign interests. We will root out the rotten crime lords of this city – in fact, I have already started.' She smirks. 'The followers of Fortune will rule the Wishes once again. And we will thrive.'

I can't help the bitter words that spill from my mouth next. 'You've destroyed everything I care for, and you expect me to be *inspired*?' A shiver runs through me, and I stand up, tugging my hand away from her grasp and hurrying down the steps. I can't be here any longer, shut up like a northern duke in his coffin. I have to reach the Scarossa I know – the city under the stars. But I stumble in my haste. The floor meets my knees, and I wince at the impact, my eyes stinging with pain.

'Stop running from your destiny, Livio,' says Shadow, approaching me slowly from the throne, her boots tapping against the floor. 'There's no point. Fate is like quicksand – the more you struggle, the tighter it draws you in.'

Suddenly, determination floods me. My fists clench and I rise up, dropping into a fighting stance. 'Let me go or kill me now,' I hiss through my teeth. 'As the gods witness it, I will never be your puppet king. I don't believe in fate.'

Silas growls, red eyes flashing.

'You don't believe in fate?' Shadow laughs humourlessly. 'You are the son of two great astromancer families. Saying you don't believe in fate is like a fish saying it doesn't believe in water! The power in you should be so much greater than fists and muscle. So much greater, even, than gods. But you are a disappointment, Livio. So much potential, squandered. I am offering you the chance to be everything you could be. If you refuse then, in Fortune's name, I'll deny your precious Contessa an honourable death. I'll string her up on the city walls until she's eaten by the gulls. *Then* we'll see if you believe in fate.'

'She'll be miles away by now,' I snap, jutting out my chin in defiance despite the icy fear in my heart.

'Sadly not. We've intercepted her at the docks,' Shadow says smoothly. 'Even now, we're holding her somewhere safe until her execution … and your coronation.'

I feel horribly, sickeningly powerless. Could it be true?

'We go tonight,' Shadow continues, 'to the palazzo, to claim it for the new kingdom. You've no choice. Come quietly, and it'll be better for you and those you care for.'

'Why are you doing this?' I ask, my voice flat and weak.

'Because it is my home,' she replies, leaning forward, eyes glowing with passion. 'I was born here, just as you were. And this is the right thing for Scarossa – it always has been. One day, you'll realise it too.'

'You know nothing about me,' I protest, hissing the words through clenched teeth. 'Nothing about this city.'

Now, finally, she faces me, her eyes flashing in an anger to match my own. 'I know everything about you. I've been watching over you your entire life. And I alone knew the secrets of Dark Scarossa. How can you say I know nothing about this city? Don't you see?'

'What?' I whisper. I'm turning the signet ring around my finger.

She breathes deeply, lets out a long sigh. It's the first time I've noticed any signs of weakness in her bearing, and I'm unsettled by whatever words are hovering behind her lips. 'I was born to a noble family, an ancient family. But ... for decades past, we had fallen on hard times – no thanks to the Contessa and her predecessors, who were jealous of our heritage. My father, however, believed in a future for our line. A greater future. He believed the Contessa's bargain with Mythris was evil. He believed in Fortune and her legacy. He taught me the ways of astromancy – how to control a sandwolf, bind it to my will. He showed me Dark Scarossa. He taught me how to act, to steal, to lie. And, before he died, he arranged a match for me with Alberto Santini. Because he knew the only way to overthrow them was from within.'

My heart is pounding so hard, I'm scared it might leap from my chest.

'I had a child, Livio. The child I always knew would be

heir to the Queens of Scarossa. The first ever to combine the powers of Fortune.'

'No,' I whisper.

'I am your mother, Livio,' she says, her voice barely louder than mine. She faces me again, her expression twisted in pain. And again, even quieter: 'I'm your mother, and you will do as I say, whether you like it or not.'

My ears roar. The world falls around my ears like the ceiling is crumbling down, stars whooshing past me like diving gulls.

Chains bind me in streaks of pure, pitiless light.

TWENTY-FOUR
No More Puppets

Beatrice

I've nothing but time in this place. No light. No footsteps. No noise. And so – I practise. I set the mask carefully aside, wrapping it in an old blanket I've been left and leaning the bundle against the wall.

At first, it's unreliable – sometimes a glowing globe hovers in my hand, strong and true. Sometimes a light no larger than a candle flame. Sometimes I feel sick, faint, like I did before. But the more I draw on the magic, the surer it feels.

Now, it flickers at my fingertips as I hold my hand palm-up – green light ricocheting from the mirror and dancing across the walls. I catch glimpses of my new face in the fractured glass – jumping at the sight of a stranger. I tip my wrist and shoot a stream of glitter at an old puppet dressed in ragged starry robes, her face blackened and stained. Her body bursts open in a shattering cloud of wood and metal, and I feel a grim satisfaction.

No more puppets.

Over the hours, the remaining hanging puppets are destroyed, one by one, by my target practice, until the room is littered with dust and debris. I lay down on the cold floor, drained. I think I can do it. I can beat Hal if I have the element of surprise.

I sleep.

And I wake, who knows how long later, to a darkness so complete that I can't tell if my eyes are open or shut. I pass my hands in front of my face: nothing.

My stomach feels so empty it's painful. Gingerly I stand, stretching out my cramped muscles.

And I see the faintest tremor of light under the door. Hear the *scuff-scuff-scuff* of footsteps.

Hal?

I lower myself closer to the ground, feeling for my magic. This is my chance – perhaps my only chance.

The light grows, hurting my eyes – but I squint into it. No lamplight, this time – the light is the colour of Hal's magic, a reddish purple like a fresh bruise.

The footsteps and the light stop outside the door, and I hear the jangle of keys. I remember how Hal summoned his attacks in the mask room, holding out his palm and letting a ball of power grow on his outstretched hand.

I hold out my palm, face up, and draw on the power – it feels eager, restless. Pushing itself from a hollow place beneath my lungs, fizzing in the pit of my stomach, tingling

297

under my skin. Light starts to fill the room. Shadows crawl across the cobwebbed walls, a huge spider scuttling across the floor by my feet.

The lock turns and – by the time the door clicks open – there's a glowing green globe the size of my head spitting like new fire in my palm.

The door creaks. I don't think. I just throw it.

Surprise is on my side – I catch a glimpse of Hal's wide eyes as the attack hits him square in the chest at close range. He doubles over, and I'm readying a second attack as he slumps forward, sliding down the door frame.

My hands tremble and the light flickers out.

Darkness consumes me again. The room is very still and a cold air whispers from the corridor. I wait a few beats, expecting a flash of bruised red light, but nothing happens. At last, I summon a shaky flame of magic in my palm – enough to see by.

I stumble across the room and kneel by Hal, rolling him on to his back by levering him with my leg. I press my head to his mouth, shakily, listening for breath …

He's alive.

I feel relief wash over me. For a moment, I feared he might be the second man I'd killed with my magic.

My resolve hardens as I gaze down at his slack face. I have to escape. I have to find the Contessa. I have to discover the truth. Or none of this was worth it.

No more puppets.

Somehow in the confusion my mask has found itself lying by Hal's side, unravelled from its wrapping of cloth, touching his hand. I draw closer to retrieve it and notice something strange: the mask is lying face up, but where it's touching Hal's hand, it appears to have absorbed a little of his darker skin colour, spreading across the surface like ink staining paper. I pick it up and, next to my skin, the colour leeches away.

I frown. Was it ... changing?

The forbidden mask she's wearing has powers they don't want out in the world.

And that's when I start to suspect what the mask is capable of. Not allowing myself to hesitate, I lower the mask on to Hal's face. At first, nothing – my old face, my sisters' faces, superimposed on his. Then ... I watch as the features of the mask shift – the nose broadening, the brows deepening, the skin darkening. My breath catches in my throat. The mask is Hal's face now.

I lift off the mask with trembling fingers, breathe deep, and press it to my own face. Power surges and I nearly scream as pain rips through my body. I fall to my knees. Faintly, I hear the tunic I'm wearing pop and tear at the seams. I black out ...

And wake, I think, a few seconds later, my lips cold and tingling. Hal lies unmoving at my side. Slowly, I rise up and draw on my power to summon a mage-light. The tiny flame that lifts from my palm is a deep, purplish red.

TWENTY-FIVE

Homecoming

Livio

We walk through Dark Scarossa, its passages strung with cobweb banners – a sad celebration for me, the new puppet king. Shadow leads the way, and I follow – Silas swirling at my side. Twelve plain-clothed Rogues strapped from head to heel with weapons walk in our wake.

For now, I'm obeying Shadow's wishes – but the thought of casting aside everything my grandmother so carefully preserved, everything she's been fighting for, sickens me. She stole a child to replace her mask-maker, yes. But good people do bad things, sometimes. I know she wants what's right for Scarossa, even if occasionally she is willing to compromise her morals to achieve it.

If I do as Shadow wants, I let Grandmother down – and that isn't an option. But if I disobey her orders, Shadow has promised a painful death to the last remaining member of my family. Except … *Shadow* is my family. The thought fills me with horror. All this time I've longed for my mother, fantasised about her return … and now … I shiver.

My head is reeling. I feel weightless, powerless. What if Shadow's right? What if this plan really is my fate? Events are aligning perfectly for her vision, circumstances slipping into place like clockwork. Are the stars on her side?

If so, I will not go down without a fight. I'll keep my eyes and ears open – searching for a way out. No chance of that here – this dark, narrow passage is winding on forever. But perhaps, perhaps when we surface in the palazzo …

Silas growls at my side, as if he can sense the direction of my thoughts. I feel his power, a pure raging swirl of Chaos, as firmly as if someone is tugging at my hand; feel the two red orbs of his eyes examining me sidelong as I walk. *I wonder* … On impulse, I reach out with my astromancy, carefully, softly, towards the wolf …

Silas lets out a shrill, rasping yap, flinching away from my astromantic touch. Shadow spins around.

'You may have the power to control sandwolves, Livio, but you can't command this one.' A flash of silver: a blade is held to my throat so fast I've no time to block it. 'Try that again, and I'll make you pay for it. Understand?'

I nod slightly, my heart hammering.

Her eyes land on Silas, next, burning. 'Quiet, beast!'

Silas whimpers and falls silent.

At last we reach an ending to the passage – a narrow

stone staircase twisting up to the underside of what looks like a trapdoor.

Shadow stops, turns to her warriors, her mage-light hovering overhead casting long shadows along the stone floor. 'Once we climb this staircase, we'll be in the kitchens. Our people are watching and waiting in the gardens for our signal. All we need to do is secure the palazzo and grounds by sunrise, when the crowning and execution will be staged in the square. We have' – she glances at a watch she pulls from a pocket of her jerkin – 'around two hours.'

'What kind of resistance can we expect?' a scarred woman asks.

'My reports suggest the palazzo has been abandoned, though largely stripped of furnishings and possessions. But stay on your guard. The Contessa is no fool, and the temples remain a force to be reckoned with in the city – though they've little business here.'

I think of the Cardinal's visit, how Grandmother had alluded to the temple's thirst for secular power. I'm not sure Shadow is right that the temple will have no business in the palazzo tonight … But she is continuing.

'If you encounter anyone, kill with knives if you can – magic is loud and bright. We don't want to raise an alarm if we can help it.'

She hands out orders, separating the small team into groups to spread out and search the building, sending signals to her Rogues outside once various areas are secured. Her knowledge of the palazzo's layout is immaculate – of course, she lived here once – but she never mentions the secret temple through Grandmother's rooms.

'Livio,' she says at last, 'you're with me and Silas. Try anything and the beast kills you – got it? We'll be waiting downstairs for the last signal.' She glances at her watch. 'Let's go.'

TWENTY-SIX
A New Face

Beatrice

I lean against the wall of the tunnel, my vision swimming.

I am Hal. His tightly muscled, tall body is my own. I'm wearing his clothes. I've stolen the colour of his magic.

I try not to think about his unconscious form, half naked and locked in the room of old puppets. The door won't hold him for long – if he survives.

Adrenalin runs through the blood of this body and sets its heart pattering – even as it fights the sensation. In fact, it feels as if it's fighting my every command. Down the dark passage I walk, my way lit by the mage-light, feeling uncomfortable and unwieldy, tall and uncoordinated. It feels as if I'm walking on stilts, and the floor is rising and falling like the surface of the ocean. Every other step I stumble, and I'm glad the passage is dark – if anyone could see me here, they'd think I was drunk.

I can understand why this magic is forbidden. I feel pulled in every direction, my identity twisted, my powers sullied. My vision blurs. My ears ring. But of course, they're not my eyes or my ears. I want nothing more than to tear this treacherous mask off my face.

No – I have to keep going.

Why didn't the mask have this effect on me before? I lurch down another passage, praying the gods will guide me to safety. I think of how the baby whose face the mask originally stole barely had a will of its own – except, in a mirror of my own infant instincts, to feed and to cry. Besides, it had already died. Whereas now, I have stolen the identity of a fully grown, living man – and an enemy. It appears his will has transferred to the mask as much as his magic.

I find a staircase, at last, my heart pounding as I stagger up the steps and shoulder open the door at the top. A foul, damp stench fills my nostrils as I enter what appears to be a sewer. I gag, but I force myself onwards. Somewhere, there'll be a way up into the city.

TWENTY-SEVEN
Fortune

Livio

Shadow pushes the door of the kitchens open, slow and careful. On the other side, the entrance hall is silent. One by one, the Rogues step silently into the moonlight, and I'm carried along in the middle, swept up in the current of a fate I never sought.

The hall feels cavernous. The marble floor, normally polished to a shine, is scuffed and grubby. White spaces linger on the walls where pictures and mirrors have been packed away, and the whole place smells of emptiness. The huge windows throw squares of moonlight on to the stairs, casting a cold white glow over the building I once called home.

Because this place isn't my home – not any more. I wonder if it ever will be again.

Shadow clicks the door shut behind us. She opens her mouth to speak … but doesn't. Instead, she sniffs the air, shuts her eyes as if honing her other senses. Silas is twisting at her side – something about his movement feels off-kilter, unsettled.

'Something is wrong,' Shadow whispers.

A blinding purple flash lights the room – bright enough for me to cower and flinch in shock, raising my hands to my eyes. I hear the swish and snap of cloth, Shadow cursing; the air hums with magic. And when I lower my hands and open my eyes, the room, though once again half hidden in the silver light, is transformed. Countless figures surround us – hooded and cloaked and terribly still, like the statues of the masked god himself.

I was right. Grandmother was right. Mythris's temple is here to claim the palazzo for itself.

One of the figures in front of the grand main entrance steps forward, his robes edge in gold. The Cardinal.

'Shadow, at last,' he says in a low, cultured voice. His eyes fix on mine – hold for a moment – and then return to the pirate queen's face. 'Or should I say, Seraphina?'

Shadow scowls. 'It's been a long time since I was Seraphina, Cardinal.'

'I remember you, even so. A good novice, once. The masked god values ambition and cunning, Sera – but yours has stretched outside the bounds of reason. You think you are more powerful than Mythris himself.'

'Fortune is the one with the power,' Shadow counters. 'I am her vessel – a messenger of her will.'

'Fortune … very well.' The Cardinal smiles indulgently.

'Regardless, you have led us a merry chase ... but for all your cleverness, you fell right into my trap. Did you really think the palazzo would be yours for the taking? That the masked god would let you claim what is his?'

As the Cardinal and Shadow exchange words, I catch sight of a face beneath the hood of the figure at the Cardinal's side. Except, it's not a face at all. Tears run down blue, cloudy cheeks, water glittering across its brow. Ice trickles down my spine. The True Masked guards are pledged to my grandmother – why is this one in the Cardinal's service, wearing the robes of Mythris's temple?

Shadow steps forward, unbowed by the unexpected arrivals or the Cardinal's speech. 'I don't care about your treacherous god,' she spits. 'And I don't care if I have to fight you. The future is ours – Fortune has declared it. All roads lead to the King of the Wishes, whether they're paved with peace or blood.' She raises an arm, Silas spinning to her side, ready for battle. 'Surrender now, crawl back to the north, to your City of False Kings and traitor gods. Or die at the hands of my beast.'

'Scarossa is ours,' the Cardinal counters. He summons a fizzing orb of dark purple magic, held in his upright palm. Every one of his mages follows suit until the hall is alive with dancing light and magic hums in the air. 'This is your last chance,' he adds softly. 'You can't win against the nine.'

'Even gods can't triumph over fate,' hisses Shadow, her arm remaining raised, poised, holding Silas at her side. Her followers summon their own attacks – every mage's magic a different colour. I feel the louder, wilder tune of their unbound power – Rogue power. And then she shouts, 'Attack!'

Silas disappears and reappears, consuming the Cardinal in his sandy whirlwind – and the rest of the hall explodes into action, a bright purple attack instantly barrelling towards me from a mage I hadn't spotted.

I throw myself to the ground, feeling the heat of the spell skim the top of my head. The air smells singed and electric. Feet pound around me. Men and women cry out in pain, frustration, triumph. Blades sing. I catch a glimpse of the True Mask, its ghastly crying face bringing one of Shadow's men to his knees, tears streaming down his cheeks in a mirror of the mask's as his emotions are twisted by Mythris's magic. Light flashes as spells are thrown, blocked, shatter into sparks against the walls, skitter over the marble floor and smash through the great arched window over the door.

Confusion reigns. And, I realise, that's an opportunity. No one's watching me – not even Shadow. The Cardinal and Shadow are fighting so fast and wild that I see nothing but flashes of purple light, glimpses of the Cardinal's gold-edged robes and Shadow's glittering rings.

I cast my gaze around the room. The fighting is blocking the exits – the front door, the servant's corridors like the one we emerged from. But the staircase … If I can get upstairs, I can climb down the bone-rose trellis and escape into the city.

I start to crawl across the marble floor towards the staircase. One of Shadow's men collapses on the floor right in front of me, eyes wide open, blood trailing from his nose. My heart pounds, stomach twisting in horror – but I force myself to crawl over him. I reach the bottom step and rise carefully to my feet, ready to run up to the first floor.

A rasping growl sounds as Silas materialises in front of me, red eyes narrowed. I stagger backwards in shock.

He's blocking my path, watching me as I stumble to the floor, helpless. A bright red attack zooms from behind me and explodes on the banister a few inches to my left – I jump near out of my skin. Despite the noise, lights and confusion at my back, the world narrows to just me and the creature, our eyes locked. The sandwolf is huge – twice the size of the yellow-eyed sandwolves I've encountered – his head reaching past my waist as I lift myself up once more.

In the underground passage, I'd managed to affect him with my astromancy. I remember how angry Shadow was – she was desperate to frighten me off. So she must've been scared I could steal Silas away from her. Which means …

I reach for my power again, feeling the otherness of the magic – the two strands of astromancy held in my heart. Somehow, this time, I can sense which is which – the textures are different: one rough and dry like a sandwolf's body; one cool and smooth like the feeling of slipping into the stars. I hold out my hand, push a thread of magic towards the sandwolf, who growls soft and low, cowering. I push harder, against the resistance I'm feeling, like a chain protecting Silas's core, determined to break it down.

Then, Silas jumps – attacks – and suddenly my world is lightning, swirling sand and pain. Choking, hot dust fills my lungs, a raw celestial magic burning my skin. I suppress my urge to panic as time is muddied, slowed. For a moment I feel like surrendering – but then a thought crosses my mind in the space of a heartbeat, clear and bright.

I'm past the chains, now. I'm *inside* the creature.

Drawing on my astromancy again, in spite of the confusion surrounding me, I reach out for Silas's spark of life, the raw intelligence I sensed in him and others of his kind. I find it … but it's shackled, bound to Shadow. The star in his heart is wrapped in another's will. But Silas has a will of his own – a will which he has been denied. I don't need to command him myself. All I have to do is set him free. I reach out, pull …

The sandwolf lifts from my chest. I glance up, panting. My face feels scratched and burned with sand, and my hands are scarred with magical streaks. But I'm alive.

'Go,' I whisper to Silas.

The creature's red eyes blink. And suddenly, there's nothing guarding the stairs but moonlight.

Not allowing myself to think, or hesitate further, I run upstairs while the battle rages on behind me.

I sprint down the empty corridor, feet thudding on the thick carpet. I consider my room but pass it – instead, I dart into Grandmother's. Her balcony and trellis are hidden from the front of the palazzo – I'm less likely to be spotted by any of Shadow's people from there. I'm through the door, running across the strangely bare room, the ghosts of furniture imprinted on the rugs – but hesitate as I reach the double windows. I glance over my shoulder. The curtain hiding the entrance to Fortune's temple swings slightly.

Where will I run? What would I achieve by fleeing? I could survive, perhaps. But Scarossa would be lost. I cannot let that happen.

Inside the temple, though, I could find answers. Direction.

The decision is instinctive. I stride over to the door, lifting the tiny key from under my clothes. I open it, step inside and lock it behind me.

Trailing my hand against the wall, I climb the stairs. Alone, I sense the age of the building like I never have before. I imagine the ghosts of my Ancestors lingering in front of me, out of sight around the tight spiral, leading my way.

Up in the temple, under the spiralling tower of blue glass, the moon is sinking and tinged with purple. Dawn approaches. The world turns, as it always does, in bad times as well as good. I lie under the stars, on the marble altar, feeling the silence like a companion at my side. Magic thrums in the air. Astromancy. I draw on my power, stronger than ever before, and open my eyes wide. The stars warp and twist in the enchanted glass, a high note chiming in my head.

Chains stretch out between the stars in a myriad of webs,

layers of near and far and possible futures stretching on into forever. I push into the chains, feel my stomach lurch as I demand answers, demand a way through. To my surprise, I'm drawn not up, further into the stars, but down …

The chains are connected to us, down here in the city of Scarossa, connecting the souls who live here to one another, to the stars, binding us to our fates … but down I go, and down again. I feel hot, shivery. Earth envelopes me – a jumbled layer of the forgotten, the lost, the discarded. I sink into the rocky no man's land beneath, old bones resting in their midst – and down, down further to the steaming streams gurgling in dripping lightless caves. Lower, lower I follow the chains until …

Soft light.

A body lies here: a woman laid out as if for a funeral pyre, hands folded over her chest, eyes shut. Roots twist around her body, gems gleaming in the walls of her berth. She's dressed in a long blue gown, and although faded by time, I can tell it's embroidered with silver and gold stars. She is beautiful, her dark hair falling long around her body in tiny, lapping waves – and the soft light spills from her skin. Her eyelids flicker as if she's dreaming. Thousands of chains fall into her body – no, I realise, they are drawn *from* her body, like beams of light. And they're not chains at all.

My vision shifts. Each link is an event, a decision, a turning point – leading to the next. The chains are paths. Choices. Opportunities.

Her eyelids flicker. Her eyes open, staring at me. She *sees* me. And in that moment, I see what I have to do.

The Cardinal. Shadow. Grandmother. Images flash before my eyes in a sequence, a chain of events, of decisions, leading into the future. My future. I feel possibilities narrowing, fading into darkness, leaving three options open to me: a future under Shadow's command; a future under the Temple's; and … another path.

The path isn't clear. In fact, it's faint, shimmering in the darkness like a distant planet. But it's something.

And as suddenly as I plunged into this dream world, I'm flung out of it. I'm not surprised when I find myself on the floor, gasping as if I've been drowning, but filled with the knowledge of what I am capable of – what I have to do to win.

I can't hesitate – I have to try. I sit on the floor and draw on my *other* astromantic power – the one that feels warm, rough and sandy, in contrast to the cold, smooth chiming sensation when I read the stars. I pull, a siren call of magic echoing through the air. A sandwolf swirls into existence in front of me, like a dust devil rising from the earth grain by grain. As it builds itself up, taller and taller, my breath hitches in my throat. When they open, flickering into existence, the sandwolf's eyes glow not yellow, but red.

'Silas?' I whisper. The huge, golden sandwolf bows its head, slightly, in assent. I've not bound him to my will. I've asked for help – and he has come. I reach out, stroke the impossible furry sand of his body, press my forehead to his. I feel his hurt, his pain, his power. His desire for revenge on the woman who held him captive.

'Soon,' I say softly. 'But not yet.'

I shut my eyes. Fortune slumbers far beneath my feet – connected to me, to the watching stars, to Silas whose head rests against my own. I probe my power, wondering at how Astromancy fills my heart with purpose, its power fizzing through my blood, raising the hairs on the back of my neck. Silas grumbles, softly, as if he feels it too. Running away isn't an option, not any more. My work here is not yet done.

TWENTY-EIGHT
Home

Beatrice

I pass two people in the sewers dressed in the plain dark clothes I associate with Shadow's gang – their eyes widen as they meet mine, their gazes quickly dropping to the sewer floor in deference as they acknowledge my presence and hurry past.

I'm glad Hal's face inspires fear. Nobody challenges me. Nobody questions why Hal is staggering, stumbling as if drunk, one hand trailing on the wall. This face, this body is protesting my control, and I don't know how much longer I can fight it.

At last I find a ladder to climb, slowly, painfully. At the top, I shoulder open the metal drain cover, glad of Hal's strength as I crawl out into the night, out of Shadow's territory. I'm surprised to find myself right outside the house I grew up in, the mascherari house. I hear no sound but the tall trees hissing in the wind and the sea crashing beyond. All of a sudden, I feel like crying. I roll on to the paving stones, unable to muster the energy or will to check if anyone is watching. My muscles are burning, the mask pulses with pain as I shift the drain cover into place. I clasp my hands to my face. I can't bear it any more. I've left Dark Scarossa now – and no one knows my true face anyway. I rip the mask away with a gasp of relief.

The pain that follows is hot, intense – running through my body like a magical attack – but mercifully brief. I lie very still for a moment, glad to feel a familiar body, an identity closer to the one I've grown up thinking was my own. I sit up and tuck the mask into an inside pocket of Hal's now ludicrously oversized yellow uniform. I bend forward to roll up the legs and then the sleeves – then I lift my eyes and finally notice lights flashing from the direction of the palazzo. If I listen closely, tinny cries and distant explosions sound beneath the waves and the wind. A fight.

Hopelessness fills my heart. Where do I go now?

But then, I notice a faint glow in a downstairs window of the mascherari house, a mere chink of light between the curtains of the dining room. I shiver, imagining my sisters sitting at the table, Valentina reading out the bulletin, and Ofelia sipping black sugared coffee and telling her everything is boring. What if I could simply slip into the seat between them? If everything could go back to how it was before?

I creep up to the house, keeping low in the undergrowth. The window, I notice, is slightly ajar. I press my eye to the gap.

An old woman is tied to one of our dining chairs, sagging into her ropes, her eyelids flickering. At first, I don't recognise her. Then it hits me – it's the Contessa. Diminished, weak. I feel an unwelcome stab of pity for the woman who stole my life.

I peer around the room, checking for guards. When I see none, I ease the window wider and climb over the sill into the room.

Despite her sorry condition, the Contessa's eyes are alert as she lifts her head and watches me drop quietly to the floor.

'Don't worry,' she says, drawing herself up until she's sitting up straight. 'There's no one here but me. I'm too weak to escape. And nobody wants to come to the mascherari house.' Her eyes twinkle. 'Except the mascherari, of course. Beatrice, isn't it?'

I blink, shocked. 'How do you know my name?' I swallow, suddenly nervous. Somehow, despite the fact that she's the one tied to a chair, she is in control of this conversion, not I. She flexes her hand, pinned to her side, the great dark mourning rings stark against her wrinkled skin. Her voice trembles as she speaks again.

'Even after all these years, I know your true face, girl. You should have fled when you could.'

My resolve hardens. I step closer, sit down on the chair beside hers. 'I couldn't run away without knowing the truth. I need to know who I am. You stole me from the life

I was born into. You failed to protect my sisters. You at least owe me this.' I steel myself. 'So tell me – who am I?'

The Contessa leans forward as best she can, her dark eyes glowing with a strange intensity. 'You think it matters whose blood you hold in your veins? You think it matters what face lies beneath the mask?' Although tremulous, her voice is full of conviction. 'Well, you are not the only one in disguise. We all wear masks, Beatrice. You won't find a person here who shows their true face to everyone they meet. And perhaps that's how it should be. Our greatness is determined not by blood, or fate – but by actions alone … by what we choose to present to the world. A mask is a truer reflection of our soul than anything we are born with.' She sags back against the bars of the chair as if the speech has drained her of energy. It's more than age and exhaustion, I realise. She's ill. Her face is damp with fever; her eyes unnaturally bright.

I can't follow the thread she's spooling out for me – part of me wonders if she's all there, or if her mind has unravelled under the pressure of her suffering. I bow my head, frustrated, then lift my eyes again. 'Please. You have to tell me.'

And she does …

I blink at the revelations. I don't know what I expected. Perhaps I thought everything would slot into place. But knowing the names doesn't change a thing: I still don't know *who* I am. Instead, I feel fragmented, broken.

'Now, I know I have no right to ask anything of you,' says the Contessa. 'But please, take me to my grandson. I want to see him … one last time.'

My heart softens. Suddenly, she isn't the Contessa. She is simply an old woman, asking me for help. Her breath is at once shallow and heavy as I lean forward to untie her ropes.

TWENTY-NINE
Dawn

Livio

In the hallway, the battle is as fierce as ever, dawn streaking the morning sky red through the huge windows over the staircase. When I peer down from the banister, I see the floor below is littered with corpses and injured mages.

The majority, I realise, are in purple robes.

Seven remaining Mythris mages, including the Cardinal and the True Masked mage at his side, fight ten of Shadow's people. Shadow herself is a blur of magic and blades. An orange-eyed sandwolf swirls in and out of the battle at her command – a new weapon for her to control. Silas growls at my side.

Shadow lets out a high battle cry and presses her advantage. She's so fast, I can't tell how it happens, but a sudden silence spills over the hall, and I realise she's holding the Cardinal tightly in her arms, a knife pressed to his throat.

One by one, the remaining mages of the masked temple drop down to their knees, hands pressed against the bloody floor in the ancient gesture of a mage's surrender. Shadow's people surround the group, drawing their knives and echoing Shadow's position, blades pressed to throats. I feel a chill of horror as I watch the robed mages' eyes widen. They're sensing what I'm sensing: they might have surrendered, but it doesn't matter. Shadow will show no mercy.

'You said I couldn't beat a god, Cardinal,' Shadow says, loud enough for everyone to hear. 'But look – I didn't need to. I have his highest order of priests and priestesses on their knees. And will Mythris come down and save you all …?' She leaves a pause. 'Come on!' she shouts to the ceiling. 'Where are you?' Her voice echoes against the empty marble walls. When she speaks again, her tone is low and mocking. 'No, I think you're all alone. Perhaps you always have been. After all, your god is a faithless betrayer.'

The Cardinal's eyes burn with rage. 'And your god is dead,' he spits. 'Old legends and half-magics are all that hold up your philosophy. You may have won the battle, but you cannot win the war. The nine won't let it happen.'

'The nine will have to watch while it does,' Shadow hisses. Her mouth twists. In one smooth movement, she draws the knife across the Cardinal's neck, a wide slice opening his gullet, blood spilling over his robes in a rush of livid red. Life drops from his eyes, quick as a diving gull. I sag against the banister, my head spinning at the ease with which she, my mother, kills. The Cardinal's body slumps to the floor.

One of the surrendered mages shouts 'No!' in a hoarse, disbelieving scream. Dark purple magic flashes from her, the knife held to her throat flying from her captor's hand and skittering across the room. The mage scrambles to her feet and rushes forward, towards the Cardinal's body. I realise with a start that it's the mage wearing the True Mask. But Shadow's magic flares, and the masked mage is flung backwards. As she hits the floor, the mask is knocked from her face, the hood from her red, flaming hair.

Carlotta.

She's dazed, slow. She half lifts herself from where she's fallen, squinting as Shadow stalks towards her, stands over her. When Carlotta reaches for the True Mask, Shadow stamps hard on her wrist and I hear a sickening crunch. Carlotta screams in pain. My stomach twists. Shadow leaves her boot in place, holding her down.

'Look,' says Shadow, glancing between the two livid shocks of red hair, bright in the dawn light. 'It's the Cardinal's child. And the last of the True Masked guards, by the look of it. What do we do with True Masked guards and their toys?'

'Destroy them,' whisper her followers in eager unison.

Keeping one foot on Carlotta's wrist, she brings down the other, hard, on the mask. One, two, three times. Blue sparks fly into the air. Carlotta cries out with every blow – as if the destruction of the mask is hurting her even more than her shattered wrist. By the time Shadow's finished, the mask is no more than a collection of blue shards. Satisfied, she lifts her boot from Carlotta's wrist, holds out her knife, and kneels down to rest the blade, point down, over Carlotta's heart. The girl's eyes are wide with fear.

The gleam of the blade – like a flame in the rising sunlight – jolts me into action. I can't let this go on.

Signalling for Silas to wait, I step out from the darkness and walk down the stairs. Shadow's eyes lift at the sound of my footsteps. I draw back my shoulders, feel my fists clench, readying for a fight. Shadow's people stand unmoving, their knives held to the remaining Mythris mages' throats.

'Son,' she says, her voice softening slightly, though her knife remains poised over Carlotta's chest. 'Just in time to claim your kingdom.'

'Let her go,' I say, glad my voice sounds stronger than I feel. I stop halfway down the stairs – I feel more powerful on this higher ground.

'*This* one?' She gazes down at Carlotta as if she's a hunk of cooked meat I've asked her not to slice. 'We killed the others. She is the last of the True Masked mages. A remnant of a dead era. Keeping her alive would be a cruelty. This is a new age, Livio. Our age.'

'Let. Her. Go,' I demand.

Annoyance crosses her face, but she smiles slightly, suppressing the emotion – I guess her victory over the masked temple has put her in a good mood that she's unwilling to let go of. 'Finally found your fire, have you?

Very well.' She steps from Carlotta, who instantly brings her broken wrist to her chest, her face drained of colour. Her eyes flit to mine, hopelessness and grief dancing in their depths.

I walk down the remaining steps slowly, starting to draw on my astromancy as I descend, holding on to the celestial visions in my mind. At my call, Silas swirls into existence at my side.

'Silas …' Shadow says as her eyes flit to the beast. The orange-eyed sandwolf she's bound to her will drifts to her side, narrowing its eyes at Silas. Shadow's smile tightens with displeasure – her voice too. 'I thought he must've perished in the fighting. But it seems you stole him.'

'I didn't steal him. I freed him,' I say. By now, I've reached Carlotta's side. I help her up – she's unsteady, leaning hard on my arm, her eyes brimming with tears. 'And I'm about to free Scarossa from you too,' I add to Shadow quietly.

Shadow's expression darkens further, any pretence at good humour now entirely fallen from her face. 'I think not, Livio. *I* am the liberator of Scarossa – from the shackles Mythris and the Santini dynasty placed upon it thousands of years ago. And it's time we sealed our victory.'

She raises her hand – a bright purple light flashes up in front of the windows, challenging the dawn. A signal? Sure enough, the hall is flooded with the remaining Rogues who'd hidden in the palazzo grounds. Shadow's eyes are oddly sad as the Rogues surround Carlotta and me, power thrumming in the air.

Shadow snarls. 'Do you still expect to beat me, Livio? You, an injured mage and a single sandwolf?'

'You're wrong about liberating Scarossa,' I tell her, my heart pounding in fear as I fight to keep my voice steady. 'Yes, we've been constrained by the bargain between my Santini Ancestors and Mythris's temple. But that age is already over.' I glance down at the shattered mask. 'And you want to replace this regime with another. What kind of kingdom do you envisage? By declaring me king, you instantly start a war on the north. You cut off the main part of our trade. You abolish the temples, leaving the city overrun with Rogues – or send away the mages, leaving us without a government structure. This would be a poor Scarossa. A diminished Scarossa.'

'It would be *our* Scarossa,' Shadow interjects, her eyes glowing. 'In pursuing this kingdom, I've followed the dream of my Ancestors for generations past, a dream passed down from father to daughter, mother to son. The dream of a great family, oppressed. We could have risen together, son. Ruled side by side. Finally we could have made up for the time we've lost.' Now her voice is tight with emotion. Around us, her mages press in closer, like an eager audience drawing in round a stage.

My heart feels heavy as I shake my head. 'I've longed for you to return ever since the day you left. But not like this.

I could never have been happy knowing you'd destroyed everything Grandmother – who has been mother, father and friend to me – worked so hard to preserve.'

At this, Shadow appears enraged, her face draining of colour, her mouth taut. After a pause, her voice is hard as she replies. 'You think you have mastered astromancy, son. But you are a mere novice in the arts of Fortune.' She stalks forward. 'So let me teach you a lesson. You hold astromancy within you, Livio, exactly like a sandwolf. Do you know what I do to sandwolves?'

My body follows the link before my mind catches up – and suddenly, it feels like my throat has closed with fear. I swallow. 'What are you saying?'

'I bind them to my will, Livio, until they are an extension of my intentions, following my every whim. If you will not obey me willingly, you give me no choice …' She raises her hand, holding it flat, parallel to the floor, magic thrumming, spitting around her fingers. 'Surrender, Livio, or I will make you a puppet king in truth. I will bind you to me exactly as I bound Silas.'

A chill of horror runs through me. I think I understand at last exactly how far Shadow is willing to go for the dream she's pursued her whole life. Whatever love she holds for me pales in comparison to her obsession. 'I won't,' I say quietly.

She closes her fist. Strange starlike sparks float around her fingers. I feel foreign power clench in my stomach, my magic churning. I gasp at the sensation, drop to one knee as the breath is knocked from my lungs, as if I've been punched hard in the gut.

Silas growls, launches himself at Shadow – but she's ready. She sends a huge surge of purple magic towards the beast. He's hit directly, lets out a rasping scream, which tears my heart. I lose sight of him – is he dead? I try to stand up, but … I can't.

Whatever spell Shadow is casting, it's keeping me on my knees. I try. Try again. I scream at myself to stand up, but it's like I'm trapped in quicksand. My leg twitches, slides a half-inch forward. A bead of sweat rolls down my cheek.

'See, Livio? How easy it is to pull your strings.' She jerks her hand and I feel myself stand, loose and uncoordinated. She twists a finger – my leg jerks forward. And then the other. I'm *walking*. I panic, but my pulse remains steady, low, as if Shadow has control of my heart, too.

Shadow walks me forward until I stand a foot in front of her – and then, leaning close, she kisses me lightly on the cheek. I smell a perfume I recognise from long ago. I smell blood. 'There, Livio. This is more like it.' She glances over her shoulder. 'Seize the temple girl. And bring the crown.'

I can't control my body. So instead, I shut my eyes, allow my mind to reach for the magic deep inside me, beyond the claws of Shadow's control. Gently, I try to do what I planned in the temple, to draw on both strands of astromancy at once.

328

I think of the Battaglia, the fight I've always had within me. I think of Elisao, kissing me. I think of Grandmother holding my hand as I summoned the stars for the first time. I picture the goddess, Fortune, sleeping far under the earth, dreaming of all our futures, offering us *choice*.

For *that*, not astromancy, was her greatest parting gift.

And I choose to be free.

The air around me dances with white sparks.

Shadow frowns. 'What—?'

I gasp as the magic surges through me, past Shadow's constraints, flooding the room with a power drawn from deep, deep inside me. From my very blood, marrying the Santini and the Lupina, uniting Fortune's power for the first time since the goddess walked the earth.

Around me, wisps of sand rise as if from nowhere, spinning, spinning. A grain multiplies into two grains – two into four – on and on until the air is full of the scent of the desert. Shadow's face falters, her eyes clouding with doubt. Her followers stagger away from the little dust devils rising all around, eyes widening as they guess what's about to happen next. Silas returns to my side, smaller, spinning slower, but *alive*. He roars triumphantly. Sandwolves spark into life, twisting into miniature tornadoes – the eyes always blinking on last, like bright lanterns in a storm.

My energy is drained. Blood leaves my face, my palms tingle. Suddenly I feel a hand on my arm, holding me steady. I glance up – it's Carlotta. She nods at me slowly, as if to tell me I can do it. As if to say, *We're going to be all right.*

For the first time, real fear crosses Shadow's face. 'How is this possible?' she breathes.

'It's exactly as you said,' I tell her, forcing myself to stand upright although I feel like falling to my knees. 'In me, the two branches of astromancy are combined for the first time. My destiny was different than the one I imagined. But it wasn't the destiny you chose for me. Only I can choose my path. As you have chosen yours. And ... Mother ... this is where it ends.'

'Livio ...' She is really scared now. More human, more *real*, than I've ever seen her.

I feel tears prick my eyes as I understand, truly, what has to be done. I have to let go of the mother I've held on to my whole life, the mother who stole herself away from me for the mad dream of her forefathers. Silently I command the sandwolves to attack.

Silas has already chosen his target.

The palazzo is alive with screams as I watch Shadow and her followers, consumed by the very land they tried to steal, by the goddess they tried to claim for their own.

One by one, at my command, the sandwolves disappear – every one except Silas, who remains at my side, spinning slow and lazy as if satiated. The floor of the palazzo hall is littered with corpses, scattered with sand. Silence reigns.

Carlotta walks over to her father's body, kneels at his side.

And I gaze down at my mother's face, a horrible mixture of grief and guilt and regret welling up inside my heart.

'Lord Livio?' A small voice at the open door. A girl I don't recognise supports a woman I do: Grandmother. I watch as both scan the hall, the destruction and death. Relief washes over their faces as they realise Shadow and the Cardinal are both defeated.

I help the girl lie Grandmother down on the threshold of the hall, her head resting in my lap. The door is wide – fresh air and sunlight spill through. Grandmother is struggling, her face unnaturally flushed, her eyes bright with fever. She's hardly able to focus on my tear-streaked face. We sit in silence for a minute or two, the girl waiting a respectful distance away, sitting on the palazzo steps.

When Grandmother finally speaks, her voice is weak. 'Livio… . I told you that destiny doesn't care what's in our hearts. It's taken me my whole life to realise I was wrong.' She breathes with difficulty. 'The stars … they are guided by our will.'

'I know,' I whisper. 'I figured it out too.' I smile down at her. 'I saw Fortune, Grandmother. She's not dead at all. She's sleeping. Dreaming. She lets us choose our fates. And …' My voice breaks. 'I choose to save you, Grandmother. I want you to be all right. You're going to be all right.' *I didn't see this*, I tell myself. *So it can't be happening. Grandmother will recover.*

She's not listening to me. Her eyes are faded, unfocused.

331

'Our desires shape our destiny, Livio. Do you understand? Your mother had a bad heart. I see that now. And perhaps … perhaps I did too. I was ambitious … hated the thought of losing power. Both of us got the destinies we deserved. But you …'

Tears are streaming down my face now. I don't know what she's trying to tell me, but I know she's dying, no matter what I want. I know it in the deepest part of my heart. 'Grandmother …'

'You saw … what you *needed* to see,' she says. A watery smile spreads across her face. 'Because… your heart is true. The stars know. Fortune knows. I am proud … so proud of you. You will be a good ruler. A good conte.'

'Don't …'

But abruptly, the smile freezes on her face. The light leaves her eyes. And I kneel in front of my city, the wreckage of the battle at my back, all alone. How can this be? Once again, the stars failed to show me the things that mattered the most. I've lost the man I love. Now I've lost my only family too.

I feel a hand on my shoulder – the girl who brought Grandmother to me.

'I'm Beatrice,' she says softly. My eyes widen and I wipe the tears from my face. The mascherari. She's removed the mask she was wearing her whole life. She kneels down beside me, loops her arm around my shoulder. 'I'm so sorry.'

332

Footsteps sound behind us. Carlotta kneels at my other side and, silently, holds my hand in her own.

'What now?' Carlotta says.

Together, we three stand up, step outside. The sun has lost its bloody hue, shining bright and golden. I hear voices, bells, the whoosh of the sea. I shut my eyes. In the palazzo, death reigns. But out here, in spite of everything, the city is coming to life.

'Now,' I say, 'we start again.'

EPILOGUE

One month later

Livio

Beatrice sits with her legs swinging over the side of the docks, boats bobbing under her feet. She's gazing out at the night sky, the early summer moon a sliver hanging low over the waves, the stars shining brightly. I join her, pushing a cold glass of sweetened lemon juice into her hand and setting a bag of spicy deep-fried prawns in her lap. We eat in silence, listening to the sounds of the city at our backs – the sizzling oil of the food stands, the clink of glasses, the shouts as a fight breaks out in the backstreets.

Eating a meal here has been a habit of ours ever since that dusk, nearly four weeks ago. The dusk of the funerals. The pyre was the largest I'd ever seen, burning like an echo of the puppet theatre in the palazzo square. We said farewell to Valentina and Ofelia, to Elisao, Grandmother, the Cardinal, even to Shadow. We said farewell to our old lives, our old world. The whole city had stood vigil – even what was left of the masked temple, including Carlotta – holding candles as the past burned before our eyes.

What next? Starting again is easier said than done. We hadn't been able to sleep, so we walked through the city, ate, drank. Sometimes, silence can be healing. But the words must always come, eventually.

Silas swirls into existence at my side, a rumbling noise starting up in his depths as he rests his head against my shoulder. I think of it, now, as a kind of purr. I stroke his head, turn to Beatrice.

'So … You set off at dawn?'

She nods, sips her drink and grimaces. 'On the *Dauntless*, for better or worse. I'm not sure any more.' She stares out at the sea.

'Why not?' I ask gently. 'I thought this is what you've always wanted.'

She sighs. 'When I thought I would be here my whole life, I wanted nothing more than to leave. It was so clear in my mind. But now …' She shakes her head. 'This city is all I've ever known. And really, I'm only just getting to know it.' She smiles faintly. 'Now that I come to leaving, I wonder if I'm making the right choice.'

'So you're only just getting to know the city. But what else is holding you back?'

'Nurse. You. Even Carlotta.' She shrugs. 'There are things I could do here. I could build a life.'

I pause, weighing my next words carefully. 'So … it's not the idea of your real family being here that's stopping you?'

She's never mentioned it – not since the time we first met, in the mask room, when she told me she was determined to find out the truth from Grandmother.

'No.' Her voice is low, careful. 'I think the Contessa was right. She said it doesn't matter who I really am. That's something I have to figure out for myself, no matter who my parents are.' She runs a hand through her hair. 'When she told me their names … it's horrible, but … I felt nothing. Whatever bonds we share through blood, whatever we might've been if I hadn't been stolen away, that's impossible to recapture now. My real family was always Valentina, Ofelia … and Nurse.' She smiles. 'I just wish I knew what to do.'

I let her words settle before I reply. 'Look … if you're after guidance … I could try to read the stars for you?' I offer.

Beatrice turns to me with glowing eyes. 'Would you? But don't we need to go to Fortune's temple?'

I gaze up at the night sky – I swear the stars have never been brighter. I've not tried reading a specific person's fate before, but I've read about it. I think I can figure it out. 'Not for this. If I need to change the future, perhaps. But we just want a glimpse, don't we?'

We set our drinks down, and I rest my hand over Beatrice's. I draw on my power, gazing up. The sea sighs in my ears, and the breeze is warm with the promise of summer. The stars shift and shimmer, pathways opening up between.

I turn my attention to Beatrice, the connection between us as I hold her hand. A path runs from her, up to the sky, branching out in a hundred different directions like a great tree.

'So many possibilities …' I inhale deeply. 'Here …' I follow one possible direction. 'I see you in Port Regal, joining the temple of Nomi. From there you travel all over the world, exploring the unknown continents to the south. Or …' I follow another path. 'Or you go to the City of Kings. There are many opportunities there … maybe even outside the temples, if you wish. And then …' I switch to another. 'If you stay – yes. There's a life for you here, too. A family, a home, a career …' I smile, let my astromancy fade away.

'Really?' She's gazing at me, her eyes shining.

'Beatrice,' I say, resting my hands on her shoulders, 'it doesn't matter what you choose. You've already been through the darkness. Now it's time for you to be free.'

ACKNOWLEDGEMENTS

My first novel, *We Are Blood and Thunder*, was six years in the making – *We Are Bound by Stars* took eighteen months from idea to publication. I only managed to write it with an enormous amount of support.

First, I'd like to thank my editor Zöe – for her patience, kindness, storytelling prowess and for knowing when to be tough. I love working with you and the entire team at Bloomsbury Children's Books: you're a dedicated and enthusiastic bunch! Special shout-outs to Fliss (Managing Editor), Vron (copy-editor), Sarah (proofreader), Bea (Senior Publicity Manager) and Siân (Marketing Brand Manager).

Huge thank you to my agent, Veronique, who could talk a lemming off a cliff-edge – you're calm, collected and wise, and I'm so glad you've got my back.

To the entire Chicken House team for putting up with my crazy schedule and deadline hysterics: Jazz, Esther, Laura, Sarah and honorary Chicken Lucy. A very big thank you to my two unbelievably understanding bosses, Rachel L and Barry.

To my writerly friends – there are a lot! I'm fortunate to work with many of you in a professional capacity – you know who you are. I feel so lucky to have you as my role models. Others I've met during my journey as an author – on social media and beyond. You're all stars and I can't tell you how valuable it has been to have travelling companions on this strange old journey. To my amazing writing group: Kat, Jess Rule, Jess Rigby, Maddy and Natasha … two down, four to go …

I've dedicated this novel to my parents, who provided me with a childhood full of books and therefore inspired my entire career – and who have continued to support and encourage me into my adult life. I love you very much and am so very grateful.

To my husband, Jeff. I could say a lot of corny stuff here, but I'll spare my poor readers! Basically – you're amazing, I love you, and thanks for putting up with my writing drama.

And, speaking of readers, an enormous thanks to YOU – telling stories is what I love, and by borrowing, buying, reading and talking about my work you're allowing me to live my dream. You're the best! I hope the stars bring our imaginations together again …

Have you read

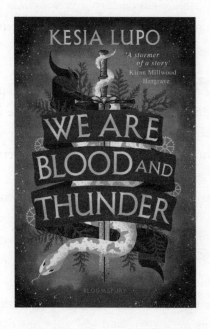

Turn the page for an extract of the gripping first
instalment of Kesia Lupo's stunning and original
YA fantasy world

PROLOGUE
A Cryptling

Before the storm cloud

Lena swept the last of the dust into her sack and stood up tall, wiping a grimy hand across her forehead. Her brass lantern flickered across the crypt's rough-hewn walls as Hunter slunk past, a twitching rat hanging from his jaws. He dropped it and purred at her, before savaging the poor creature's torso. The largest mouser prowling the crypts, Hunter was vicious, ginger and apparently immortal. For the hundredth time, Lena wondered why he'd picked her bed in which to sleep, leaving dubious gifts of rodents and birds at its foot.

Lena tied the dust sack shut and hoisted it over her shoulder, casting one last look at the empty, fresh-polished sarcophagus where the body would be laid in the morning for its last rites, the Descent. Her stomach twisted and she swallowed hard as bile rose in her throat. Earlier in the afternoon, she'd been allowed to watch while Mortician Vigo prepared the body in one of the special rooms beneath the gardens. She had managed – but only by digging her nails hard into her palms – to stop herself from fainting.

The dead man's Ancestors lay all around, stretching into darkness. Now, attuned to the scent of the morticians' special preserving ointments, Lena picked out sharp herbal smells beneath the ever-present musk of her world. The tomb itself was relatively small, and while noble families had the luxury of individual sarcophagi, the stonemason's family – like most others – had cut long body-shaped niches into the walls, one over another, or shared two bodies to a resting place. Husband with wife. Sister with brother. Baby with mother.

Each body's empty eye sockets had been sewn open, their eyes replaced with smooth rocks painted as eyes, or sometimes glittering gemstones. Mortician Vigo said that the Ancestors were sleeping, but Lena didn't think so. They were staring at the ceiling, at the floors of the living world above. Waiting.

Waiting for what?

A chill ran down her spine. She touched her forehead, lips and heart in the old sign of reverence. When she'd been very little, the Ancestors had frightened her – she'd had nightmares about the staring stone eyes, about the way the older corpses' flesh and skin were shrunken and leathery, but their hair as thick and lustrous as the day they died. How, from certain angles, even the oldest of the Ancestors looked like living people lying in the dark. But now she was eleven, almost a grown-up, and she wasn't afraid of anything.

4

Hunter mewed and Lena nearly jumped out of her skin. *I'm not afraid of anything*, she reminded herself firmly, calming her racing heart.

'All right – let's go,' she whispered to the cat, after a deep breath. 'It's a long walk back.'

She tried not to hurry as she started down the passages under the upper town, leading to the network of small cellars beneath the castle that the cryptlings called home. You weren't meant to hurry – it wasn't respectful, Mortician Vigo said. Hunter weaved through her legs, in and out of the lantern light, very nearly tripping her up.

For a time, everything was quiet and ordinary, the only sounds the occasional scuttle of a rat, or the snap of one of the mousetraps Lena had set out on her way down – the cryptlings and the cats were supposed to keep the vermin at bay. But as she drew further through the cobwebbed passages, she started to hear something strange … a voice. It grew louder, gradually: a low, rhythmic murmur, drifting from somewhere up ahead.

Lena frowned and stopped. Who else might be down here in the dead of night? As far as she knew, the stonemason's was the only funeral tomorrow, and she was the only cryptling on duty. No one else was allowed down here.

Suddenly she was frightened. She flicked off her lantern and stood in the dark for a few moments. She didn't like the thought of being seen – didn't like the way people's eyes settled on her, on the black mark on her cheek. She felt

5

Hunter slide past her legs, hurrying ahead impatiently, as she stood listening in the quiet. The voice carried on – distant and musical. A sad song, perhaps … or a poem. But Lena couldn't make out the words. She wondered if they were in another language.

She continued down the familiar passages in darkness, trailing her fingers along the wall, her footsteps silent in the padded canvas slippers they had to wear in the crypts. The voice grew closer, louder as she neared the passages she knew were directly beneath the castle itself, where the noble Ancestors and their households were interred. But she saw nothing – and after a time, the voice stopped.

Her heart beat faster. Somehow the silence and darkness were more unnerving now that she knew someone, somewhere, was sharing them with her. And that's when she saw it: the flicker of light. She clutched tightly to the iron handle of her lantern and to her dust sack, half-convincing herself to run. Cold sweat broke out across the back of her neck.

At first, she wondered if it was a trick of her eyes in the dark – she'd known it to happen before, green-purple shapes blooming like strange flowers, disappearing and re-forming at a blink. But this was real, she saw, as it grew closer – a clumsy, winding speck of light, fluttering on and off, bright then dim. A … butterfly?

She watched, her heart hammering. She'd never felt so terribly alert, every sense sharp, nearly painful.

The creature was made of metal – filigree wings, a smooth brass body. It landed on the edge of a sarcophagus nearby, its wings gently rising and falling, rising and falling, like the breath of a tiny animal.

It was beautiful.

Lena set down her things and stepped closer. The light emanating from the creature's body was flickering, like a sputtering candle. She reached out to touch it ... but hesitated, fingers outstretched.

All the rules Vigo had ever told her ran through her mind at once, like a flock of startled birds. *Don't reveal your face above ground. Don't touch anybody, especially not anybody who's not a cryptling. Don't touch the Ancestors, except as your duties demand. Don't touch the grave goods. Don't touch anything. To other people, Lena, you are dirty. Everything you touch is sullied.*

And yet ... she'd never seen anything so beautiful. Lena stopped thinking. She reached out and cupped the butterfly in her hands. She felt its delicate legs like feathers on her palms. It was incredibly light and made a faint whirring sound like a watch as its wings fluttered weakly.

Suddenly its little light extinguished and the crypt was plunged into darkness. Lena shivered. The creature was silent and still, the slight warmth quickly fading from its body, as if it had never been.

Is it broken?

She waited a few moments more, her heart in her mouth. Somewhere, she could hear hurried footsteps, a voice calling – but if they were searching for the butterfly, they were moving in the wrong direction, some way off to her left. Lena opened her palms and ran her fingers along the butterfly's body. Its wings were fully outstretched, and she liked the feel of the filigree patterns against her fingertips. It was strangely soothing.

But the butterfly didn't belong to her. She should drop it here and go home.

Even though her mind had decided, her body didn't move. She shouldn't take it, should she? She couldn't. If anyone found out she had removed anything from the crypts, she'd be in trouble. Even if she hadn't found it on a body, it was still grave goods. Who would believe her when she said it had been flying towards her, as if it had chosen her, as if it had *wanted* her to take it?

Somehow it didn't matter: the determination was already hardening in her heart. She wasn't allowed to have things of her own: even her clothes were shared hand-me-downs, her soft shoes worn thin by other cryptlings' feet. And above ground, she knew, the un-Marked children of the upper town had rooms filled with toys and trinkets – and even clothes that only they had worn. Except for the dark birthmark on her cheek, she wasn't any different from them. So why shouldn't she have the butterfly? She felt her breath quicken. It was only one thing. Such a small thing. She'd keep it secret of course. She'd never tell a soul. It would be something hers and hers alone – her only possession. Was that so much to ask?

Lena slipped the metal creature into the inside pocket of her habit, picked up her lantern and sack, and carried on through the tunnels.

ONE
The Hounds

Sixth year of the storm cloud

Lena ran until her lungs felt close to bursting, her feet thumping, sliding on the steep cobblestone road, down the peak of the city towards the walls and the forest beyond.

The Justice's words rang loud in her ears.

You have been found guilty of magecraft.

The storm cloud was all-encompassing, a thick, poisonous gauze clinging to her clothes, obscuring her path.

I sentence you to die.

Islands of muffled light trembled in the gloom – a lit window here, a patch of fading sunlight there. Her feet thumped into greyness, invisible.

The hounds will eat your flesh.

She could hear them – howling, growling. Had they finished off Vigo? Or had they grown tired of his old flesh, now lusting after hers? He'd bought her time, but it was all for nothing. Tears stung her eyes as she pushed herself faster.

Your bones will lie bare under the sky, banished from the sacred crypts.

She could never outrun them. Nobody could. At seventeen, she was far from the youngest to have fallen under the hounds' vicious teeth; you only had to see the chewed-up remains at the foot of the city walls to know that. But there was a chance – just a chance. She had to try.

Your soul will never join the Ancestors, will never feast on the glories of ages past, will never guide the fates.

Lena found herself down in the lowest tier of the city. The fog was thicker here. She stumbled to a halt, suddenly unable to breathe, a crushing pain in her side. Pulling up the neck of her habit to cover her mouth and nose, she felt tears welling behind the glass of her shield-eyes.

You will be dead, in this world and the next.

A howl broke the gloom, then a chorus of howls, swiftly followed by frenzied barking; the hounds were gaining. No time to cry. She turned and ran, harder than ever, hobnailed boots clacking against the pavement.

Soon the city walls loomed above, a small bone crunching under her foot. She felt sick, but pressed on round the curve of the wall, desperately scanning the base where the dark stone met the bone-littered ground. The gates had been locked for two years, bolted with broad beams of oak, ivy grown over the rusted locks – but nearby … Vigo had told her …

Lena scanned the rotted undergrowth for the outline of the old rose bush – and found it, her heart no more than a hollow, fluttering thing in the back of her throat. She could so easily have missed it altogether, a tangle of bare thorns almost lost among the skeletal remains of its neighbours. Parting the branches with her thick leather gloves, she spotted a slight dip in the earth. So small.

I used it as a child, he'd said, in the few moments they'd had together before the hounds. *I would slip out into the forest to play when I was supposed to be at my lessons. It was before my … deformity.*

She'd shaken her head wordlessly, clutching at his old arthritic hands, the hands which had first picked her up from the steps down to the cryptling cellars as a baby, wailing into the dawn. She'd been crying again, then.

Lena, I cannot run. But you might just be fast and small enough to escape.

It was her only chance.

Lena threw herself to the ground as the howls behind her grew in intensity – along with the clink and scratch of claws on the cobblestones. She pressed herself under the bush, the old thorny stems snagging at her habit and showering her with rot, and scrabbled into the musty darkness beneath the wall. Curling her fingers as best she could into the damp soil, Lena pulled herself forward, wriggling until her feet were almost concealed under the rose bush, the weight of the great thick wall bearing down over her head, dark and cold and ancient.

The gap was tight, her lungs constricting as she forced her shoulders further, her arms outstretched. She thought she could feel a wisp of air from the other side – but it was then that a bark came from close quarters, followed by a frenzy of growls, a snapping of teeth. Something closed around the tough leather heel of her boot; a surprising strength pulled her backwards. Panic fuelled her. She gripped on to the wall's slick underside with clawed hands. Her shield-eyes snagged on a root, the leather strap snapping. She let them fall, kicked out hard and redoubled her efforts, squirming frantically under the wall until she could see the light filtering through the other side. She squeezed her shoulders forward and, with more difficulty, her hips, ripping the coarse material of her habit. By this time, she had begun to sob – but somehow she forced her way out.

Lena staggered to her feet, half-falling into the forest. Her heart plummeted as she absorbed the sight confronting her. The forest was a picture of decay, the trees visibly withering. A grey residue veiled their bark and occasionally bumped outwards in a strange fungus. The storm cloud was as thick as it was within the walls of the city, flashing and rumbling between the trees. She thought of her shield-eyes, fallen under the wall – but where she had crawled, the hounds could surely follow: she couldn't risk retrieving them. She ran instead, stumbling over roots, slipping on wet leaves. Here and there, a rotted trunk had fallen across the path, or a branch half-snapped from a larger tree threatened her head.

Gradually, the howls and barks faded altogether, but it was a long time before Lena allowed herself to be certain she had not been followed – perhaps the dogs, penned for so long within the city walls, had been spooked by the alien scents and noises of the forest. Or perhaps the houndmaster had assumed her dead and called them off, or perhaps he'd feared losing them forever among the trees, as so many travellers had been lost before. In any case, she was painfully grateful. She slowed down, rubbed her stinging eyes and caught her breath. She rested her hands on her knees for a moment, her heartbeat slowing – and then she reached for the brass butterfly she kept in the pocket of her robe. It was as big as the palm of her hand, warm from her body. Tracing the delicate filigree of its wings, she felt her breathing slow.

Whenever she held the butterfly, she remembered how she had felt the night she'd found it – or rather, the night it had found her. She had felt wanted. Calm. Secure in the knowledge that she was worth something, because she had something of worth.

Out of the corner of her eye she saw a shape – a human shape, hunched at the foot of a tree. Her stomach convulsed and she ducked behind a rotten tangle of undergrowth, pressing her hand against her mouth to stifle a rising scream. But the figure didn't appear to have noticed her. The cloud shifted, alternately revealing and concealing a long cloak, brown boots, large leather gloves. So still, so quiet, his hooded head resting on his chest. Sleeping? But she saw no movement, not a twitch, no rise and fall of breath. Slowly, Lena realised the man was dead.

She slipped the butterfly in her pocket, stood up and walked towards him, her whole body still trembling – but gradually calming as she approached the corpse. She wasn't afraid of the dead – not unless they … She shook her head, not wanting to think about it. No, it was the living who frightened her.

She crouched, examined a blade dropped near the body, glinting in the faint evening light filtering through cloud and trees. It was a short dagger, the hilt twined with a dragon motif in silver, its eye picked out with a green gem. Hardly thinking, she picked it up, slid it carefully into her belt. As she carried on, she realised the man had been resting on the edge of a small clearing. And she saw another body. A woman, her back turned to Lena, marked out by her perfectly preserved, long red hair, splayed in the mud. And another – a man curled up under his cloak by the blackened remains of a fire. Without meaning to, she glimpsed his face, decayed and ghastly.

These bodies had been here for a long time. Had they been trying to reach the city? They were strangers, surely. What had killed them?

She didn't want to wait to find out.

She returned to the narrow path and carried on at a stumbling run.

After a time, it grew so late that she could barely distinguish the trees from the darknesses in between – but soon she began to see other things, shapes in the fog twisting into suggestions of hands, eyes, mouths. She blinked, rubbing her eyes and cursing the loss of her shield-eyes. No one in Duke's Forest would step outside with their eyes unprotected – the toxic storm cloud caused visions if they were exposed for too long. Every now and then, larger shapes loomed from between the trees, and she could not prevent herself from starting backwards before they dissipated, even though she knew they weren't real.

She imagined the strangers' bodies in the clearing moving, rising up, following her. *Don't. Think.* But despite her stern thoughts, and the exhaustion screaming at her to stop, she quickened her pace.

Eventually, Lena could continue no longer. Her legs gave out, and she felt her fingers burrow into the mossy mulch of the forest floor. The hallucinations were worsening. She knew she was vulnerable out here – to *real* threats – if she wasn't able to run. She remembered Vigo's tales of the giant snakes and wild boar that infested the wood, and screwed her eyes shut against a wave of terror. She took a deep breath. She needed her wits now more than ever.

But the forest stretched in all directions, and she had long lost the road – how would she escape? And even if she were to find her way out, what fate could a girl like her expect in the wider world? She felt for the birthmark on her cheek, several shades darker than the brown of her skin. Even the people of Duke's Forest had regarded cryptlings – marked out by their various deformities – with a mixture of disgust and begrudging respect for their duties. Vigo had said the gods were cruel, their followers toying with dangerous magic. What would they make of her? What did they do to Marked people outside of Duke's Forest?

15

Would *they* try to execute her too?

Lena felt a sickly chill spread from her throat to her stomach as she considered the most terrible possibility of all: what if the storm cloud had swallowed everything, leaving the city of Duke's Forest the lonely centre of the universe? What if those people had been trying to reach Duke's Forest to save themselves?

No – she could not give up. Lena opened her eyes and dragged her exhausted body upright once more, determined to continue, but now she was surrounded, not by trees, but by a mass of people, each one of them turning towards her – each one of them familiar. These were the dead of Duke's Forest, the dead the Pestilence had taken, the dead she had helped to undress, wash and embalm, replacing their eyes with the painted stones and glittering gems that now bore into her.

She was a convicted mage, and an outcast, and the Ancestors were angry.

She stumbled back against a tree, touched her forehead, lips and chest in a silent prayer, her hand shaking. 'Please …' she managed, but the Ancestors' hearts were hollowed out. The world turned black.

Lena had been sixteen the first time it had happened, a year before the Justice had condemned her to die. She'd been helping Vigo embalm an old guardsman, dead of the Pestilence, in one of the special preparatory chambers beneath the castle's gardens. Thick glass bricks had been set in the ceiling, allowing weak light – and the occasional flash of the storm cloud's blue-green lightning – to filter down on their delicate work.

She had pulled up the guardsman's left eyelid to sew it in place with the curved needle and special white thread. Eyes were something of a specialty of Lena's, with her slender, accurate fingers – and although she had once hated the feel of the cold gems slotting into empty sockets, in time she had come to find it satisfying.

'Have you thought about what you're going to do?' Master Vigo had said, in the manner of one who had asked the question a hundred times. He was in the process of removing and potting the organs, a special stoneware jar for each one. The smell of spoiling flesh filled the air, but Lena had grown used to it long ago. 'You ought to. You've barely a year until you come of age.' He deftly pulled the liver through the small incision he had cut in the body's side and slipped it into the waiting vessel, already packed with the sharp-smelling preservative oils and herbs.

'I haven't thought about it,' Lena lied, trying to sound dismissive. 'A year is a long time.' In fact, she'd been thinking about it a lot recently. She'd never chosen this life. The birthmark on her face had chosen it for her – or rather her parents had, whoever they were, when they decided to abandon her to the fate of a cryptling rather than raise a Marked child.

'It's not, and you're a fool to pretend you can put it off for much longer.'

17

Lena shrugged as she pulled the fourth stitch neatly through the thin skin of the lid. Vigo was a miserable old goat, but she'd come to love him, and she knew he was right. As she leaned forward to make her fifth and last stitch, she felt the weight of the brass butterfly in her pocket. Her secret, ever since she had found it fluttering in the catacombs. She knew if anyone saw it, she'd be accused of stealing grave goods, a terrible crime for a cryptling – but somehow she couldn't bear to let it go. It was the only thing she had.

'You'd make a good mortician,' said Vigo, limping around the body to inspect her work as she tied the thread and snipped it with a pair of small, sharp scissors. 'You've a steady hand, Lena – and you're quiet, respectful.' She glanced up at him. She could tell his leg was hurting him today – the tension around his eyes and mouth showed itself in hard lines through his pale, papery skin. He had a wooden peg from the knee down to replace the limb they'd had to amputate, but no matter how hard Lena tried to find him the right kind of padding, and the right sort of salve, the place where it met the stub was nearly always sore.

She smiled at him weakly and shook her head, setting down her needle. She couldn't tell him the truth. She couldn't admit that because every option involved working in the crypts for the rest of her life, she didn't feel like she had a choice at all. Subconsciously, she touched the mark on her face, a black stain as big as a child's clenched fist. If it weren't for the mark, she'd be ordinary. Imagine. Where would she be now? *Maybe with my parents in a mansion in the upper town, eating sweets and laughing* ... Lena pictured strong sunlight spilling through tall windows, no cowl to shadow her face. She tilted her head slightly towards the glass roof, imagining how the warmth would feel against her skin.

'Lena?' Master Vigo shot her a concerned glance. 'Are you all right?'

'Sorry,' she said, returning her attention to her task, slotting more of the white thread through her needle. It was stupid to fantasise as she had done when she was younger. Life was difficult for everyone now: for a year, the city had been under quarantine. Instead of eating sweets in sunny rooms, half the people of the city were dead, rich and poor alike, and the other half lived in fear. As the cloud had deepened and darkened, strange flashes and rumbles disturbing its noxious peace, the Pestilence raged through the population, spreading its fever of hallucinations and shivers that left each victim dead in a matter of hours. The disease had visited three times – always in the warmest months, as if it thrived on the meagre heat of a mountain summer. It was September, and the latest flurry of deaths was drawing to an end.

'Why not be a mortician?' Vigo went on, warming to his subject as he pulled out the intestines. 'People need us more than ever. We are busier than we've ever been. And the Justice knows he won't find any mages among our number. You'll be safe here.'

'The Justice,' Lena whispered. 'Yes ... I am glad to be safe from him.' Ever since the Duke had fallen ill, the Justice had

19

ruled the city with a cold, hard grip. Like most of his citizens, the Justice knew the unnatural storm and Pestilence could have but one cause: magic. Unlike most of his citizens, the Justice had dedicated his attention to searching for the mage or mages responsible. He was obsessed, the other cryptlings whispered, ordering his guards to search for evidence of magic, burning the few magical books and toys in the city, his vicious hounds chasing suspect after suspect to an early, gruesome grave at the city walls. Lena could hear the dogs sometimes, howling in the kennels at dawn, and the sound chilled her to the core. But the cryptlings, dedicated to serving the Ancestors, had never suffered under his rule. The Justice *loved* the Ancestors. Since he'd accepted the reins of power, the ceremonies and rituals dedicated to their honour had grown threefold – old prayers and ceremonies resurrected, new ones invented.

Vigo slid the remains of food from the intestines on to the floor, a system of flowing drains transporting the waste out of the city. 'But what do you say, Lena? Would you like to be a mortician?'

Lena wasn't listening. All right, so she was safe down here – but it still wasn't enough, was it? What if she wasn't meant to be here at all? What if this was all some big mistake – like her parents had left her little basket on the steps just for a moment, and returned to find it gone? Or she'd been swapped with another child by accident? What if there was some other life she should be living, some other place where she would belong? She didn't feel like she belonged here, that was for sure – and yet this was where she was trapped. She found her vision blurring, frustration trembling her fingers.

'Why aren't you answering?' Vigo snapped. Quickly he tried to soften his voice, though he still sounded irritated as he packed the intestines into their stoneware grave. 'If you want to try something else, you only need say.'

He'd misunderstood her silence completely. Lena felt instantly sorry: it wasn't his fault she felt this way. She gathered herself together and spoke at last. 'I would like to stay with you, Vigo, of course I would. I just wish … I just wish there were more options to choose from. Before the quarantine …' She looked down at the corpse. One eye sewn open, one eye shut, his face was frozen in a grotesque wink.

Vigo sighed, sealing the intestine jar with a deft twist of his swollen-knuckled hand. 'Before the quarantine, you would have had the option to leave Duke's Forest altogether, is that what you're saying?' As he set the jar down and wiped his hands, he looked very old and tired, and Lena knew he understood.

'No, I just …' She shook her head. 'This is my home, Vigo. But it sometimes feels like a prison too.'

He sighed. 'People like us are marked out for the life we lead, Lena – marked out by the Ancestors themselves. I understand your frustration. When I was your age, I wanted to see the world too – but what was I to do, as a cripple? It is cruel, in a way, the fate that we are handed. My parents abandoned me after my accident. I was a child of six, old enough to remember who they were, to remember their love, our home, my brothers and sisters, my name.' Lena said a silent prayer of thanks that she had been so young when she was abandoned. It was easier not quite knowing what you had lost – and although Vigo spoke briskly, in his usual matter-of-fact tone, she could hear the pain beneath his words. 'It is cruel,' he carried on, his voice quickening, 'to give it all up. But it is also an honour. Our families abandon us, divest us of our names and sever our ties to our own blood Ancestors – but it's only in order that we might serve *all* the Ancestors. Think on it.'

Lena thought on it, but found herself wondering which of the corpses under the mountain were related to her by blood – and whether she'd prepared a body for a grave that was an aunt, or a cousin, or a brother, without ever realising. Had Vigo ever prepared one of his parents or siblings, recognising their faces but unable to acknowledge them for who they were?

'Ordinary people *never* see the Ancestors,' Vigo continued, 'except at funerals. Are we not blessed to be around them constantly? The work we do is the most sacred of all work. I have been here seventy years, Lena, and I feel my life has had purpose, and joy, and sorrow, as much as any other life. I had a wife for many years.' His eyes grew suddenly watery and he turned aside. 'I had a child.'

Despite the sincerity in his voice, the suppressed tears, she wasn't in the mood to play along. Not today. 'Seventy years in darkness,' Lena said, setting down her needle and picking up the green painted eye-stone, not caring if she hurt the old man's feelings. 'A wife and child who lived and died in darkness. Sounds bad enough to me.'

'It is not as if we never go outside, Lena,' he snapped.

'Hidden under a cowl!' she protested, grasping the eye-stone tightly, feeling it cold and hard in her palm. 'We might as well be underground. It's like *they*' – she gestured at the frosted glass ceiling, at the city above – 'can't bear to see us. Like we shame them. I don't feel chosen at all. I don't feel special. I feel the opposite of special.' She turned to the opened eye, scooped out the eyeball with a spoon and slotted the gem in its place. She sullenly plopped the eyeball in a copper dish.

Vigo went quiet for a moment, studiously tending the herbal mixture with which he would pack the dead man's cavities, the whisper and rattle of the pestle and mortar the only sound in the preparatory chamber. In the silence, Lena grew to regret her words about his wife and son, who had died years before she was born, but she wasn't sure how to say sorry. Eventually, Vigo apologised instead, his voice slightly unsteady. 'I am sorry you feel this way. If not for the quarantine, you would have had the opportunity to leave forever. But now …'

'I never said I wanted to leave forever.' Lena hung her head, feeling shame burn tight and hot in her chest. 'I don't. No one should have to face such a stark choice – to stay forever or leave forever. What kind of a choice is that? I just … I just want a *real* choice. I want to feel like I'm in control for once.'

She picked up her needle again and started to pull back the second eyelid to sew it into place.

That's when it happened.

That's when the dead man's eye turned to her face and looked right at her, accusingly. She felt the swivel of it under her touch.

She leaped backwards, dropping her needle and thread and knocking an urn of priceless embalming oil with her elbow. It toppled and shattered.

Vigo looked at her as if she'd gone mad.

'He ...' Even as the words started to leave her lips, she swallowed them. The man's eye was dead and sightless once more. 'I ... I'm not feeling well.'

It was true: she felt sick. She had imagined it. She *must* have imagined it. Vigo sent her back to her cell and cleaned up the mess – despite his infirmities – insisting that she rest. Lying on her bed like a corpse herself, staring at the ceiling, she had felt terrible. She played the moment over and over in her mind. Even when Hunter had sat on her chest, purring like a furnace, she'd felt somehow detached from the world, trapped in that moment of horror. *Was* she going mad?

Later, in the refectory at dinner, she'd asked the other cryptlings if they had any stories – Ancestors moving or twitching as they were prepared ... But it was the usual stuff. The hunchbacked boy who sat opposite Lena told her he'd prepared a corpse that farted. The deaf girl next to her mimed how she'd watched as a dead man's arm had risen up like a

24

balloon, and everyone laughed. Lena nodded, smiling, pretending her experience had been similar. It was true: the contents of bellies could sometimes flood the body with gas, and that could make a corpse move. She told herself that was what had happened. But deep down she knew it was different. Who had ever heard of gas moving eyes? And besides, the man's eye had fixed on her like he knew what she was doing – what she was *thinking*. Gas couldn't do that.

Next thing Lena knew there were footsteps, and she started from the forest floor, spitting dead leaves from her open mouth, scrambling back towards the protection of the tree trunk behind her. A shadow began to emerge from the fog. Lena tried to raise herself to her feet, tried to run, but she could not, her legs cramped with cold.

The shadow solidified into a darker mass, holding a bulb of purple light. The figure stopped before her, as if Lena had been its destination all along. She recoiled. There was something wrong with the face of this creature – a smooth brass surface with glassy black eyes and a gaping mouth. A faint *tick-tick-tick* noise appeared to emanate from the face, a cog turning somewhere at its jaw. Lena's hands scrambled at the sides of the tree as she pulled herself upright, shivering, and she hurriedly drew the knife from her belt.

ABOUT THE AUTHOR

Kesia Lupo studied history at the University of Oxford and creative writing at Bath Spa. She lives in Bristol with her husband and works as a children's book editor, writing in the mornings before work. Her debut novel, *We Are Blood and Thunder*, was a fan favourite. *We Are Bound by Stars* is her second novel set in her same highly original fantasy world.